Duncan expecte
though

Instead, Moira locked gazes with him, then reached back and unfastened her hair. As it fell over her shoulders in a shining dark mass, the smell of summer wildflowers brought back memories so strong Duncan's knees nearly buckled.

His breathing grew shallow as she ran her fingertips over the bare skin above the neckline of her gown. When she reached the valley between her breasts, she looped her finger round and round the little tie at the center of her bodice. Duncan was vaguely aware that his mouth was hanging open, but he did not have the concentration to close it.

"I know what ye want," Moira said in a throaty voice and gave the tie a little tug. "And I'll give it to ye, if ye take me to my son."

Praise for the novels of Margaret Mallory

The Sinner

"Sizzling and captivating...Mallory weaves a fine yarn with plenty of spice and thrills."
—Publishers Weekly

"4½ stars! Mallory's portrait of 16th-century Scotland and the lively adventures she creates for her characters certainly engage readers' emotions. The sizzling sexual tension between the hero and heroine will leave readers breathless."
—RT Book Reviews

"*The Sinner* is perfect! Alex and Glynis are sexy, stubborn and simply divine together. *The Sinner* should not be missed!"

—JoyfullyReviewed.com

"A wonderful novel led by two powerful personalities...*The Sinner* is an exciting, turbulent read from beginning to end. I will be waiting impatiently for the next installment of this story."

—FreshFiction.com

"Captivating...Alex is a delicious male lead that would send any woman's heart aflutter...The chemistry and the fire that this couple had was explosive and just seemed to leap off the page...This book needs to be savored with a nice glass of wine...I am anxiously awaiting Duncan's story."

—NightOwlRomance.com

The Guardian

"4½ stars! Top Pick! Mallory imbues history with a life of its own, creating a deeply moving story. Her characters are vibrantly alive and full of emotional depth, each with their own realistic flaws. Her sensuous and highly passionate tale grabs the reader and doesn't let go."
—RT Book Reviews

"Masterfully written...Mallory has created a series that every romance reader must read. *The Guardian* is truly a sizzling romance with high-impact adventure that captures the Scotland readers long for. The characters created by Mallory have found places in my heart, and I am impatiently awaiting the next of this spectacular series!"
—FreshFiction.com

"A must-read for all historical and highlander fans...Ms. Mallory weaves a gripping story of heartbreak, intrigue, and trust...This one is a keeper. I'm looking forward to the next installment."
—TheRomanceReadersConnection.com

"The story line and writing were fantastic...The love scenes were very hot, and the historical elements...added a ton of flavor to the story."
—Romanceaholic.com

"An amazing introduction to what is fated to become a dangerously addictive series. With characters capable of breaching the most impenetrable of readers' defenses, riveting story lines (and even more intriguing subplots), quick, witty dialogue, as well as wild sexual tension—the only thing readers will crave, is more."
—RomanceJunkiesReviews.com

"Five stars! I fell in love with this novel!...The characters in this story really touched me...This is a wonderful start of a series and I can't wait to read the adventures of the MacDonald brothers."
—**NightOwlRomance.com**

Knight of Passion

"Top Pick! As in the previous book in her All the King's Men series, Mallory brings history to life, creating dramatic and gut-wrenching stories. Her characters are incredibly alive and readers will feel and believe their sensual and passionate adventures. Mallory raises the genre to new levels."
—*RT Book Reviews*

"I really enjoyed this story...Very intense...Fans of medieval historicals will especially love this one."
—**CoffeeTimeRomance.com**

"An amazing story...a series that readers won't want to miss...Filled with hot romance as well as adventure with a fascinating historical background."
—**RomRevToday.com**

Knight of Pleasure

"4 Stars! A riveting story...Such depth and sensuality are a rare treat."
—*RT Book Reviews*

"Fascinating...An excellent historical romance. Ms. Mallory gives us amazingly vivid details of the characters, romance, and intrigue of England. You're not just reading a novel, you are stepping into the story and feeling all the emotions of each character... *Knight of Pleasure* is amazing and I highly recommend it."

—TheRomanceReadersConnection.com

"An absolute delight... captivating."

—FreshFiction.com

"Thrilling, romantic, and just plain good reading... An enjoyable, historically accurate, and very well written novel."

—RomRevToday.com

Knight of Desire

"An impressive debut... Margaret Mallory is a star in the making."

—Mary Balogh, *New York Times* **bestselling author of** *At Last Comes Love*

"5 Stars! Amazing... The fifteenth century came alive... *Knight of Desire* is the first in the All the King's Men series and what a way to start it off."

—CoffeeTimeRomance.com

"A fast-paced tale of romance and intrigue that will sweep you along and have you rooting for William and his fair Catherine to fight their way to love at last."

—Candace Camp, *New York Times* **bestselling author of** *The Courtship Dance*

"4 Stars! Mallory's debut is impressive. She breathes life into major historical characters... in a dramatic romance."

—RT Book Reviews

Also by Margaret Mallory

The Return of the Highlanders

The Guardian
The Sinner

All the King's Men

Knight of Desire
Knight of Pleasure
Knight of Passion

THE
WARRIOR

The Return of the Highlanders

MARGARET MALLORY

FOREVER

NEW YORK   BOSTON

Copyright © 2012 by Peggy L. Brown
Excerpt from *The Chieftain* Copyright © 2012 by Peggy L. Brown

Forever
Hachette Book Group
237 Park Avenue
New York, NY 10017

www.HachetteBookGroup.com

Printed in the United States of America

First Edition: October 2012
10 9 8 7 6 5 4 3 2 1
OPM

Forever is an imprint of Grand Central Publishing.
The Forever name and logo are trademarks of Hachette Book Group, Inc.

The Hachette Speakers Bureau provides a wide range of authors for speaking events. To find out more, go to www.hachettespeakersbureau.com or call (866) 376-6591.

The publisher is not responsible for websites (or their content) that are not owned by the publisher.

ATTENTION CORPORATIONS AND ORGANIZATIONS:

Most Hachette Book Group books are available at quantity discounts with bulk purchase for educational, business, or sales promotional use. For information, please call or write:

Special Markets Department, Hachette Book Group
237 Park Avenue, New York, NY 10017
Telephone: 1-800-222-6747 Fax: 1-800-477-5925

This book is dedicated to my dad,
Norman J. Brown,
who never, even when I begged, told a story
the same way twice.
He taught me all I needed to know about heroes.

ACKNOWLEDGMENTS

I spend a lot of time with my fictional MacDonald heroes in sixteenth-century Scotland. Perhaps it is not surprising, then, that my first thought when I received an offer of help out of the blue from a Jamie MacDonald who was a descendant of the Lord of the Isles and spoke Gaelic was that I was living in a time-travel novel. Fortunately, Dr. James R. MacDonald turned out to be a real person with a PhD in Scottish studies from the University of Edinburgh. I am very grateful to him and also to Sharron Gunn for their generosity in helping me with Gaelic phrases and in answering my odd questions about Scottish history. Any mistakes in the book, however, are mine.

The other new acquaintances I made in the course of writing this book include the four-legged variety. I want to thank Mary Horton for letting a stranger into her house to meet her incredible wolfhounds, Connery, Lena, and Galen. Mary was very kind to answer all my questions about this wonderful breed and even invited me back to see Lena's puppies.

My heartfelt thanks, as always, to my editor, Alex Logan, and to the rest of the hardworking and remarkable staff at Grand Central Publishing. The art department deserves special mention for another gorgeous cover. (No, I don't get to meet these guys—but I should.)

My love and thanks to my family, especially my long-suffering husband, for their support and patience. I'm forever grateful to my friends Anthea Lawson, who is my critique partner, and Ginny Heim, who has read my manuscripts for me from the beginning. My warm thanks also to my agent, Kevan Lyon, for her wise counsel and enthusiastic support.

Finally, I want to thank my readers, who make the long days hunched over a laptop worthwhile. Like a kid, I hang your messages on the fridge to keep me going on the days when the words don't come easy. Thank you!

Bidh an t-ubhal as fheàrr air a' mheangan as àirde.

The best apple is on the highest bough.

THE
WARRIOR

PROLOGUE

Duncan MacDonald could defeat any warrior in the castle—and yet, he was powerless against his chieftain's seventeen-year-old daughter.

"As soon as my father leaves the hall," Moira whispered, leaning close enough to make him light-headed, "I'll meet ye outside by the ash tree."

Duncan knew he should refuse her, but he may as well try to stop his heart from beating.

"I've told ye not to speak to me here," he said, glancing about the long room filled with their clansmen and the chieftain's guests from Ireland. "Someone might notice."

When Moira turned to look straight at him with her midnight-blue eyes, Duncan felt as if a fist slammed into his chest. That had happened the first time she looked at him—*really* looked at him—and every time since.

"Why would anyone take notice if I speak with my brother Connor's best friend?" she asked.

Perhaps because she had ignored him the first seventeen years of her life? It was still a mystery to him how that had changed.

"Go now—Ragnall is watching us," he said when he felt her older brother's eyes on him. Unlike Moira and Connor, Ragnall had their father's fair hair, bull-like build, and short temper. He was also the only warrior in the clan Duncan was not certain he could defeat at arms.

"I won't go until ye say you'll meet me later." Moira folded her arms, but amusement quirked up the corners of her full lips, reminding Duncan that this was a game to her.

Yet if the chieftain learned that Duncan was sneaking off with his only daughter, he would murder him on the spot. Duncan turned and left the hall without bothering to answer her; Moira knew he would be there.

As he waited for her in the dark, he listened to the soft lap of the sea on the shore. There was no mist on the Misty Isle of Skye tonight, and Dunscaith Castle was beautiful, ablaze with torchlight against the clear night sky. He had grown up in the castle and seen this sight a thousand times, but Duncan was a young man who took nothing for granted.

His mother had served as nursemaid to the chieftain's children, and he and Connor had been best friends since the cradle. From the time they could lift wooden swords, the two of them and Connor's cousins, Alex and Ian, had trained in the art of war. When they weren't practicing with their weapons, they were off looking for adventure—or trouble—and they usually found it.

Moira had always been apart, a coddled princess dressed in finery. Duncan had little to do with the lovely, wee creature whose laughter often filled the castle.

Duncan heard the rustle of silk skirts and turned to see Moira running toward him. Even in the dark and covered head-to-toe in a cloak, he could pick her out of a thousand women. Though she could not possibly see what was in her path, Moira ran headlong, expecting no impediment. No stone tripped her, for even the faeries favored this lass.

When Moira threw her arms around his neck, Duncan closed his eyes and lost himself in her womanly softness. He breathed in the scent of her hair, and it was like lying in a field of wildflowers.

"It's been two whole days," she said. "I missed ye so much."

Duncan was amazed at how unguarded Moira was. The lass said whatever came into her head, with no caution, no fear of rejection. But then, who would refuse her?

The chieftain had sent Duncan to attend university in the Lowlands with Connor and Connor's cousins, and he'd learned about Helen of Troy there. Moira had a face like that—the kind that could start a clan war. And worse for his jealous heart, she had lush curves and an innate sensuality that made every man want her.

The other men only lusted after her for her beauty. But for Duncan, Moira was the bright spark in his world.

Moira pulled him down into a deep kiss that sent him reeling. Before he knew it, his hands were roaming over the feminine dips and swells of her body, and she was moaning into his mouth. They were in danger of dropping to the grass at their feet, where anyone could happen upon them, so he broke the kiss. One of them had to keep their head—and it wouldn't be Moira.

"Not here," he said, though he knew damned well what

they would do if they went to the cave. Anticipation caused every fiber of his being to throb with need.

For the first weeks, they had found ways to please each other without committing the last, irrevocable sin—the one that could cost Duncan his life if his chieftain knew of it. He felt guilty for taking what rightfully belonged to Moira's future husband. But it was a miracle that he'd held out against her as long as he had.

At least he was confident that Moira would not suffer for what they had done. She was a clever lass—she would not be the first to spill a vial of sheep's blood on her wedding sheet. And Moira was not one to be troubled by guilt.

Once they were inside the cave, they spread the blanket they kept there, and Duncan pulled her onto his lap.

"The Irish chieftain's son is rather amusing," Moira said, poking her finger in his side.

Moira's father had not taken another wife after Connor and Moira's mother died. So when they had guests, Moira sat on one side of her father, charming them, while her older brother Ragnall sat on his other side, frightening them.

"The man was looking down the front of your gown all through supper." And Duncan thought Moira let him. "I wanted to crush his head between my hands."

All his life, he'd minded his temper, both because he was bigger than other lads and because his position was precarious. He hated the way Moira made him lose control.

"That's sweet." She laughed and kissed his cheek. "I was trying to make ye jealous."

"Why would ye do that?"

"To make certain ye would meet me, because we need

to talk." Her voice was serious now. "Duncan, I want us to marry."

Duncan closed his eyes and, for one brief moment, let himself pretend it was possible. He imagined what it would be like to be the man so blessed as to sleep with this lass in his arms each night and to wake up each morning to her sunny smile.

"It will never happen," he said.

"Of course it will."

Moira was accustomed to having her way. Her father, who had no other weakness, had spoiled her, but he would not give in to her on such an important matter.

"Your father will never permit his only daughter to wed the nursemaid's bastard son," he said. "He'll use your marriage to make an alliance for the clan."

Duncan pulled out his flask of whiskey and took a long drink. With Moira talking such nonsense, he needed it.

"My father always lets me have what I want in the end. And what I want," she said, her breath warm in his ear as she ran her hand down his stomach, "is you, Duncan Ruadh MacDonald."

With all his blood rushing to his cock, he couldn't think. He pulled her into his arms, and they fell across the blanket, their legs tangled.

"I'm desperate for ye," she said between frantic kisses.

He still found it hard to believe Moira wanted him— but when she put her hand on his cock, he did believe it. For however long she wanted him, he was hers.

* * *

Duncan ran his fingers through Moira's hair as she lay with her head on his chest. He fixed every moment of their time together in his memory to retrieve later.

"I love ye so much," she said.

An unfamiliar sensation of pure joy bubbled up inside Duncan.

"Tell me ye love me," she said.

"Ye know I do," he said, though it made no difference as to what would happen. "I'll never stop."

His feelings didn't come and go like Moira's. One week, she loved her brown horse, the next week the spotted one, and the week after that she didn't like to ride at all. She had always been like that. They were opposites in so many ways.

Duncan forced himself to sit up so he could see the sky outside the cave.

"Ach, it's near dawn," he said and cursed himself. "I must get ye back to the castle quickly."

"I will convince my father," Moira said as they dressed. "He's no fool. He can see that one day you'll be a famed warrior known throughout the Western Isles."

"If ye tell your father about us," he said, cupping her face in his hands, "that will be the end of this."

Moira could not be as naïve about it as she pretended.

"He would let us wed if I carried your child," she said in a small voice.

Duncan's heart stopped in his chest. "Tell me ye are taking the potion to avoid conceiving?"

"Aye," she said, sounding annoyed. "And I've had my courses."

He brushed his thumb over her cheek. It was strange, but he would love to have a child with her—a wee lass with Moira's laughing eyes. He had no business having thoughts like that. It would be years before he could support a wife and child, and he'd never be able to provide for a woman accustomed to fine clothes and servants.

The scare she gave him made him resolve, yet again, to end it. Moira could hide the loss of her virginity, but a child was another matter.

"If my father won't agree, we can run away," she said.

"He'd send half a dozen war galleys after us," Duncan said as he fastened her cloak for her. "Even if we escaped—which we wouldn't—ye would never be happy estranged from our clan and living in a humble cottage. I love ye too much to do that to ye."

"Don't doubt me," Moira said, gripping the front of his shirt. "I'd live anywhere with ye."

She believed it only because she'd never lived with hardship. Duncan had known from the start that he could never keep her. Moira was like a colorful butterfly, landing on his hand for a breathless moment.

The sky was growing light when they reached the kitchen entrance behind the keep.

"I love ye," Moira said. "And I promise ye, one way or another, I will marry ye."

Duncan was a lucky man to have her love, even for a little while. He pulled her into one last mindless kiss and wondered how he would last until the next time.

He lived on the precipice of disaster, never knowing which would befall him first—getting caught or having her end it. And yet, he had never felt happier in his life. He had to stop himself from whistling as he crossed the castle yard to his mother's cottage.

Damn, there was candlelight in the window. Duncan was a grown man of nearly twenty and didn't have to an-

swer to his mother. Still, he wished she were not awake to
see him come in with the rising sun. She would ask questions, and he didn't like to lie to her.

Duncan opened the door—and his stomach dropped
like a stone to his feet.

His chieftain and Ragnall sat on either side of his
mother's table with their long, claymore swords resting,
unsheathed, across their thighs. Rage rolled off them.
With their golden hair and fierce golden eyes, they looked
like a pair of lions.

Duncan hoped they would not kill him in front of his
mother and sister. Though he did not take his eyes off the
two warriors dwarfing the tiny cottage, he was aware of
his mother hunched on the floor in the corner, weeping.
His eleven-year-old sister stood with her hand on their
mother's shoulder.

"The old seer foretold that ye would save my son Connor's life one day." The chieftain's voice held enough
menace to fell birds from the sky. "That is the only reason
I did not kill ye the moment ye walked through that door."

Duncan suspected he would be flogged within an inch
of his life instead. But a beating, however bad, meant
nothing. He was strong; he would survive it. What
weighed down his shoulders was the realization that he
would never again hold Moira in his arms.

His chieftain was speaking again, but Duncan found it
hard to listen with the well of grief rising in his chest.

"I suspect Connor and my nephews knew ye were *violating my daughter*!"

When the chieftain started to rise from his chair, Ragnall put his hand on his father's arm.

"We are taking Knock Castle from the MacKinnons today, so fetch your sword and shield," Ragnall said. "As soon as the battle is over, you, Alex, and Ian will sail with Connor for France. Ye can hone your skills there, fighting the English."

"By the time ye return," the chieftain said, his eyes narrow slits of hate, "Moira will be far from Skye, living with her husband and children."

Duncan had known from the start that he would lose Moira. And yet, he felt the loss as keenly as if he'd been the expectant bridegroom whose bride is torn from his arms on his wedding night.

The bright spark was gone from his life forever.

CHAPTER 1

The Isle of Skye is there." Moira stood at the edge of the sea holding her son's hand and pointed at the empty horizon to the north. "That is our true home. Never forget that we are MacDonalds of Sleat."

Her son Ragnall, whom she named for her older brother, gave her a grave nod. After a moment, he asked, "If they are our clan, why don't they come for us?"

Why indeed. She hated this feeling of being trapped. If she ever escaped from her husband, she would never let it happen again. Never. All she wanted in this life was to be safe with her son at Dunscaith Castle. Once, she had wanted more. Nay, she had expected it as her due.

Unbidden and unwanted, the image of Duncan MacDonald, the man whose desertion had led to all this misery, filled her head. No one had seen a young warrior of such promise since her brother Ragnall, who was ten years older. Moira remembered Duncan's copper hair glinting in the sunlight, the hard lines of his face that softened when he looked at her, the warrior's body that had taught her pleasure.

She would be better off without these memories. Ach, she had been a foolish and trusting lass at seventeen. She had read devotion in Duncan's silences, mistaken his lust for love, and counted on his strength to fight for her. Alas, she had been wrong in every regard.

"Damn ye, Duncan Ruadh Mòr!" Moira said under her breath as she stared out at the empty sea. "How could ye leave me?"

Duncan had brought her worse luck than a broken looking glass. Seven years of misery, with no end in sight.

Moira recalled the day of her wedding. Everyone was gathered in the hall waiting for the bride while she stood on the castle wall still watching for a sail in the distance. Up until the last moment, when her father came himself to fetch her, she was hoping and praying Duncan would return in time to save her. Even then, she would have sneaked down to the beach and—after giving him a tongue-lashing he would not soon forget—she would have climbed into his boat and gone anywhere with him.

She had been so certain he would come back for her. But it was five years before Duncan MacDonald returned to Skye. She would never forgive him.

Moira pushed away the old pain and watched Ragnall throwing a stick for his dog, Sàr, a giant wolfhound twice Ragnall's weight and the size of a small pony. For a moment her son looked as if he were a carefree lad, and she felt guilty that he could not be. His sweet young face had an old man's eyes.

Ragnall raised his arm to throw the stick again but stopped and stared up at the top of the bluff. "Father is here."

Moira flinched as she always did when she heard Ragnall call that foul man his father. When she turned and saw Sean's bearlike shape above them, she fought back the wave of nausea that rose in her throat. Even from this distance, she sensed trouble. She did not want Ragnall here.

"Ye know how he hates Sàr. Take him away," she said. When Ragnall hesitated and gave her a worried look, she pushed him. "Quickly now!"

"Come," Ragnall called, and Sàr loped beside him down the beach.

Moira forced her body to relax as Sean came down the cliff path toward her. Showing fear only emboldened him. Unfortunately, Sean could smell fear on you like the wild beast he was. When Sean reached her, he stood too close, towering over her with his hands on his hips and his legs apart in a wide stance. She smiled up at him.

"My dear wife," Sean said, his eyes as cold as the icy wind coming off the winter sea, "have ye something to tell me?"

Fear closed her throat, so she brightened her smile until she could speak. "Just that I'm pleased ye could come out to take a stroll with me. I know what a busy man ye are."

The smell of whiskey wafted off him, heightening her alarm. It was early in the day for strong drink, even for Sean.

"I saw the way my brother Colla was looking at ye in the hall at breakfast," Sean said.

Not this again. There was a time when Sean liked that men looked at her, and even provoked it by making lewd remarks about her. Now it only made him angry.

Sean had always been difficult, but he had grown

worse since the deaths of her father and brother Ragnall at the Battle of Flodden. As a result of their deaths, the fortunes of her clan fell, and with them, her own. Sean respected power, and she had lost hers.

Moira had heard rumors that her clan was slowly recovering its strength under her brother Connor. Yet Connor had not visited her once to demonstrate to Sean that he placed a high value on her welfare. She would have begged her brother to come if Sean had allowed her to send a message.

"I can't help it if men look at me," she said in what she hoped was a light voice.

Sean grabbed her arm in an iron grip, sending apprehension thrumming through her.

"Ye encourage them," he said. "I see how ye flaunt yourself at them."

"I don't." She should have kept silent, but she could not seem to help herself. She was tired of the false accusations, weary of pretending he was always right, and sick to death of *him*.

"Are ye calling your husband a liar now?"

She squeezed her eyes shut and steeled herself for the slap.

"Stop!" Ragnall shouted. "Let go of her!"

Moira snapped her eyes open when she heard her son's voice. Ragnall stood with his feet apart and with the stick he had been tossing to his dog clenched in his fist, a small boy mimicking the battle stance of the warrior he would one day be.

Dread weighed down on Moira's chest. "I'm all right," she said, meeting Ragnall's worried glance. "Put that down. Please."

Fear turned Moira's insides to liquid as she watched Sean's face fill with impending violence. Her world hung suspended by the thin thread of her husband's control.

When Sean threw his head back and barked out a laugh, Moira's knees felt weak. For once, Sean's unpredictability had worked in her favor.

"Ye will be a fierce warrior like your father," Sean said.

Ragnall clenched his jaw as Sean roughed his hair.

"One time, I'll let ye get away with challenging your father," Sean said, pointing his finger in Ragnall's face. "But if ye ever raise your hand to me again, I'll teach ye a lesson ye won't soon forget."

Moira heard the low rumble of a growl and turned to find Sàr approaching with his teeth bared.

"But as punishment, you'll get rid of that dog," Sean said.

"Please don't," she said. Ragnall loved Sàr. It would break his heart to lose him.

"Enough," Sean said, glaring at her.

"I won't do it," Ragnall said. "Ye can't make me."

Oh, no. "Sean, he's just a bairn," she pleaded, "He doesn't mean to challenge ye—"

Sean jerked Moira's head back by her hair so hard that tears sprang to her eyes. Despite the pain, her first thought was that she had succeeded in diverting him from taking his wrath out on Ragnall. But renewed panic flooded through her when Sean began dragging her across the rocky shore to the water.

"Let me go! Please!" she cried as he pulled her into the frigid water.

Ragnall was trying to follow, but the wolfhound blocked his path each time he got close to the water.

"Make a choice, Ragnall," Sean shouted. "Your mother or that dog?"

The weight of the water dragged at Moira's skirts as Sean hauled her into the surf. She stumbled over the rocks and fell to her knees, then gasped as an icy wave caught her full in the face. When Sean jerked her to her feet, her headdress fell off and was carried away with the next wave.

She could hear Ragnall screaming over the crash of the surf as Sean dragged her out farther still. When he finally halted, they were waist-deep, and the waves crested over her head.

"Shall I give her the witch's test?" Sean called out to Ragnall. Then he grabbed Moira by the back of her neck and said, "We'll see if ye are lying to me about Colla."

Witch's test? Did he mean to drown her?

Moira barely had time to take a deep breath before Sean plunged her head under the water. The shock of the cold nearly caused her to suck in seawater in a gasp. He held her under so long that her lungs were screaming for air. In sheer panic, she flailed her arms and scratched at him, but to no avail.

When he finally pulled her head up, she coughed and wheezed. She could not get enough air. She felt as if the cold had frozen her lungs, allowing her to take in only short breaths. Her hair streamed over her face, blinding her, as she choked and shook uncontrollably.

"Stop! Stop!" Ragnall's wails came to her over the water. Through rivulets of seawater and strands of wet hair, she saw her son crying on the beach. He was still trying to come in after her, but the wolfhound barred his way.

"I'll give Sàr up!" he shrieked. "I will, I will!"

"Are ye certain?" Sean's voice boomed beside her. "I don't want to find you've changed your mind later."

Ragnall darted past Sàr and into the water.

"Ragnall, no!" Moira cried out just before Sean plunged her head underwater again.

CHAPTER 2

Clank! Clank! Clank!

The rain pelted Duncan's face as he fought back-to-back with Connor against the ten warriors encircling them. Not good odds, but their opponents' number made them far too sure of themselves. As Duncan blocked one blade after another, he watched for the first man to make a fatal mistake.

He did not have to wait long. The instant one of their attackers swiped at the rain running into his eyes, Duncan swung his claymore so hard against the man's shield that he landed on his arse and bounced off the ground.

"Have ye paid no mind to what I've been teaching ye?" Duncan leaned over and shouted at the man sprawled at his feet. "You'd let yourself get killed over a wee bit of rain in your eyes?"

Duncan rammed his shoulder into another young warrior who was gawking at his friend on the ground when he should have been swinging his sword. Duncan's mood was as foul as the weather.

"Do ye think the MacLeods will wait for a dry day to attack us?" Duncan asked as he struck another man with the flat of his blade. Then he forced a pair of them back, shouting, "Or the MacKinnons? Or the Macleans? Or the—"

"That's enough for today, lads," Connor called out and held up his hand. As the others moved away, he lowered his voice and said to Duncan, "No need to take your temper out on them when it's me you're angry with."

Duncan dropped the point of his sword to rest on the ground. "Don't ask me to go to Ireland."

He could not bear to see Moira living there with her husband. It had nearly killed him when he learned that she had married the Irish chieftain's son only a fortnight after he left for France. Her heart had changed that quickly. Yet seven years later, her memory still walked beside him every day.

"I wouldn't ask," Connor said, resting his hand on Duncan's shoulder, "but ye are the only man I can send."

"I'm the captain of your guard," Duncan said. "Ye need me here to train the men. As ye can see, they've a lot to learn."

Even as he said it, Duncan was aware that it was a lost cause. Connor was his best friend as well as his chieftain. They both knew he would do whatever Connor needed, no matter what it cost him.

That didn't mean Duncan had to like it.

"Can I wipe the rain from my eyes now," Connor asked, "or are ye going to take a swing at me?"

Duncan swung so hard and fast that he nearly caught Connor off guard. For the next several minutes, they

crossed swords up and down the courtyard and showed
the others how true fighting was done. By the time they
stopped, the rain was coming down in icy sheets, and
steam rose from the heat of their skin.

"I enjoyed that." Connor grinned at him as he swiped
at his face with his sleeve. The responsibilities of the
chieftainship weighed heavily on Connor, so it was good
to see him looking carefree.

"After wasting my day attempting to forge warriors
from the likes of those," Duncan said, casting his gaze at
the men who had remained in the pouring rain to watch
them, "'tis a relief to see that my chieftain still knows
how to fight."

"They are fine warriors," Connor said, slapping Duncan on the shoulder. "They're just not as good as we are."

As they walked through the puddles to the keep, Duncan remembered splashing through them one day when
they were young lads. Duncan had come to a dead halt
when Moira skipped down the steps of the keep looking
like a sparkle of sunshine in her bright yellow gown. Connor didn't notice her and sprayed her head-to-toe with
mud. Ach, that lass could shriek! Moira pounded on Connor until their older brother Ragnall lifted her off her feet
and carried her inside.

Yet most of his memories of Moira were not from their
childhood, but from the summer she was a breathtaking
seventeen. As he climbed the steps of the keep, Duncan
glanced up at the window of the bedchamber that had
been hers. Moira told him how she had looked out of it
one day that summer, seen him practicing with the other
men, and decided he was the one she wanted. From that
moment on, she had turned his world upside down.

It had been two years since they had returned from fighting in France and taken Dunscaith Castle back from Connor's uncle. And still, every corner and every stone of the castle reminded him of her. And damned fool that he was, he nurtured the memories. He could not give them up because they were all he had of her—and all he ever would.

And the lass had forgotten him in a fortnight. Moira's father spoiled her shamelessly. If she had not been willing to wed the Irish chieftain's son, he would not have forced her.

As Duncan entered the keep behind Connor, he saw that his sister Ilysa was fussing at the men, handing them towels and advising them not to bring mud into the hall or she'd forget where she hid the whiskey. Duncan was not sure how it had happened that Ilysa had taken over the management of the chieftain's household—and he suspected Connor didn't, either. Regardless, his slight, eighteen-year-old sister performed the duty with a firm hand. When she pointed at their muddy boots, both the chieftain and the captain of the guard wiped them before entering the hall.

"Can ye have someone bring us whiskey?" Connor asked her.

"'Tis on the high table waiting for ye, if your two cousins haven't drunk it all," Ilysa said with a small smile.

With their mother dead, Duncan should speak to Ilysa about her future, but he felt wholly inadequate to the task. It seemed odd that his baby sister had been married, albeit briefly, while he was in France. Though she had lost her husband more than two years ago in the Battle of Flodden, she showed no interest in remarrying. Still, she would have to find something to do with herself once Connor finally took a wife.

Connor's cousins, Ian and Alex, were lounging by the hearth with their long legs stretched out before them and cups of whiskey in their hands. Ian had the same black hair as Connor, while Alex had the fair hair of the Vikings who spawned children while terrorizing these coasts in the old days. Though they still looked like the sort of men a wise father kept away from his daughters, Ian and Alex were both devoted family men now.

"Ye should have joined the practice," Duncan said by way of greeting. "If all ye do is make babies, you'll grow weak and be no use to us in a fight."

"Great warriors like us?" Alex unfolded himself from his chair and stretched. "Ach, we don't need practice."

Alex tossed his cup in the air, whipped his sword through the air several times, spun in a circle, and then caught the cup by the handle with his teeth, barely spilling a drop. The hall erupted as the men shouted and pounded the hilts of their swords on the floor, but Duncan ignored the display. Despite Alex's foolishness, he kept his skills razor-sharp.

Connor stood by the head table, his wet hair as black as a seal's, and filled the two empty cups waiting there with whiskey from the flask. When he signaled for his cousins and Duncan to join him, the others in the hall moved away a respectful distance. Everyone understood that they were the men the chieftain trusted to advise him on important matters.

The four of them had been closer than brothers since they were bairns. The bond forged in their boyhood had been strengthened by fighting side by side in countless battles. If they lived to be old men, they could bore young men with their tales for hours around this hearth on long winter nights. And Alex probably would.

"We have accomplished much since we returned from France to find my father and brother dead and our clan in peril," Connor said after they had settled at the table. "Our lands here on the Sleat Peninsula of Skye are protected by Dunscaith Castle on the west and Knock Castle on the east."

They raised their cups to Ian, who deserved most of the credit for their success in wresting Knock Castle from the thieving MacKinnons and Dunscaith Castle from Connor's uncle Hugh. Unfortunately, after losing both Dunscaith and the chieftainship, Hugh had escaped and returned to pirating, which caused them a good deal of trouble.

"Our people on the isle of North Uist are safe now as well," Connor continued.

This time they raised their cups to Alex, who was the new keeper of the clan's castle on North Uist. While they had succeeded in driving off the pirates who had been raiding North Uist and the neighboring islands, Hugh had escaped that time as well.

"But we cannot rest until we take back the lands the MacLeods stole from us," Connor said. "'Tis time we did."

This was what they had all been waiting for. As one, they raised their cups and chanted, "*A' phlàigh oirbh, a Chlanna MhicLeòid!*" A plague on the MacLeods!

The MacLeods of Dunvegan were their chief rivals on the Isle of Skye, and there was a bloody history between them. Most recently, the wily MacLeod chieftain, Alastair Crotach, had taken advantage of the MacDonalds' weakness after the Battle of Flodden to capture the

MacDonald lands and castle on the Trotternish Peninsula of the island.

"It won't be easy," Ian said, leaning his forearms on the table. "The MacLeods have more men and war galleys than we do. Also, Alastair MacLeod doesn't have his miserable relatives trying to take the chieftainship from him like Connor does."

"*Am fear nach eil làidir 's fheudar dha 'bhith carach,*" Alex said. He who is not strong must be cunning.

"The MacLeods are too strong for us to take them alone," Connor said.

"We have a powerful alley in the Campbells, especially now that they have the Crown's authority over the Western Isles," Ian said. "Can they be persuaded to fight with us?"

"Only if we are attacked," Connor said, running his hands through his damp hair. "They won't send warriors to help us recover our stolen lands."

"There's a risk the other rebel clans will side with the MacLeods against us," Duncan said, and immediately regretted speaking up when Connor fixed his gaze on him.

"That is why I need ye to visit our 'allies' in Ireland," Connor said. "We must know which side they will be on when the fighting starts."

"Send someone else," Duncan said and took a drink.

"Hugh has spies here at Dunscaith." Connor leaned forward and spoke in a low voice. "Until I discover who they are, I cannot trust anyone but the three of ye. I need Ian here on Skye to defend Knock Castle and Alex on North Uist to protect our people there. That leaves you, Duncan."

"Maybe if ye see Moira, ye can finally forget her," Alex said with his usual lack of tact. At least this time he did not add his personal nickname for her, *Sea of Sorrow*. "Isn't it time both you and Connor took brides?"

"Aye," Ian said. "Connor, ye put the clan in jeopardy by not having an heir."

"I must make the best alliance possible with my marriage," Connor said. "I can't know which clan to choose until the dust settles after this damned rebellion is ended."

"I suppose that leaves Moira's son as your heir for the time being," Ian said.

"That is another reason I'm sending Duncan to Ireland," Connor said, turning back to him. "Hugh has shown he is willing to murder anyone who stands between him and the chieftainship. The lad's father must be warned of the danger."

Damn. Damn. Damn.

"So you're going to Ireland." Alex raised his cup to Duncan and winked. "Good luck telling Rhona. Ach, that woman of yours scares me."

"'Tis time ye showed her the door anyway," Ian said. "But I'd advise ye to take her dirk from her first."

They were talking nonsense, but Duncan let them have their laugh.

Suddenly the doors to the keep burst open with a rush of wind and rain and banged against the walls. Duncan was on his feet with his claymore in his hands before he saw the tiny hunched figure silhouetted in the doorway.

God in Heaven, what is the ancient seer doing at the castle? Teàrlag was as old as the mist and older by two, as the saying went. She had not left her cottage in Duncan's memory.

"I've had a vision!" Teàrlag wailed. "Woe, I bring terrible news!"

CHAPTER 3

Sean finally released Moira and left her to make her own way back to shore. She glared at his back as she coughed up salt water and fought the pull of the undertow.

"If I see that dog again, I'll slit its throat," Sean shouted at Ragnall as he passed him in the water. Ragnall was in up to his knees, with each wave threatening to knock him over, but Sean continued to shore without looking back.

"Don't come any farther!" Moira called out to her son.

She stumbled and fell headlong into the water and came up gasping. Her knees and palms were cut and bleeding from the barnacles, but she concentrated on her son's face and kept moving. Finally, when she was within a few feet of him, Ragnall ran into her arms. A wave crashed into her from behind, nearly causing her to lose her footing again on the slippery rock.

Ragnall took her hand and pulled her toward shore.

Once they were on the beach beyond the reach of the

waves, she collapsed onto the sand. Ragnall ran to fetch the blanket they had brought to the beach, then dropped it around her shoulders and crawled into her lap. Her teeth chattered uncontrollably as she rocked her son, a ball of heat that she enveloped in her icy body. Seawater from her hair streamed down to mix with the tears on his face.

"We cannot stay here any longer," she said.

Moira had felt the lash of Sean's tongue almost from the start of their marriage, but this was the first time she had been in fear for her life. Though Sean had become increasingly volatile these last months, she had fooled herself into believing she could control him by cajoling and flattering him, as she always had.

The moment Ragnall raised the stick at Sean, everything changed. She should have known her son would try to protect her. Ragnall had an innate sense of honor that Sean could not comprehend—and it would put her son in danger.

"I don't know how yet, but we will go home to Dunscaith Castle. We'll be safe there." She rubbed her son's head and stared out at the empty sea toward Skye. Whatever she had to do to get her son to safety, she would do it.

"I wish he weren't my father." Ragnall paused, then asked in a small voice, "Will I be like him?"

"No." Moira took Ragnall's face in her hands and looked hard into his eyes. "You're nothing like him, and ye never will be."

"How do ye know?" Ragnall asked, worry tinting his dark blue eyes, the only part of him that he got from her.

"Because at six you're already a better man than he is." She brushed his hair back from his face. "Ye will grow up to be a fine warrior and the best of men. Ye will make your mother proud."

Sàr reappeared and lay down next to her, smelling of wet dog.

"He's trying to warm ye," Ragnall said.

"He's a good dog," she said, scratching the wolf-hound's shaggy head, "but you'll have to let him go. Sean will kill Sàr if he sees him."

Ach, Sean was a demon to force a child to choose between his beloved dog and his mother's life.

"My father will never catch him," Ragnall said. "Sàr is too fast."

"Until we can make our escape, we must do our best not to provoke Sean," she said. "Do ye understand?"

Ragnall buried his face against her. "But how will Sàr eat?"

"Whenever we can, we'll leave food for him in our special place in the old fort."

Ragnall was quiet for a long while, then he asked, "Can we take Sàr with us when we go to Skye?"

Moira was tempted to lie, but she had been raised on lies and false hopes, and she would not do the same to Ragnall. She brushed the hair back from his face with her fingers and kissed his forehead. "I don't think so, *mo chroí*." My heart. "But you and I will escape."

No matter what she had to do, she would save her son.

CHAPTER 4

While they all gaped at Teàrlag, who stood at the entrance to the hall moaning and waving her arms, Ian's seventeen-year-old brother Niall came in behind her and pulled the doors shut.

"Are you the fool who brought Teàrlag out in such weather?" Ian asked him while Connor and Ilysa helped the old seer to the chair closest to the hearth. "Ye could have killed her."

Niall looked sheepish and came to stand next to Duncan. "I tried to tell her no," Niall whispered to him, "but the old woman threatened to cast a spell that would make my manly parts shrink to nothing."

Duncan chuckled. Teàrlag was well known for her foretelling and no doubt had the gift, but she made use of her reputation to suit herself.

"What have ye seen that is so important that ye left your cottage, and in such bad weather?" Connor asked, kneeling beside the old seer.

She looked around her with her one good eye. "Will no one fetch an old woman a cup of whiskey before I die of a chill?"

Ilysa retrieved the flask from the head table and poured Teàrlag a small cupful. All eyes were on the old seer as they waited to hear her news while she downed her drink.

Teàrlag wiped her mouth on the back of her hand and gave Connor a mournful glance. "My own jug is pathetically low…"

"I'll send a new jug home with ye," Connor said, patting her arm and showing the patience of a saint. "Are ye ready to tell us now?"

Duncan did not trust what he could not see. His mother had had strange visions on occasion—or thought she did—and the whole business made him uneasy. And he sure as hell did not like that his sister was learning the Old Ways from the seer.

"I saw a great storm at sea." Teàrlag swayed in her seat and waved her gnarled hands in the air. "Thunder came rolling over the water, and lightning cracked."

It didn't take *The Sight* to see the storm outside. Duncan glanced toward the stairs, wishing he could leave the hall unnoticed, though with his size that was never possible. Ach, he was leaving anyway.

Before Duncan had taken two steps, Teàrlag's next words stopped him in place.

"Just before the storm, I heard Moira's voice."

"My sister?" Connor asked. "Is she safe?"

"Would I leave my cottage for the first time in a dozen years to tell ye all was well?" Teàrlag snapped.

Duncan crossed the room and pushed the others aside to stand in front of Teàrlag. "What do ye see?" he asked.

Teàrlag closed her eyes and made a humming sound before she spoke again. "I can't see Moira, but I hear her voice...and then I see a pool of blood."

Duncan felt as if he had taken a blow to the chest.

"So much blood!" Teàrlag wailed.

"But is it Moira's blood?" Connor asked.

"I've no notion whose blood it is," Teàrlag said, coming out of her "trance" with alarming speed. She got to her feet, but she was so hunched over that she looked no taller standing than sitting. "Now I'll have a wee nap before I return to my cottage."

"Stay here tonight," Ilysa said, resting her hand on the old woman's shoulder.

"No. My cow will need milking." Teàrlag fixed her good eye on Duncan. "You, lad, help me upstairs to a bed."

Duncan walked her across the hall to the stairs at an excruciatingly slow pace and wondered if it would hurt the old seer's pride to pick her up and carry her.

"Do ye remember," Teàrlag said between wheezing breaths as they climbed the circular stone staircase, "when I predicted ye would suffer great sorrow?"

"Aye." That wasn't something a lad of eleven was likely to forget.

Teàrlag had seemed older than the mist even back then, so he, Connor, Alex, and Ian had gone to her cottage hoping she would predict their future before she died. Being lads, all they had wanted to hear was what great warriors they would become. Instead, her predictions had been about love and women. The old seer had always been contrary.

"I told ye then that sometimes a man can change his

fate," she said when she stopped to catch her breath. "'Tis time ye changed yours, Duncan Ruadh MacDonald."

He had changed it—he was no longer just the nurse-maid's fatherless son. Whoever sired him had violated the Highland tradition that required a man to claim his child, regardless of whether he was wed to the mother. Duncan had risen from that shame to become captain of his chieftain's guard, a respected warrior with a fearsome reputation.

"Ye try an old woman's patience. Ye were fated from the start to be a great warrior." Teàrlag stretched her arm above her head to tap her knobby finger on his chest. "But are ye brave enough to trust in a woman's love? Because that is your only hope of truly changing your fate."

That would change his fate, all right. For the worse.

"Do ye still carry that old bone whistle?" she asked.

Ach, the old woman's mind was growing weak with the way it wandered.

"Aye," he said, touching the eight-inch whistle that was tied to a leather thong around his neck. It was a gift from his mother, and he always carried it with him.

"Good," Teàrlag said. "Ye will need it before your trip is done."

His whistle?

"And in our clan's time of need, your music will provide the answer."

* * *

Moira hated having to do this. Her heart pounded in her ears as she glanced at Sean again to be sure he was immersed in the fabricated tale he was telling the men on the other side of him. Then she met Colla's eyes across the table and slowly ran her tongue across her upper lip. Colla leaned forward with his mouth hanging open like a fish.

Ach, she should have chosen a man capable of subtlety. Once she scratched the men with wives and children off her list, there were few to choose from who owned their own boats. Besides, Colla had wanted her for years. It should not take long to convince him to take her away, and she was in a hurry.

Moira stood up from the table and put her hand on her husband's shoulder. When Sean turned his face toward her, she remembered how handsome and charming she had thought he was when she first met him. The charm had evaporated a long time ago, but his drinking had not yet softened his warrior's body or made the skin over his broad cheekbones blotchy.

He had the eyes of a snake.

"The wine is getting low," she said. "I'll see that the new barrel is opened."

"Be quick about it," Sean said.

She clenched her teeth as he slapped her bottom. Ach, he had the manners of a pig.

She could not risk a quick glance at Colla on her way out of the hall. Even blind drunk, Sean might notice. She hurried down the stone steps into the damp coolness of the undercroft. To her left, the kitchen was noisy and lit with torches and cooking fires. She turned to her right, into the dark corridor that led to the storerooms.

Using the key tied to her belt, she unlocked the door to the room in which they kept the whiskey, wine, and ale. The smell of spirits and dank earth filled her nose as she slipped inside. Her heart hammered as she waited and watched through the crack in the door.

Would Colla come? She did not know which she feared more—if he did or if he did not. Playing on a man's desire without letting him have what he wanted was a difficult game to play, and the stakes could not be higher.

Footsteps echoed against the stone walls. Her chest tightened while she watched the boots and then the legs of a man appear as he descended the stairs. A moment later, she saw that it was Colla. After pausing to glance furtively toward the kitchens, he strode toward the store-rooms.

"Quickly!" She opened the door for him and then shut it behind him.

Colla pulled her against him at once, before she was prepared for it. She turned her face when he tried to kiss her.

"Did I misread ye?" Colla's breath in her face smelled of onions and ale. "Or are ye playing coy with me?"

She tried to ease him away. "Ye didn't misread me, but—"

"God, how I've wanted ye," he said as he began planting sloppy, wet kisses down the side of her throat. When she shivered, he mistook her revulsion for excitement and increased his efforts. Ach, men saw what they wanted to see. They were all vain as peacocks.

"We don't have time for this now." Moira gripped his shoulders and gave him a hard push. "And 'tis not safe here."

"Can ye get away and meet me in the field behind the castle tonight?" Colla asked, breathing in her face again.

"In the field behind the castle? Is that all ye think of me?" She did not have to pretend to be affronted.

"I think the world of ye," Colla said, leaning too close again.

"'Tis too dangerous for us here," she said. "If Sean caught us, he'd murder us both."

"If ye could slip away for an afternoon," Colla said, "there's a quiet bay a couple of miles to the west."

"Do ye think I'd leave my husband for a man who only wants to roll around on the grass with me a time or two?" she asked.

"Leave your husband?" Colla straightened and blinked at her.

Had she misjudged how badly he wanted her? Moira did not have much time to persuade Colla to take her and her son away. Sean was like a pot of oil on a hot fire ready to explode. She took Colla's hand and placed it on her breast.

"*O shluagh*," Colla murmured, calling on the faeries for help.

Moira swallowed back her distaste. Even through the cloth of her gown, his hand felt hot and damp.

"Please, Moira, I've wanted ye for so long. Just tell me where ye want to meet."

When will this be over? His hand was on her breast like a limpet.

"I want ye to take me far away from here," she said, "to a place where Sean could never catch us."

"Meet me tomorrow and we'll talk about it." Colla's breathing grew harsh as he rubbed his thumb over her nipple. This was taking longer than she'd anticipated.

"The only place we'll be safe is at my brother's castle on Skye," she said and removed his hand from her breast. "My brother is chieftain of my clan and would welcome us."

Connor damned well better welcome her, after all she'd been through.

"Ye would take me as your new husband?" Colla asked. "My heart has been yours for years, but I didn't dare hope ye would consider marrying me."

Colla may have convinced himself that his heart was engaged, but Moira knew precisely what part of him he hoped to engage with her. And, typical man, he did not even notice that she had failed to answer his question.

"I won't be parted from my son." She folded her arms beneath her breasts to draw his attention to them.

"Ach, I don't know about taking a man's child from him..."

"I will not go without Ragnall," she said.

Colla dragged his gaze from her breasts to her face. "Whatever ye want, Moira."

She let her breath out slowly. This time, when Colla pulled her into his arms, she gritted her teeth and let him for a moment.

"I must wait for an opportunity," she said, leaning back from him. "Ye cannot tell a soul. Sean is a dangerous man."

"Ach, I'm no afraid of Sean," Colla said, puffing out his chest. "I'm willing to fight him for ye."

Men. She had told him that to make him cautious, not to prick his pride. She cupped his jaw with her hand and smiled up at him. "Please. I don't want a fight."

"All right," he said.

Panic rose in her throat when Colla crushed her against him. She felt cold and clammy as he began running his hands over her.

"I must go before Sean sends someone looking for

me." Feigning reluctance, she eased him away. "We'll have all the time we want once we are away from here."

"How will I know when and where to meet you?" Colla asked.

"When I wear my dark red gown, that means I will try to get away that night," she said. "Ye know where the old wooden fort is?"

"Aye."

"I'll meet ye there at midnight."

CHAPTER 5

I'll leave for Ireland in the morning," Duncan said.

He and Connor were sitting alone having a last drink. Alex had taken Teàrlag home to her cow, and Ian had gone home to Sìleas and their babies. After all the commotion earlier, the hall had settled down to a quiet hum of voices.

"The winter storms are still upon us," Connor said. "Wait another month or two."

"After what Teàrlag said, ye know I can't," Duncan said.

"The meaning of Teàrlag's vision wasn't clear, and she's getting old and confused," Connor said. "I expect you'll find that all is well with Moira."

For all Duncan's years of misery, his one consolation had been that he had done the right thing in leaving. He had believed that Moira would wed a chieftain and have the kind of life that would make her happy—the kind that he could never give her. A thousand times he had imagined her as mistress of a fine castle, with servants, jewels, and pretty gowns. And in his mind's eye, she had always been smiling and laughing.

If he had been wrong and he had made the sacrifice for nothing, he could not bear it.

"All the same, I'll be going in the morning," Duncan said, looking into his cup.

Duncan's affair with Moira was the only secret he had ever kept from Connor. Ian had been at court in Stirling that summer, so he had not known of it, either. But Alex had been around Dunscaith and, being Alex, had guessed what was going on between Duncan and Moira long before Connor's father did.

Their chieftain had waited to tell Connor until they were boarding the boat for France. Connor refused to believe his father until he confronted Duncan, and Duncan admitted it was true. That was the only time Connor had ever struck Duncan in anger. Even as a young lad, Connor always had a cool head.

When Connor knocked him to the bottom of the boat and started punching him, Duncan did not defend himself. He knew he deserved it. Eventually, Alex and Ian managed to drag Connor off him.

"Use your head," Alex had shouted in Connor's face as he flung his arm out to point at Duncan. "Who do ye think did the seducing? Our man, death-before-dishonor Duncan? Or Princess Moira, who expects the world to bend to her will? Ach, I tell ye, Duncan didn't have a chance."

"Do ye love her?" Connor asked him.

"Aye," Duncan answered.

And that was the end of it. As close as he and Connor

were, they never spoke about Duncan's relationship with Moira again.

Months later, though, Connor shared the battered letter from his father with the news of Moira's marriage. The letter had taken far longer to reach them than the mere fortnight it had taken for Moira to say wedding vows to another man after professing her love to Duncan. Connor had put his hand on Duncan's shoulder as he read the letter. But he said nothing, because there was nothing to say.

"I am grateful to ye for going to Ireland," Connor said. "When you see my sister, you'll know if something is wrong."

Just because they never spoke of Duncan's feelings for Moira, did not mean that Connor did not know them.

"I'll take the galley we stole from Shaggy Maclean," Duncan said. "It's small, but it's fast and glides through the water like a sea otter."

"Ye can't take many men on it," Connor said.

"That's an advantage," Duncan said. "Since ye can't spare enough men for me to do battle with the Irish, 'tis better to have too few to put them on their guard."

"How many men do ye want?" Connor asked.

"I could use a second pair of hands on the boat," Duncan said. "That's all."

"Ye know I can't spare Ian or Alex." Connor narrowed his eyes as he stared into the fire. "Take Ian's brother Niall."

Duncan suppressed a groan. Ian's seventeen-year-old brother was becoming a fine warrior, and he had plenty of courage, but he was so damned earnest.

"Niall is not much younger than we were when we left for France," Connor said. "He fought at Flodden."

"Aye, but..."

"I know, he's so naïve as to be painful." Connor took a drink from his cup. "'Tis hard to believe we were that young not long ago."

Duncan had never been naïve, and he took nothing at face value. Unlike Niall and Ian, who had grown up in a loving home with parents who protected them, Duncan had to learn to watch out for himself at an early age. He did not regret it; the hard lessons had made him strong.

"People trust Niall," Connor said. "They'll tell him anything, and that could be useful."

Duncan leaned forward and rubbed his head. "He's a good lad, I suppose. Niall will do."

"Your first task is to find out if the MacQuillans and the other Irish will fight for or against us when we take on the MacLeods," Connor said. "I don't want to risk our alliance with them over a wee spat Moira is having with her husband."

"And if it's more than a wee spat?" Duncan asked.

"We have too many enemies already," Connor said. "Do whatever ye can to get her home without starting a clan war. I don't care if ye have to lie, cheat, or charm them to do it."

"Hmmph. Lie, cheat, or charm? You should send one of the others," Duncan said. "I'm a fighting man."

"You're that and more," Connor said, squeezing his shoulder. "Be careful. I can't afford to lose ye."

* * *

"*Mìle fàilte oirbh*." A thousand welcomes. Moira bit out the traditional greeting to the MacLeod chieftain. She was furious that Sean had invited her clan's worst enemy to their home. This was one more affront, and hopefully the last.

She brushed her fingers over the skirt of her wine-red gown to remind herself that she was leaving tonight. Twice before, she had worn it. Both times she had had to call off her plan when Sean came upstairs instead of falling asleep drunk in the hall as he usually did. Tonight she was determined to succeed. She caught Colla's eye and gave him a slight nod.

"*Beannachd air an taigh.*" A blessing on this house. Alastair Crotach MacLeod spoke in a deep, raspy voice while he appraised her with his cold eyes. He did not appear to be any more pleased by the prospect of sharing a meal with a MacDonald than she was at sharing it with him.

The MacLeod chieftain carried a constant, and likely painful, reminder of his hate for her clan. He was called Alastair Crotach, Alastair the Humpback, because a terrible axe wound he had received as a young man, from a MacDonald, had left his shoulder deformed.

Alastair MacLeod had been chieftain of his clan for nearly forty years, and he wore his power like a second skin. He was sixty-odd years but looked far younger. Paradoxically, his deformed shoulder made him seem more formidable and added to his mystique.

"Ye look like your mother," the MacLeod said.

"Ye knew her?" Moira had not intended to converse with the man, but his remark startled her into blurting out the question.

"She was the youngest and prettiest of the three beautiful Clanranald sisters," he said. "I saw her but once, but she was not a woman a man forgets."

Moira had no memory at all of her mother.

"Shame she left a good man for the likes of your father," the MacLeod said, "and then died trying to leave him."

How dare he speak ill of my family to my face? Only the dead knew the truth of what happened between her father and mother at the end.

"And they say 'tis women who spread rumors and gossip," Moira said, giving the MacLeod chieftain a falsely sweet smile.

"Moira!" Sean squeezed her arm painfully and marched her out of the hall. "I expect ye to be courteous to my guests."

Moira bit her tongue to keep from saying that his guest was rude first.

"I will deal with ye later, woman." When Sean had her through the door to the stairs, he gave her a shove. "Go upstairs. I have important business to discuss with the MacLeod, and I can't have ye causing trouble."

She would never have guessed that she would be grateful for the MacLeod's visit or his rudeness. But thanks to him, she would have more time to make her escape. The two chieftains were likely to talk and drink far into the night, and Sean would not discover she was gone until morning.

Ragnall was asleep on the pallet on the floor next to the bed.

"Wake up," she whispered and shook his shoulder. When he opened his eyes, she said, "We're leaving, *mo chroí*."

She gathered the last of their things, shoved them into her cloth bag, and flung it over her shoulder. After taking her son's hand, she put her ear to the door. She heard no one in the stone stairwell, so she eased the door open.

With her hand on the latch, she paused to glance back at the bedchamber that had been the source of such misery to her.

Good riddance, Sean MacQuillan. May ye burn in hell for all eternity.

CHAPTER 6

"Y ou're packing?" Rhona asked.

"Mmph." Duncan grunted in the affirmative, though it was obvious what he was doing.

"How long will ye be gone this time?" she asked.

"I don't know." He took an axe down from the wall and tested the sharpness of the blade before setting it on the table with the other weapons and supplies he was taking.

"Where can ye be going in the midst of the winter storms?" Rhona asked.

He shot her a glance. Asking so many questions was contrary to the understanding between them. He never told her the chieftain's business. In fact, he never discussed it with anyone, except for Ian and Alex. And he wouldn't even tell them if Connor asked him not to.

"Perhaps I won't be here when ye return," Rhona said, folding her arms.

"Do as ye wish." They got along well enough, but if she wanted to go, she could.

"Is that all ye have to say to me?" she said and grabbed his arm. "I've been sharing your bed for two years."

Duncan had thought their arrangement suited her. He should have listened when Alex warned him that Rhona might think there was more to it than there was. Alex understood women. Duncan sighed. It was not Rhona's fault that there was only one woman he would ever want for more than a bedmate.

And that one woman had forgotten him in a fortnight.

"You'd be sorry to find me gone when ye return," Rhona said.

Duncan strapped his sword on his back, picked up his bag, and turned to face her. It was ironic that he had been sleeping with Moira's former maid. Of course, it was Moira who had developed the plan that Rhona pretend she was the one slipping out of the castle and carrying on with him. Rhona had none of Moira's vibrant beauty, but she was a curvy lass with dark hair and blue eyes. It was because of Rhona's superficial resemblance to Moira that they had been able to carry on as long as they had without discovery.

It was also the reason he had let Rhona into his house when she kept coming around after he returned from France. Ach, he was a sorry man. At least he never pretended that she was Moira in the dark anymore.

Well, almost never.

* * *

Moira hugged herself more against the chill growing inside her than the bitter wind coming off the sea as she watched for Colla's boat. Seven years she had waited. Surely, God should not ask one more day of her.

For the first hour she and Ragnall waited, Moira had to force herself not to think about the price she would have to pay with her body for this boat ride home to Skye. Colla was not a bad sort, but she did not want him touching her. Perhaps she could persuade him that a good deed was its own reward. Ha.

They had waited so long now that she feared Colla was not coming.

"Where is the boat?" Ragnall asked in a sleepy voice. He sat on the ground leaning against the wolfhound, who had joined them shortly after they entered the ruins of the old fort.

Moira dug her fingernails into her palms to keep from crying in front of her son.

"We'll wait a wee bit longer," she said. "If he doesn't come, we'll find another way."

Clump, clump, clump.

Moira jumped at the sound of footsteps on the stone slabs that had once been the floor of the old fortress. Finally, Colla had come. She wanted to believe it, but with every echoing footstep, she felt disaster coming closer.

Clump, clump, clump. Mary, Mother of God, please let it be Colla.

Out of the shadows the figure of a man emerged. It was not Colla.

She heard Ragnall whisper "Go!" and the wolfhound disappeared into the darkness.

Despite the numbing cold, Moira's palms were clammy, and sweat prickled under her arms. Her mind worked feverishly to find an explanation she could give Sean for their being at the old fort in the night. But there was none.

"Expecting someone else?" Sean's voice came out of the blackness.

The calmness of Sean's voice frightened her more than if he had shouted. She did not want her son here.

"Go ahead, look for Colla's boat," Sean said, swinging his arm out toward the sea.

How had he discovered that it was Colla who was taking her away?

"Ye won't be seeing him again." Sean paused. "No one will. Colla's feeding the fish."

Moira sucked in her breath. "No! Ye wouldn't. Not to your own brother."

But she knew in her heart that Sean spoke the truth. Dear God, she had not meant to cause Colla's death.

She told herself to brazen it out, to pretend that she did not know why Sean had murdered Colla, but she could not. Instead, she sank down on her knees on the cold, hard ground and bent over, trying to get her breath back. Ragnall ran to her and threw his arms around her.

Although Moira had no real memories of her mother, she had been plagued as a child by dreams of her mother's body floating facedown in the sea with her long dark hair swirling about her. Those images of her drowned mother came back to her now, but with Colla's body floating beside her.

Mary, Mother of God, please help me. Would she ever have the chance to attempt an escape again? Sean would watch her even more vigilantly than before. All was lost.

She was too drained to fear Sean's temper. Surely, there was nothing worse he could do to her than keep her trapped with him in his castle.

CHAPTER 7

Moira heard the *clink-clink* of the key turning in the lock and pushed Ragnall behind her.

When Sean stepped inside, his large frame seemed to take up all the empty space in the bedchamber. He had left her all night to wait and wonder what her punishment would be for attempting to leave him. In the gray morning light coming through the narrow window, Sean's expression still appeared unnaturally calm. It did not bode well. Whatever evil he had set his mind to, it pleased him.

"I've decided to foster our son," Sean said.

It was a common practice for highborn families to foster their children with other clans as a way of strengthening their alliances. Months ago, Moira had suggested that Sean foster Ragnall with her own clan. Though she knew better, hope rose in her chest against all odds, like a blade of grass that grows out of rock.

"My brother would teach Ragnall to be a strong warrior," she said, trying to keep her voice steady.

"I wouldn't send a son of mine to your clan," Sean said. "The MacDonalds of Sleat are weak and doomed."

She wanted to argue, but that would work against her. "Where then?"

Ragnall was all she had to live for, and she would miss him with all her heart. Still, she wanted him away from Sean, anywhere he would be safe.

"The MacLeod chieftain has agreed to foster Ragnall."

"Ye can't send him to the MacLeods," she blurted out. "They are my clan's worst enemies!"

"They aren't my enemy," Sean said, with a self-satisfied smile. "The MacLeods will be a useful ally to us MacQuillans."

"What of the alliance your father made with mine? You've no cause to break it." Despite the danger, Moira was raised a chieftain's daughter, and it was her duty to speak for her clan. "Ye can't send Ragnall to the MacLeods—he's my brother's heir." At least, she had not heard that Connor had a son of his own.

"Ragnall is *my* son and *my* heir." Sean leaned forward, his pretense of good humor cracking. "I can send him to the MacLeods or to the devil himself if I choose."

Ragnall was clinging to her waist and weeping. Moira held him against her, trying to comfort him, as her mind whirled. It struck her that Sean was not doing this to threaten her brother and her clan, but her.

"You'd best learn to treat me with the respect I deserve," Sean said between tight lips. "If ye ever attempt to leave me again, I'll make certain ye will never see our son again."

"Punishing me is more important than protecting our son?" Even as she asked the question, she knew the answer. Sean had found the one punishment that would make her suffer every hour of every day, and he meant to use it.

"Ragnall, say good-bye to your mother," Sean said. "And stop weeping like a damned lass."

"Don't do this. Please," she begged Sean as she held her son against her side. "Ye can't trust the MacLeods with my precious boy."

"The MacLeods are ready to set sail," Sean said. "Ragnall, gather your things and get down to the beach, or your mother will pay for your disobedience."

Sean slammed the door behind him, leaving them alone to say good-bye. For a long moment, she and Ragnall wept and clung to each other. Then Moira wiped her nose and eyes on her sleeve and took her son's face between her hands. She knew that what she said to him now was important. It would have to sustain them both until they could be reunited.

"Never forget that ye are a MacDonald of Sleat and that ye come from a long line of famed warriors, including Somerled and the Lords of the Isles," she said. "Learn all ye can from the MacLeods, for it could prove useful one day, but don't trust anyone except a MacDonald."

Ragnall wiped his eyes and nodded, but his bottom lip was quivering. "I don't want to go."

"I don't know how long you'll have to stay with the MacLeods." She brushed his hair back and looked into his eyes. "But I promise, I will come for ye or send someone to bring ye to me as soon as I can."

Ragnall nodded again. Ach, he was such a brave little boy. She pulled him close and kissed his hair.

"Don't forget me," she whispered, though it was too much to ask. He was only six.

"I won't," he said. "I love ye, Mother."

"You are the pulse of my heart, *a chuisle mo chroí*," she said and embraced her son for the last time.

CHAPTER 8

Another wave crashed over the bow, drenching Niall from head to toe.

"This storm will pass soon," Duncan called out over the wind whipping against his face. "The sky is clear up ahead."

"I don't mind a wee bit of weather," Niall shouted back with a grin.

Niall was a good lad, though a mite too cheerful. Duncan did not mind the foul weather, either. Navigating through rough seas diverted his thoughts. Once they passed through the squall and the sailing became easy, he could not keep himself from thinking about seeing Moira for the first time after all these years of longing.

If God had any mercy, she would have grown plump and lost her looks.

Yet it would make no difference. Moira was imprinted on his soul, and there would never be another woman he wanted in the way he wanted her.

That did not mean he would let her make a fool of him again. Not that she would bother trying. Despite the old seer's vision, Duncan expected to find Moira living happily in her fine castle with her chieftain husband.

"I see it," Niall called out and pointed to where a castle sat high on the red cliffs emerging from the clouds.

"We'll stow our boat out of sight up the shore and walk back to the castle," Duncan said.

Niall cast him a questioning look. "Ye don't trust this clan?"

"I don't trust any clan but ours," Duncan said. "And I don't trust all of our own clansmen, either."

Duncan steered the boat into a small cove, and they hauled it up the shore and into the brush.

"I suppose you'll have us sleeping out here in the cold and wet," Niall said, "when we could be sleeping beside the roaring hearth inside their keep."

"A cautious man lives longer."

Ach, he sounded like an old man. But castle walls only protected those who belonged within, and Duncan generally avoided being closed in with men he did not trust. Besides, he could not bear to sleep in the castle's hall knowing Moira was in bed with her husband on one of the floors above him.

A cold drizzle was falling in the bleak winter afternoon as he and Niall trudged up the path that ran along the top of the red cliffs. Ahead of them, the MacQuillan castle looked dark and ominous sitting on an outcrop that jutted out to sea.

"We've come on behalf of our chieftain, Connor MacDonald of Sleat," Duncan told the guards when they reached the gate. "Take us to your chieftain."

The guards reeked of whiskey, a sure sign of a lax leader. As they escorted Duncan and Niall across the bailey yard to the keep, Duncan steeled himself to see Moira with her husband and the children she and Duncan should have had together.

"'Tis a dreary hall," Niall said in a low voice as they entered the keep. "It could use the flowers and such your sister puts about at Dunscaith."

Flowers? God save him. "Keep your hand near your dirk, Niall."

Duncan scanned the warriors who were gathered in small groups at the long tables or by the roaring fire in the hearth.

"Which one is Moira's husband?" Niall asked in a low voice.

One of the guards who had brought them from the gate spoke to a tall, dark-haired warrior who stood with his back to them.

"That's him," Duncan said when the man turned around and fixed cold gray eyes on them.

This was the handsome chieftain's son Moira had sat with at supper on their last night together. The memory of her laughing and flirting while this man stared at her breasts would never leave him.

Moira's husband was chieftain now, which must please her. As their host crossed the hall to greet them, Duncan noted that his face was harder and his body more heavily muscled than seven years ago.

"A thousand welcomes to you," the man said, though there was nothing welcoming in his expression. "I am Sean, son of Owen, and chieftain of the MacQuillans."

"This is Niall. He is cousin to your wife and to our

chieftain, Connor MacDonald of Sleat," Duncan said, dispensing with the usual useless greetings. "I am Duncan Ruadh MacDonald, captain of our chieftain's guard."

"Not much good to your chieftain here, are ye, Captain?" Sean said.

The man was drunk—not swaying, slobbering drunk, but obstreperous, fighting drunk. And Duncan was tempted to wipe the sneer off the Irishman's face with his fist.

"Ye look familiar," Sean continued, narrowing his cold, gray eyes at Duncan. "Did I meet ye when Moira and I wed at Dunscaith?"

"No," Duncan said. "We carry a message from our chieftain for his sister."

"Ye can tell it to me." Sean planted his hands on his hips and rocked back on his heels as he spoke. "Moira is not well today."

"Well or no, we must see her," Duncan said. "Our chieftain expects us to pay our respects to his sister."

"I can't let ye disturb my wife's rest when she's ill." Sean did not seem the least bit worried about his wife's health, and Duncan wondered why he did not want them to see Moira. Regardless, Duncan was losing patience with this game.

"It would be a shame if my chieftain had to make this trip himself with a dozen of his war galleys." Connor didn't have a dozen war galleys, but Duncan was hoping Sean did not know that.

Sean locked gazes with Duncan for a good long while. Apparently, he was persuaded that Duncan did indeed mean his words as a threat.

"Ach, no reason to get upset over so trifling a matter,"

Sean said, waving his hand. "Moira has a wee headache. Ye know what complainers women are." He turned and shouted at one of the serving women, "Tell my wife to come down to the hall at once."

Duncan half turned from his host so that he was positioned to see Moira when she came through the doorway from the stairs. Seven years he had waited for this. He needed to see what was in Moira's eyes the very first moment she saw him, before she had a chance to cover her reaction.

"I'm surprised ye made the sail from Skye this time of year," Sean said while they waited. "Did ye get caught in any storms?"

Duncan ignored Sean's attempt to engage him in conversation. He had a mission here, and discussing the weather was not part of it. Niall gave him a sideways glance and raised an eyebrow, but Duncan ignored that, too.

"I see your friend is a man of few words," Sean said to Niall.

"Aye," Niall said. "But Duncan's eloquence with a sword more than makes up for it."

If Duncan had known Niall had a silver tongue, he would have left all the talking to him. Sean fidgeted in the silence that fell between them in the wake of Niall's remark. Sean was uncomfortable with silence, and Duncan preferred him to be uncomfortable.

Through the open doorway, Duncan heard a light step on the stairs. The pain in his heart told him it was Moira.

* * *

Moira buried her face in one of Ragnall's shirts and breathed in deeply, but it had been a week since her son had been taken from her, and the smell of him was nearly gone. Sean had promised to take her to the MacLeods to see Ragnall in a year or two, but he was always threatening to change his mind.

She quickly tucked the shirt away as the bedchamber door opened.

"The chieftain wants ye in the hall," the maid said from the doorway. "Your clansmen have come."

The saints be praised! Moira pictured her brother in the hall dressed in his chieftain's finery and flanked by two dozen of his warriors, with a hundred more waiting on the shore with his war galleys. Conner would take her home and help her get Ragnall from the MacLeods.

"How many warriors did my brother bring?" Moira asked as she straightened her gown.

"Your chieftain did not come himself," the woman said. "He sent two men."

Moira blinked at the woman. "Two?"

What use is that? Two men could never get her out of this castle. Her only hope now was to give them a message for Connor, begging him to send his war galleys to rescue her. As Moira hurried down the stairs, she tried desperately to think of how she could do it. She paused at the bottom of the stairs to school her face before entering the hall.

When she walked through the doorway, she felt as if all the air was sucked from the room. She could not breathe. Duncan MacDonald, the man responsible for ruining her life and for taking every happiness from her, filled her vision.

At nineteen, Duncan had already been a fierce and powerfully built warrior. Now he carried an additional twenty pounds of hard muscle and exuded the confidence of a warrior who had defeated so many men in battle that he no longer needed to prove himself.

His auburn hair brushed his broad shoulders, and he wore gold bands around his biceps as if he were one of the ancient warriors of legend. Yet there was no mistaking him. This was the man whose desertion led her directly to her current wretched existence.

When she met Duncan's hazel eyes, they burned with a hunger that made her pulse leap wildly. How could he look at her like that after what he'd done? How dare he? She swept past him to stand beside her husband.

Moira made herself smile up at Sean by imagining she was sticking a dirk into his eye. "Ye wished to see me?"

"These men of your clan are here to greet ye."

Moira avoided looking at Duncan and instead fixed her gaze on the lean, younger man next to him who had chestnut hair and deep brown eyes.

"Don't ye recognize me?" the young man said. "I'm your cousin Niall."

"Niall?" She broke into a wide smile. "Ach, ye must have grown a yard since I saw ye last."

"Well, you haven't changed. You're as pretty as ever." Niall was well over six feet, but he blushed as if he were a lad of twelve.

"'Tis good to see ye, cousin." Moira decided she must take the chance to give him the message that she needed help and leaned forward as if to kiss Niall's cheek. But before she could whisper in her cousin's ear, Sean put his arm around her and pulled her tight against his side. The bastard had a sixth sense that allowed him to foresee her every attempt to escape.

"And what of me?" Duncan asked.

With a false smile pasted on her face, Moira took her time shifting her gaze to Duncan. She steeled herself to show no reaction, and yet she faltered for an instant. This close, Duncan was everything she remembered, magnified. He was bigger, taller, more handsome. His powerful presence radiated through the room, drawing every eye.

"Tell me ye remember who I am," Duncan said when she failed to answer.

She remembered everything. Every touch, every look, every conversation, every pleasure he gave her. But her clearest memory of all was standing on the wall at Dunscaith on her wedding day with her insides cut and bleeding as if she had swallowed shards of glass.

"I fear I have no recollection of ye at all," she said.

"I'm a close friend of your brother," Duncan said as the tension snapped between them. "Surely ye remember something of me."

She heard the challenge in his voice and shrugged, as if he were beneath her notice. But when the light from the candles glinted in his auburn hair, she felt a sharp pang as she recalled how it felt between her fingers. Duncan's hair had the same texture as her son's...

God have mercy!

What if Sean saw the resemblance between them? Ragnall's hair was several shades brighter and his eyes were blue, but his face was a softer, boyish version of Duncan's. The likeness was plain to anyone looking for it.

Moira tried to calm herself. Red hair was common among those of Celtic blood, of course, and Duncan was a giant compared with Ragnall. There was no reason for Sean to make the connection.

Moira's heart hammered, but she kept the bland smile fixed on her face. Over the course of her marriage, she had become practiced at putting up a false front. Sean was like a hound, though, sniffing out any slight against him. If he suspected who Ragnall's father really was, he would not let her live.

"Truly, I don't remember ye," Moira said in a clear voice. "'Tis such a long time since I left Skye."

Duncan was staring at her like a starving lion and frightening her half to death. God help her, he was going to give her away. Moira risked a sideways glance at her husband. A frisson of fear went through her when she saw the ugly red blotches on Sean's face and neck. She prayed they were due to his usual angry jealousy—and not because he had guessed the truth she had hidden from him all these years.

Sean squinted at her, the question in his snake eyes. "Now that our guests have satisfied their curiosity, ye may return to your sickbed."

"We want a word alone with Moira." Duncan's deep voice reverberated through her.

"No need," Moira said quickly, knowing Sean would never permit it. Fear made her mouth feel dry and her tongue thick as she patted Sean's arm. "There's nothing I'd tell ye that I couldn't say in front of my dear husband."

Duncan never took his eyes off her. "Connor is concerned about you."

"He's been home well over two years," she said, the hurt making her voice tight. "If he wanted to see me, he knew where to find me."

Her emotions were running far too high. She had to leave the hall before she lost control.

"I must rest now," she said. "Whatever business ye have ye can discuss with my husband."

Moira felt Duncan's gaze drilling into her back as she left the hall. Please, God, had she not suffered enough? She hardly knew which was worse—feeling like she was dying inside from seeing Duncan after all this time or fearing Sean had guessed the truth.

* * *

Duncan had not thought it possible, but Moira was even lovelier than before. The girl had given way entirely to woman, and the result took his breath away. Her body was fuller, with curves so voluptuous that his palms itched to run over them. Though her face had lost its youthful softness, the stronger lines gave her a regal beauty that would have a prince bending his knee to her.

But the woman Moira had become was serious and cold. He missed the flashes of mischief and joy he used to see in her violet eyes.

"Ye are welcome to stay the night," Sean said, drawing Duncan's attention from the empty doorway through which Moira had gone.

By suggesting they were only invited to remain at his home for one night, the MacQuillan chieftain was perilously close to violating a Highlander's almost sacred duty to welcome guests.

"We don't wish to impose upon your generous hospitality," Duncan said.

"If ye have any business to discuss, let's hear it." Sean glanced meaningfully toward the stairs and said, "With a wife as beautiful as mine, I'm sure ye understand why I want to get to bed."

Duncan's anger, already burning bright, flared like a raging inferno at the thought of Sean touching Moira in all the ways that Duncan once had—and desperately wanted to again.

Niall saved Duncan from punching Sean's smug face by poking his elbow in Duncan's side and saying, "Our chieftain asks that ye consider fostering your son at Dunscaith."

Connor had them make this request as a means of determining if the MacQuillan chieftain was still committed to the alliance.

"We can take the lad with us now," Duncan said, "unless ye think he's too young to be parted from his mother."

"Ragnall is already fostered," Sean said.

"Who did ye send him to?" Duncan asked.

Sean paused before answering, his eyes glinting with amusement. "I sent him to the MacLeod chieftain."

"MacLeod of Lewis?" Niall asked, referring to the branch of the MacLeods with whom the MacDonalds were on good terms.

Sean shook his head, a smile tugging at the corners of his mouth. "MacLeod of Harris and Dunvegan."

When Duncan wrapped his fist around the handle of his dirk, the MacQuillan chieftain's guards took their places beside him.

"Ye must have known what a grave insult it would be to our chieftain to send his only nephew to foster with his worst enemy," Duncan said. "Did Moira agree to this?"

"Ye seem overly concerned about my wife's opinion." Sean narrowed his eyes at Duncan, examining him as if he were seeing him for the first time. Then his eyes suddenly widened, and his face flushed a dark red.

Duncan smiled because he thought Sean was going to give him the fight he longed for. *One move, and my fist will be in your face.*

"We'll bid ye good night and farewell," Niall said, grabbing Duncan's arm. "We'll be gone in the morning."

CHAPTER 9

Moira!"

The hair on the back of Moira's neck stood up as her husband's voice thundered up the stairs and echoed off the stone walls. Before she could prepare herself, the door crashed open. Sean stomped into the bedchamber and slammed the door behind him.

"What is troubling ye, dear?" She attempted to make her voice calm, but it came out high and thin.

"Don't ye play games with me!" Sean shouted. "I know what ye did."

Moira took an involuntary step back as he came toward her. "I don't know what ye mean, Sean."

"Ye pretended ye were an innocent virgin while ye carried that man's child! Ye whore!"

He backhanded her across the face so hard that Moira staggered backward and fell against the side of the bed. She grabbed the bedpost and struggled to keep her feet. In the last week, she had learned that there was nothing worse than to fall to the ground and try to protect her head from kicks. Her ribs had not healed from the last time.

"Ye will pay for this," Sean said as he shoved her against the bed.

Sean was always accusing her of perceived wrongs or slights, and she had seen him angry countless times. But this was different. The rage in his eyes glowed like a wild beast and bespoke murder.

Moira looked about her desperately for something to use to protect herself.

"I should have known the boy wasn't mine. He's nothing like me." Sean grabbed hold of her shoulders and shook her. "Ye told me he was born early!"

"Ye remember the blood on the sheet," Moira said. "Of course Ragnall is yours."

"Then why does he look exactly like that big redhaired MacDonald warrior?" Sean demanded.

"He doesn't!" Moira said, her voice sounding far too desperate. "Ragnall takes after my father and older brother. They were both fair."

"Ye lie," Sean hissed an inch from her face. "That Duncan MacDonald looked at ye as if he believed ye belonged to him."

"I've told ye that I can't help if men look at me."

"Other men look at ye as if they want ye," Sean said. "But that man looked at ye as if he'd touched every inch of your skin and memorized it."

Moira shivered as Sean slid his hand around her neck in a menacing caress. His thick fingers curved around the back of her neck as he rubbed his thumb up under her chin, forcing her head back.

"Don't, Sean. Please."

"Ye made a fool of me for all these years." He kissed her roughly on the mouth.

She squirmed and tried to push him away. When he began to slowly squeeze her throat, she tried to scream, but it came out as a pathetic muffled sound against his mouth. Finally, she managed to sink her teeth into his bottom lip.

He jerked back with a yelp and released her. "Goddamn ye!"

She gasped for air. But then he punched her in the eye so hard that everything went black. She felt herself falling. Sean caught her and slammed her against the wall. Her head bounced against it, dazing her again. She blinked to clear the stars sparking across her vision in one eye. The other eye she couldn't see out of at all.

"You'll never see Ragnall again!" Sean shouted. This time he hit her in the jaw. Pain jutted upward and exploded inside her head.

Moira felt as if she were watching herself from a distance. *He's going to kill me this time* drifted through her thoughts, but she felt indifferent to it.

"Did ye hear me?" Sean shouted. His face was only inches from hers, but she could not see it clearly.

When her head lolled to the side, he gripped her chin and held it. His fingers dug into her cheek, sending shooting pains from her injured jaw to her ear. She tasted the tang of blood on her tongue.

"I'm going to kill your son, too," Sean said.

"Ragnall?" Her voice was a scratchy whisper. "No, ye can't!"

"I will," Sean said. "And when he's dead, there will be nothing left of ye on this earth."

Moira fought her way through the layers of fog in her

head. She knew she must do something, but her body was slow to follow her commands. She had to concentrate to hit her fists against Sean's chest, but her efforts were feeble.

"I'll bring Ragnall home and squeeze the life out of the little bastard," Sean said through clenched teeth. "Just like this."

As Sean closed his hands around Moira's throat, panic surged through her and blasted away the fog that had debilitated her. She had to live so she could protect her son from Sean. She scratched and clawed at his hands around her throat. When that did not stop him, she kneed him in the groin.

"Huh!" Sean grunted and doubled over.

Moira sucked in lungfuls of air. When he came at her again, she fought him off, kicking and raking his face with her nails. But Sean was far heavier and stronger, and soon he had his hands around her throat again. His eyes were wild and bulging. Drops of spittle came from his mouth like a mad dog.

Her lungs burned as she fought for air against his ever-tightening hold. The bright sparks crossed her vision again, and she knew she was close to blacking out. *Please, God, help me!*

Something hard poked her stomach. The hilt of his dirk! Her hands were going numb as she closed her fingers around it and jerked the dirk free. Then, with a last surge of strength born of desperation, she plunged it into Sean's side.

"Argh!" Sean made a loud animal sound between a roar and a groan and threw his hands up.

Moira's throat burned, and her head pounded with a

violence that made her stomach roil. Still, she held on to the hilt of the blade when Sean jerked away. He staggered and bent over, holding his side. Blood seeped between his fingers.

But Sean kept his feet. He was not badly injured.

When he raised his head, rage glowed in his eyes like a demon from hell. If she was very lucky, she would have one more chance. Only one. She still held the dirk, but she had no idea where to stick him. She cursed her father and brothers for not teaching her how to protect herself.

Her head was starting to spin, and she was weaving on her feet. With desperation clawing at her belly, she held the dirk in front of her.

Then everything happened at once. Sean roared and launched himself at her with such force that she was hurtling through the air backward. Her screams echoing off the walls seemed as if they came from someone else. The back of her head banged on the floor, jarring her injured jaw and setting off a burst of blinding pain. An instant later Sean slammed on top of her, his weight forcing the air out of her lungs with an *oof*.

God, no. She did not want to die with Sean lying on top of her.

* * *

Across the flames of the fire, Duncan saw the wolfhound's eyes glinting in the darkness. He took another piece of dried meat and tossed it over the fire into the darkness beyond and was pleased when he did not hear it hit the ground. The dog was quick.

"I've never seen ye like that," Niall said, giving him a sideways glace. "It looked as though ye intended to fight their chieftain in his own hall with a hundred of his warriors watching."

"Hmmph." Duncan prided himself on never letting his temper interfere with his judgment or cause him to forget his duty. But he had failed to control it tonight. In truth, his hands still itched to murder Moira's arrogant husband.

"Moira wasn't at all like I remember her," Niall said. "What did ye think?"

"About what?"

"About Moira," Niall said, sounding as though Duncan was trying his patience.

Moira had given him nothing. Not so much as a soft glance. *I have no recollection of ye at all.*

"Do ye suppose she is all right?" Niall asked. "That Sean is an arse."

"That he is." Duncan took a swig from his flask. "But he's the man Moira wanted." Her father doted on his little princess—he would not have forced her to marry Sean MacQuillan against her wishes. There were other suitable chieftains' sons.

An icy rain started up, causing the campfire to hiss and smoke. As Duncan's temper cooled with the temperature, he thought back on that first moment when Moira entered the hall and saw him. In that brief instant, everything that had once been between them flashed in her eyes.

It was gone almost before he saw it, and then Moira was as cold as this winter rain running down the back of his neck. Niall was right; Moira had changed. Though her eyes were the same astonishing shade of violet, they carried no laughter in them. The cautious woman he had met in the hall who measured her words was a far cry from the carefree lass who ran headlong through the dark, believing nothing and no one could stop her.

Duncan threw bits of dried meat to the wolfhound, drawing the dog ever closer, while he pondered the question of what could have caused such a change in Moira's nature.

As a quiet man who kept his own counsel, Duncan was usually a keen observer of others. He had been so angry and absorbed in his own pain that he had failed to examine Moira's demeanor with his usual cool perception. Going over their brief encounter in his mind now, he recalled the tension in Moira's neck and how she repeatedly smoothed the skirt of her gown with her hands.

Her aloof and dismissive manner had fooled him. Though she had covered it well, *Moira was frightened.* Who or what could make her fearful? And why in the hell did her husband not make her feel safe?

Only one answer came to him.

Duncan got to his feet. "Stay here with the boat and be ready."

"Ready for what?" Niall asked, sitting up straight.

"A quick departure." Duncan leaned inside the boat for a coil of rope and stuck it inside his plaid. "Can ye handle the boat alone?"

Niall shrugged. "If I have to. Why?"

Ach, Duncan did not like the idea of Niall sailing alone such a distance in the stormy sea, but if Duncan was dead or in the castle dungeon, Niall would have to do it.

"If I'm not back by an hour before dawn," Duncan said, "set sail for Skye without me and tell Connor what's happened."

"How can I tell Connor what's happened," Niall asked,

spreading his arms out wide, "when I have no notion myself?"

"Something's amiss," Duncan said. "Moira may be in danger."

While they talked, the wolfhound had quietly come to stand beside Duncan, probably for what little warmth their sputtering fire gave off. The dog was thin and ragged.

"Leave the extra meat for the wolfhound." Duncan patted the dog's head as he left.

He hoped the guards would let him in without any trouble since their chieftain had welcomed him earlier, but he picked up a rock just in case. If he had misread Moira, he was about to cause a lot of unnecessary trouble for Connor. He could not feel too badly about it. Sean had thrown his lot in with the MacLeods, which made him an enemy.

When Duncan banged on the gate, one of the guards opened the small door next it. The light from his torch spilled out into the rainy night.

"Changed your mind about sleeping out in the cold rain?" the guard asked.

"Aye," Duncan said. "No need to disturb anyone. I'll just go into the hall and sleep on the floor with the rest of the men."

"Ye made your choice and can freeze to death for all I care," the guard said. "I can't let ye in without my chieftain's permission, and he's gone to bed."

Before the guard could close the door or take a breath to shout, Duncan pulled him outside by the front of his shirt, locked an arm around his throat, and knocked him on the head with the rock.

"Simon?" another guard called from inside.

Duncan flattened himself against the castle wall and waited. As soon as the second guard poked his head out the small door of the gatehouse, Duncan hit him with the same rock. Working quickly, he tied the two men together with his rope and dragged them a few feet into the darkness away from the castle wall.

He drew his dirk and entered the gatehouse without making a sound. Anticipating he might need to make a quick escape, he removed the heavy crossbar that held the gate closed. When he heard footsteps, he paused until they passed. A single set of boots. Duncan trained his men to work in pairs when they stood guard—not that two men could have stopped him.

The guards up on the walls would be looking outward for attackers, if they were awake at all. To avoid raising suspicions, Duncan walked across the yard as if he belonged there.

Inside the keep, a few men were still drinking near the hearth. Sean was not among them. Staying in the shadows, Duncan followed the wall around the room until he reached the doorway that led to the stairs. This was the riskiest part so far because no one but family members and a few trusted servants would have good cause to go to the rooms above at this late hour.

Duncan waited until there was a burst of laughter from the men around the hearth, then strode through the doorway and started up the stairs.

When he was halfway up, a woman's scream came from above, piercing the air—and his heart. It was Moira. Duncan charged up the spiral stone stairs three at a time. The door on the next floor was closed. Without pausing, he slammed his shoulder against it. The door crashed open and banged against the wall.

Moira lay on the floor in a pool of blood with a man on top of her.

Duncan was across the room in two strides. He jerked the man up by the back of his tunic with one hand while he brought up his dirk with his other to slice the man's throat. He stopped his arm midswing. The man he was holding was Sean, and he was already dead.

Duncan looked down at Moira. *Oh, Jesu.* One of her eyes was swollen purple like a ripe plum, and the rest of her face was battered. Her gown was torn and gaping open.

Blood was everywhere. In her hair. On her hands and face. Soaking her gown. Duncan dropped to his knee beside her. Grief swept through him. *God, no!* He was too late to save her.

CHAPTER 10

Moira moaned and struggled to sit up.

Praise God, she is alive. Duncan put his arm beneath her shoulders. "Are ye hurt badly, *mo leannain*?" My sweetheart.

"Is Sean dead?" She sounded dazed.

"Aye," he said. "Can ye walk? We must leave the castle at once."

Even while he said it, he heard boots on the stairs. If the men found Moira covered in blood and their chieftain dead, it would not go well for her.

Duncan lifted her to her feet. Holding her with one arm and his sword in the other, he started out with her just as one of the MacQuillan warriors filled the doorway. Two more were right behind him. Duncan needed to dispatch them quickly before they raised the alarm and brought the fifty men sleeping in the hall into the fight.

"What have ye done to—"

Duncan cut the first man down before the words were

out of his mouth. Then he shoved the next one backward
into the third, sending the pair tumbling down the stairs.

Holding Moira to his side, Duncan leaped over the
flailing men and continued down the stairs. The noise had
drawn three more warriors into the bottom of the stair-
well. But the fools did not have their blades at the ready.
Before they could unsheathe them, Duncan kicked one in
the gut, swung his claymore into another, and rammed the
third with his shoulder.

Damn. The commotion was waking the other
MacQuillan men. When Duncan started through the hall,
some of them were already on their feet and reaching for
their swords. Duncan lifted Moira over his shoulder and
ran like hell for the door.

He burst through it, cleared the steps in one leap, and
ran hard through the darkness of the bailey yard to the
gate. Knowing he had removed the bar, he hit the gate
running. It was made of heavy oak, but it swung open
against his weight.

After a few yards, he was in pitch blackness. The
MacQuillan men were on his heels, and Duncan could not
see the path to the beach. He was running blind.

A dog barked. A moment later he saw the wolfhound
in front of him, leading the way, his golden fur just visible
in the night.

Moira moaned, and Duncan thought of her bruised and
battered face bouncing against his back. But he had no
choice. He must get her away from here at all costs. The
shouts behind them were growing closer, but so was the
sound of waves crashing on the beach. As he crested a hill
behind the dog, he saw the white foam of the curling sea
swells through the darkness.

"Niall!" he shouted as he followed the wolfhound down the bluff to the beach.

"Over here!" Niall called.

Duncan saw the black shape of their boat.

"There they are!" a voice came from behind him. "Stop them!"

Niall was already pushing the galley out when Duncan reached it.

"Get in!" Duncan shouted. As soon as Niall jumped into the boat, Duncan thrust Moira into Niall's arms and took hold of the side of the boat.

"Get ready to raise the sail," Duncan called to Niall. As he strained to push their galley farther out to the sea, a huge dark shape sailed past him and landed inside the boat. The wolfhound.

Over his shoulder, Duncan saw men with torches coming down the bluff and onto the beach.

"Now!" Duncan shouted as he flung himself into the boat.

Niall unfurled the sail in the gusting wind, and the vessel lurched forward. It listed to the side before Duncan could grab hold of the rudder. He straightened the boat quickly, and they headed out to sea.

When Duncan looked back again, torchlights filled the beach. The MacQuillans knew these waters far better than he did. But with any luck, they would wait until daylight to set sail after them.

He wished Alex were with them. The old Viking blood was strong in Alex, giving him a sixth sense on the water that would be useful sailing through unfamiliar shallows in the dark. Twice the boat scraped rocks, and it was only by the hand of God that they made it out to deep water.

As soon as it was safe to do so, he fastened the rudder in place, found a blanket, and went to check on Moira. She was shaking and weeping when he wrapped the blanket around her, so he put his arms around her as well. Despite the danger they were in, a fleeting sense of peace settled over him. This was not how he'd dreamed it would happen, but he had Moira in his arms again.

* * *

Moira slept fitfully, plagued by dreams that made her feel as if she were falling through time. She dozed and awoke so often that she did not know what was real and what was dream.

No! No! Sean's weight was crushing her, and she was begging God not to let her last moment on earth be with Sean's smell in her nose and his body touching hers. Then the weight was gone, and Duncan MacDonald stood above her in all his glory. Duncan had fire in his eyes and his blade brandished, just as she had imagined him every time she had hoped and prayed he would come.

But she must have dreamed him, called him up into the nightmare that was her life. As always, Duncan was too late to save her. Moira felt the motion of the waves beneath her, and she was floating in the sea beside her mother.

Then Sean was alive again, and his hands were closing on her throat.

* * *

"It's all right." Duncan held Moira against him, stilling her flailing arms.

He hated to awaken her again, but it was dangerous to

let her sleep for more than a short time after how hard she had been hit on the head.

"Drink," he said, holding the flask of ale to her lips. Moira drank it greedily, but half went down her chin because the side of her mouth was swollen. He dabbed it gently with the corner of the blanket.

"Duncan?" she said.

"Aye, it's me."

"You're too late," she murmured. "I watched for ye, but ye didn't come."

Moira was out of her head. She had been saying that to him all night.

He batted away the wolfhound, who kept nosing her face. "Leave her be or I'll toss ye over the side."

"No!" Moira wailed.

"Shh. I didn't mean it." Duncan brushed his fingers through her hair, which was still sticky with blood, as he rocked her in his arms. "He's a good dog. He led me down the path to the beach."

"He's my son's dog," she said in a choked whisper.

The next time Duncan checked on her, dawn was breaking, and Moira seemed alert. Ach, her lovely face was a mess. He helped her sit up.

"Tell me where you're hurt, Moira."

"My head hurts like the very devil, and I can't open my left eye," she said in a strong voice, "but I don't think he broke any bones."

God in Heaven. If Sean were not already dead, Duncan would go back and kill him now. "There was a lot of blood. If ye have a wound, we should bind it."

He had checked her for fresh bleeding as best he could in the night and found none, but he needed to be sure.

"The blood is his," she said. "The blade I was holding must have gone into him when he knocked me over and fell on top of me."

Duncan had fought all kinds of men, good and bad, and he had seen plenty of evil. Still, it shocked him how any man could violently attack a woman.

"Had he hurt ye before?" he asked.

"Not like this," she said.

He swallowed. "What happened?"

Moira pulled away from him and drew the blanket tightly around her. "Sean saw how ye looked at me, that's what happened," she said in a hard voice.

She blamed him.

"Sean was always getting jealous for no cause," she snapped.

Duncan let that sink in. "I'll get ye another blanket, then ye should try to rest some more."

"I must bring my son home to Dunscaith," she said as she stared out to sea.

"I'm sure the lad is safe," Duncan said. "Even the MacLeod would not harm a child he had agreed to foster."

That was the only reassurance he could give her. Even if there were not such animosity between the MacDonalds and the MacLeods—and there was soon to be more—a boy belonged to his father's clan. The MacQuillans were unlikely to agree to let Moira have their chieftain's son, especially when they believed that she, or the man she left with, had murdered their chieftain.

"Duncan!" Niall called from the front of the boat. "They're following us."

CHAPTER 11

Erik MacLeod narrowed his eyes as he watched his chieftain's guards escort the visitor into the Great Hall of Dunvegan Castle. The guards brought him to a halt a respectful distance from the dais, where Alastair Crotach MacLeod sat looking every inch the great chieftain he was, despite his hunched shoulder.

It was unusual, to say the least, to see a MacDonald of Sleat in Dunvegan Castle, except in the dungeon. If the chieftain was surprised, he did not show it.

The visitor was a big, fair-haired man in his midthirties who had earned the name Hugh Dubh, Black Hugh, for his black heart. If rumors were to be believed, Hugh had a hand in the deaths of his former chieftain and the chieftain's eldest son, who were his half brother and nephew.

Erik admired the man's ruthlessness in pursuing his ambitions. Erik's chieftain disapproved of Hugh, but then, Alastair MacLeod had never had to fight for his place in this world. He was born to be a chieftain and would die one. Of course, the MacLeod's dislike of Hugh would not prevent him from using the man to benefit his clan.

"My nephew Connor is scheming to take the Trotternish Peninsula from ye," Hugh said after the formal greetings. "If I were the chieftain of the MacDonalds of Sleat, as I ought to be, I'd be content with the lands we have."

"As the keeper of Trotternish Castle," the chieftain said, turning his gaze to Erik, "are ye worried about this pup Connor taking Trotternish from us?"

Erik had worked single-mindedly for years to earn his chieftain's trust and respect. He'd had much to overcome. His father had been a warrior better known for his drinking than for his skill with a sword, and his mother was a woman of no consequence at all. After Erik had led the attack when they took Trotternish Castle from the MacDonalds, his chieftain had finally given him his just reward.

There was *nothing* Erik would not do to retain the castle and his position as its keeper.

"I haven't lost a wink of sleep over it," Erik lied and forced a laugh. "From what I hear, the new MacDonald chieftain has so few men and war galleys that he'd be a fool to launch an attack against us."

Erik knew his chieftain was pleased with his response, though the MacLeod's face remained expressionless. His chieftain did not want Hugh to believe he had anything of value to offer them.

"I'd advise ye not to underestimate Connor," Hugh said. "Through surprise and cunning, he has won battles against greater numbers before."

"Why do ye warn us?" the MacLeod asked.

"Connor is responsible for the deaths of two of my half brothers," Hugh said. "I want him to pay for that with his life."

The MacLeod raised an eyebrow. "I had the impression ye weren't overly fond of your brothers."

Erik snorted. It was rumored that Hugh had murdered a second brother in addition to the one that had been chieftain.

"How do ye know your nephew's plans?" the MacLeod asked and signaled for his cup.

"I have spies in his castle," Hugh said, looking a mite too pleased with himself.

When his cupbearer brought him his intricately carved wooden cup, the chieftain took a deep draught. Though he never permitted himself to drink in excess, he did take whiskey for the lifelong pain he suffered from the MacDonald axe that had split his shoulder.

"I supported ye once before against your nephew. It cost me the lives of some of my best warriors and gained me nothing." The MacLeod stared down at Hugh from his high chair, the heat of his temper burning in his eyes. "What is it that you've come to ask me for this time, and why should I give it to ye?"

"I hear ye are fostering my niece Moira's son."

The MacLeod narrowed his eyes at Hugh.

"The lad is Connor's heir," Hugh said. "I want him."

* * *

Damn, the MacQuillans were persistent.

Duncan glared at the three war galleys that had been following them for two days, then turned around to watch the black clouds rolling toward them from the west. Bolts of lightning flashed in the narrow band of horizon between the thunderclouds and the sea.

This had the makings of a storm that sailors would talk about for years afterward. Unfortunately, the MacQuillans had cleverly positioned their war galleys between Duncan's boat and the shelter of the islands to the east. They were forcing him to choose between going to shore where they were sure to catch him or sailing directly into the storm.

Risking his own life was one thing, but Duncan could not sail into this gale with Moira and Niall. He turned their boat toward their pursuers and the nearest island.

"When the MacQuillans take us," he said to Niall, "I killed Sean. Understood?"

Niall nodded.

The only good news was that Moira seemed to be recovering from her injuries. Duncan watched her now as she leaned into the wind and crossed the boat to where he and Niall stood at the stern.

"What are ye doing?" she asked when she reached them. When Duncan did not answer, she grabbed his sleeve. "No, I won't go back. I'd rather die."

Her hair was snapping across her bruised and battered face. One of her eyes was no more than a slit. Even with Sean dead, he could understand why she was loath to return.

"I expect they'll throw us all in their dungeon to rot," Niall said. "I'm for taking our chances at sea."

If Duncan could be certain the MacQuillans would punish only him for their chieftain's death, he would sail for the island and let them take him. But Niall was right.

After their chieftain had been murdered under their noses, the MacQuillans might not be in a mood to distinguish guilt among the three of them.

Praying he was not making the wrong choice, Duncan turned the boat again, this time toward the open sea and the gathering storm. Before long, the war galleys behind them tacked eastward to take shelter in one of the protected coves of the islands. The MacQuillans were not foolish enough to risk their lives and boats to capture them.

As they sailed closer to the storm, the wind drove hard pellets of rain against Duncan's face. *Thump. Thump. Thump.* Their galley rose and fell in the waves.

Before long they collided with the storm, and the sea became a torrent. The wind whirled about them and tossed their boat with increasing violence.

"Niall, take the rudder." Duncan had to shout to be heard. "I'm taking the sail down before the mast snaps."

He took Moira's hand and wrapped it around the piece of rope he had tied around the wolfhound's neck. "Stay down and hold on to Sàr until I come back for ye."

The sea crashed over the boat, drenching Duncan while he dropped the sail. Working fast, he retrieved two coils of rope from the bottom of the boat and returned to the others.

"Moira, I'm tying ye to the mast so ye don't get washed overboard," he shouted. "So long as we all stay in the boat, we'll be fine."

If the boat capsized, it would not matter that she was tied and could not swim. There would be no hope. Duncan led Moira to the mast, then tied the rope around her waist, taking care to avoid her bruised ribs.

"Stay," he ordered the dog, who obediently sat and leaned against Moira.

"We will make it," he said, and cupped Moira's cheek for a moment before he left her.

The boat creaked and shook as each cresting wave pounded into it. Duncan had to hold on to the side of the boat as he worked his way back to Niall.

"I'll steer," he shouted. When he took the rudder from Niall, he felt the full power of the sea pushing against it. "Now tie yourself to the mast with Moira."

As he thrust the rope at Niall, a wall of water twenty feet high crashed over the side of the galley.

"Niall!" Duncan shouted and reached for him.

Time moved slowly as Duncan watched Niall spread his arms wide trying to catch hold of something before the mammoth wave hit them. Then the wall of water crashed over the boat, lifting Niall off his feet and tossing him head over heels like a twig in a whirlpool.

The rushing surge of water swept Duncan after Niall and slammed him against the side of the boat. Duncan held on to the rail, his arms straining against the force of water sweeping past him. As the swell receded, washing back across the top of the boat, Duncan heard Moira's screams over the wind. That meant she was still safe, tied to the mast.

But Niall was gone.

CHAPTER 12

Niall! Niall!" Duncan shouted as he leaned over the side of the boat searching the swirling sea for him.

A lifetime seemed to pass before Niall's arm popped out of the next swell. A moment later, a dark head bobbed to the surface and went down again. Niall was still alive.

Somehow, Duncan still held the rope in his hands. He quickly tied a loop at one end and fastened it over a hook on the side of the boat. But the boat was drifting dangerously. Before it took the next wave sideways and capsized, Duncan threw his weight against the rudder.

The boat shook as Duncan turned it against the force of the sea pushing it sideways.

The next wave crashed over the bow. When he glanced at Moira, she looked like a rag doll with her hair and limbs flailing in the wind.

Duncan fought to keep the bow hitting the waves head-on, while easing the boat closer to where he'd last seen Niall in the water. Then he saw Niall's head bob to the surface again, thank God. Niall started swimming toward the boat, but he looked hurt. His strokes were awkward.

A giant swell curled and crashed over Niall, taking him under. Duncan's heart stuttered in his chest as he watched for Niall's head to reappear. When it finally did, Niall started swimming again, but his strokes seemed weaker than before. His head went down again and again, and each time Duncan feared Niall was lost.

"Niall!" Duncan shouted and tossed the rope with all his might. It uncoiled, carried aloft in the wind, and fell into the roiling sea not far from Niall. But as Niall swam toward it, the current carried the rope farther and farther from his reach.

Duncan pulled the rope in, coiling it around his arm. Before he could try again, he had to grab the rudder to steady the boat for the next swell. As soon as the galley crashed through the wave, Duncan turned to toss the rope. Niall had disappeared. Long, long moments passed before his head popped up again. The lad did not appear able to lift his arms to swim.

Niall did not have much strength left. If he did not catch hold of the rope this time, there would not be another chance. Taking careful aim, Duncan flung the rope out to him.

This time, the end landed close enough for Niall to grasp it.

"Hold on!" Duncan shouted as the boat crashed through another rolling swell. Then, holding the rudder steady with his leg, Duncan began pulling the rope in. Duncan was not a man who prayed much, but he was praying for all he was worth.

Give the lad the strength to hold on.

Another wave broke over the bow, and the tension in the rope grew slack for a sickening moment. When it jerked in Duncan's hands, relief surged through him. Niall still held the other end.

Duncan pulled the rope in hand over hand until Niall was next to the boat. Duncan waited for the next wave to pass so that Niall would not be hit by the force of it while Duncan pulled him out of the water. Niall was close enough now that Duncan could see that his lips were blue and he had blood running down the side of his face.

Duncan heaved the rope, lifting Niall out of the water. As he watched, Niall's hands began slipping down the rope. Duncan leaned over the side of the boat to help him, but Niall was just out of his reach.

"Hold on, damn it!" Duncan shouted.

The next wave caught Niall broadside, and he started to fall.

* * *

Moira felt helpless tied to the mast as she watched Duncan trying to save Niall's life. When Niall started falling back into the water, she thought all hope for him was gone. Her scream of anguish was lost in the wind. But when the wave passed, Duncan was hanging dangerously over the side of the boat—and he was holding Niall's wrist. She could see Duncan's muscles strain beneath his soaked tunic as he held Niall's deadweight against the force of the burgeoning sea.

Moira untied the rope around her, took hold of Sàr's makeshift collar, and started across the boat to help Duncan. The galley rocked sideways, knocking her to her knees. When she looked up, Duncan was still leaning precariously over the side of the boat. Over the wind, she heard him shouting Niall's name. Leaning on Sàr for support, she pulled herself to her feet and stumbled toward the back of the boat.

At last, she reached Duncan and wrapped her arms around his legs to help anchor him with her weight. With his every muscle straining, Duncan held Niall as another wave crashed over them. He grunted with the final effort of hoisting Niall's limp body up and over the side of the boat. All three of them fell into the bottom of the boat as it rocked back.

Before Moira could right herself, Duncan had turned Niall onto his stomach and began rhythmically pushing on his back. Moira crouched beside him while he worked to save Niall. He pushed once, twice, three times.

O shluagh! Breathe, Niall, breathe! It could not be too late.

Finally, Niall coughed and choked and threw up seawater.

"God help me, I thought I'd lost him," Duncan said, looking up at her. "Can ye take care of him? I must take the rudder."

Moira had been so focused on Niall that she had not noticed that the boat was listing dangerously to the side again.

"Go. I've got Niall," she said.

Niall gasped and coughed as Moira rubbed his back.

"Can ye see where he's bleeding from?" Duncan called out above her.

Niall had a long gash along the side of his face, but it did not look deep. She scanned the rest of him, trying to discern where all the blood was coming from. A dark red cloud was spreading through his wet tunic over his thigh. When Moira lifted the cloth, she had to swallow back the bile rising in her throat at the sight of the torn flesh.

"We need to stop the bleeding," Duncan said, glancing down at Niall's leg. "Take my dirk and cut a strip of cloth for a bandage."

She reached over Niall's prone body to take the dirk from Duncan's hand, then quickly cut two long strips of cloth from the hem of her gown. When she had them ready, Duncan dropped to his knee to help her wrap the makeshift bandage around Niall's thigh.

"We're past the worst of the storm," Duncan said. "With luck and God's grace, we'll ride out the rest of it."

When Moira glanced up, she saw that it was true. The swells were not so high, and the sky was light up ahead. She had been certain they would all die. Her hands shook as she wrapped the second strip around Niall's leg and tied a knot to bind it.

Niall groaned as Duncan helped her tug the knot tight.

"You'll be all right," she told Niall, and prayed it was true.

She stole another look at Duncan. It was thanks to his skill with the boat, his exceptional strength, and the force of his will that they had survived.

Moira lifted Niall's head onto her lap and wiped the blood and vomit from his face. "He's still so cold," she said.

Duncan fetched a blanket and gently tucked it around Niall. Then he snapped his fingers at Sàr and the wolfhound lay down beside Niall. "The dog will help keep him warm."

Niall opened his eyes and gave Duncan a faint smile.

"Ye looked like Cúchulainn himself when ye were pulling me in on that rope."

"Lie still and rest." Duncan spoke in a soft voice as if he were putting a wee bairn to bed. He smoothed the wet hair back from Niall's face until Niall closed his eyes again.

Niall's comparison of Duncan to the mythical Celtic warrior of legend was apt. His powerful build and in-domitable will were what had drawn Moira to him and stirred her blood when she was seventeen.

But it was this gentle side of Duncan that had stolen her heart.

* * *

Duncan bailed the boat with one hand while steering as best he could with a broken rudder. The little galley, as fine a boat as he had ever sailed, was holding together with spit and a prayer. At least the sea was calm now. If they hit another squall, he feared the galley would break into pieces.

Duncan took a deep breath. That had been far too close. God help him, he had almost lost Ian's brother. And Niall was not out of danger yet. The wound in his leg was deep, and he had lost a lot of blood.

Moira hovered over Niall, who was moaning in his sleep. Her brows were pinched together with worry, and her beau-tiful face looked painful. The swelling had gone down a bit, but the bruises would color her skin for a long time.

"We stole this little galley from Shaggy Maclean when we escaped from his dungeon," Duncan said in an attempt to take her mind off Niall and their precarious situation. "The four of us had a long-running argument over who had the better right to it."

"How did ye end up in Shaggy's dungeon?" she asked.

"We left France as soon as we heard about the disastrous battle against the English at Flodden." Duncan looked off at the horizon, remembering it all. "We didn't know that your father and brother Ragnall were dead or that your uncle Hugh Dubh had taken control of Dunscaith Castle and proclaimed himself the new chieftain."

"I did not hear of it myself until afterward," Moira said.

"Hugh feared the clan would choose Connor as chieftain if he returned," Duncan continued. "He knew we would have to sail past the Maclean fortress on our way home, so he asked Shaggy to keep watch for us and see that we never made it to Skye."

"My uncle wanted Connor murdered?" she asked.

"He still does." Duncan continued bailing as they talked, but the water was seeping in through the cracks almost as fast as he scooped it out. "We managed to toss Hugh out of Dunscaith, and Connor was made chieftain. But Hugh is still a threat. He's tried to kill Connor more than once, and he'll try again."

"Surely the clan wouldn't make Hugh chieftain if he murdered Connor," she said.

"They wouldn't have much choice," Duncan said with a shrug. "The clan will follow tradition and choose a man of chieftain's blood. If Connor were dead, that would leave only Hugh and your other miserable half uncle."

"And my son," Moira said.

"Aye," Duncan said.

Moira rubbed the wolfhound's ears while silence fell between them.

"Ragnall loves this dog." Moira's lip trembled as she spoke. "Sean made Ragnall give him up."

That explained why the dog was so thin.

"He's a big dog for a wee lad." Duncan turned his gaze to the sea and asked his question as if the answer were not important. "How old is this son of yours?"

"Five," she said. "Ragnall is five."

* * *

Moira lied instinctively to protect her son, but she did not regret it. Duncan did not deserve the truth. After living with Sean, Ragnall was hungry for a man he could look up to. He would take to this big man who had a quiet strength and the fighting skills of the warriors of legend.

She would never give Duncan the power to disappoint Ragnall as he had her.

"Ye said the four of ye had a dispute over this boat," she said to change the subject. "How did you get it?"

"I made a wager with Alex that he would wed within six months." A rare smile lit Duncan's face. "He was wed in three."

"Ach, the poor woman." Alex was her cousin, but he was a born philanderer.

"His wife Glynis is happy," he said. "Alex is a devoted husband and father."

So many changes at home. She reminded herself that she had missed them all because of Duncan. While she was exceedingly grateful that he'd rescued her, she would not have needed rescuing if he had done the right thing seven years ago. He had failed her when it mattered most.

Moira looked out at the empty sea and wondered if she would die out here with him. She could almost hear the faeries laughing.

CHAPTER 13

Moira was desperate to get out of this damned leaky boat. Duncan was wearing her down with his kindness and self-sacrifice. After handing her half of their remaining dried meat and soggy oatcakes, he packed the rest away, saving it for when Niall woke up.

"Aren't ye going to eat any of it?" she demanded.

"I don't need it," Duncan said. "I've gone without food far longer than this. I'm trained for it."

"You're a liar. Your stomach has been growling like a bear since yesterday."

"I didn't say I wasn't hungry," he said with a half smile.

Ach, the man thought he was invincible. It was beyond annoying. She shared her meat with Sàr, hoping to get a rise from him, but Duncan did not appear to begrudge the dog a share.

Duncan put his arm beneath Niall's shoulders, gently lifted him, and held the last of their ale to his lips. Niall was burning with fever, and she suspected worry was half the reason she was snapping at Duncan.

"'Tis good we're nearing land," Duncan said. "We need to find help for him."

Moira leaped to her feet. When she saw land in the distance, her heart beat fast. Seven years she had waited to see her home again.

"Is that Skye?" she asked. "It doesn't look like I remember it."

"The storm blew us miles off course," Duncan said. "That is Skye, but we're headed for the MacLeod end of the island."

"My son is with the MacLeods," she said

"Our being taken hostage would not help bring your son home to Dunscaith," Duncan said.

But perhaps she could be with him. She wished she knew whether the MacLeods had Ragnall here on Skye or at their fortress on the isle of Harris.

"See that small bay?" Duncan pointed toward the shore. "It belongs to the MacCrimmons. The MacLeod chieftain gave it to them as reward for serving as the MacLeods' hereditary pipers. That's where I'll try to land."

"Won't these MacCrimmons deliver us to the MacLeods?" she asked.

"I'm hoping they won't since I'm kin of sorts," he said. "My mother's mother was a MacCrimmon."

Why did she not know that? What else didn't she know about him?

"All the same, let's not tempt them by telling them ye are the MacDonald chieftain's only sister," Duncan said.

Not that Connor cared what happened to her.

Duncan touched the back of his fingers to Niall's forehead. Then, using an oar in place of the broken rudder, he guided the boat toward the MacCrimmon cove. At the same time, he minded the sail and bailed with one hand. Did he think she was useless?

"Let me do that," Moira said, snatching the bucket from him.

Duncan picked up a large wooden bowl that was floating in the bilge and began to bail with that. The land was farther away than it looked, and it seemed like they bailed for hours. Despite the cold winter mist, Moira was sweating when they finally drifted into the cove. A small crowd had gathered on the shore. The men had their blades drawn.

"Your MacCrimmon relations don't look friendly to me," she said.

* * *

Duncan grounded the boat and hopped over the side. As he dragged it up on shore, several men with unsheathed blades surrounded him. The women and children gathered on the beach stared at him from behind their men.

"I am the great-grandson of Duncan MacCrimmon," Duncan said. "I have an injured man in desperate need of a healer."

Without waiting for permission, Duncan lifted Niall's limp body out of the boat.

A young, fair-haired woman pushed through the men and peered down at Niall. "He's in a bad way," she said and then turned to one of the warriors. "Take him to my cottage."

Luck was finally with them. They had found a healer.

Duncan let the MacCrimmon man take Niall from him so he could help Moira out of the boat.

"Ye must come to my cottage as well." The young woman took Moira's arm and gave Duncan a sour look. "Big fellow like you should be ashamed of yourself."

By the saints, the healer thought he had done that to Moira's face.

Moira touched her swollen jaw, as if she had forgotten her injuries. "I'm fine," she said. "And it wasn't him that did it."

"Wasn't your husband?" Duncan heard the healer say as he followed behind the two women toward a line of cottages built along the shore. "That's a story I want to hear."

It was odd to hear the healer mistake him for Moira's husband. For the first time, it struck him that Moira was free. Hope was a foolish thing. He had no reason to believe Moira would have him now, or if she did, that he could keep her. Yet, despite the unremitting disasters since they were reunited, hope sparked in Duncan's chest for the first time in seven years.

* * *

Moira sat on the edge of the bed holding a vile-smelling compress to her eye while she felt Niall's forehead with her free hand. Praise God, his fever was down. Despite all the commotion in the little cottage, he was sound asleep. Duncan had had to hold Niall down while the healer cleaned and sewed up the wound on his leg, and the process had sapped Niall's strength.

"How do we know you're who ye say ye are?" one of the men asked Duncan.

"My mother gave this to me." Duncan pulled the six-hole whistle he always carried on a leather cord around his neck from inside his shirt and held it out for them to see. "She told me it belonged to her grandfather, the one I'm named for."

An ancient woman with wild white hair shuffled up to Duncan and examined the whistle an inch from her nose. As she turned it in her hand, Moira remembered that the whistle had a thistle carved on the back of it.

"This is Old Duncan's whistle, but ye could have stolen it." The old woman leaned her head back and scrutinized Duncan as carefully as she had the whistle. "If ye are his grandson, ye didn't get your size from him."

The MacCrimmons whispered among themselves for a time, then a handsome man with graying hair asked, "Can ye play that wee whistle?"

Duncan sat down on a stool that was far too small for him, placed his fingers on the holes of the whistle, and began to play. His music was so entwined with Moira's memories of the summer they were lovers that the first note took her back to that time.

"Ach, he's got MacCrimmon blood in him for certain," the man with graying hair said when Duncan had finished the song. "Ye should have learned to play the pipes."

"I do play the pipes a wee bit," Duncan said, "though not as well as the harp."

"The man is boasting now," the old woman said. She waved to a lad in the corner. "Fetch Caitlin's harp, and let's see what this big fellow can do."

When Duncan strummed the strings of the harp, the sounds made Moira think of delicate faery wings and the fields aflower on a high summer day at home. She closed her eyes and let the music take her back to a time when she was a young lass with nothing to worry her but which gown to wear.

"Who taught ye to play?" the same man asked after Duncan finished the tune.

"One of the MacArthurs taught me the pipes," Duncan said, referring to another well-known piping family. "My mother played the harp a bit. I figured the rest out on my own."

"I remember your mother well," the man said. "She was a fine woman and a beauty, but she didn't have the gift."

"'Tis in his blood," a plump woman standing next to Moira said. She waggled her eyebrows and nudged Moira. "MacCrimmon men have music in their souls and magic in their fingers."

Moira remembered. The memory had blighted her marriage.

"Shame your mother didn't send ye to us," the man said.

"I was born to be a warrior, not a piper," Duncan said.

"Ach, the Highlands are filled with warriors," the man said, waving his hand. Then he grinned. "If ye had the training ye should have, ye could be a famous piper like me. My name is Uilleam, by the way. I'm Caitlin's father."

"I've heard of ye," Duncan said. "I hope I have the pleasure of hearing ye play before we leave."

"Ye won't be taking your friend anywhere for a few days," the healer interrupted. "Now, if ye all have satisfied your curiosity, let me tend to this poor injured man in peace."

Duncan expected to be sleeping with the cow in one of the cottages. Instead, one of the women led him and Moira to the last cottage in the little row.

"We keep this cottage ready for visiting pipers," the woman explained as she opened the door for them. "We have pipers from all over the Highlands come here to improve their skills, though we have none staying with us at the moment."

The woman opened the door and bustled about the tiny cottage, lighting the lamp on the table and pouring the pitcher of water she had brought with her into a bowl for washing.

"You'll find peat by the hearth and warm blankets on the bed," she said.

There was only the one bed. Duncan told himself that nothing interesting was going to happen in that bed. For one thing, Moira was widowed but three days.

But his cock was not listening to reason. As he looked at the bed, seven years of pent-up yearning had him nearly shaking with desire. His body prickled with awareness of Moira's as she stood so close to him. When his arm brushed hers, a jolt went through him like the lightning in the storm they had sailed through.

"Caitlin said to give ye this salve," the woman said, handing a pot to Moira.

"Thank you," Moira said as the woman left.

Duncan heard the door close. The two of them were alone.

CHAPTER 14

Moira glanced about the tiny cottage, but there was only the one bed. Duncan was looking at her as if he were dying of thirst and she was the last drop of water on God's earth. If ever there was a man who could tempt her, it was Duncan MacDonald.

"Moira." He said her name as if she were all he wanted in this world.

But she knew better. She had been down that road before.

"The ladder to the loft is there." She pointed to it and turned her back on him.

As she listened to Duncan climbing the ladder, she forced herself to recall how she had stood on the wall at Dunscaith in all her wedding finery, still hanging on to hope like the foolish and trusting lass that she had been.

"How could he do this to me?" Moira had said to her maid, Rhona, who had been her confidante from the start of her affair with Duncan. "How could he leave me?"

"This Irish chieftain's son is a handsome man—he'll make ye a fine husband," Rhona said, patting her arm. Then her eyes got big as she looked over Moira's shoulder. "Your father's coming. I'll wait for ye down in the hall."

Moira turned and saw her father. Rhona bobbed her head and hurried past him.

"What are ye doing up here?" her father asked. "Everyone's waiting for ye."

"Da!" She threw her arms around his waist.

"There, there." Her father brushed her hair back. "What's this about?"

"He didn't come," she said against his chest.

"Is it that damned Duncan you're still fussing about?"

She wept for three days after Duncan left before she confessed to her father that she was in love with Duncan. He had been the angriest she had ever seen him when she told him she had given Duncan her virginity and would marry no one else. But that was before she discovered she was with child. When she told her father she was pregnant, he had quickly arranged a marriage to a man who happened to be their guest at the time and who had the appropriate pedigree.

"I thought Duncan would come back for me," she choked out.

"Ye can see now that he didn't deserve ye."

"Duncan's the one I want, Da," she said into his shirt.

He leaned her away from him and wiped the tears from her cheeks. "I'm telling ye, that Duncan is bad seed."

"Ye don't know that, Da," she said. "And I don't care who his father is, anyway."

"Ye should. Blood will out." Her father took her face

in his big, rough hands and looked straight into her eyes. "I didn't tell ye before to spare your feelings, but I gave Duncan the choice of going with the others to France or staying. He chose to go."

Now Moira pushed the painful memories of that day aside and took off her gown to wash up in the water the woman had so kindly left for them. She gingerly washed the cuts and scrapes on her body that the healer had not seen. Even after being drenched to the skin in that storm at sea, she found blood in the creases inside her elbows.

Moira covered her face with her wet hands, sank to the floor, and wept. She did not regret killing Sean, but the memory was still terrible. Then she cried for all those years of trying to appease him, of always having to be careful and constrained. And now Duncan was here, bringing back those other memories. And then there was Niall to worry about. And hardest of all, she missed her son.

She was not one to give in to self-pity, but she was just so damned tired of being strong.

* * *

Duncan lay staring up at the thatched roof above his head. His every muscle tensed as he strained to listen to the soft splash of water each time Moira wrung the towel out in the bowl. As she washed herself, he tortured himself imagining her long, slender fingers running the wet towel over her throat and down her breasts.

His erotic thoughts were interrupted by another sound, like a mewling kitten. Was that Moira weeping?

Ouch! Duncan hit his head on a wooden beam when he sat up. The roof was so low that he had to crawl across the straw on his hands and knees to the hole where the ladder was. Peering through it, he saw Moira sitting on the floor with her head on her knees. Her shoulders were shaking.

She did not look up as he climbed down. When he sat beside her and put his arms around her, she leaned into him. Duncan's heart beat too fast, and his chest felt too tight to breathe. She was just in her shift.

"Shh. You're all right now," he said as she wept her heart out. Words rarely helped anything, but he gave it a try. "If it's Niall you're worried about, he's tough. It takes more than a wound like that to kill a MacDonald."

There was nothing he could say about her dead husband except good riddance.

He kissed the top of her head. Memories of kissing her creamy skin flooded his mind as he breathed in the smell of her hair. His hand shook as he ran his fingers through the shining black locks. He should not take advantage of her being distressed to touch her, but he could not help himself.

When she buried her face against his chest, the heat of her breath through his shirt set his skin on fire. He never thought to hold her again, and he told himself to be content with this. But having her in his arms only made him long to touch her in all the ways he had during that long-ago summer. He wanted to kiss every inch of her skin and make her his a thousand times over.

When she leaned her head back and looked at him with her deep violet eyes, he cupped her cheek with his palm and marveled at its softness. The black soot lashes framing her eyes were wet. He caught a tear with his finger before it fell.

The bruises on her face pained him, and he wanted to kiss every hurt away. He pressed his lips lightly to her forehead, and the soft sound of her sigh was like an answer to every prayer he'd made for the last seven years. Time held still as he leaned down closer and closer to her mouth. He hesitated just above her red rose lips to give her a chance to say no.

Kissing her would be a mistake. It would only make him miss her worse afterward.

His heart clenched as his lips touched hers. They were as sweet as in his memories. Since she was sad and wanted his comfort, he made himself keep the kiss soft. But his heart was bleeding for her, as it always had. He would let her cut it to shreds again.

When he broke the kiss, he stared into her lovely eyes and wondered what she was thinking. Probably that Duncan MacDonald was the most foolish of the many fools who had loved her.

But then she slid her hands up his chest, clasped them at the back of his neck, and pulled him down into another kiss. Her mouth softened against his, and he died a little more inside. He cupped the back of her neck and deepened the kiss.

For a long time, he was lost in a mindless, neverending kiss. But when she groaned into his mouth and pressed her breasts against his chest, lust too-long denied surged through him like a roaring river. And that river of desire swept away all the barriers he had built through all the years away from her.

To have this woman, he would die a thousand deaths, face any enemy, fight the very devil himself. He could never have enough of her.

Duncan drank in her sighs and whimpers as he kissed her mouth, her arched black eyebrow, her perfect nose, her determined chin. Very, very softly, he brushed his lips over her injured jaw.

"Moira," he said her name over and over. He ran his tongue over her, tasting her skin, as he moved down the side of her throat. Then he leaned her back onto the floor and buried his face between her breasts.

Please, God, let me have her again just this once. He had waited so long and missed her so much. Even as he pleaded with God for one more time, he knew once would never be enough.

Moira should be his. She should belong to him, now and forever.

Her hands were under his shirt, on his skin. *Aye, aye, aye.* Hope and desperate desire took hold of him as he tugged at the skirt of her gown. At last, his hand was on the silky skin of her bare thigh. Paradise was within his reach.

"No!"

Through the blood pounding in his ears, Duncan barely heard her. But he could not miss how Moira stiffened beneath him. And just like that, she was weeping again.

Oh, Jesu, what had he done wrong?

He rolled off her and tried to pull her onto his chest, but she strained against him.

"Don't touch me! Don't!" She sat up and covered her face.

He sat up beside her but dropped his arms to his sides. She did not want him after all. Though he had known she was distressed and seeking comfort from him, he had let foolish hope blind him.

"I'm sorry. I shouldn't have..."

He stopped himself. Though he felt badly that he had

upset her, he would not be her fool again—no more than he already was, anyway. Duncan got up and stoked the fire, then climbed the ladder to the loft. He stretched out on the straw and listened to the wind whistle through the thatched roof over his head. Despite her rejection, he still wanted her so badly he ached.

Duncan had not met a man who could defeat him since he was full grown. And yet, this black-haired lass half his size could rip out his heart with her velvet touch.

* * *

Moira hugged her knees to her chest.

When Duncan had wrapped his arms around her, she had felt safe for the first time in years. She should have left it at that and been grateful. But when she looked up at him and saw the longing in his eyes, it stirred feelings she had believed were buried too deep for any man to awaken. She had wanted to know those feelings again.

And she did, for a while. When Duncan kissed her, she felt that wonderful, long-ago sensation of being swept away and yet aware of every inch of her body. His fevered touches burned through the layers and layers of the protective cocoon she had built between herself and her body to survive the life she had.

But when Duncan pulled at her skirts, images filled her head of Sean grunting over her. Her throat closed, and panic surged through her veins.

She had survived living with Sean. More than that, she had not let him destroy her pride or her sense of her own worth. She was proud that she had been strong enough to be the mother her son needed.

But Sean had ruined her for a better man's touch. He

had ruined her for pleasure. That was the part of herself she could not save. To feel those wonderful, intense feelings again, she would have to make herself vulnerable to a man. And for that, she would have to trust him.

Moira never intended to trust a man again. Least of all, Duncan MacDonald.

CHAPTER 15

Duncan hoped Niall healed quickly so they could get the hell out of here. The tension between him and Moira was thick as a dense fog as they walked to the healer's cottage in the morning.

"How is he?" Duncan asked the healer as soon as she opened her door.

"Ye can ask him yourself," she said, waving her arm to where Niall lay in the bed propped up with pillows.

Duncan was relieved to see that Niall was alert and his color much improved. The only other person in the room was the old woman who had recognized his great-grandfather's whistle. Duncan nodded to her.

"Caitlin is as good a healer as old Teàrlag," Niall said, looking at the young woman with calf eyes. "But she has a far gentler touch."

Ach, Niall was thoroughly enjoying his injury. "How soon will he be ready to travel?" Duncan asked.

"Not for a few days," Caitlin said.

"I'll have the boat repaired by then." He turned to leave. "I'll be on the beach."

"If you'll take a seat," Caitlin said, gesturing to her small table, "I'll give you and your wife some breakfast."

His wife, ha.

"Thank ye kindly," Moira said and sat at the table with the old woman.

Duncan was starving, as usual, so he joined them and made quick work of the steaming bowl of porridge Caitlin set in front of him. When he glanced up, hoping there was more, the old woman was staring at him with her bulging eyes. She appeared to have forgotten the spoonful of porridge she held in her quivering hand halfway to her mouth.

"Ye were born here, ye know," she said.

He did not. So far as he knew, his mother never told a soul where she had been the year she was gone. She certainly had not told him.

"Ah, I see that she kept her secret," the old woman said. "A woman's allowed."

"I remember our bard telling the tale of Duncan's mother disappearing from the beach one day with a secret lover," Moira said with a faraway look in her eyes. "It was a great mystery and a favorite tale on long winter nights in our castle."

"The truth is no romantic tale," the old woman said, shaking her head.

"I never believed it anyway." Duncan hated that this strange old woman knew more about his birth than he did. And he hated it even more that he wanted to know. He ground out the words, "What did happen?"

Duncan stiffened when the old woman reached across the table and touched his arm with her clawlike hand. He did not need pity from an old woman.

"All I want is the truth," he said.

"Your mother was stolen from the beach near Dunscaith Castle one day, that much of the tale is true," she said. "A MacLeod took her."

"My mother ran off with a MacLeod?" Ach, this was worse than he thought.

"She didn't go willingly." The old woman paused, giving him time to absorb that. "Your mother was a dreamer and didn't notice the galley full of MacLeod warriors until they were upon her. At sixteen, your mother was a rare beauty, to be sure. One of the MacLeod men decided to take her away with him."

Duncan leaned his elbows on the table and held his head in his hands. His father was a MacLeod and a rapist. Christ, help him. No wonder his mother had refused to tell him.

"What was this MacLeod called?" he asked without looking up.

"The devil's name is Erik," the old woman said. "And he's no dead, if that's what ye think."

Duncan sat up straight. "He's alive?"

"Aye," the old woman said, bobbing her head.

Erik MacLeod. Duncan rolled the name of his father and enemy over in his head. He was going to kill this man. "Where will I find him?"

"Erik is the keeper of the MacLeod Castle at Trotternish," the old woman said.

The very castle the MacLeods had stolen from his clan. When the MacDonalds fought to take it back, Duncan would kill Erik MacLeod and avenge his mother.

"How did Duncan come to be born here among the MacCrimmons?" Moira asked.

"His mother's grandfather, Old Duncan, was the MacLeod chieftain's piper at the time. As I'm sure ye know, that is a position of great respect," the old woman said, settling back in her chair. "When Old Duncan heard that his granddaughter was being ill used by one of the MacLeod warriors, he went to someone in the chieftain's family, who ordered Erik to marry her or release her to her grandfather. The swine chose to release her, which I'm sure was better for the poor lass, and Erik was forced to make a payment for what he'd done."

A payment. Bitterness ate at Duncan's stomach as he recalled his mother's pitiful hoard of silver coins. He understood now why she sometimes looked at him the way she did. While Duncan knew she loved him, he was also aware that he made her uneasy. She must have feared he might become like his father.

* * *

Moira spent the day helping Caitlin crush herbs and mix them for healing remedies.

"How far are we from the MacLeods' stronghold?" Moira asked Caitlin as they worked.

"Dunvegan Castle? 'Tis just a short sail from here," Caitlin said.

"What about walking?" Moira asked.

"Ach, I don't know. A day, maybe more," Caitlin said. "The path that goes along the coast starts behind the cottage you're staying in, but I've never taken it all the way to Dunvegan."

In the isles, people rarely traveled by foot when they could take a boat.

"Why do ye ask?" Caitlin asked.

"I just wanted to know that we're a safe distance from the MacLeod chieftain's lair." Moira gave her a wink. "Ye see, I was raised on tales of him eating small children."

Niall, who was lying on the bed behind them, laughed. "We were told he prefers to eat MacDonald children roasted."

Moira turned and smiled at him, grateful for the diversion. Her cousin had turned into a charming young man, and she was enjoying getting reacquainted with him.

"Where have all the lasses gone?" she asked to tease him.

"Every MacCrimmon female between the ages of twelve and eighteen has already visited my cottage today," Caitlin said. "They'd be here still if I hadn't shooed them out before supper."

"I should go as well so ye can get to bed," Moira said. "Unless ye think I should stay here so people won't talk."

"So long as Niall can't walk, I think I'm safe from him," Caitlin said, suppressing a smile.

"I'd never press my attentions on a lass," Niall said, looking so offended that Moira could not risk meeting Caitlin's eyes for fear of laughing.

"Besides," Caitlin said, "my grandmother is here."

Moira glanced at the old woman, who had been snoring on a pallet in the corner for hours, and this time she did laugh. It struck her that she could not recall the last time she had laughed. It felt good.

She was putting on the old cloak Caitlin had lent her when Duncan came to the door.

"Evening," Duncan said to Caitlin and Niall, then to her, "Let's go."

Judging from Duncan's stony expression, he was still thinking about what the old woman had told him about his father.

"Have ye had anything to eat since breakfast?" Moira asked as they walked to their cottage.

"Some women brought me food while I was tarring the leaks in the boat."

Some things had not changed. Moira recalled how women at Dunscaith were always bringing food to Duncan, hoping to draw his attention.

"I'm sorry about your father," Moira said.

Duncan gave her a fierce, sideways glance that would have discouraged a lesser woman. "'Tis always best to know the truth," he said.

"Is it?" She wasn't so sure. "Ye know, Duncan, you're nothing like him."

"*Hmmph.*"

They walked the rest of the short distance in silence. When they reached the cottage, Duncan made her wait outside while he went in with his dirk in his hand.

"That can't be necessary," she said as she hung her borrowed cloak on the peg by the door.

"It's what a man does." Duncan said with his back to her as he knelt by the hearth and prodded the fire to life.

"It isn't what all men do," she said. "Do ye think that Erik would put the safety of others before his own? Sean never did."

Duncan continued poking at the fire, so she pulled up a stool beside him. The firelight set off the warm reds in his rich auburn hair, but his face was all hard lines.

"Ye are your own man, Duncan MacDonald," she said. "Your father's shame is not yours."

"I am a man of the sword like he is," Duncan said without looking at her. "No matter how hard I try to be different or what I accomplish, his blood runs through my veins."

Without thinking, Moira leaned forward and touched his cheek with her fingers. She felt the muscles of his jaw tighten beneath the rough beard. Before she could pull away, Duncan covered her hand with his and closed his eyes. He turned his head and pressed a kiss to her palm that sent warm tingles all the way up her arm.

Then he opened his eyes and looked straight into hers. The desire burning in them was like a hot fire sucking air from the room. Clearly, Duncan was not thinking about his father anymore.

How could she let herself forget, even for a moment, the wrongs Duncan had done her? He seemed so straightforward and trustworthy, but then, he always had. It was so easy for a woman to mistake a man's lust for something more.

"I have a weakness for ye, as ye well know," Duncan said, his voice rough and dangerous. "I don't need your sympathy. And if ye aren't careful, I could mistake it for something I do need."

Duncan wanted her badly. And there was something she wanted from him as well. Anxiety balled in her stomach. This would cost her dearly, but she had to try.

"Take me to Dunvegan Castle to get my son."

"Ye want to go to the MacLeod stronghold?" Duncan pulled away from her. "We can't do that."

"Why not?" she asked. "Niall seems to be out of danger. Surely ye can leave him long enough to take me to Dunvegan."

"It would be pure foolishness for a MacDonald of Sleat to willingly walk into the MacLeod stronghold," he said, raising his voice. "There is no fortress in all the isles stronger than Dunvegan. And ye don't even know your son is there. He could just as well be on the island of Harris."

But Ragnall *could* be at Dunvegan. If there was a chance he was there, Moira had to go to him.

"Ye needn't go inside Dunvegan with me," she said. "Just get me within sight of the castle and leave me."

"Leave ye there?" Duncan asked, sounding affronted. Then he rested his hands on her shoulders. "Once I have you and Niall safely home at Dunscaith, I'll talk to Connor, and we'll figure out how to get your son for you."

* * *

Duncan expected Moira to continue arguing, though it would be pointless.

Instead, Moira locked gazes with him, then reached back and unfastened her hair. As it fell over her shoulders in a shining dark mass, the smell of summer wildflowers brought back memories so strong Duncan's knees nearly buckled.

His breathing grew shallow as she ran her fingertips over the bare skin above the neckline of her gown. When she reached the valley between her breasts, she looped her finger round and round the little tie at the center of her bodice. Duncan was vaguely aware that his mouth was hanging open, but he did not have the concentration to close it.

"I know what ye want," Moira said in a throaty voice and gave the tie a little tug. "And I'll give it to ye, if ye take me to my son."

With all the blood rushing to his cock, it took some time for Duncan's addled mind to take in Moira's words. And it took him longer still to comprehend that she was offering herself to him, not because she wanted to, but because she wanted something from him.

"You're offering an exchange?" He could not believe it. "Ye gave yourself to me freely before. Don't ye dare play the whore with me."

Duncan was so angry his vision blurred. He stormed out of the cottage, slamming the door behind him. *How could she?*

CHAPTER 16

Moira pretended to be asleep when Duncan returned to the cottage an hour or two later and climbed the ladder to the loft. After waiting for the sounds above her to quiet, she slipped out of bed and stepped into her shoes. She was already fully dressed. Moving quickly, she lifted the cloak from the peg and eased the door open.

Sàr lifted his head from where he lay in front of the warm hearth. When she signaled, he got up and trotted out in front of her. She closed the door behind her and paused to listen. All was quiet. She released the breath she had been holding and started out.

The moon shone between the clouds racing across the night sky, giving her just enough light to follow the path. The sounds of the wind blowing over the hills and of the surf on the shore below seemed louder. Animals scuttled through the bushes along the path, making her glad for Sàr's company.

Traveling at night was eerie, but Moira was determined to be far enough away when Duncan awoke in the morning that he could not catch up to her before she reached Dunvegan.

Moira would wager she was the only lass in all the islands who did not know how to sail a damned boat. If she knew how, she could have "borrowed" one of the MacCrimmons' and arrived at Dunvegan in no time. How could her father and brothers leave her so ill prepared?

Once again, she cursed her pampered upbringing. If she ever had a daughter, Moira would make certain she knew how to kill a man with a dirk and sail a boat by herself. In the end, a lass could count on no one but herself.

"I'm done with waiting for men to help me," she said aloud.

Sàr gave her a worried look over his shoulder.

Moira still wore the delicate slippers that went with her now-ragged gown, and her feet hurt like the devil. She was freezing as well. Sàr pranced ahead of her, unperturbed by the cold.

She walked for what felt like hours and was tired to the bone when the sky turned a lighter shade of dismal gray, signaling the coming dawn. When her foot caught in a hole, she heard her gown rip as she fell on her hands and knees in the mud. Her gown was such a rag already that she would be half-naked by the time she arrived at Dunvegan. At least she'd be noticed.

Sàr paced around her until Moira picked herself up out of the mud.

"Time for a rest and breakfast, wouldn't ye say?" She found a rock to sit on. Then she gave Sàr half of the dried fish and oatcakes one of the women had left in the cottage for Duncan. He would have no trouble getting more.

"Ye miss Ragnall, too, don't ye?" She rubbed Sàr's ears. "Well, we won't see him any sooner sitting here."

They drank from the little cricks and waterfalls that were running down the hills everywhere from the winter rains. Her slippers and the bottom of her skirts were a muddy mess.

Moira trudged behind Sàr as the path climbed a steep hill. At the top, where the trail narrowed and ran along the edge of a steep ravine, Sàr came to an abrupt halt.

"Ye big baby," she said, laughing at him. "All right, I'll go first."

Sàr barked and bit at her skirt.

"Quit it! You're as bad as Duncan," she said. "If ye don't want to go to Dunvegan with me, ye can turn around."

Suddenly Moira's feet went out from under her, and she was hurtling down the ravine backward. She flung her arms out, trying to grab hold of something as she crashed through the brush. Branches cracked. Her body thumped and bounced as she careened down the hillside like a falling rock.

* * *

"Hugh MacDonald could be of use to us," Erik said and watched his chieftain carefully for his reaction.

"I don't trust a man who is a traitor to his own clan." Alastair MacLeod's glare deepened. "He insulted me, suggesting I would hand Sean MacQuillan's son over to him after I agreed to foster the lad."

"The boy *is* the MacDonald chieftain's heir...," Erik ventured.

"And he is under my protection," the chieftain snapped.

Erik feared he had gone too far. While his chieftain was ruthless in battle, he had an unnatural softness when it came to women and children. Erik had suffered for this weakness of his chieftain before.

"In any case, the lad will not be the MacDonald heir for long," the chieftain said. "Connor MacDonald is a young man and will have sons of his own."

"Not if he's dead." Erik paused. "If Hugh were their chieftain, we'd have a good chance of driving the MacDonalds out of Skye altogether."

"That's true enough." The chieftain drummed his fingers on the arm of his elaborately carved chair. "But if Hugh hasn't succeeded in killing his nephew yet, he's unlikely to."

Erik waited while his chieftain took a long drink from his cup.

"According to Hugh, Connor has three warriors who have been his closest companions since they were young lads. Hugh says that no one can get to Connor without killing them first."

Hugh also said that the four who returned from France were willing to die for even the lowliest members of their clan, but that was too foolish to believe.

Alastair MacLeod steepled his hands under his chin and fixed his ice-blue eyes on Erik. "What else do ye know of them?"

"They have trained and fought together for so long that they can read one another's minds," Erik said. "Fighting the four of them is like fighting a score of warriors."

"I've heard the same," the chieftain said.

"Two are Connor's cousins," Erik said. "Their mothers were sisters."

"The Clanranald sisters were famous beauties in their time," the chieftain said, nodding.

"One cousin holds Knock Castle and the other is keeper of Dunfaileag Castle on the isle of North Uist, so they are no longer part of Connor's personal guard," Erik said. "Still, if there is a battle, they will both join in the fight."

"What of the third man?" the chieftain asked, raising one shaggy eyebrow.

"He is captain of Connor's personal guard and the most formidable warrior of the four," Erik said. "Hugh says the man's never been defeated, but he's probably lying."

The chieftain stared into the hearth, leaving Erik to wonder at the direction of his thoughts.

"'Tis good you're keeping a close eye on Hugh Dubh," the chieftain said at last. "I don't like that he learned so quickly that the MacQuillan lad was here. Find out how he knows MacLeod business."

"I will." Erik had told Hugh himself, but it would be easy to find someone else on whom he could lay the blame.

CHAPTER 17

Duncan was still angry when he woke up, so it was just as well that Moira had already left for the healer's cottage. He steeled himself to see her when he went to see how Niall fared.

When he ducked his head under the doorway, he found Niall on the bed, surrounded by half a dozen giggling young lasses.

"I see you're well cared for," Duncan said.

"Aye," Niall said with a wide grin. "I'm nearly mended."

"Good. Then we'll be leaving soon." Duncan turned to Caitlin. "Where's Moira?"

Caitlin shook her head. "I haven't seen her yet today."

Uneasiness settled in his stomach. Where would Moira go? Duncan started to leave to look for her, but halted with his hand on the latch. "Is there a walking path nearby?"

"Aye, the path that leads to Dunvegan starts just behind the cottage you're staying in," Caitlin said. "Moira was asking about it yesterday."

God preserve him, Moira had gone alone to get her son.

The lass was as unpredictable and as dangerous to herself as ever. As captain of his chieftain's guard, Duncan was accustomed to having his judgment respected and his orders obeyed. He had told Moira that going to Dunvegan was pure foolishness, but did she listen? No. She did precisely as she pleased with no consideration of the consequences.

"Niall," he said. "I'm going after Moira. The fool has headed off for Dunvegan by herself."

"What?" Niall flinched as he swung his legs off the bed. "I'll come with—"

"Ye will stay right there in that bed," Duncan said, pointing his finger at him. "Ye re-injure yourself, and you'll answer to me."

The pair of them was more trouble than Hugh MacDonald and his pirates.

* * *

Something rough and wet kept rubbing against Moira's face. When she opened her eyes, Sàr's black nose was an inch above her, and his tongue covered half her face.

"Bleck!" Moira tried to sit up, but it hurt too much to move. She felt as if a herd of cattle had trampled over her.

"Stop licking me," she said, batting at the dog.

Sàr rested his head on his paws next to her ear and proceeded to whine until the sound was so annoying that she forced herself to sit up. She spit out the bits of dirt and leaves in her mouth and looked up the hill—or cliff—she had fallen down. It was so steep she could not see the path above.

"We are in a fine fix," she said to Sàr.

She had scratches from head to toe, though it was a miracle she had not broken her neck. Sàr stuck his nose in her face until she hauled herself to her feet. She felt stiff, as if she had lain on the cold ground for a long time. She probably had.

What was wrong with Sàr now? The wolfhound had ceased whining, but he was pacing back and forth in front of her and growling.

Then she heard it—a long, high howl that sent a shiver of terror up her spine. A wolf. There was no mistaking the sound, for there was nothing else like it. Heart hammering, Moira picked up a stick.

Two answering howls echoed against the hillside. The wolves were close.

* * *

Duncan had been running along the path for an hour. Without slowing his pace, he took a drink from his flask and wondered how far ahead Moira was. He cursed himself again for not hearing her leave the cottage. It was not like him to be so slack.

Duncan thought of Moira's fancy slippers. At least she could not be making good time in those. He should catch up with her soon.

Up ahead, at the top of the hill, the path had been washed out in a mudslide from the rains. Duncan scanned the hills, looking for another way across. Then, over his breathing, he heard a dog bark. Praise God, he had found them. He halted and listened. The barking was coming from the trees at the base of the ravine.

O shluagh! Moira and the dog must have gone down in the mudslide.

Duncan's blood froze when he heard the yips and eerie howls of wolves, calling to one another.

He left the path and scrambled across the hillside toward the ravine. Judging by Sàr's steady barking, the wolves had not attacked yet. Duncan had to believe that. He did not let himself consider that Moira could already be dead from the fall.

"Moira!" Duncan leaped over fallen trees and rocks and crashed through the brush as he entered the vortex of the ravine.

Suddenly Sàr's barking became fierce and frantic. Duncan pulled his claymore from his back and ran harder. Through the trees, he saw the dog and a gray wolf fighting. The two animals were on their hind legs, locked in a death struggle, trying to bite each other's throat.

Behind them, Duncan caught a glimpse of Moira's blood-red gown.

From the corner of his eye, he saw a movement and turned. Four wolves were slinking through the trees toward Moira.

* * *

Moira did not see the wolf until it sprang through the air, lunging at Sàr's throat. She screamed and gripped her stick, ready to hit it and protect her dog. But before the wolf's jaws reached his throat, Sàr attacked the wolf with a viciousness that startled her. This snarling and snapping beast was a different animal from the gentle giant dog she knew.

The two fought on their hind legs, biting at each other in a brutal dance. With a ferocious lunge, Sàr caught the wolf's neck in his jaws. Moira's stomach turned as Sàr shook his head back and forth until the wolf's body went limp.

Moira sagged, relieved that the fight was over and that she and Sàr were safe.

But then she saw two sleek gray forms sliding through the trees. When one of the wolves turned its head and fixed its yellow eyes on her, Moira's blood froze. The next moment, Sàr was in front of her, growling and baring his teeth. She screamed as the two wolves attacked Sàr at once. While Sàr fought one wolf, the other tried to bite the back of his leg.

Moira heard a yip and turned to find another pair of sleek dark forms in the trees. While Sàr fought for his life, the two new wolves watched and waited.

Moira prayed. *Jesus, Mary, and Joseph, protect us.*

A roar filled the air, and Duncan burst through the trees brandishing his claymore. With the flat of it, he slammed first one and then the other of the wolves attacking Sàr. The wolves turned on Duncan, snapping and darting at him between his swings with the claymore. One jumped, and its teeth were an inch from sinking into Duncan's arm. But Duncan was lightning-quick and blocked it with the flat of his sword.

In quick succession the two wolves gave up the fight and withdrew to find easier prey. When Moira turned to look where the other wolves had been waiting, their dark shapes were already slipping through the trees like seals in the water.

* * *

Moira threw herself into Duncan's arms, and he held her tight. His heart flipped over in his chest as he thought about how close he had come to seeing her ripped apart before his eyes.

"Are ye all right?" he asked.

When she nodded, Duncan picked her up and whistled to Sàr. He was anxious to get her out of the wood before the wolves decided to return. He was relieved when the dog ran ahead, showing no sign of serious injury.

"I can walk now," Moira said after they left the ravine, and he was carrying her across the grassy hillside.

"I saw the cliff ye fell down, and you're not walking anywhere until I have a good look at ye."

When he judged they were a safe distance, Duncan unfastened his mantle, spread it on the ground, and set her down on it. He knelt on one knee beside her, while Sàr lay down on her other side. The dog had survived his battle with nary a scratch.

Moira, however, looked like hell. He could hardly see the bruises on her face for the mud, and she had twigs in her hair.

"I'm perfectly fine," Moira said. "I've nothing worse than a scratch or two."

Duncan snorted.

"What could ye possibly find amusing about this?" she demanded.

"'Tis just that ye don't look much like a princess at the moment."

Moira leaned forward and glared at him. "I know that's what you lads used to call me."

Duncan fought a smile as he ran his hands over her ankles.

"What are ye doing?" She slapped at his hands as he started up her legs.

"Checking to be sure nothing is broken."

"Nothing is broken." As if to prove it, she started to hoist herself up, but gasped, "Aah."

"If it hurts, I'll carry ye," Duncan said as he helped her to her feet. "We'd best get started back."

"Thank ye for coming to my aid," Moira said. "But I'm continuing on to Dunvegan."

Duncan grabbed her arm before she took a single step. His humor was gone.

"Have ye no sense at all, woman?" he said. "It was only by the grace of God that ye didn't kill yourself already."

"I did ask ye to come with me," Moira said. "'Tis not my fault ye didn't."

"Ye can't just do what ye please, every time the notion strikes ye," Duncan said. "The last thing Connor needs is to have his closest relation held by his worst enemy. Don't ye see what that would do?"

"I do," Moira said, her eyes spitting fire. "The MacLeods would learn what I already know—that Connor doesn't give a damn what happens to me."

"Of course he does."

"Connor didn't trouble himself to visit me and his only nephew in the two years since he returned from France."

"Can ye not see beyond yourself when there is so much at stake?" Duncan asked. "Ye don't understand the danger to both Connor and the clan."

"Then perhaps ye should explain it to me," she said, putting her hand on her hip, "instead of shouting at me."

"I don't shout at women," he said.

"Ye were shouting," she said.

Duncan sighed because she was right. Moira was the only woman who could rile him. "I'll tell ye anything ye want to hear while we walk back to the MacCrimmons," he said.

"What about my son?"

"'Tis unfortunate the MacLeods have him, but as I told ye, he is safe under Alastair MacLeod's protection." Duncan took her hands. "The same cannot be said for you. What do ye think the MacLeods would do with ye when they heard about Sean's death? Most likely, they would return ye to your husband's clan for punishment."

Duncan thought they would first use the threat of returning her to the MacQuillans against Connor—and after they got what they wanted from him, they would send Moira to the MacQuillans anyway.

"That would not help your son," he said.

"I suppose not." Moira had not shed a tear before, despite the fall and the wolves, but a wet streak was working down her muddy cheek now. "I miss him."

Duncan lifted her chin with his finger. "We *will* get your son back."

"Promise?" she asked, her solemn gaze fixed on him.

Duncan paused. He did not give his word lightly, but he could not take away her hope. "I promise."

CHAPTER 18

Connor is the only hope for our clan," Duncan said after taking her arm and starting down the path. "Our enemies know this, and so should you."

"My brother has been fortunate to always have your loyalty." Moira failed to keep the bitterness from her tone.

"He merits my loyalty—and yours as well," Duncan said.

"Connor and I were never close as children," she said.

"He kept his distance to avoid getting in trouble with your father," Duncan said. "One word of complaint from you, and Connor would be punished."

Moira had always known, as children do, that her father favored her and her brother Ragnall over Connor. But she never gave it much thought. It was just how her family was, like her mother being dead.

"He must resent me," she said.

"Connor never held it against you," Duncan said.

As they walked, Duncan explained what dire straits the

clan had been in when the four of them returned from France. Though Moira had heard bits of this before, she had been far away and absorbed by her own troubles. Duncan answered all the questions she put to him about the dangers their clan still faced.

"Ye only had the one child?"

Duncan's question startled her and brought back the old familiar ache.

"I conceived two other times, but lost the babes," she said, fighting to keep her voice even. "Sean even blamed me for that."

"I'm sorry," Duncan said.

It had been hard, very hard. Moira turned her face away and pretended to look up at the hills until she could trust her voice again. Then, to change the subject, she asked Duncan about their clansmen—who had married or died or had more children. Duncan's answers were exceedingly brief and uninformative.

"What of my former maid?" she tried again. "Rhona must be long since wed."

"No."

Ah well, Duncan was never one to engage in what he viewed as idle gossip.

Moira did not ask him why he left her, though it was on her mind. His question before about Ragnall's age had made her uneasy. She could not risk a discussion that delved into their past and might lead him to discover her secret. Besides, she did not trust Duncan to tell her the truth; nor did she want to hear his excuses.

And was there any answer he could give her that would make a damned bit of difference? Was there anything he could say that would erase the suffering of the last seven years? No, there was no point in upsetting herself. Her father had given Duncan the choice, and he chose Connor and pursuing a warrior's glory in France.

The past could not be undone.

When she and Duncan lapsed into a long silence, Moira did not mind. With Sean, every conversation had been fraught with hazards. He had been so volatile that she had to watch her every word, never knowing what might set him off. In truth, she found it soothing to walk with Duncan and not talk at all.

Her body ached, and she was growing wearier with each step. She had been beaten, lost at sea, swept down a cliff, and attacked by wolves. This time, when Duncan lifted her off her feet, she did not object to being carried.

Before she knew it, he was setting her down in front of Caitlin's cottage. Judging from the way Niall's eyes widened when she stepped through the doorway, Moira knew she must look a fright.

"What ye need is a good long soak," Caitlin said. "I expect ye don't want to bathe in front of Niall, even if he is your cousin—"

"Definitely not," Duncan interrupted.

"Then you're welcome to roll my washtub down to the other cottage." Caitlin handed Moira a small pot of a creamy substance that smelled of heather and honey. "After you've bathed, have your husband help rub this salve on ye. It will soothe your aches and pains from that fall."

Moira swallowed. After she had already slept alone in the cottage with Duncan, she supposed it was too late to confess that they were not married and ask Caitlin to help her with the salve.

"'Tis a lovely salve," Caitlin whispered in Moira's ear while Duncan retrieved the washtub from the far corner of the cottage. "I believe you'll thank me in the morning."

As she and Duncan went out the door, she heard Niall's voice behind her, "But he's not her husband."

"Hush," Caitlin said.

* * *

Moira had a hundred scratches, and her gown stuck to her in all the places she had bled.

"Ouch!" she said as Duncan peeled it off, leaving her in just her shift.

Before Moira could give him instructions, Duncan lifted her up and set her feet down into the tub of warm water. She wiggled her toes and sighed. "Ach, it feels heavenly."

Duncan held a towel up between them. "Do ye need me to help ye take your shift off as well?"

She did not miss the hopeful note in his voice.

"No." But her shoulder hurt so badly that she got stuck with the damned shift half off and covering her head. "I do need a hand, but don't look."

One tug and the shift was over her head—and she was naked as the day she was born. She winced as she dropped down to sit in the tub. The hot water made her scratches sting for just a moment, then the heat began soaking through her sore muscles.

"Ahh, that feels good," she said on an exhale as she leaned her head back and closed her eyes. She heard Duncan pour in another bucket of water that he had heated over the hearth.

"Shame I can't tell everyone at Dunscaith how the captain of the guard waited on me hand and foot better than any maid I ever had." She smiled to herself. After a while, she slit her eyes open to see what Duncan was up to. "Ye didn't close your eyes!"

Duncan snorted. "Did ye expect me to?"

"Ye could at least pretend ye were," she said and covered her breasts with her hands.

"Let me wash your hair for ye." He picked up a long strand and twirled it between his fingers. "Ye still have twigs in it."

Her hair was so filthy that it itched unbearably. Keeping her arms crossed over her chest, she sat up and leaned her head over. Duncan's strong fingers massaged her scalp as he washed her hair with the soap. It felt so good.

He gave her a folded cloth to cover her eyes before pouring the bucket over her head. When he was finished rinsing her hair, Duncan eased her back and put the cloth behind her head to cushion it against the rim of the tub. The gesture was so kind.

Tears slid down the sides of her face as Duncan rubbed her temples and then her shoulders and neck. No one had taken care of her in such a long time.

"Shh," he shushed her. "You've been a brave lass."

Moira must have dozed, for she awoke with a start when Duncan said, "The water's getting cold. Let's get ye out."

She was too limp to fight him when he slipped his arm under her, lifted her to her feet, and wrapped the towel around her. When she slumped against him, he scooped her up and carried her to the bed.

"We've nothing clean for ye to put on." Before she could gather herself to protest, he removed the towel and slid her under the bedclothes naked. "Here's a warming stone."

"Mmmm," she whimpered when he put the wrapped stone next to her swollen feet.

Moira fell asleep to the soft splashing of water. When she awoke, Duncan sat on the edge of the bed wearing nothing except the towel wrapped around his waist. His wet hair was slicked back from his handsome face, and the muscles in his arms and shoulders were impressive.

Duncan eased one of her arms out from under the blankets and began rubbing Caitlin's salve over it. As he worked the salve in, warmth spread through the muscles of her arm, and the fragrance of honey and heather filled the room.

Duncan glanced up and met her eyes. "Am I hurting ye?"

Moira shook her head a fraction. How did a man who looked every inch the powerful warrior have such gentle hands?

She watched, mesmerized, as Duncan massaged each of her fingers and then her palm. She stifled a sigh as he slowly worked his way up her arm, soothing every ache with the magic in his hands.

Moira had never thought she would enjoy having a man touch her again. What was even more surprising was that she longed to touch him. She imagined running her hands over his broad chest and how the rough hair and hard muscles would feel beneath her palms.

She dropped her gaze to his hard-muscled belly. When she saw his shaft pushing up against the towel, she did not feel the usual surge of panic and disgust. Far from it. She wanted to remove the towel.

When Duncan tucked the arm he had been working on under the blankets and reached for the other, Moira lifted it out for him. She held his gaze as he massaged her fingers, one by one. Her breasts ached and her breathing grew shallow as he slowly worked his way from her wrist to her shoulder. She wanted to drown in the longing in Duncan's eyes, to feel all the things he used to make her feel.

Before she could stop herself, she lifted her hand to his cheek. It was wrong to mislead him, wrong to let him believe she was a whole woman who could give him all he wanted. But she wanted badly to be whole again.

She had built so many layers between herself and her body to survive the years with Sean. Bedding Duncan MacDonald would be altogether different. He was the only man who had ever given her pleasure, and she desperately wanted him to awaken her body from its dead sleep.

But could she give herself to him without losing her heart again?

"I've watched ye mulling it over," Duncan said in a rough voice that reverberated somewhere low in her belly. "Which is it, Moira? Aye or nay?"

* * *

Duncan waited for her answer, wanting her so much his hands were shaking. But, God help him, he would not plead with her.

"'Tis a simple question," he said. "Either ye want me or ye don't."

"Will ye hold me?"

He groaned. Must she make it so difficult for him?

She'd had a rough time, and if she wanted comfort, he should give it to her. He drew in a deep breath, lay down on top of the bedclothes, and enfolded her in his arms. When she leaned into him, all her soft curves pressing against him, he buried his face into her neck and breathed in her scent.

"Your skin smells just the same," he murmured.

When Moira put her arms around his neck, he decided that served as an aye and kissed her. He did it slowly and deeply, savoring the taste of her. Her breasts, soft and full, pressed against his chest as their tongues moved together in a slow, tantalizing rhythm. On top of the bedclothes, he ran his hand up over her hip, down the dip of her waist, and up her side until he felt the swell of the side of her breast. He needed more.

He eased the bedclothes out from between them and groaned with pleasure as he pulled her against him. Skin to skin, at last. His shaft throbbed against her belly, and she was making those erotic little sounds that had always driven him wild with lust. Duncan reached between them, his fingers seeking her damp heat.

"No! I can't do this." Moira struggled to sit up, but Duncan held her fast in his arms. She let her head fall back and said, "I'm sorry, I thought I could."

"What do ye mean ye can't?" Duncan asked, keeping his voice low and calm.

"I want to," she said. "But I just can't."

Duncan brushed a strand of wet hair back from her face. "Tell me why."

Moira squeezed her eyes shut and shook her head. Duncan waited, and finally she said, "Sean ruined this for me. I…"

The bastard. Duncan finally understood. He took her hand. "But ye do want to?"

"I don't know," she said, turning her face away from him. "I do, but... I'm afraid."

Could he do this for her? Was he strong enough to give her this and then lose her again? To show her the pleasure of being with a man only to have her go off and marry someone else again?

Ha, who am I fooling? If Moira gave him the chance to touch her, to be with her, he would take it no matter what hell came after.

"We'll take this slowly, bit by bit," Duncan said as he ran a finger up her arm. "And we'll stop whenever ye say."

He leaned down and brushed his lips against the sensitive spot just below her ear, then he whispered, "Remember all the things we did that summer?"

* * *

Moira remembered. For weeks, they found ways to please each other before she finally persuaded him to take her virginity.

"It wasn't me wanting to stop that summer," she said, attempting a smile.

The side of Duncan's mouth quirked up. "Now you're hurting my manly pride."

"I have a confession to make. I put a potion in your ale that night." Moira had been desperate. Duncan's sense of honor had held him back, despite all her efforts.

Instead of being angry, Duncan chuckled deep in his throat. "Ach, lass, I was done with being virtuous. Ye didn't need a potion. I couldn't have made it another day."

Moira's skin prickled when he leaned down and breathed in her ear.

"Will ye trust me?" he asked.

That was the question. After she had given him everything before, Duncan had left her. She could not—*she would not*—trust him with her heart and soul again.

But she believed she could trust him with her body. In bed, he had only ever given her pleasure, and she longed to feel that again. After all the suffering he had caused her, did he not owe her this? All he had ever had to give her was lust and passion, and that was all she wanted from him now.

"I'll try," she said.

Duncan began with the tips of her fingers. She felt his breath on each one first, then the softness of his lips brushing the top—a powerful, passionate man, touching her as lightly as butterfly wings. He was telling her that she could trust him to be gentle.

When he scraped his front teeth over the pad of her thumb, she felt it all the way to her toes.

"Is this all right?" he asked.

She nodded, and he sucked her forefinger into his mouth. His tongue ran over it, calling to her mind their tongues entwined in deep kisses. Duncan did it as if he had all the time in the world—unlike Sean, who had no patience or interest in anything but grabbing her breasts and pushing inside her.

At first, she had been foolish enough to think Sean would want to please her. When she tried to show him how, he had been insulted and extremely annoyed. He was a selfish pig, and that was the least of his faults.

"Whatever you're thinking about, stop." Duncan held

her face, forcing her to look into his eyes. This close, she could see the warm golden flecks in them.

With his magic fingers, he began rubbing her temples, soothing the ugly memories away. He massaged her forehead and the tightness in her neck, then pressed a tender kiss to her bare shoulder.

"On your stomach," he said. "I need to rub the salve on your back."

He rubbed firmly, easing all the aches and pains. Gradually, Moira gave herself over to the rhythm of his hands. She felt weak, but her weakness did not make her feel endangered. Hours seemed to pass. When Duncan pushed her hair to the side and kissed her neck, she started, but then relaxed again.

"Your skin is like satin," he said, running his fingers over her back in wide, arcing circles.

Moira felt vaguely guilty, as if she should be doing something to earn his attentions. But she felt so good, and it had been such a long time since a man had made her feel good.

Since the day Duncan left her, to be exact.

When Duncan leaned over to kiss her, his hair brushed her shoulder and sent tingles across her skin. His big hands gripped her hips as his mouth moved down her back. Old longings stirred deep inside her as his lips reached the base of her spine.

"Mmm" came out of her mouth when he wrapped his hand around her thigh and lightly bit her bottom. The deep relaxation gradually gave way to a sensual tension that started between her legs. She wanted him to touch her there like he used to. Instead, he teased her, holding her thigh in his big hand while running his lips and tongue along the back of her leg.

He sat up and soothed her once again by massaging her feet and toes. She felt as if she were floating in a pool of liquid warmth while he moved up her legs with his sure hands. He could touch her anywhere now, and she would not object. Though she suspected there was much she did not know about the man Duncan had become, she believed she still knew him here, in bed.

And the Duncan she knew would want more than her compliance. He would want a full joining, their pleasure pounding through their bodies and resonating in their hearts and souls.

Moira rolled onto her back and held her arms out to him.

Duncan made a low sound deep in his throat, and the hungry way he looked at her made her nipples stand up and tighten. Anticipation and trepidation filled her in equal measure as she waited for him. Except for the rise and fall of his chest, he remained frozen above her.

"I want to feel ye on top of me," she said.

"That would be a verra poor plan," he said in a strained voice.

"Why?"

"Because I said we would take this bit by bit, and I'm a man who keeps his word."

Was he? Duncan had not promised that he would marry her, but he had said he would love her forever, which to her mind amounted to the same thing.

Those hurts drifted from her mind as Duncan lowered his head to her breast.

"Aye," she said on a breath as he circled and flicked his tongue over her nipple. Finally, he sucked the tip of her breast into his mouth. Pleasure sang through her as her body awakened under his ministrations. Soon she was moaning and arching and gripping his hair in her hands.

His hand slid up her thigh, and she gasped when his fingers found her center. Tension built inside her as his fingers circled round and round endlessly. He sucked harder on her breast, and she felt on the brink of release. She remembered what it was like and wanted it. Wanted it *right now*.

And yet, flashes of times with Sean made her feel embarrassed and awkward over her body's reaction, even while she was so frustrated that she wanted to scream and kick her legs.

Duncan rose up on his hands and knees and blew on her damp skin, bringing all her attention to the sensation. Then he lay beside her and began whispering things in her ear—soothing words at first and then ones that aroused her.

I love the feel of your skin, your hair. Ye are so beautiful, m' eudail. My treasure. *It feels so good to touch ye.*

While he spoke to her fears and desires, he traced his fingers over her face and throat and then over her breasts, making her ache for him.

"I want to hear ye find your release," he said. "Ye know it makes me mad for ye."

He kissed her hair and the side of her face as he began moving his hand between her legs again. After all this time, Duncan knew exactly how to touch her.

"Trust me." His breathing was ragged in her ear as the tension built and built until she thought she would break in two.

"Oh! Oh!"

Duncan held her tight as her body convulsed in waves

of pleasure. *At last.* She felt like weeping with the joy of
it. At the same time, her barriers were shaken, leaving her
heart far too vulnerable to him.

Duncan pulled her hard against his chest and kissed
her with a fierce passion that left no doubt that giving her
pleasure had excited him. If he wanted to make love to
her fully now, Moira would not be able to say no. But she
was afraid to be that close to him, to be joined as one. She
wanted to be like a man and give in to lust without losing
herself.

When Duncan pulled away and took several slow, deep
breaths, Moira was both relieved and disappointed. Then
he tucked her head beneath his chin and ran his fingers
through her hair.

As she lay enfolded in his arms, the question pounded
in her head like an echo of his heartbeat against her ear
until she had to ask it, though she knew it was a mistake.

"Why did ye leave me?"

His chest rose and fell on a deep breath. She lay very
still while Duncan kept her waiting for an answer he
should have had ready.

"Your father found out about us," he said in a flat
voice. "He ordered me to go with the others to France. He
gave me no choice."

That was not what her father told her, and her father
had never lied to her. *Never.* She knew she should not
have asked.

Against her will, the things her father said about Duncan on her wedding day went through her head over and
over. *He didn't deserve ye. That Duncan is bad seed.
Blood will out.* Had even her father betrayed her trust? It
was one more bitter disappointment, but she finally ac-

cepted that it was possible her father had lied to her.

Yet it changed nothing if Duncan had been commanded to leave. This was the man who managed to sneak into an unfamiliar castle, pull her dead husband's body off her, and carry her away with a hundred warriors chasing them. If Duncan had wanted to, he could have found a way to come back for her or get word to her to meet him. Instead, he had sailed off and not returned.

"I missed ye every day," Duncan said in a soft voice.

He sounded so sincere. Perhaps he had missed her— or at least missed bedding her—but that had not brought him back any sooner. Nor could it undo one day of her or her son's suffering.

Moira was grateful to Duncan for the healing pleasure she found in his arms, and she would let herself enjoy it. But she would never give him the power to hurt her again.

* * *

Duncan watched Moira sleep in the morning light. How long would he have her this time? He knew he must take her home to Dunscaith as soon as Niall was well enough to leave and the boat was repaired—but he dreaded it. She was in his arms because she wanted to forget the terrible things that had happened to her, at least for a while. But it would end when they left here. Duncan did not know how he would bear it.

Connor had always been a better judge of character than his father and older brother, and he would make sure that the next chieftain or chieftain's son she wed was a good man. Duncan tried to take comfort in this, but he failed miserably.

It made him furious to see the deep purple bruises marring her perfect skin. The bumps and scratches from her fall yesterday would heal quickly, but he feared the marks Sean left on her—inside and out—would be with her a long time. Before they parted, there was something more he needed to do for her.

Moira opened her eyes and stretched, giving him a slow grin.

"Out of bed with ye," Duncan said. "'Tis time for your lessons."

"What?" Moira asked with a laugh in her voice, then she waggled her eyebrows at him. "Will this lesson involve getting splinters in my backside from the door?"

"Is having your wicked way with me all ye can think of, lass?" Duncan asked.

Moira rolled her eyes at him.

"A lass should know how to protect herself," he said. "Your training in this regard has been sorely lacking, so I'm going to teach ye how to kill someone with a dirk."

"That's the sweetest thing a man has ever said to me," Moira said in a dead-serious voice.

Duncan threw his head back and laughed out loud. When Moira laughed with him, Lord above, it felt good.

"What was your father thinking, not teaching a lass like you how to use a blade?" he asked.

"A lass like me?" she asked, tilting her head.

"Aye. A lass who runs headlong into danger without a second thought." Duncan pointed his finger at her. "Falling down that ravine was not the worst thing that could have happened to ye roaming about the hillsides on your own."

"Ach, don't give me another tedious lecture." Moira got out of bed naked and stood with one hand on her hip, as if she meant to torture him. "Just show me how to use the dirk."

Duncan retrieved her gown from where it had been drying in front of the hearth and tossed it to her. "Put it on quickly, or I can't guarantee we'll get to the lesson."

CHAPTER 19

I'll be away from Skye for a time," Alastair Crotach MacLeod told Erik. "When I return, I'll want ye to report to me on Hugh Dubh."

Erik had cultivated informants and heard a whisper that his wily chieftain was negotiating to change sides in the rebellion and throw his support behind the Crown— for a price. That would be a wise move now that it was clear the rebellion was failing. What troubled Erik was that his chieftain had not confided his plans to him.

Still, his chieftain's absence from Skye would give Erik the opportunity he needed.

"I could take the MacQuillan lad off your hands while you're gone," Erik said, taking care to make it sound as if it were a burden he did not relish.

"Aye, take the lad to Trotternish Castle." The corner of the chieftain's mouth lifted a fraction in what passed for a smile. "We have a duty to train him, but don't teach him all ye know—he may be our enemy one day."

Erik wouldn't be teaching him anything for long. One less MacDonald male of chieftain's blood would be good for the MacLeods, as far as he was concerned. His chieftain didn't have the stomach to do what needed to be done, so Erik would do it for him.

At Trotternish Castle, Erik had both the power and the distance from his chieftain to handle matters as he saw fit. He would be careful, of course, so that the blame could not be laid at his door.

"No one could match ye as a warrior in your prime," his chieftain said, standing up to clamp a hand on Erik's shoulder.

Erik nodded to acknowledge the compliment, but the *in your prime* remark had cut. Although Erik was closer to fifty than forty now, few men were willing to challenge him to a fight. He was still stronger than most and twice as devious as the rest.

* * *

Duncan awoke with Moira in his arms. He rested his cheek against the top of her head and watched the late-afternoon light sift through the crack in the shutters. It had been years since he felt this content.

For the last three days, he and Moira had barely left the cottage. They had spent their time alternately napping, practicing with the dirk, and rediscovering interesting things to do in bed, short of a full joining of their bodies, that, in the end, were quite satisfying for both of them. It brought him untold joy to watch Moira's innate sensuality blossom under his hands.

Bang! Bang! Bang!

Duncan sprang out of bed and picked up his claymore from where he kept it at the ready on the floor.

"What is it?" he called through the closed door.

"'Tis me, Uilleam."

Duncan opened the door a crack.

"Not dressed, and the day's nearly over?" Uilleam said. "I suspected that the two of ye weren't wed yet, and now I know it for certain."

Duncan could not help cracking a smile. "What urgent business has ye getting me out of bed now?"

"Niall has recovered so well that the neighbors are starting to talk about my daughter Caitlin," Uilleam said. "If ye don't get him out of her cottage by morning, they'll expect me to demand a wedding—not that Caitlin would agree to it."

"My boat is ready, so we'll set sail first thing tomorrow," Duncan said. "I'm grateful to your daughter. I hope Niall isn't troubling her too much. He seems taken with her."

"He's not the first," Uilleam said, shaking his head. "Bring your whistle to Caitlin's cottage tonight. We'll have ourselves a good time drinking whiskey and playing music."

Duncan felt like celebrating.

* * *

Moira tapped her foot to the lively tune the men were playing as she sat with Caitlin by the hearth. In the morning, they would be on their way home to Dunscaith.

Home. It had been such a long time.

She glanced at Duncan, and he winked when he caught her gaze on him. She could not remember ever seeing him so carefree. Playing music brought him such pleasure, and he truly had a gift for it.

The other men stopped playing, and Duncan strummed his harp.

"Ach, I know this song," Caitlin said and elbowed Moira.

Goose bumps rose on Moira's skin as Duncan's strong voice filled the small cottage. It was an old tune, but she felt as if he had made up the words to sing just for her.

Black is the color of my true love's hair
Her lips are like some roses fair
She has the sweetest smile and the gentlest hands
And I love the ground whereon she stands

I love my love and well she knows
I love the ground whereon she goes
I hope the day it soon will come
When she and I will live as one

Duncan set his harp down, said something in Uilleam's ear, then came to stand in front of Moira. When she looked up at him, he gave her one of his rare smiles that went straight to her heart and held out his hand.

"Dance with me, Moira MacDonald."

"I—"

"Go on, lass!" one of the women called out. "When a man that handsome asks ye to dance, ye must jump to your feet before he goes looking for a lass who will."

"There's only one lass I wish to dance with," Duncan said, his eyes warm on hers. "'Tis Moira and none other."

He said it as if he meant more by it than dancing. Duncan kept saying things like that to her, suggesting he had not put her out of his heart—as if he were not the one who left.

"Hurry up lass," Uilleam said. "We're ready to play."

Moira gave Duncan her hand and let him pull her to her feet. A couple of the men moved the table against the wall, and the small cottage filled with a burst of music.

The joy in life that she used to feel every day spread through her as she and Duncan skipped and hopped, arm in arm, in a tight circle in the tiny room. Duncan made a travesty of the footwork, but his body moved with a natural grace to the rhythm of the music. When he twirled her in his arms, Moira let her head fall back, laughing.

The door opened and closed as people from the neighboring cottages squeezed in to hear the music and watch the dancing. Those who weren't playing clapped. Moira and Duncan danced until she was sweaty and breathless. Duncan was not even breathing hard.

"Please," she gasped, "I can't anymore."

Duncan found an empty space on one of the benches and pulled her onto his lap.

"I can sit on my own," she said.

"There aren't enough seats," he said, still smiling. She couldn't resist him when he was lighthearted like this; it was so unexpected.

Caitlin came around with cups of whiskey.

"*Cha deoch-slàint, i gun a tràghadh!*" It's no health if the glass is not emptied!

Moira tossed it back. The third time the whiskey was passed, Moira shook her head. Her head was spinning pleasantly.

"Ach, I'm so hot!" She fanned herself with her hand.

"Let's take a stroll outside to cool off," Duncan said.

Before she could answer, he was walking her out the door. When he paused to lift their cloaks from the pegs, Moira thought she caught Uilleam giving Duncan a wink.

The cool night air felt good on her hot cheeks. For once, it wasn't drizzling or blowing.

"Ah, that was lovely," she said. Except for Ragnall not being here, everything was perfect tonight.

Moira felt a bit unsteady on her feet and was grateful when Duncan put his arm around her. Being with him was so easy. She did not have to watch what she said or even speak at all. Though she knew she had felt exactly this way before he left her, she pushed that worry aside for now. Tonight she felt happy, and she was just going to let herself enjoy it.

"That was a short walk," she teased him when he took her straight to their cottage at the end of the row.

Anticipation ran through her as she watched Duncan light a candle, poke at the burning embers in the hearth, and put fresh peat on the fire. The light from the flames glinted in his hair. He moved with the ease and sureness of a man whose body was honed and trained as a weapon to do whatever he asked of it.

Once he had the fire going, Duncan came to where she stood and put his hands against the wall on either side of her head. She found it hard to breathe as he gazed into her eyes for a long moment.

"There are a few things we haven't tried yet," he said and trailed his finger along her jaw. "Things ye used to be quite fond of..."

Instead of kissing her right away, he let the tension grow between them until she wanted his kiss so much that she grabbed hold of his tunic and pulled him to her.

For such a hard-muscled, uncompromising man, his lips were soft. She leaned into him with a sigh. His arms came around her, not constraining her, but enveloping her in a delicious warmth.

* * *

Duncan held Moira as she slept and wondered if this would be his last time.

He had little more to offer her now than he had when he was nineteen. Though he held a position of respect as captain of her brother's guard, respect was not enough to hold a woman like Moira. She was meant to grace a high table, wear the finest silks, and have servants to wait upon her. She carried the blood of the Lord of Isles and the ancient kings before them, while he was the unclaimed son of a MacLeod rapist.

Still, he whispered, "Please God, don't take her from me. Not again."

CHAPTER 20

Moira blinked against the sting in her eyes at her fist sight of Dunscaith Castle sitting majestically on its rock island off the headland. As they sailed nearer, the rain cleared, revealing the green hills behind the castle and the purple mountains across the bay to the northwest.

"I'd forgotten how beautiful it is," she said. Growing up, Moira had taken both the beauty of her home and her happiness for granted.

"Aye, 'tis a lovely sight," Duncan said, standing beside her. "And Dunscaith is a strong fortress as well."

It had been easy to be fearless here.

The guards standing on the castle wall recognized Duncan's boat and waved. Moira waved back with both arms. At long last, she was coming home. If only Ragnall were here with her, all would be well.

"Once I have my son safely behind the walls of Dunscaith," she said, "he'll never be in danger again."

"Ragnall has MacDonald blood in him," Niall said

from behind her, where he was sitting with his injured leg propped up. "Once he's grown, he'll not be content to hide behind walls when it's time to fight."

Moira was not going to think about that now.

"It looks as though the whole household is coming out to greet us," Duncan said.

A steady stream of people were crossing the narrow bridge slung between Dunscaith and the main island and coming down to the shore. Moira's heart beat fast as she tried to pick out her brother. Connor was chieftain now, so perhaps he would wait to greet her formally in the hall.

Despite Duncan's explanation for Connor's failure to visit her, Moira felt uneasy about whether he would be pleased to see her.

"Moira!"

She heard someone call her name, and then she saw Connor running into the surf to meet the boat with his black hair blowing behind him. When he reached it, he held out his arms to her. Laughing, she jumped down and threw her arms around his neck. She thought of her beloved father and older brother Ragnall, who were not here, and held on more tightly to Connor as he carried her to the beach.

"Welcome home," Connor said and gave her a broad smile as he set her on her feet.

They held each other's hands and leaned back to gaze at each other. Connor looked much the same, lean and hard-muscled, but his face had sharper angles and the lankiness of his youth had given way to a powerful presence.

"'Tis good to have ye back," Connor said, and he seemed genuinely happy to see her.

"I'll never leave again," she told him. "Never."

Connor raised an eyebrow, but then his gaze shifted to something behind her.

"Is that a horse or a dog with Duncan?" he asked with a laugh in his voice.

Moira turned and saw that Sàr, the traitor, had remained at Duncan's side in the boat. "That's my son's wolfhound."

"Is Niall hurt?" Connor asked as Duncan helped Niall off the boat.

"Aye," she said. "He would have died if not for Duncan."

"Duncan is the best man to have with ye when trouble comes," Connor said and ran off to help him with Niall.

Moira proceeded to greet everyone who had come down to the shore to welcome her. From the way they stared at her, she must have changed more than she realized. But the women gave her affectionate smiles as Moira exclaimed over all the new babes and the children grown up in her absence.

After some time, a brisk young woman in an ugly brown gown took her arm. "Ye must be weary from your journey," the young woman said. "Would ye like to go inside now?"

"Do I know ye?" Moira asked.

"I expect ye don't recognize me because I was only eleven the last time ye saw me," the young woman said with a warm smile. "I'm Ilysa, Duncan's sister."

It was hard to believe this wisp of a lass was Duncan's sister.

"I'm sure we can find one of your old gowns for ye to change into," Ilysa said.

Moira looked down at the bedraggled garment she had worn through the disasters of the last several days and laughed. No wonder everyone had stared at her. "A fresh gown and a bath would be lovely."

* * *

Duncan watched as their clansmen surrounded Moira, welcoming their returning princess home. She had always been a favorite. Smiles and bursts of laughter followed her as she worked her way slowly through the crowd. Moira spoke to each one, doing her duty as a member of the chieftain's family without making anyone feel that was why she did it.

Sàr whined beside him.

"No need to fret," Duncan said and patted the dog's head. "She's safe now."

Duncan wondered if he had brought her to safety only to lose her. Now that they were back among their clan, their time at the MacCrimmons seemed a world away. Perhaps if Moira had given herself to him wholly, Duncan would know she wanted more than to forget Sean for a few days. He had been patient, waiting for her to tell him she was ready.

She never did.

Connor signaled to Duncan, Niall, and Ian to remain on the beach while the others drifted back to the castle. Duncan watched Moira's back as she and his sister walked arm in arm up the hill to the castle's bridge.

"'Tis safer to talk here," Connor said when the beach was empty except for the four of them. "The walls of Dunscaith have ears."

"You and Moira both look like hell," Ian said to Niall,

who had his arm slung over Ian's shoulder to take the weight off his injured leg. "But I can tell somebody fed ye well."

"That would be Caitlin MacCrimmon," Niall said in a wistful voice. "I'm in love with her."

This was a fairly common ailment for Niall, so they ignored the remark and went on to discuss serious matters.

"I want to know why my sister has come home without her husband," Connor said, "and how she and Niall came to be injured."

Connor's expression grew darker and darker as Duncan told him of Sean MacQuillan's mistreatment of Moira and how Sean had died.

"There will be hell to pay for it, but ye did well to bring her home," Connor said.

Duncan then gave a brief account of the storm and their stay with the MacCrimmons—leaving out the parts that he and Moira spent naked. He gave Niall a hard look to encourage him to keep his mouth shut about them sharing a cottage.

"Did ye learn anything about the MacLeods from the MacCrimmons?" Connor asked.

"I did," Niall piped up. "The lasses who visited Caitlin's cottage—that's where I stayed because she's a healer—were loose-tongued about the MacLeods."

Duncan felt Connor's gaze on him and feared he was about to ask where he and Moira had slept. Fortunately, Niall kept talking.

"They heard that the MacLeod chieftain left Dunvegan with a dozen of his war galleys," Niall said. "They didn't believe he was going to his fortress on the isle of Harris, because he left his wife and daughters behind."

"People will say anything to my charming brother," Ian said. "Especially twittering lasses."

"I wonder where the MacLeod was going with so many war galleys," Connor said, narrowing his eyes. "If he was attacking us, he would already be here."

"If ever there was a time for us to try to take Trotternish," Duncan said, "'tis now, while Alastair MacLeod and hundreds of his warriors are away causing trouble for some other clan."

The others were quiet for a long moment as they considered his suggestion.

"We must take the castle first," Ian said. "Without it, we have no hope of taking the peninsula—or of holding it once we do."

"I agree," Connor said. "We've all been inside the castle, but we know nothing about how many men the MacLeods have there, how well trained they are, or what sort of man commands them. We could have a bloodbath going in blind."

"Shame we don't have spies there," Ian said. "That's one lesson we could learn from Hugh."

"Aye," Connor said. "What I wouldn't give to know if the MacLeods had shored up that weak wall my father never had repaired."

Niall had been glancing at Duncan ever since Connor had mentioned the keeper of the castle. Duncan hesitated to tell what he knew, but he was already keeping one secret from Connor and did not wish to keep another.

"I know something about Trotternish Castle," Duncan said.

"What is that?" Connor asked.

"The keeper is my father."

* * *

Moira stood in the center of her old bedchamber and turned slowly in a circle. "'Tis almost as I left it, except that there are no gowns strewn across the bed and the bed curtains are a bit faded."

It was odd to find her old chamber had changed so little when she could hardly remember the lass she had been when she lived here.

Moira smiled at Ilysa when she noticed the branch of holly in a jug on the side table. "This must be your doing."

"'Tis hard to come by anything in bloom this time of year, so I thought the holly berries would brighten the room," Ilysa said and dropped her gaze to her feet. "Connor never mentions the flowers I put out on the tables and in his chamber in summer, but I think he appreciates them all the same."

Moira doubted it. "The holly is lovely."

"I've been managing the castle household for Connor as he had no one else to do it," Ilysa said with a slight quiver in her voice. "I hope you'll find everything in good order."

"I'm certain you've done a fine job."

"When you're planning the menus with the cooks," Ilysa hurried on before Moira could say more, "Connor doesn't care at all for goose liver, though he'd never say so. He's never one to complain."

Ach, no. Did the poor lass fancy herself in love with Connor? That would never do. Even if Ilysa caught Connor's eye—which seemed unlikely in that old woman's cap and ill-fitting brown gown—Connor would never act on it. Her father had no such scruples when it came to women, but Connor would never dally with his best friend's sister. And when he wed, he would put duty first and make an alliance for the clan.

"I should warn ye that Tait is the orneriest of the guards," Ilysa rattled on, "but he's always the first to lend a hand when ye need it. And then there's..." Ilysa stopped speaking and clasped her hands together. "I'm sorry. I'm sure ye don't need my advice."

Clearly, these responsibilities had become very important to Ilysa.

"Good heavens," Moira said. "I hope Connor doesn't expect me to manage his household for him."

"Ye don't wish to?" Ilysa asked, her eyes going impossibly wide.

"Would ye mind doing it awhile longer?" Moira asked. "I'm so distracted with worry over my son that it would be an unwelcome burden to me."

"I'd be happy to," Ilysa said.

"Duncan told me ye lost your husband at Flodden," Moira said. "You're so young. Surely ye will want to marry again and set up your own household before long."

Ilysa dropped her gaze to the floor again and shook her head.

"Well, Connor *is* bound to marry soon—he should have already," Moira said in a soft voice and touched the younger woman's arm. "Ye do know that when Connor weds, his wife will take over these duties?"

"Of course," Ilysa said.

Connor had always been tediously responsible. In fact, Moira suspected the only reason Connor had waited this long to wed was that the time was not yet ripe to make the best match possible.

How different she and Connor had been as children. Moira had rushed headlong into things, letting her heart lead her wherever it would, while Connor thought things through. Living with Sean had taught Moira to be cautious and calculating like her brother.

Moira could not help Ilysa win Connor, but there were plenty of fine warriors in the castle. Ilysa was a pale thing, but she had a pretty face. If only she didn't wear the drabbest colors and loose gowns that did nothing to flatter her slender figure.

Intent on giving Ilysa some pointers, Moira pulled her over to the standing mirror, a gift her father had brought all the way from Edinburgh for her.

"God have mercy!" Moira cried when she caught her own reflection in the mirror. "Look at me!"

"Is your face as painful as it looks?" Ilysa asked, scrunching her delicate brows together.

"Painful? It's hideous!" Her face was a misshapen mass of bruises, ranging in color from purple to a sickly greenish yellow. And her gown looked even worse than she had imagined.

Moira sat down on the nearby bench with a thump. Ach, she must have looked even worse before. She thought of all the hours she'd spent with Duncan. Especially the hours in bed. In the afternoon, when it was light.

Moira did not pretend she didn't know she was beautiful. Men had lusted after her since she was thirteen, so she was well aware it was her looks that drew them to her.

But despite how revolting she looked now, Duncan had wanted her. In truth, no one had ever made her feel more beautiful—not even Duncan himself when she was seventeen and the prettiest she would ever be. She was touched by it. Did it mean he truly cared for her?

Moira was not sure, but she suddenly wanted to see Duncan. It seemed as if it had been hours since she was standing beside him on the boat.

"Ah, here's your bath," Ilysa said, waving in the servants carrying the washtub and buckets of hot water. "Before I leave ye, I'll lay out a few of your old gowns for you to try."

Moira hurried through her bath and, with the servants' help, squeezed into an old velvet gown in a midnight-blue that matched her eyes. After searching the hall for Duncan, she went out into the courtyard to look for him. She found Connor instead.

"Ye look a wee bit better," Connor said with a smile and kissed her cheek.

"Where is Duncan?" Moira asked.

"He's gone home," Conner said.

"To his mother's cottage?" They had always called it a cottage, though it was just two rooms built against the outer wall of the castle.

"No, Ilysa lives there," Connor said. "Duncan often sleeps in the hall with the men, but he has his own house."

"Where?" she asked.

Connor pointed to a white cottage she could barely see near the top of the hill behind the castle. "Duncan says that he can keep a lookout for anyone approaching Dunscaith from up there, but I know he just needed a place of his own."

"The view must be lovely," she said. "I'd like to see it. I think I'll pay him a wee visit."

"Why?" Connor asked, narrowing his eyes at her. "Is

there something between the two of ye I should know about?"

"Of course not." It was none of Connor's business.

"Ye should wait until you're invited," Connor said.

"Whatever for?" Moira asked with a laugh.

"Duncan likes his privacy. Ye should—"

"He'll be happy to see me." Moira winked at her brother over her shoulder as she left, feeling like her old self.

* * *

Duncan opened the door to his cottage. He had been proud to have a home, a place that belonged to him. He kept it freshly whitewashed and in good repair, and his sister had planted a dog rose by his door that bloomed in summer.

But as he stood in the doorway and looked at it with different eyes—with her eyes—he saw that it was just a humble, two-room cottage. Two chairs and a small table fit comfortably in the main room with the hearth. Ilysa had proclaimed it cozy, but he could see now that it was simply tiny.

He sat down on one of the chairs and rested his head in his hands. What a fool he'd been. Moira had lived her entire life as the mistress of fine castles. He could never ask her to live with him here. Her gowns alone would take up the entire second room.

"Duncan, you're home!"

He started at the sound of the voice coming from the other room and turned. What in the hell was Rhona doing here?

CHAPTER 21

Before Duncan could stop her, Rhona bolted across the room and threw herself at him. He unlocked her hands from around his neck and set her on her feet.

"Ye said you'd be gone when I returned."

"A woman can change her mind," Rhona said, cocking her head to the side, "and a wise man doesn't remind her that she has."

When she reached up to run her fingers down his cheek, Duncan caught her hand. "It's finished between us."

"Finished?" Rhona's eyes widened.

"It was done before I left."

"Ah well, I decided to forgive ye." She looked at him from under her lashes and gave him a slow smile. "I know how ye can make it up to me."

"I want ye to go," Duncan said. "Now."

"Ye don't mean it," she said giving him a coy smile.

Duncan paused. He may as well make it plain. "Moira is here."

"Moira?" Rhona said her name in a shriek, then she narrowed her eyes to slits. "I should have known. Ye were always such a fool for her."

He was, but there was no point in discussing it.

"And did the little princess let ye pleasure her in bed like she used to?" Rhona said. "That's all Moira thinks you're good for. She won't be seen with ye in the light of day."

"Don't," Duncan warned her.

"Ye don't like hearing the truth?" Rhona's eyes were snapping fire as she poked her finger into his chest. "Moira never thought ye were good enough for her."

"If ye have anything in my house, take it with ye now," Duncan said. "You're not coming back."

When Rhona did not budge, Duncan took the large cloth bag from the hook on the wall and started tossing in the odds and ends she had left in his house. He'd never really noticed them before.

"As soon as ye left for France, Moira started sneaking off with that handsome Irish chieftain," Rhona said. "She used my clothes, pretending she was me, just like she had with you."

"That's enough." Duncan did not want to hear it, did not want to believe it.

"While ye were bleeding for her as ye crossed the sea to France, I had to listen to Moira prattle on about what an important man her Irish lover was," Rhona said, waving her hand in the air, "and all the things he could give her."

Duncan shoved the bag at Rhona and opened the door. "Out!"

"She forgot ye like that." Rhona snapped her fingers in front of his face as she left. "And she'll do it again."

* * *

A hint of spring was in the air, and the view from the path to Duncan's cottage was indeed wondrous. Moira spread out her arms and drank it in. When she was near the top of the hill, she paused in the middle of the open field to look back at the Cuillins and was pleased with herself when she could remember the names of most of the peaks. There was no place on God's earth she would rather be than right here.

She smiled as she continued up the path. Just ahead, Duncan's cottage was a pretty sight with its fresh white-wash and thatch. Sàr lay on one side of the door, and someone had planted a dog rose on the other side that would be lovely come summer. Who would have guessed the fiercest of the MacDonald warriors had a soft spot for dogs and flowers?

As she drew nearer the cottage, she heard raised voices. Rather, one voice. A woman's.

Her stomach dropped. Duncan had not mentioned that he had a woman waiting at home. When Duncan touched her, he made her believe there was no other. Perhaps she had just wanted that to be true.

Only now did Moira admit to herself why she had come to his cottage. She had wanted to take that last step and let him make love to her fully. She was no longer a seventeen-year-old lass in the blush of first love. She thought Duncan did not have the power to hurt her now.

But she was wrong.

She should have known that a man as fine looking as Duncan would not be alone. Even apart from his hand-some face and warrior's body, Duncan was the sort of man who intrigued women—at least the brave ones. They were drawn by his darkness and silence, each hoping to be the one woman he would share his secrets with.

Before Moira could start back down the hill, the door opened and a black-haired woman came out. Her head was turned, and she was shouting back toward the cottage.

"Ye are a damned fool, Duncan Ruadh! Princess Moira would never have stayed with ye before, and she won't now."

The woman adjusted the large cloth bag that weighed down her shoulder, then started marching down the hill with her head down. Moira had nowhere to hide in the open field. After a few steps, the woman looked up, and they both sucked in their breath.

"Rhona!" Moira could not think of a single other word to say to her former maid.

"Duncan will come crawling back to me after you've broken his heart again," Rhona said.

Moira stood there, too stunned to move, as Rhona brushed past her. Then she watched Rhona's figure, swaying under the burden of the heavy bag, as it disappeared down the hill. After a while, she felt eyes on her and turned to find Duncan standing in front of the door of his cottage.

"Don't mind her," he said.

Moira waited for Duncan to give her an explanation, but the man said nothing. This was one of those times when she found his dark silence far more annoying than intriguing.

"So ye missed me every day, did ye?" she snapped. "I see your suffering did not include sleeping alone."

Duncan shrugged. "Rhona and I met each other's needs for a time, that's all."

"Is that all ye have to say about it?" Moira put her hands on her hips. "Judging from how upset Rhona was—and that heavy bag slung over her shoulder— you've been meeting each other's needs for some time."

Ach, she sounded like a harpy. Did she expect Duncan to have lived like a monk these past seven years? But knowing she had no cause to feel aggrieved did not make her feel less so. Moira turned her head and fixed her gaze on the sheep grazing across the hillside.

"Are ye coming in?" Duncan asked.

Well, she had come all the way here, and she was curious about where he lived. Besides, she was not done with this conversation.

Duncan stepped to the side to let her in and then shut the door behind them. Sàr, who must have come into the cottage during the confusion, was lying in front of the hearth and taking up half the room. He raised his scraggly brows at her and wagged his tail.

"Outside," Duncan said, and the wolfhound slunk past her with a guilty look.

Moira perched on the edge of one of the two chairs and took in the room, which was small but clean and pleasant. She drummed her fingertips on her knee and waited to speak again until Duncan sat as well.

"Why Rhona?" Moira asked.

"I'm sorry if she upset ye," Duncan said, which was no answer.

"She's an angry woman," Moira said. "And she was wrong. I would have stayed with ye forever if ye hadn't left for France."

She was not speaking to Rhona's accusation that she would not stay with him now. If Moira had any sense, she would be running down the hill.

"Ye weren't here," Duncan said.

"What?" Moira asked.

"That is the reason I was with Rhona," Duncan said, meeting her eyes with his direct gaze. "You are the only woman who ever mattered to me. Rhona knows it. Everyone does."

"*O shluagh.*" Just when she was ready to storm off, he said something like that to her. Worse, Duncan thought he believed it.

And for the next few hours, Moira was going to let herself believe it, too.

She picked up the harp from where it rested beside her chair and handed it to him. "Play that song for me," she said. "The one about the black-haired lass."

Duncan strummed the strings a few times as he tuned it. Then he looked at her with his warm hazel eyes, and his rich voice filled the small cottage with the song of love and longing.

> *Black is the color of my true love's hair*
> *Her lips are like some roses fair*
> *She has the sweetest smile and the gentlest hands*
> *And I love the ground whereon she stands*
>
> *I love my love and well she knows*
> *I love the ground whereon she goes*
> *I hope the day it soon will come*
> *When she and I will be as one*

* * *

Duncan should not have sung that song to her again and bared his soul to her so utterly. Yet there was no point in attempting to hide his feelings. Moira knew he had lost his heart to her seven years ago, and he was not a man whose feelings changed.

Seeing her here in his humble home made the situation clear to him. Yet when Moira stood in front of his chair and looked down at him with violet eyes as soft as her velvet gown, Duncan knew he would give his life to keep her.

She took his harp from him, set it on the floor, and held out her hands to him. "Take me to bed."

CHAPTER 22

I'm glad ye came." Duncan framed her face in his hands and gave her a long, lingering kiss.

When he picked her up and carried her into the other room, Moira laughed because he had to turn sideways and duck his head to get through the low doorway. A simple, wood-framed bed covered with thick blankets filled most of his bedchamber, which Moira guessed had been converted from what was usually the cow's half of a cottage.

Behind the bed, the single window was tightly shuttered against the winter winds. Moira imagined that when it was open on a fine day, Duncan could lie in bed and have a grand view of the sea and mountains.

Without exchanging a word, they undressed quickly in the small space beside the bed. As they crawled under the heavy blankets, the ropes holding the mattress creaked beneath their weight. The bedchamber was so small and the bed so cozy that Moira felt as if she were locked away with Duncan in a warm cocoon.

She put her arms around his neck and gazed into his face. His features were all hard angles and his expression was serious, but his gold-flecked hazel eyes were warm. When he slid his hand over the curve of her hip, she sighed.

With the MacCrimmons, Duncan had been patient with her, giving her time to trust his touch. Under his gentle ministrations, her body had come alive again. And now that she had seen herself in the mirror, she knew that it was not just her beauty that made him want her.

You are the only woman who ever mattered to me. Rhona knows it. Everyone does.

The cottage, the creaking bed, and Duncan's strong, warrior's body all made her feel protected. And after Sean, she needed to feel safe and wanted for herself before she could share her body fully.

Was she ready? She ran her hands over Duncan's chest, enjoying the feel of the taut muscles and rough hair beneath her palms. When he splayed his hand against her back and drew her into a deep kiss, she closed her eyes and melted into him. Aye, she was ready.

Moira moved against him like a cat to feel the friction of his chest on her sensitive breasts. He groaned and pulled her more tightly to him. Their kisses grew more fevered, and the hardness of his shaft poking against her belly aroused a deep need in her. She held him tightly, needing to be closer still, as their tongues moved together in a rhythm as old as time.

When he rolled her on her back, she wrapped her legs around his waist, instinctively urging him forward. Aye, this was what she wanted. No more waiting. Flashes from that long-ago summer came back to her—of Duncan deep inside her, crying out his love for her when he could not say it any other time. How she wanted him like that again.

She moaned aloud when the tip of his shaft touched her center. For a long, long moment, Duncan held still above her, the muscles of his shoulders straining beneath her fingers. As the tension between them became unbearable, she dug her fingers into his shoulders and lifted her hips.

"Please, Duncan."

Instead of doing as she urged, he covered her breasts with his callused hands and moved down her body. He teased her nipples between his fingers and thumbs while he kissed her throat and ran his tongue down her breastbone. Liquid heat pooled deep in her belly as he moved lower and lower with his warm lips and tongue.

Anticipation sang through her body as he lifted her leg over his shoulder and kissed the inside of her thigh. A high moan came from the back of her throat when he finally ran his tongue over the sensitive spot between her legs. As he worked his magic with his lips and tongue, she gripped the bedclothes in her hands and bit her lip.

She came in waves of white light.

It was wonderful, but this time it was not enough.

* * *

When Duncan moved to lie beside her, Moira pulled him down on top of her.

"I want to feel ye inside me," she said, still breathing hard.

Oh, Jesu. Did she mean it?

"Are ye certain?" Duncan forced out the question. "We don't have to do this yet."

"I want us to be as one," she said, echoing the words of the song he had sung to her. "And I don't want to wait another moment."

This time, when she tightened her legs around him, urging him forward, Duncan did not resist her. They both gasped as he thrust deep inside her in one stroke. Sweat beaded on his forehead as he forced himself to take long, deep breaths and hold still. His body was so hungry for her, and for release, that the urge to pound into her again and again until he exploded was nearly irresistible.

And Moira was not making it any easier for him. She was hot and wet and squirming beneath him.

Slowly, slowly, he pulled out almost all the way. When he slid back inside her, the rush of pleasure almost blinded him. He held her face between his hands and stared into her midnight-blue eyes as he moved in and out with excruciating slowness.

"Is this good?" he asked, though he could tell that it was.

"Aye," she said and gasped as he thrust deep into her again. "And for you?"

He almost laughed. "Nothing has ever felt this good."

As he increased his pace, she made those high-pitched sounds that drove him wild. She raised her hips to meet him as he thrust into her faster and harder. He could hold back no longer. He had wanted her forever. Through the blood pounding in his ears, he heard Moira cry his name as her body clenched around him.

At long last, Moira was his again. He let go, exploding inside her.

* * *

Duncan wanted her again.

He had been deprived of Moira for so long that he was like a starving animal. When he ran his finger up the silky skin of her inner thigh to ask the question, her breath hitched. Then she rolled on top of him, giving him precisely the answer he wanted.

Miraculously, Moira seemed almost as hungry for him as he was for her. They made love all afternoon until they were too sore and weak to do it again.

But afterward, while she dozed in his arms, Rhona's words echoed round and round in Duncan's head.

Did the little princess let ye pleasure her in bed like she used to? That's all she thinks you're good for… Moira forgot ye like that, and she'll do it again.

Duncan had thought if she gave her body fully to him, she would give him her heart as well. But he'd had her love once, if briefly, and he knew the difference.

He looked about his tiny bedchamber, barely large enough for his bed. How long would Moira want to sneak out of the castle to seek pleasure with him here? Their clan needed allies, and Connor would surely pressure her to make a new marriage to benefit the clan. And Connor had a way of getting what he wanted. Eventually, Moira would agree to wed one of the men Connor invited to visit, a chieftain who could give her all the things she was accustomed to.

Duncan had not sung the last verse of the song to her, the sad one. But he heard it in his head now.

> *I go down to the sea, and I mourn and weep*
> *For satisfied, she'll never be*

So I write a song to her, just a few short lines
And suffer death a thousand times

Duncan was not sure he could survive being parted from her a second time. He was willing to suffer the thousand deaths to be with her now.

But damn it, that was not enough. As he lay watching the only woman he would ever love sleep on his chest, Duncan made up his mind. He was not giving her up. This time, he would find a way to give Moira all the things she needed.

This time, he would find a way to keep her.

* * *

When Moira opened her eyes, she found Duncan standing beside the bed fully dressed and smelling of the outdoors. In his hand, he held a cup with a clump of heather in it. He kissed her forehead and leaned across the bed to set the heather on the windowsill.

"I didn't know the heather was blooming already." She sat up and put her nose in it to breathe in the scent.

"Ye just need to know where to look," Duncan said and sat on the edge of the bed.

Moira felt her defenses crumbling. After making love to her until she was senseless, Duncan was showing her this gentle side of him that squeezed her heart. When he was like this, she could almost trust him. Almost.

Moira felt a twinge of guilt for not telling him about Ragnall. She knew that the longer she waited to tell him that Ragnall was his son, the harder it would be.

But despite his passionate lovemaking and kind gestures, a part of her still did not believe he deserved to know. She had not forgotten that Duncan had left her or all that she had suffered because of it—the years of living in fear and having her body used by a man she loathed. And how she'd had to fight in a thousand subtle ways against Sean's influence over her son. She had won the battle for her son's soul, and she had done it all on her own.

Duncan took a strand of her hair between his finger and thumb and twirled it. "You're even more lovely than ye used to be."

She snorted. "I've seen myself in a looking glass."

"I think ye know I would want ye no matter what ye looked like," Duncan said, making Moira feel all soft inside again.

While Moira could not forget the past, neither did she want to let bitterness ruin her happiness of the moment. And, miraculously, she was happy.

"I expect to be gone for a few days on an errand for Connor," Duncan said.

"Must ye go?" she asked and ran her hand up his chest.

"Aye," he said and brushed her hair back from her face. "Before I go, I need to tell ye that I lo—"

Moira put her fingers over his lips. "Don't say it."

Meaningless words, that's all they were. She did not want him to ruin what was between them with words of love that amounted to false promises. All those years ago, she had believed those words meant that he would stay with her, that he would always be there, that he would not fail her.

"Let's make the most of this while it lasts," she said.

"While it lasts?" Duncan asked, with an edge to his voice.

"Aye." That's all anyone could count on. Expecting more just led to disappointment.

"And how long do ye think that will be?" Duncan said between his teeth.

"I don't know." He was growing angry, but she was not going to lie. Until she had her son back, she did not want to think about the future any more than the past. She rubbed her hand up Duncan's thigh. "All I do know is that I am happy with ye now."

"Ye like sharing a bed with me."

"I do." She could not help the grin spreading across her face, despite the forbidding look Duncan was giving her. "I want to stay here at the cottage with ye until ye go. Perhaps I'll stay here while you're gone as well. Can ye help me bring some of my things up?"

* * *

"Ye can't stay here," Duncan said, his voice rising, despite his effort to be calm. "And ye can't be living in my cottage while I'm gone."

The woman would drive him mad. No matter what else she said, her plan to stay in his cottage had to mean she intended to marry him. Since she did not care to hear his words of love, he could only assume he pleased her in bed even more than he thought.

"Why can't I stay here?" she asked.

"For one thing, 'tis safer in the castle. For another, it would be improper. And for a third, Connor would have my head on a platter."

"Improper?" Moira asked, sounding outraged. "I'm no unmarried lass of seventeen."

She leaned over the side of the bed and started gathering her clothes from the floor.

"Come, Moira, ye know ye can't stay here without us being married."

Duncan had formed a plan, but he did not want to

discuss marriage with her until he was certain his plan would succeed—and until he had Connor's permission. That was the only honorable way to do this.

"I know nothing of the kind," Moira said as she jerked her shift over her head. "No one—not you, not my brother, not anyone—is going to tell me what I can and cannot do."

"We can't have everyone believing you're giving yourself to me without us being wed."

"But I *am* giving myself to ye without being wed." She squeezed past him with the rest of her clothes in her hands.

"That is no the point," Duncan said, following her into the other room. "Have ye no concern for your reputation?"

"No," she said, turning to look straight at him. "I. don't."

She stepped into her gown and, leaving it unfastened in the back, threw her cloak over it.

"If you're going to act foolishly with no regard for the consequences," Duncan said, shaking his finger in her face, "then ye can expect those who care for ye—*and who have a good deal more sense*—to tell ye what to do."

"You're a pigheaded arse, Duncan MacDonald!" Moira shouted. "For the last seven years, I've been under a man's thumb, my every move watched and censored, and I shall never let that happen again."

"I'm not like Sean," Duncan objected, spreading his arms out. "But I won't have all our clansmen thinking ill of ye because of what you're doing with me."

"I thought this is what ye wanted," she snapped. "Ye certainly seemed to like it—repeatedly—a short time ago."

"I do want ye," he said. "Ye know damned well I do."

She ignored him and headed for the door. "I doubt I'll have any trouble," she said over her shoulder as she opened it, "finding a man who appreciates an improper lass like me."

"Ye let another man *appreciate* ye, and I'll kill him."

The door slammed behind her.

CHAPTER 23

Erik stood waiting on the rocky shore below Trotternish Castle on the appointed night until he saw the outline of Hugh's boat hovering offshore.

"Here," Erik called, after glancing behind him again to make certain no one had followed him. "Leave your men on the boat."

He heard a splash and saw Hugh's dark shape coming toward him.

"Where's the boy?" Hugh asked when he reached Erik.

"I didn't bring him," Erik said.

"Ye told me he would be here. We had an agreement." Hugh sounded outraged—as if he had never altered a deal.

"I can't give him to ye yet," Erik said.

"Then when?" Hugh demanded.

"When ye give me information that makes it worth my while," Erik said.

"I thought ye wanted to be rid of the lad as much as I did."

"I don't care one way or the other," Erik lied. "But my chieftain will be displeased if something *unfortunate* happens to the lad. I need a very good reason to take the risk. I need information."

"Losing Trotternish is like a festering wound to my nephew," Hugh said. "I know he is planning to take it back."

"And maybe I'm planning to fook the faery queen," Erik said. "If ye want the MacQuillan lad, you'll have to tell me more than what your nephew is dreaming about."

"Connor will attempt to take the castle," Hugh said. "When he decides to make the attack, I'll hear of it."

He sounded confident, but Erik did not trust Hugh any more than Hugh trusted him.

"When ye bring me your nephew's plan for attacking my castle," Erik said, "I'll give ye the lad."

* * *

Duncan flinched as another bloodcurdling scream echoed down the stairs of Knock Castle. He glanced at Ian to see if they should see to the injured, but Ian lounged back in his chair and sipped his whiskey, showing no concern for the mayhem upstairs.

"Those wee lasses of yours have good lungs," Connor said, raising his voice so he could be heard over the twins' continuing objections to their nap.

"Aye," Ian said with a grin, as if it were a compliment. "They're strong-willed lasses like their mother."

Connor winced as another screech reached them. And Duncan had thought it would be good for Connor to escape Dunscaith for a couple of hours rather than send for Ian.

"Now that we're here," Connor said, turning to him, "what did ye want to talk about?"

"I know how to get inside Trotternish Castle," Duncan said.

"How?" Connor asked.

"With my pipes," Duncan said.

"Your pipes?" Ian laughed. "I thought ye were serious."

"I am," Duncan said. "When Teàrlag came to Dunscaith before I left for Ireland, she told me that my music would provide the answer we need."

That silenced them for a time. Teàrlag's predictions usually came true, though not always as one would expect.

"Teàrlag was right about Moira being in danger, and I found her in a pool of blood, just like Teàrlag said," Duncan told them. The old seer had also predicted Duncan would need his whistle—and indeed, it had led the MacCrimmons to accept him. "So she could be right about my music as well."

"Go on," Connor said.

"Well, I've been thinking about what Ian said about us needing spies on our enemies," Duncan said.

Ian groaned. "I can guess what you're going to propose."

"I'll pretend I'm a piper making my way to visit the MacCrimmons," Duncan explained. "Once I'm inside, I'll have a look around. If they have a weakness, I'll find it."

"Ye believe ye can fool them?" Connor asked.

"I'm a fair piper," Duncan said with a shrug.

"Ye play well enough, but ye look like a warrior." Ian squeezed Duncan's upper arm. "A man doesn't get muscles like this from blowing on pipes."

"People see what they expect to see," Duncan said. "If I carry pipes and dress the part, no one will look beyond that."

"Someone could recognize ye from a battle or gathering," Connor said. "I don't like the idea of ye going in there alone."

"One man is less likely to draw suspicion," Duncan said, telling Connor what he already knew. "And neither of ye could play a tune to save your lives."

"I don't like him going in alone, either, but it is a good plan," Ian said, looking at Connor. "We don't have another way to find out if the castle is vulnerable."

"It's too risky," Connor said, shaking his head. "If the MacLeods find out who ye are, they won't give ye an easy death."

That was a risk a warrior faced.

"I need to take the castle from Erik MacLeod," Duncan said, meeting Connor's gaze. "I have fought for this clan since I was old enough to swing a claymore. You owe me this chance at vengeance."

"All right." Connor blew out his breath and rested his hand on Duncan's shoulder. "If ye do discover a weakness in the castle's defenses, we'll need to gather every warrior we can spare for the battle. I'll send word to Alex on North Uist. By the time you're back, he'll be here with his men."

"I will find a weakness," Duncan said.

"In the meantime, we must keep this among the three

of us," Connor said. "If a whisper of it reaches the MacLeods, we'll find Duncan's broken body in the sea below the cliffs of Trotternish Castle."

Duncan leaned back in his chair. If they succeeded in taking Trotternish Castle, Connor would surely make him the new keeper. Then he would finally be in a position to marry Moira.

All would be well. Even the twins had stopped screaming. Surely that was a sign.

CHAPTER 24

Duncan hauled his boat to shore in a quiet cove a couple of miles from Trotternish Castle and hid it in the low shrubs. With a sigh of regret, he unstrapped his claymore and laid it carefully in the bottom of the boat.

"Guard it well while I'm gone, Sàr." He scratched the wolfhound's ears and picked up his pipes.

No one was supposed to know Duncan was going, but his sister Ilysa had shown up at his cottage with the dog just as he was leaving. She claimed she had seen a vision, or some such foolishness, and insisted he bring the wolfhound with him. Though Duncan did not believe Ilysa had The Sight—or at least, he hoped not—he was happy for the dog's company on the two-day sail.

He let Sàr accompany him until they were in sight of Trotternish Castle, then ordered him to stay. Because wolfhounds usually belonged to the highborn and were distinctive, he could not take the dog with him.

As Duncan walked across the wide grassy field that

led up to the castle, he could see the whitecaps of the sea stretching out for miles, all the way to the outer isles. Up here on the bluff, with the fierce wind blowing his hair back, he had the sensation of being at the edge of the world. He understood the pull his Viking ancestors must have felt to sail ever westward into the unknown.

Duncan had been to Trotternish Castle several times when it was in the possession of the MacDonalds. But this time, he came as an enemy.

The castle was perched on a point of the bluff, with sheer, fifty-foot cliffs on three sides. There were only two ways to attack it. From the sea, warriors had to climb single-file up steep steps that were cut into the rock and curved up the cliff from the adjacent crescent beach. The sea approach was nigh onto impossible unless you had a great many men—and you were willing to lose a lot of them.

From what Duncan had heard, that was what the MacLeods had done.

The only other approach was through this wide-open expanse on the bluff, which gave the castle defenders plenty of forewarning. In fact, Duncan could feel the guards watching him now. An attack from here would have to be made under cover of darkness or in extremely poor weather.

As Duncan crossed the last several yards to the castle, the land fell away on either side of him. This final stretch of land leading up to the point on which the castle stood was narrow and had a ditch dug across it, enhancing the defensibility of the castle.

Duncan did not bother calling out or banging on the gate since the guards had been watching his slow arrival for some time. Instead, he opened his bag and held up his pipes for the guards to see. He felt half naked without his claymore strapped to his back. Entering his enemy's lair with no weapon but his pipes—he may as well be holding his cock in his hand.

The guards swung the gate open without even questioning him. When Duncan returned to Dunscaith, he would make damned sure the MacDonald guards were not so easily deceived by appearances.

"Hope you're better than the last piper who came through here," one guard said. "Go in the hall and someone will feed ye."

Duncan pulled his cap low over his eyes as he entered the keep. He had become fairly well known for his fighting skills. He was counting on the MacLeod warriors inside, like the guards at the gate, to see a man with pipes—and no claymore—and not look closer.

The hall was noisy, and it appeared the midday meal had just ended. Near-empty platters of food were on the tables, and about half the people in the hall were still sitting at them, while the others were milling about before setting to their afternoon tasks.

As Duncan made his way to a table, a few people looked at him curiously, but no one tried to stop him. He decided he may as well eat while he observed the MacLeods and found an empty seat in front of a platter that still had a goodly amount of food on it. He stabbed a hunk of roasted pork with his eating knife. Before the juicy meat reached his mouth, a deep voice rumbled across the hall.

"Ye must play for your dinner first, piper!"

There was one MacLeod, after all, who had the wits to

test a stranger entering the castle. Reluctantly, Duncan set his knife down.

As the noisy room grew quiet, Duncan's senses went on alert. Slowly, he turned in the direction from which the voice had come. The blood drained from his head as he met the gaze of the man seated at the center of the high table.

If the MacLeod chieftain were in the castle, he would be sitting in the decorative, high-backed chair at the center. But Duncan had seen Alastair MacLeod before, a man of sixty-odd years with a hunchback, and this was not him.

In the absence of the chieftain, the man who would have the honor of sitting in that chair would be the keeper of the castle—and the man Duncan had been looking for all his life. For the first time, Duncan stared into the face of his father.

His enemy.

Erik MacLeod was probably in his forties, though he still looked strong as an ox. Except for his build, the likeness between him and Duncan was not strong. Erik had steel-gray hair that he wore shorn short, and a beard to match. Still, Duncan could see himself in the hardness of the older man's eyes.

Every fiber of his body urged him to reach for the dirk hidden in his boot and charge his enemy, shouting his war cry. Duncan was quick with a blade. He could sink his dirk into Erik's throat before anyone could stop him. But he was here on a mission for his clan, and his personal revenge would have to wait awhile longer.

Your time will come, old man. And soon.

All these thoughts rushed through Duncan's head in an

instant. Quickly he dropped his gaze and forced his muscles to relax as he leaned over and removed his pipes from the oiled leather bag he carried them in.

"Your size is wasted on a piper," Erik said in a booming voice. "Who are ye, piper?"

"I'm a MacKay." Duncan had considered choosing the MacArthurs, another piping family in the isles, but he settled on the MacKays because their lands were far away, up in the north of the Scottish mainland.

"You're a long way from home," Erik said, narrowing his eyes at Duncan.

"I'm on my way to the MacCrimmons," he said. "With your permission, I'll pass this way again on my return as well."

Duncan hoped when he returned he would be storming the gates, rather than carrying his pipes, but it seemed wise to smooth his path should he need to use the ruse again.

"What is your business with the MacCrimmons?" Erik asked.

"I hear they claim to be the very best pipers," Duncan said. "I want to see for myself if it's true and trade a few tunes with them."

"I'm not a trusting soul, either," Erik said. "Let's hear ye play those pipes."

Erik was straining the rules of hospitality by demanding his guest perform, but then the man had committed far worse sins.

Duncan's fingers found their places on the melody pipe, or chanter, from long habit. As he took the blowpipe in his mouth, he closed his eyes to concentrate. If he wanted to stay out of the castle's dungeon, he needed to give a persuasive performance. As usual, his mood affected his music, and he played a tune that sounded like a pounding storm with driving rain and sleet.

When he finished and opened his eyes, the hall was dead silent. The applause started with a few claps and then spread through the room.

"I've never heard a tune quite like that one before," Erik said when the cheers had died down. "But you've earned your dinner, piper."

And you've earned death at my sword. Before you feel my blade, I'll make certain you know who took your castle from you.

* * *

Duncan left the hall as soon as he had finished eating. He had counted a hundred MacLeod warriors inside. That would be more than sufficient to hold such a strong fortress, unless he discovered a weakness—a crumbling wall, a weak door, drunken guards.

As he strolled about the courtyard, pretending to enjoy the freezing cold, Duncan noted that the heavy oak doors of the gate were reinforced with iron. He glanced along the top of the walls; the half dozen guards all appeared to be alert and watchful. Damn. If the castle had a weakness, he could not see it. Vile as Erik was, he did his job of maintaining the castle's defenses. After dark, Duncan would go inside the storage rooms built against the outer wall and look for poorly patched holes. He did not expect to find any.

He must find a way to take this castle. Everything depended upon it.

When one of the guards noticed that Duncan was examining the castle structure a mite too closely for a musician, Duncan turned to go back inside. As he went up the steps, he ran his gaze first over the old, four-story keep and then over the two-story building attached at a right angle to it. This lower building ran along the edge of the cliff overlooking the sea.

An idea began to form in Duncan's head.

* * *

"I believe we have enough ale and wine to last till spring." Ilysa narrowed her eyes as she ran her gaze along the row of barrels, then clicked her tongue. "But we're down to one small barrel of whiskey. That will never do."

Moira had found Ilysa in one of the storage rooms in the undercroft, assessing what was left of the castle's winter supplies, and offered to help.

"The men can survive without whiskey for a few weeks," Moira said.

Ilysa gave her a doubtful look. "They do call it *uisge-beatha*, water of life."

Moira laughed. "I assume ye have a plan to get more."

"I'll send word to Father Brian asking him to bring a barrel when he comes on his annual visit to the island," Ilysa said.

Ach, Duncan's sister was a model of competence. Moira hoped her brother appreciated how good Ilysa was, but she suspected that Connor, like most men, did not notice a smooth-running household as much as he would notice one that wasn't.

"Do ye know where your brother has gone or when he'll be back?" Though Moira was still mad enough at him to spit, she felt uneasy not knowing where he was.

Duncan had surprised her by leaving without attempting to speak with her again—and he had even taken her dog!

"I don't know where Duncan is," Ilysa said.

It made Moira furious every time she thought about Duncan lecturing her about propriety and what she could and could not do. How dare he? She was a grown woman. If she chose to share a bed with a man, it was no one's business but her own.

If she wanted to be ordered about and criticized, she'd take another husband. By the saints, she would not suffer that misery again.

"Tell me," Moira said. "Does your brother try to tell ye what to do?"

"Aye," Ilysa said as she brushed the dust from her hands.

"Does it not annoy ye?" Moira asked.

"Not much."

"What do ye do?" Moira asked.

"First, I smile at him, because I know he means well," Ilysa said as she led Moira into the next storeroom. "And then, unless he has persuaded me by raising some point I hadn't thought of already—which is rare—I do as I intended in the first place."

Moira burst out laughing. "That is far more clever than arguing with him."

"Ye know what my mother was like," Ilysa said with a shrug. "I learned to make decisions for myself at a young age."

While Ilysa counted the sacks of oats stacked against the wall, Moira thought about Ilysa and Duncan's mother, a kind but fearful woman. Moira felt guilty for how she had ignored the poor woman's attempts to guide her. She had been far too spoiled and strong-willed for such a meek nursemaid.

"When I was a bairn, Duncan was usually off with the other young men," Ilysa said when she had finished counting the bags of oats. "And then he left us."

Moira had given no thought to the consequences of their affair on Duncan's mother and sister. At the time, Moira had been only a year younger than Ilysa was now, but she could not have been more different from this contained, responsible young woman. But as wild and undisciplined as Moira was, she had loved Duncan deeply.

Moira glanced at Ilysa's delicate features and hoped Ilysa would not suffer as much for love as she had.

* * *

Duncan went inside the keep, but instead of going straight through the second set of doors into the hall, he opened the door to his right that led into the adjacent building. When the MacDonalds held the castle, the chieftain's private rooms were here, and Duncan had never been inside before.

If anyone saw him in this part of the castle, he would need an explanation. Duncan regretted not paying attention when Alex had talked at length about which lies worked best in such situations. Before his marriage, Alex was always sneaking in and out of bedchambers he should not be in.

Luckily, the building appeared to be empty. Whoever had these rooms now must still be in the hall. Duncan glanced into the large room that made up the first floor. The wall facing the courtyard was covered with tapestries and windowless, as he had known it would be. But he cursed under his breath when he saw the narrow, arrow-slit windows on the sea side. Most likely, the windows on the floor above would be the same, but he wanted to check before giving up on his plan.

Duncan went up the stairs quickly, keeping his ears open.

When he heard the voices of children, he hesitated. But he only needed one quick look, and the children sounded absorbed in their play. When he leaned around the doorway from the stairwell, he saw a boy and girl playing with wooden swords. The boy wore a hood and had his back to Duncan. The girl, who was half a foot shorter, had summer-blue eyes and fair, bouncing curls.

The room they were playing in spanned the width of the narrow building, like the room below, but it had windows on both sides. One set overlooked the sea cliff, while the ones on the opposite wall looked out toward the castle walls and the grassy fields beyond.

Damn, damn, damn. The windows were all less than a foot wide. He would have to find another way.

Duncan knew he should leave before the children saw him, but something made him pause in the doorway to watch them.

"Not like that, ye wee fool!" the boy said.

Duncan considered intervening until he saw the amusement on the girl's face.

"Hold it like this so I can't plunge my blade into your belly." The boy took the girl's arm and showed her how to hold her wooden sword. "Ye wouldn't like that, would ye?"

The lass shook her head, sending her fair curls bouncing. "Ye wouldn't do that to me."

"Of course I wouldn't," the lad said. "But someone else might try it one day, and I won't be here to protect ye."

The girl dropped the point of her sword to the floor. "Why not?"

"I told ye before," the lad said. "I'm going back to Ireland."

The girl stuck out her bottom lip. "I don't want ye to leave, Ragnall."

Ragnall. Duncan's heart stopped in his chest. Had he stumbled upon Moira's son?

"I must go back," the lad said. "My mother needs me."

CHAPTER 25

"Lad, are you Ragnall MacQuillan?" Duncan asked as he stepped into the doorway to show himself.

The children stopped their play, and the boy turned around to look at him. Duncan fell back a step, as if he had taken a heavy blow—and he felt as if he had.

In that instant, he knew the truth.

And that Moira had lied to him.

The boy had Moira's midnight-blue eyes, but all his other features were Duncan's—including his bright red hair. Although Duncan's hair was a deep auburn now, it had been that exact color when he was a bairn.

"Aye, I'm Ragnall." The lad's stance was stiff, his eyes cautious. "Who are you?"

Duncan was too stunned to speak for a moment, and then he was not sure how to answer. Finally, he said, "My name is Duncan. I play the pipes."

He understood now that it was no coincidence that Moira's husband had exploded in a murderous rage on the very night that Duncan arrived. When Sean saw Duncan, he must have come to the same conclusion that Duncan had just now.

"How old are ye?" Duncan asked, needing to confirm it.

"I'm eight," the girl said, tilting her head and sending her curls bouncing again.

"And you?" Duncan asked Ragnall.

Ragnall paused, as if weighing whether to answer, before he said, "Six and a half."

Duncan heard Moira's voice in his head. *Ragnall is five years old.* She had purposefully deceived him, and she had continued the deceit every day since.

If Moira would lie to him about his son, she would lie about anything.

How could she do it? It was not for lack of opportunity that she'd failed to tell him the truth. Duncan thought of all the times she'd mentioned her son—and worse, all the hours she lay in his arms—and chose not to tell him.

How could Moira let him touch her in every intimate way and still keep this secret from him? When they made love, he had believed their souls touched, but now he could see that it was only his that was laid bare.

"What is your name?" Duncan asked the little girl.

"I'm Sarah," the girl said with a bright smile.

"Someone downstairs was calling for ye," Duncan said.

"Ach, that's my nursemaid," Sarah said and rolled her eyes.

Duncan would wager Sarah ran the poor woman ragged. "You'd best go to her."

"Wait here," Sarah said to Ragnall as she flew out the door. "I'll be back as soon as I can."

Ragnall gazed up at him as if Duncan was a puzzle he was trying to solve.

"I'm a MacDonald," Duncan said, "and a friend of your mother."

"Where is she?" Ragnall asked, his eyes wide. "Is she safe?"

Ragnall looked so worried that Duncan instinctively put his hand on the lad's head. An unexpected rush of warmth went through him. This was his son, a gift Moira would deny him no more.

"Your mother is safe with our clan at Dunscaith Castle," Duncan said.

Ragnall studied him. "Ye could be lying."

He was mistrustful for such a young lad. That was Sean's doing.

"Come look out the window, and I'll show ye that I speak the truth." Duncan led the boy to one of the windows that faced the wide fields behind the castle and lifted him up on his knee.

"Look closely over there, to the southeast, at the edge of the field." Duncan leaned close so that their heads just touched as he pointed. "Can ye see him? He's there, crouching in the grass."

The boy was quiet and squinted his eyes as he searched the distant field, then he sucked in his breath.

"Sàr!" The single word was so full of emotion that Duncan felt his own throat close.

Whether it was The Sight or something else that made Ilysa suggest he bring the dog, Duncan was grateful.

Ragnall turned to him so that they were eye-to-eye with their faces just inches apart when he asked his question. "Have ye come to take me to my mother?"

Ragnall's young face looked so hopeful that it pained Duncan. He wanted to take his boy out of the castle this very moment, but he could not. The guards would not let him take the MacQuillan chieftain's son, and fighting his way out would be foolish. Not only would he fail in his mission for his clan, but he would put the boy in danger. He reminded himself that Ragnall was under the MacLeod chieftain's protection here and was safe.

"Can ye keep a secret?" Duncan asked, knowing he was taking an enormous risk trusting a young child with such important information. "Even from your friend Sarah?"

Ragnall nodded. "I'm good at keeping secrets."

Duncan was betting his life on it.

"I can't do it now," he said, "but I'll be returning soon with a great many MacDonald warriors to take this castle from the MacLeods. I'll take ye home to your mother then."

Ragnall's eyebrows shot up. "An attack?" he asked, sounding excited. "How will ye do it?"

"I'd hoped to find a window facing the sea that is wide enough for a man to fit through," Duncan said. "But the windows are all too small."

Ragnall was quiet for a moment, then his face brightened. "The window in the tower is bigger."

"What tower?" Duncan asked.

"Ye can't see it from the front of the castle," Ragnall said. "No one goes there because it's haunted, but Sarah showed it to me. We play there sometimes."

Duncan tried not to hope too much. "Can ye show me?"

"It's through there," Ragnall said, pointing to a low door in the far corner of the room.

Duncan ducked his head as he followed Ragnall through the low doorway and up three steps into a small, round room. The curved window looked to be two feet wide and two feet tall. Duncan leaned out and looked down the sheer cliff to the sea below.

It just might be possible.

"Sarah says the nursemaid dropped the baby out that window," Ragnall said. "That's why she can't rest."

Duncan was sorry for the woman and the babe, but the ghost story would be useful. Ragnall listened with a serious expression as Duncan explained his plan.

"I'll leave first thing in the morning," Duncan said. "When I return, I'll still be pretending to be a piper. Ye must be careful not to give me away."

Ragnall nodded.

"There will be a battle for the castle," Duncan said, "but I will get ye out safely."

It was Duncan's first promise to his son, and he meant to be a father who kept his promises.

In the meantime, he had a few choice words to say to the lad's lying mother.

* * *

Erik's gaze kept returning to the piper as he played for them after supper. The big, red-haired musician puzzled him, and Erik had not risen to his position by ignoring puzzles.

Listening to him play, Erik had to admit that the man was a true musician. In fact, the piper was so caught up in his music that he appeared to be unaware of all the lasses sighing over him. Still, the piper did not get the muscles rippling across his broad back from blowing on his pipes.

He moved with the grace and power of a lion—or a Highland warrior.

It was time for a test. Erik picked up an apple from the platter in front of him and waited until the piper was in the midst of a lively tune.

"Piper!" Erik called out as he threw the apple fast and hard straight at his head.

The piper caught the apple with one hand without dropping his instrument, took a bite, and continued his tune, barely missing a beat, to a roar of applause. Erik narrowed his eyes. Just as he suspected, this piper had the quick reflexes of a man who needed them to stay alive.

Perhaps it meant nothing. But with that warrior's build, Erik would wager this piper could fight. He was like a man with a debauching nature who becomes a priest. Though the priest might say fine prayers, he'd still have his hands on the lasses.

The piper said he was leaving in the morning, and Erik would be glad to see the back of him.

CHAPTER 26

Moira still felt strange sitting in her old place at the high table when everything else had changed—especially her. She glanced at Connor, who sat next to her in her father's chair. There was an awkwardness between them, and it was not just because she was not accustomed to him being chieftain or because they had been apart for seven years. Fair or not, Moira had not quite forgiven him for waiting so long to send someone to Ireland to check on her welfare.

Sadness settled over her as she looked past Connor to where their older brother, as *tànaiste*, the chieftain's successor, had always sat. Ragnall had been so like her father—brash and bold and full of life.

Connor caught her eye, and said, "I miss him, too."

Connor had always been both observant and perceptive. When they were young, she felt as if he judged her and found her lacking. But then, she had been spoiled by her father, who never found fault with her at all.

She remembered that Connor had also been close to Ragnall, though they could not be more different, and put her hand over his.

"I'm glad you're home," Connor said and smiled at her.

Moira had been holding back from asking him about Duncan. She had not liked Connor's tone when he pressed her on that first day about whether there was something between her and Duncan, but her brother's warmth made her set aside her caution.

"Where did ye send Duncan?" she asked.

Connor's expression did not change except for a slight tightening around his mouth, but the warmth she'd felt from him a moment before was gone.

"I've been meaning to talk with ye about your future," Connor said, ignoring her question completely. "Let us speak in private."

He stood and held out his hand, giving her no choice. With her fingers resting lightly on Connor's arm, they crossed the hall to the arched doorway that led to the chieftain's bedchamber.

A swell of emotion rose in Moira's throat as she entered what had been her father's private sanctum. She could almost hear his booming voice calling for her. Shock replaced fond recollections as she glanced about the once-grand chamber. Connor had stripped it bare.

Gone were the beautiful tapestries, the ornate side tables, the velvet cushions, and the enormous curtained bed. In their place were plain, rough-hewn chairs, a small table, a battered chest that looked as if it had been retrieved from the sea, and the bed she recognized as the one Connor had slept in as a boy.

She was both hurt and curious as to why her brother

had been so intent on removing every scrap of their father's memory from his bedchamber. Before she could remark upon it, Connor shut the door and spoke first.

"Ye must be more cautious about what ye say and where ye say it," Connor said, fixing his intent, silver-blue eyes on her. "Someone could have heard ye ask where I sent Duncan."

"Where did ye send him?" she asked.

"You're not hearing me, Moira," Connor said. "Hugh has spies in the castle. Ye could endanger both Duncan and the clan by talking out of turn like that."

"If anyone had told me where he's gone and why," she said, crossing her arms, "I wouldn't have to ask."

Connor sighed as if she were a trial. "He's on important clan business, and that's all ye need to know."

"I was helping Father with important clan business while the four of ye were off having your adventures," she said, "so don't give me that look as if I won't understand."

"If our father had wanted my help, I would have given it." Connor spoke in a tone devoid of emotion as he poured himself a cup of whiskey from the jug on the table. He took a drink, and then said, "I sent Duncan alone into Trotternish Castle."

Moira put her hand to her heart. "You what?"

When Connor told her the rest, Moira sat down hard on one of the chairs. She had trouble getting her breath as she thought of Duncan in a castle full of their enemies, his life dependent on this ruse.

"Ye must not breathe a word of this," Connor said. "If Duncan is found out, the MacLeods will skin him alive."

"So why did ye send him?" Moira demanded. "He's been your best friend all your life."

"It was his idea," Connor said.

"How can ye be so cold?" she asked. "Do ye not care about any of us?"

"I care about every member of this clan, which is why I let him go," Connor said in a voice so calm Moira wanted to slap him. "And while we're discussing Duncan, just what do ye plan to do about him?"

"I don't know what you're talking about," Moira said, getting to her feet.

"Ach, ye were better at covering your tracks when ye were seventeen." Connor took another drink of his whiskey. "Do ye want to marry him?"

"I'm never getting married again," Moira said, putting her hands on her hips. "Not to Duncan. Not to anyone."

"So you're just toying with him again?" Connor said.

"*Toying with him?*" she said, her voice rising. "Who do ye think ye are, speaking to me like that, Connor MacDonald? What I do is none of your concern."

"I am chieftain of this clan, which means everything is my concern," Connor said in that same aggravatingly calm tone. "And, as my sister, what you do reflects on me."

"If our clansmen don't respect ye for yourself, nothing I do will change it." And because she was angry, she added, "Even after what our mother did to him, our father commanded the respect of all the clans of the isles. So don't blame me if they don't respect you."

"I suppose you're right about that." Connor heaved a sigh and turned to look out the narrow window.

Suddenly Moira noticed how careworn her brother looked and realized how heavily the burden of leading their clan weighed upon him. Her father had not suffered the same.

"If we take Trotternish Castle, I expect we'll have a few MacLeod hostages," Connor said. "I'll try to make a trade for your son."

"Thank you," she said.

"That was Duncan's idea as well," Connor said, still looking out the window. "He said he made a promise to you."

"With all the plans to take Trotternish, I feared he had forgotten," Moira said in a soft voice.

"Duncan does not forget promises," Connor said as he turned and fixed his penetrating gaze on her. "And I've never known him to fail to keep one."

A short time ago, Moira would have disagreed. But Duncan had only said he would love her always. She was the one who thought that was a promise of marriage and a lifetime together.

"I would still need to persuade the MacQuillans to let the lad foster here," Connor said, rubbing his forehead.

"I fear that will be no easy task," Moira said.

"One thing is for certain—" Connor gave a dry laugh and shook his head. "—unless I want a trail of dead MacQuillans, I won't be sending you and Duncan to talk with them."

* * *

Duncan stormed across Dunscaith's courtyard and banged through the doors of the keep. As he entered the hall, he did not notice—or care—if there were ten people or a hundred in it. There was only one person he was looking for.

After learning he had a son, he'd had to suffer through an endless evening at Trotternish Castle, playing tune after tune like a king's fool. Then it had taken him two days to travel home, with impatience and outrage burning at his soul the entire way.

As he crossed the hall, Ilysa appeared at his side. "Ye seem a bit upset," she said, picking up her skirts to walk fast enough to keep up with him. "Is there something I can do?

"Where in the hell is Moira?"

"She's in with Connor, but—"

That was all he needed to know.

The men guarding Connor's door scrambled to step aside. Duncan pounded on the door and did not wait to open it. As soon as he did, Moira filled his vision. She stood in the center of the room with the light from the long, narrow windows playing across her features.

The fury Duncan had banked since he learned the truth about Ragnall burst to the surface, making his head pound and his skin feel too tight. In the far recesses of his mind, the ever-alert warrior in him was aware of someone closing the door behind him. He marched up to Moira until he was close enough to scorch her skin with the heat of his temper.

Moira's eyes went wide, but she stood her ground. It was never courage she lacked, but any sense of loyalty and honor.

"Why did ye not tell me that Ragnall was mine?" Duncan asked, clenching his fists to keep from picking her up and shaking her.

Moira's mouth fell open, and her hand fluttered to her chest. "You saw Ragnall?"

"I did," Duncan bit out, "and the lad is six and a half years old, not five as ye told me. He has flaming red hair, Moira!"

"Where is he?" Moira leaned to the side to look behind him. "Did ye bring my son home to me?"

Duncan jerked her in front of him to get her full attention. "Ragnall is at Trotternish Castle, and he is not just *your* son."

"Ye weren't here to claim him," she said, narrowing her eyes to angry slits. "So, aye, Ragnall is *my* son."

"How could I claim him if I didn't know about him?" Duncan shouted. "Ye didn't tell me ye were pregnant."

Moira wrenched free of him. Her breasts rose and fell in harsh breaths as her eyes burned holes into him. "Ye didn't bother staying to find out, did ye?"

CHAPTER 27

Duncan stormed out, slamming the door behind him. Moira had forgotten Connor was in the room until he ran out after Duncan and the door slammed a second time.

Moira sank into the closest chair, her heart beating wildly in her chest. Too many emotions swirled inside her. Relief that Duncan had found her son. Anger that Duncan had left Ragnall at Trotternish Castle. Confusion over Duncan's knowing he was Ragnall's father. And, finally, regret over how he had learned the truth.

She did not know how long she had sat there, unable to gather herself to leave, when she heard the latch on the door. Startled from her thoughts, she looked about her and saw that the light filtering through the narrow windows had dimmed from midday to late afternoon.

Connor came in alone, looking grim. In the tense silence that hung between them, the gurgle of the whiskey as he refilled his cup from the jug seemed unnaturally loud. Then he leaned on the table and fixed his hard, steely-blue gaze on her.

"I thought you'd grown up, but you're as selfish as ye were as a child," he said, in a tight voice. "How could ye not tell Duncan he had a son?"

She should have known her brother would take Duncan's side in this.

"Don't ye dare judge me, Connor MacDonald," she said, clenching the edge of the table. "Ye don't know how it was for me. Ye know nothing at all about it."

"Ye did not deny that ye knew the child was Duncan's all along," Connor said. "Ye should have told him."

"I had my reasons not to." Moira went to stand by the window and folded her arms.

"I hope they're good ones, but it's not me ye need to explain it to," Connor said. "We're leaving soon to take Trotternish Castle, so ye don't have much time."

"Don't play chieftain with me," she said.

"I *am* your chieftain," Connor said, in a commanding voice, "and I'm telling ye to make this right."

Moira pressed her lips together and glared at her brother.

"When a man goes to fight for his clan, ye can never be certain he'll return," Connor said. "Don't leave it like this."

Ach, it was not fair for Connor to use that argument against her.

"Where is he?" she snapped.

Connor picked up his drink and sipped it. "I expect he's gone up to his cottage."

Moira climbed the hill, mud clinging to her skirts like the guilt and resentment she carried. When she reached the cottage, she pulled the door open without bothering to knock. Duncan stood in the center of the room. His rage was like a living creature filling the small cottage.

"I'll ask ye again," he said. "Why did ye not tell me I have a son?"

"I might have told ye before ye went to Trotternish Castle," she said, "if ye had bothered to share the news with me that ye were paying a visit on the MacLeods."

"That was clan business," Duncan said. "I couldn't tell anyone, and I didn't lie to ye."

"I'd wager ye trusted Ian with the information," she said. "And Alex, too, if ye saw him."

"Ye lied to me about my son," Duncan said, clenching his fists. "I want to know why."

"All right, I'll tell ye." It was time to get it all out on the table and see where the pieces fell. "Ye didn't deserve to know the truth."

Moira was furious that tears were stinging the back of her eyes.

"Ye took your clothes off for me, but ye couldn't tell me the truth about Ragnall?" Duncan said, his voice growing louder.

"Going to bed with ye has nothing to do with it," she said.

"Nothing to do with it?" he shouted.

"Why should I trust ye with my son, who is more precious to me than anything in this life, after ye left me alone and pregnant?"

"I asked ye that last night before your father sent me away," Duncan said, "and ye told me ye weren't with child."

"I didn't know until after you'd gone," Moira bit out.

Duncan raked his hands through his hair as he started pacing the tiny room, making it seem even smaller than it was. "Then how can ye blame me for not knowing?"

"Did it never occur to ye that I might discover I was with child after ye left?" Moira asked, her voice strained. "Could ye be that ignorant?"

Duncan stopped his pacing. He did not answer her for a long while, and when he did, it sounded as though the words were torn from his chest. "I did not think you were. But aye, I did know it was possible."

She'd known it all along. "But ye didn't care enough for me or our child to stay," she said, choking on the words. "Ye left me to face all that alone."

Duncan looked away from her, but she could see his raw emotion in the tension in his jaw and the wildly beating pulse at his throat.

"Why did ye leave me?" Moira stepped close to him and clenched her fists in his shirt. "Why, Duncan, *why*?"

The silence stretched out between them like a fraying rope while she waited for him to finally tell her.

"I told ye before. Your father found out about us," Duncan said in a quiet voice. "He was my chieftain, and he commanded me to go with the others to France. It was obey or die."

Moira stared into his eyes searching for the truth. Duncan was holding something back.

"You're the most stubborn and determined man I know," she said. "If ye truly wanted me, ye would have found a way."

Duncan pressed his lips together in a tight line.

"Ye owe me the truth, Duncan."

"I cared enough to leave," he said between his teeth.

"No," she said. "Ye didn't care enough."

"Do ye think leaving ye was easy for me?" he shouted, his control snapping. He took hold of her arms and backed her against the door. "Do ye think I wanted to let some other man have ye?"

"You are the one who left me," she said, her voice thick in her throat.

"I wanted to die rather than leave ye," he said, his eyes wild.

"Then why did ye do it?" she shouted back.

"Because we would have had to leave the clan," he said, "and I couldn't do that to you."

"I don't believe ye," she said. "Even if my father did threaten to banish us, that would not be reason enough."

His eyes burned into her and the pulse at his temple throbbed, but he said nothing.

"I've waited seven years for the truth," Moira said. "You tell me all of it, Duncan MacDonald."

"All right," Duncan said in a hard voice. "I loved ye with all my heart, but I knew ye for the spoiled lass that ye were. Ye were used to having everything come easy and just as ye wanted it. Ye liked your jewels and silk gowns, servants to wait on ye hand and foot, and sitting at the high table. I couldn't give any of that to ye."

"Ye left me so I could have silk gowns and servants?" Moira could not believe she was hearing this. "*That* is why ye deserted me?"

"Ye hadn't suffered a day in your life," he said. "Ye would have left me in a week."

"I would never have left ye."

"Ye could not have lived the kind of life we would have had, ostracized from our clan and living from place

to place while I fought for whoever could pay me most."
Duncan rested his hands on the door on either side of her
head and leaned his face close to hers. "I'm telling ye, I
had no choice."

"No, Duncan. You made a choice," she said, tapping
her finger against his chest.

"Leaving ye was the hardest thing I've ever had to do,"
Duncan said, his voice strained. "It nearly broke me."

"I would have lived anywhere, gone anywhere, just to
be with ye. That's how much I loved ye," she said, choking back tears. "But ye had no faith in me."

"I didn't have faith in ye, and I wasn't wrong," Duncan
said, his eyes fierce. "You've changed, Moira. Perhaps ye
would be willing to make those sacrifices today, but not
then."

"Ye never gave me the chance," she said. "Ye should
have."

"All I wanted was for ye to be happy," Duncan cupped
her cheek with his palm. "I couldn't be responsible for
making ye suffer."

"That is precisely what ye did," she said, her voice
cracking.

"Your father doted on ye so," Duncan said. "I believed
he would marry ye to a good man, when the time came."

"Well, he didn't." She shoved him away with both
hands and jerked the door open.

CHAPTER 28

Duncan's hopes and dreams were crumbling beneath his feet as Moira opened the door. He was losing her again, and this time it would be forever.

"Don't leave me." He grabbed her hand and dropped to his knees. "I'm sorry for the unspeakable things that happened to ye after I left for France."

Though Duncan had not meant for any of it to happen, he understood why she blamed him. He had been too concerned about defending his decision, when he should have apologized to her from the start.

"I would never hurt ye on purpose," he said. "Ye know that."

Moira's eyes were swimming with unshed tears, but her back was stiff, and she still had one hand on the door.

"I love ye, Moira MacDonald. I always have," he said. "We have a son we should raise together. I'm asking ye to trust me and give me another chance."

"I can't be with ye, unless ye trust me as well," Moira said.

Duncan had no notion what she meant, but if Moira was setting conditions, instead of refusing him, that was a very good sign. He got up off his knees, reached around her, and closed the door.

"I love ye," Moira said, her eyes flashing, "but I will never again be with a man who does not respect me."

She loved him. Duncan had feared he would never hear her say those words to him again. Despite her angry tone, they were a healing balm to his soul.

"Tell me what ye want, *mo leannain*," my sweetheart, he said, taking her hand again, "and I'll do it."

"I'm no fragile flower. I fended for myself for seven long years without ye," she said. "Don't ye dare treat me as if I were a spoiled lass who could not survive without fine gowns and silver cups."

Did he think of her that way still? Duncan reflected on how he had found her in Ireland, battered and lying in a pool of blood; the dangerous trip to Skye, which she endured without complaint; and her foolish, but brave attempt to reach Dunvegan Castle by walking all night on her own.

"Ye said I am a stubborn man, and you're right," Duncan said. "Ye have changed, and I've been slow to accept it."

"I mean it, Duncan," she said, pinning him with a hard look. "I won't have ye thinking of me as an irresponsible child who will run when things get hard."

Duncan loved to see her full of life like this. By the saints, she was gorgeous when she was angry, though he was not foolish enough to say it.

"I know ye are as strong and brave as ye are beautiful," he said, pulling her hard against him. "And believe me, I don't think of ye as a child."

Duncan clamped his mouth over hers and kissed her with all the passion welling up in his heart. After a moment, she twined her arms around his neck and kissed him back with such fire that he wanted to drop to the floor and take her right there.

When she pulled away, he was breathless. Duncan had not believed he could love Moira more than he had when she was an enchanting lass of seventeen, but he loved this passionate woman in his arms even more.

"If ye leave me again," she said. "I swear, I'll murder ye."

Given what she'd done to her last husband, Duncan believed she meant it.

* * *

As they made love, Moira finally let go of her heart.

She was aware that Duncan, being a man, assumed she had given it to him when they made love for the first time since finding each other again. But trusting him with her heart was a much bigger leap for her than trusting him with her body.

After all she had been through, it was not easy to stifle her fears that marriage would suffocate her. But Duncan recognized that the scars on her soul had made her strong, and he did not need her to be weak. He would not try to make her be something less, a shadow of herself, as Sean had tried to do.

She let all the layers of protection slowly melt away in his arms.

"I love ye," Duncan said over and over as he moved

inside her, quelling her last shred of doubt. "I love ye forever. No matter what comes."

No matter what comes.

"I love ye, too," she said, holding his face between her hands. "Always and forever."

For the first time since Moira was seventeen, she gave herself to Duncan without holding back any part of herself.

* * *

"The captain of Connor's guard disappeared again, and no one knows where," Hugh said. "I'm certain his coming and going in secret is leading up to an attack."

"Sounds to me as if he's sneaking off to fook another man's wife," Erik said.

"Not Duncan MacDonald," Hugh said with a laugh. "He's straight as an arrow, the sort who would choose death over dishonor."

"Hmmph," Erik snorted.

"This Duncan is a fearsome fighter—I've seen him," Hugh said, shaking his head. "And there's no one Connor trusts more."

Erik shrugged. What could a lone man do?

"I suspect Connor has sent Duncan to your clan's other enemies to seek their help in an attack on Trotternish."

"Your suspicions are useless," Erik said. "I've told ye before, I need information."

"I have my spies watching," Hugh said, "but Connor is keeping this very close."

* * *

Moira stood outside the cottage with the wind whipping her hair around her face as she watched for Duncan. Since his return from Trotternish yesterday, her emotions had been as wild as the weather, constantly fluctuating from anxiety over her son, to fear for Duncan and the other men who would soon be going into battle, to a daze of happiness over the love between her and Duncan.

Aye, she did love him.

Even so, putting her trust in Duncan felt like closing her eyes and jumping off a cliff. But she was making that leap of faith.

"Duncan!" she called, waving her arms when she finally saw him coming up the path. When she ran to meet him, he lifted her off her feet.

"Ye shouldn't be waiting outside in the cold," Duncan said, but from the way he was smiling, she knew it pleased him. "I wish I had more time, but Ian sent word that Alex has arrived at Knock Castle. Connor and I are riding over there this afternoon."

Despite what Duncan said about not having much time, they wound up in Duncan's bed. Moira lay warm and cozy in his arms, listening to the wind pound against the shutters and thinking how happy she was. Though she had no doubt that Duncan wanted to marry her, she was starting to wonder why he did not speak of it.

"Is Connor being difficult about giving his approval for us to wed?" Moira tilted her head back to smile up at Duncan. "I told him I would never wed again, so perhaps he needs to hear from me that I've changed my mind."

"I haven't spoken to Connor yet," Duncan said, sounding distinctly uncomfortable.

Moira got up on one elbow to have a better look at him. "Why not?"

When Duncan pressed his lips together and did not answer, Moira felt as if the ground were sinking under her.

"Fool that I am," she said, "I thought ye meant to marry me this time."

"There is nothing I want more in this life." Duncan reached for her hand, but she jerked away.

"Then what are ye waiting for?" she asked.

"I must have a better home for ye than this," Duncan said.

"You'll marry me when ye have a better home?" she asked with an edge to her voice. "What if ye never do?"

"I will."

"Ye can't know that," she said.

"We'll get married as soon as I'm keeper of Trotternish Castle," Duncan said. "That won't be long at all. We're planning our attack today."

"Are ye saying ye won't marry me unless ye take the castle and Connor makes ye the keeper of it?"

"I'm just saying we need to wait a wee bit," he said.

"Why?" Anger started in her belly and spread out through the rest of her body until she felt as if she would burst with it. "As long as I have you, Ragnall, and a roof over our heads, I'll be happy."

"Damn it, woman," Duncan said. "Have ye no respect for a man's pride?"

"I think ye care more for your pride than ye do for me," she said, her voice low and thick with emotion. "Ye want to marry me one day when it is convenient for ye, after you've done every other bloody thing that is more important to ye."

"'Tis because I care so much that I want to wait," he said.

"And ye left me to go to France because ye cared too

much," she said, fighting the well of emotion that threatened to choke her.

"Can't ye understand that I need to be able to provide ye with a proper home?" Duncan asked.

"Why?" she demanded. "If I don't care, why do you?"

"I can't explain it any better." He held her face between his hands. "It matters to me. It just does."

"The truth is that ye don't trust me to know my own heart and ye never have," she said.

"I didn't say that," he said.

"Ye think I'll change my mind about ye if ye can't give me a fine castle to live in," she said. "That's why ye left me before and why ye won't marry me now."

"Moira, I just want to be able to make ye happy," he said in a soft voice.

"Ye still don't believe I'm capable of loving ye without all that?" she said. "After what I've been through, ye think I care about *gowns and servants*?"

"I—"

"I won't marry a man who thinks so little of me." She threw the bedclothes off, jumped to the floor, and started dressing. "Ye could be the king of Scotland, and I wouldn't have ye!"

"I think the world of ye," Duncan said.

"Ye don't," she said. "I lived with a man for seven years who treated me as if I were nothing, and I won't do it again."

Duncan got out of bed and grabbed her arm as she started to leave the bedchamber.

"Get your damned hands off me!" She was so angry her vision was blurred. "I trusted you! How could ye do this to me again?"

"I want to give ye all the things ye ought to have—the things ye deserve," he said.

"Ye still think of me as a shallow, spoiled girl," Moira said. "I was never just that, and it is certainly not who I am now."

She grabbed her cloak from the peg and opened the door without taking the time to put it on.

"Don't leave like this," Duncan said. "I love ye, Moira."

"You're no different from the other men who wanted to bed me," she said over her shoulder. "Ye don't love me. For God's sake, Duncan, ye don't even know me."

CHAPTER 29

Moira was so confused and upset she did not know what to do with herself. How could Duncan believe he loved her and yet think so poorly of her? She dried her tears before she entered the castle to pay a visit on Ilysa. Perhaps Duncan's sister could help her understand him.

After searching the keep and not finding Ilysa there, Moira crossed the courtyard to what had been her nursemaid's home.

"Do ye mind a bit of company?" Moira asked when Ilysa answered her door.

"I'd enjoy it," Ilysa said. "I'm just doing a bit of stitching."

Moira suspected that if Connor were home, Ilysa would be doing the chore in the keep.

"I sense ye came here with a purpose," Ilysa said after Moira sat down with her. "Is it about my brother?"

Moira appreciated the younger woman's directness.

"Duncan said my father forced him to leave," Moira said, deciding to start with that. "I wish I knew if it was true."

"My brother has his faults, but he doesn't lie," Ilysa said in her quiet, sure voice.

"I didn't think my father would lie to me, either," Moira said.

"I wouldn't know what that feels like, as I never knew my father," Ilysa said, which reminded Moira that, though Ilysa looked young, she'd had her share of sorrows and struggles.

"The loss of your mother must have been difficult." Moira turned to look out the small window and sighed. "If she were here, I would ask her what happened that day between Duncan and my father."

"I was here and saw it all," Ilysa said. "What do ye want to know?"

"You?" Moira asked. "Why, ye were still a child."

"I was old enough," Ilysa said. "Ach, your father was in a dreadful fury that morning."

"Can ye tell me what happened?" Moira asked.

"The chieftain and your brother Ragnall woke my mother and me while it was still dark." Ilysa stopped stitching but kept her gaze fixed on the shirt in her hands. "I know ye loved them, but they were hard men, and they were angry. When they asked where Duncan was, my mother started weeping."

"I'm sorry they frightened you," Moira said.

"I tried to comfort my mother, but she was inconsolable," Ilysa said. "We told the chieftain we didn't know where Duncan was, but I suspect now that my mother guessed he was with you."

"What did my father and brother do when they saw that Duncan was not here?"

"They sat in these chairs at our wee table," Ilysa said, nodding toward it. "It felt as if the walls of our cottage would explode with their anger."

Moira could well imagine it. Her father and older brother had been powerful warriors long accustomed to their authority over the clan.

"When Duncan opened the door"—Ilysa paused and licked her lips—"I thought your father was going to murder him right here in this room."

"He would not have," Moira said.

"He said that the only reason he didn't was that Teàrlag had predicted Duncan would save Connor's life." Ilysa met Moira's eyes with an unwavering gaze. "I believed him then, and I still do."

Moira leaned over and touched Ilysa's hand. "I'm sorry I caused such grief for you and your mother."

"Ye can't help who ye love." Ilysa cleared her throat. "Your brother Ragnall told Duncan he would be sailing for France that day, right after the battle for Knock Castle. Then he and the chieftain took Duncan away, without even letting him kiss our mother good-bye."

Moira and Ilysa sat in silence for a long while.

"My father could force Duncan to leave the clan, but he could not force him to go to France—or to stay there," Moira said. "Duncan could have gotten word to me to join him somewhere, but he didn't believe in me."

"I don't think that was the reason," Ilysa said in a soft voice. "It was himself he didn't believe in."

"What do ye mean?" Moira asked.

"Duncan left because he believed your father was right

to send him away," Ilysa said. "He thought he did not deserve you."

Moira stared blindly out the small window. Though she had not paid much attention at the time, she remembered hearing the men make gibes about Duncan's unknown parentage when they were children. Perhaps there was some truth to what Ilysa said about why he left her.

"That does not explain why he lacks faith in me now," Moira said. "Duncan is captain of our chieftain's guard and has a fearsome reputation as a great warrior."

"That's how others see him," Ilysa said. "But Duncan is still trying to prove to himself that he is worthy."

A sharp knock at the door interrupted their conversation. Without waiting for an answer, Tait, a short, wiry member of the guard, barged in.

"I've been looking everywhere for ye," he said to Ilysa.

"What is it?" Ilysa asked.

"There's a fleet of war galleys headed this way," he said.

Cold fear licked its way up Moira's spine. She had thought she would be safe here at Dunscaith.

"Have ye told Connor?" Ilysa asked.

"He and Duncan rode across the peninsula to Knock Castle," Tait said. "I sent a man after them, but those war galleys will arrive before they do."

"Do ye recognize the boats?" Ilysa asked, calm as could be.

"I know the banner," Tait said. "It belongs to Alexander of Dunivaig and the Glens."

Moira's hands went cold as ice. Alexander was the chieftain of a more powerful branch of the MacDonalds and a descendant of a Lord of the Isles, which made them distant relatives. In addition to his lands in the Western Isles of the Scottish Highlands, he ruled over the Glens in Ireland, where he was an ally of the MacQuillans.

"He's come for me," Moira said.

* * *

"Are we under attack? What is happening?" women called out to Moira and Ilysa as they raced behind Tait across the courtyard to the castle wall.

"We don't know yet," Ilysa told them. "Stay calm, but take the children inside the keep."

The courtyard was in confusion, with men shouting and running to gather weapons. Moira picked up her skirts and climbed the ladder up the side of the castle wall. The wall walk that ran along the top was crowded with warriors, and she had to push her way through them to look out.

When she caught sight of a dozen war galleys sailing straight for the castle, Moira sucked in her breath. The first ones were so close that she could see the fierce faces of the warriors above their shields. She was aware when Tait and Ilysa joined her, but she kept her gaze on the galleys filling the bay.

"That one is their chieftain's," Tait said, pointing to the galley with the warrior's cross on its sail and a dragon head on its bow.

A tall man with dark golden hair stood in the center of the chieftain's boat, a little apart from the other warriors, and scanned the hills like a hawk. When the boat glided into shore, escorted by a galley on either side of it, he was the first to vault over the side.

"I'm going down to the beach," Moira said and turned to go down the ladder.

"No, ye mustn't!" Ilysa said, gripping Moira's arm.

"There is no point in sacrificing the lives of our men when it's me they want," Moira said. "If there is a price to be paid for taking my husband's miserable life, I'll be the one to pay it."

CHAPTER 30

Duncan's thoughts were on Moira as he and Connor rode back to Dunscaith escorted by a dozen members of Connor's guard. There was no use talking to Moira until he took Trotternish Castle. Teàrlag told him he could change his fate, and she was right. Taking the castle would settle everything—with his father, with the MacLeods, and with Moira.

But what in the hell did Moira mean by saying he did not know her? He knew her every mood, every expression that crossed her face, how her breathing changed when he touched her.

Still, he had to admit there was one thing he had not understood before. Her blind determination to walk through the night and enter the MacLeod chieftain's lair alone to get Ragnall had seemed utter foolishness to him. But the moment he met his son, Duncan understood why she did it. Though Duncan knew that Ragnall was under the protection of the MacLeod chieftain, whose word was law within his clan, Duncan shared Moira's driving need to bring him home.

Ragnall was one more reason Duncan was relieved he would be sailing for Trotternish Castle tonight.

Duncan saw a rider crest the hill coming toward them and pulled his claymore before he recognized the man as one of their own.

"Looks like trouble," Connor said and held up his hand, signaling the guardsmen to halt.

The rider came toward them at a full gallop, then pulled his horse up hard, causing it to rear.

"War galleys are approaching Dunscaith!" the man shouted.

Duncan dug his heels into his horse's side, took the lead, and rode for Dunscaith at breakneck speed. Though they were only two miles from the chieftain's castle, it seemed like fifty. When Duncan finally broke over the last hill, the familiar vista of Dunscaith on its protruding rock in the midst of miles of coastline spread before him.

But this time, a swarm of war galleys loomed just offshore, threatening Dunscaith and everyone in it, including Moira and Ilysa.

"This visit must relate to Sean MacQuillan's death," Connor shouted as he brought his horse up beside Duncan's.

They both had recognized the ships at once, of course, as belonging to the powerful MacDonalds of Dunivaig and the Glens, who were allied with the less powerful MacQuillans. Before the rebellion, their two branches of the MacDonalds had been allies as well.

"They haven't attacked yet," Connor continued, "so they may be willing to talk."

"'Tis worth a chance," Duncan shouted back.

"I'll invite the chieftain in as my guest," Connor said.

The Highland customs of hospitality were sacrosanct. If the other chieftain accepted Connor's offer, there would be no attack today. Of course, the constraint lasted only until the guests departed.

"What in the hell is my sister doing?" Connor shouted.

Duncan snapped his gaze from the war galleys to the castle and saw a figure stepping off the castle's bridge. *God have mercy*, it was Moira!

Protecting his chieftain was Duncan's first duty, but he had to stop Moira.

"Send her back inside!" Connor shouted. "If they see her, they'll try to take her!"

Duncan veered his horse toward the castle, and they flew over the tall grass. Moira's eyes went wide as he bore down on her. Leaning low over the side of his horse, he caught her around the waist and lifted her in front of him. He continued up to the castle bridge and then dismounted with her.

"Were ye trying to make it easy for them to take ye?" he shouted, shaking her by the shoulders.

"I know him," Moira said. "I was just going to talk with him."

Duncan let out a string of oaths that would make the devil blush. "You're endangering yourself and everyone else. Get inside *now*!"

CHAPTER 31

Moira pressed her face to the peephole, which provided a good view of the high table.

"I used this peephole many times at my father's request," she whispered to Ilysa, who crouched beside her. Unlike Duncan and Connor, her father had valued her assistance with difficult guests.

Just now, it looked as though Connor was badly in need of help. Her brother's and his guest's expressions were coldly polite, but they had daggers in their eyes. As she had guessed when she saw him standing in the galley, the tall, golden-haired visitor was not the clan chieftain, but his eldest son, James.

"You'll have to take the word of the captain of my guard regarding what happened at the MacQuillan castle that night," Connor said, sounding as immovable as granite.

Moira was sorry she had missed hearing Duncan's version of events while she changed her clothes.

"I don't know your captain," James said, his tone equally unbending. "I must hear it from your sister directly."

"I vouch for my captain's word," Connor said, raising the stakes. "And I will not permit ye to upset my sister by questioning her. She has suffered enough."

Ach, she did not need Connor to protect her from answering James's questions, any more than she needed Duncan to protect her reputation from gossip.

Where had the two of them been when she truly needed their protection?

* * *

Duncan's teeth ached from clenching his jaw so hard. He wished the ironclad rules of hospitality did not prevent him from challenging this James with the jewel-studded brooch and the too-handsome face to settle the matter with swords.

When the hall suddenly went quiet, Duncan turned to see who had drawn everyone's attention, half fearing he would see old Teàrlag waving her arms and wailing in the doorway again.

Instead, Moira entered the hall looking like a faery queen, covered head-to-toe in a silvery cape and matching hood, with the wolfhound at her side. The cape floated out behind her as she swept across the room and came to a halt before the center of the head table.

"A thousand welcomes to you, James, son of Alexander of Dunivaig and the Glens and great-great-grandson of John, the first Lord of the Isles," Moira said, giving the formal greeting. "'Tis an honor and a pleasure to see you again. It has been far too long."

James leaped to his feet and started around the table. Duncan was half out of his seat with his hand on the hilt of his dirk before Connor stopped him.

"James will not harm her here in my hall," Connor said in a low voice, with a steel grip on Duncan's arm. "Moira's made her choice. Let's see how this plays out."

Duncan gritted his teeth when James reached Moira and kissed her hand like a courtier.

"These are not the circumstances under which I had hoped we would meet again," James said. "It is, of course, the *unfortunate* death of your husband that brings me here to speak with you."

James had not let go of her hand.

"I see ye brought the wolfhound I gave your son," James said.

"I'm very attached to Sàr," Moira said, running her slender fingers over the dog's head. "I could not leave him behind."

"Moira has him in the palm of her hand," Connor whispered to Duncan, sounding inordinately pleased.

"If ye had a justification for what ye did, ye should not have run off," James said. "I—and my father—have always been fond of ye, but we could only think the worst."

"Alas," Moira said, looking up at James from under her lashes, "Sean's men were in no mind to listen to explanations that night."

"Come, Moira," James said, his tone far too familiar. "Tell me what happened."

Moira stepped back from James. Slowly, she pushed back her hood and unfastened the cape that had been tied snugly beneath her chin. She let the cape fall to the ground and stood before them all in a low-cut gown that revealed the bruises on her neck.

Several people at the table gasped, and Connor swore under his breath. Hearing that Moira's husband had tried to kill her was not the same as seeing the evidence of it on her slender neck.

"Jesu!" James's nostrils flared and the muscles of his jaw flexed as he clamped his lips together. After a long moment, he asked, "Sean did this to you?"

"He tried to strangle me," she said. "Ye can see his finger marks."

She turned her head to the side and pulled her hair back. Most of the bruising to Moira's face had healed, thanks to Caitlin's and Ilysa's skills and smelly poultices, but the left side of her face still showed the damage Sean had done to her.

"I am so sorry he hurt ye," James said.

"'Tis much improved," Moira said, her voice wavering a bit. "Ye can imagine what I looked like the night I escaped. If I had not killed Sean first, he would have murdered me."

"But why would Sean harm you?" James picked up her cape, wrapped it around her, and rested his hands on her shoulders. "How could any man harm you?"

Duncan ground his teeth to keep from shouting at the man to get his hands off her.

"Sean was afraid to hurt me while I had powerful protectors. I wasn't safe from him once you and your father left Ireland." She turned her gaze on Connor. "Sean did not believe my own clan was concerned with my wellbeing."

Connor was gripping his cup so tightly that his knuckles were white. He worked with such single-minded devotion to protect their clan that Duncan knew what a blow Moira's words were to him.

"I believe ye, Moira," James said and blew out his breath. "But it's no that easy. Having their chieftain killed by a lass in their own fortress humiliated the MacQuillans. They want retribution."

"What if my brother was willing to make a modest payment to the MacQuillans?" Moira asked. "To compensate them for their . . . 'loss.'"

Such payments were sometimes made in cases of rape and murder, to avoid blood feuds.

"That was clever," Connor said under his breath to Duncan, before he finally intervened in Moira's play. "James, I am prepared to offer a modest sum, as my sister suggests."

"That would help soothe their pride," James said.

"Though I will expect one in return for the harm their chieftain did to my sister," Connor added.

"I'll leave now and let you men discuss it," Moira said as if she had not orchestrated it all. "Thank you, James, for listening to me with an open heart."

"You're a brave lass," James said and kissed her hand again, quite unnecessarily. "I've always admired ye."

Duncan wanted to gag—or better yet, slice James's silver tongue from his throat.

* * *

Moira lay on her bed, exhausted. Before her marriage, she could have carried off that performance without feeling like her soul was bleeding out on the floor. The display of her wounds was necessary and the drama effective, but she had underestimated the toll it would take on her. Making love with Duncan had made her believe she had recovered from Sean. But though she had always liked James, she found herself feeling faint when he stood too close and kept dropping his gaze to her breasts.

The mischievous faeries must have cast a spell on her for their amusement. Not only did she love a man who thought she was useless, silly, and wholly lacking in character, but it appeared that no other man could touch her without sending her into a panic.

A knock on the door made her sit up straight. "Who is it?"

She squelched her disappointment when Connor stuck his head through the door.

"Can we talk?" he asked.

When she nodded, he came inside and closed the door behind him.

"I appreciate what ye did," Connor said. "I suspect you were more of a help to our father when he was chieftain than I ever realized."

At least her brother was beginning to see her value, if belatedly.

"I am so sorry I didn't send Duncan to Ireland sooner." Connor came to stand by the bed and took her hand. "I believed you were safe, and there were so many dangers facing our clan that I... Well, there is no excuse for it. I should have found a way."

Connor had such sadness in his eyes that she felt her own tearing up. "Thank you for saying that. I thought ye didn't care at all."

"It was never that," Connor said as he brushed a lock of her hair off her forehead. "Growing up, it always seemed as if ye had a special magic around ye, and that nothing bad could ever happen to ye."

Moira gave a humorless laugh. "What the faeries give they take away twice."

"Duncan loves ye, and he's a good man," Connor said.

"Hmmph." Moira crossed her arms and looked away.

"Give him a chance, Moira."

"Is that an order from my chieftain?" she asked.

"It's advice from a brother who wants to see ye happy," Connor said. "And now, if you'll have pity on me, I'm desperate for your help with our guest."

"I do have something else I need to discuss with James," Moira said, smiling at her brother. "And I think I might enjoy aggravating Duncan a bit more."

CHAPTER 32

Duncan sat by the hall's great hearth sharpening his dirk on a whetstone while he watched Moira flirt with James. At least she had changed out of that low-cut gown, though nothing could hide curves like hers.

He emptied his cup of whiskey and refilled it. If everything went well, he would be the keeper of Trotternish Castle in a week's time. Then he could marry Moira and give her the kind of home she needed.

If she didn't run off with that damned James, son of a chieftain, first.

Connor strolled over and sat next to him. "I had a long talk with James," he said in a low voice. "Thanks to Moira, he's verra cooperative now."

"Hmmph." Duncan took another long drink of his whiskey.

"According to James, Alastair MacLeod and Shaggy Maclean have left the rebellion and are proving their new-found loyalty to the Crown by chasing after their former ally Donald Gallda," Connor said, referring to the leader of the rebellion. "They haven't caught Donald yet, but they captured his brothers and turned them over to the Crown to be executed."

"Now we know where Alastair MacLeod went with his war galleys," Duncan said. "'Tis good news for us that he's busy elsewhere."

"The bad news is that the Crown has rewarded Alastair MacLeod by granting him a royal charter to the lands he stole from us on Trotternish."

"But we never joined the rebellion!" Duncan said, slamming his cup down. Connor had taken a considerable risk by not taking up arms with their neighboring clans against the Crown.

"Surely ye remember the parable of the prodigal son," Connor said, shaking his head.

"Forget the damned charter," Duncan said. "What matters most is who holds the land."

It had proven far easier for the Crown to issue royal charters—in fact, it had been known to issue charters to the same land to rival clans—than to remove a clan from its lands.

"I should help my sister with our guest," Connor said, shifting his gaze to Moira, who was still having an excessively friendly chat with James on the other side of the hall. "I know it's soon to ask her, but I wonder if she would consider James for her next husband."

Duncan squeezed the cup in his hand pretending it was James's neck.

Rhona came into the hall from the kitchens carrying a jug of wine and cups. After serving Moira, James, and Connor, she ambled over to where Duncan sat.

"I see she's even quicker to find a new man this time," Rhona said, leaning down to speak into his ear. "I told ye this would happen."

Rhona gave him an amused glance over her shoulder as she pranced off.

Duncan watched how Moira and James leaned their heads together and looked into each other's eyes while they talked about God knew what.

But it was her laugh a moment later that sent him over the edge. As her face lit up, he could feel the pulse in his temples throb. Her shining black braid fell over her shoulder as she leaned closer to James and laughed. That last night before he was forced to leave for France, Duncan had watched her laugh just like this with the man who became her husband.

The temper Duncan had spent his youth learning to control exploded. It surged through his veins, pounded in his ears, and tunneled his vision until all he could see was the two of them laughing.

Duncan marched across the hall, aware but not giving a goddamn that he was causing a disruption. He'd had enough. As he neared the pair, some of James's men started to rise from their seats

"Stay where ye are!" Duncan said, turning to glare at them. "It's not James I'm after."

At least not yet. James was just a pawn in Moira's game.

When Duncan reached Moira, he grabbed her by her arms and lifted her out of her seat.

"What do ye think you're doing, Duncan MacDonald?" she said, as he dragged her away. "Connor! Do something!"

"Halt!" James called and started after them, but he thought better of it when all of the MacDonalds of Sleat began hooting and clapping.

Duncan was too full of fury to feel gratified by the cheers.

"I'll strangle ye in your sleep! I'll burn your cottage!" Moira was spewing a stream of useless threats.

He hauled her through the arched doorway to the stair-well, then tossed her over his shoulder and headed up the stairs. She was pounding his back and calling him all manner of vile names, which for some perverse reason did bring him a measure of satisfaction.

Duncan flung open the door to the sacrosanct bed-chamber belonging to the adored chieftain's daughter, the room he was never permitted to violate with his lowly presence even as a child. As a young man, he would have been beaten within an inch of his life if he had been caught invading this hallowed place.

Well, he was here now.

Duncan kicked the door shut behind him. As soon as he set Moira on her feet, he grabbed her arms before she could scratch his eyes out. Judging from the fire in hers, that was precisely what she wished to do to him.

Good. He was in the mood for a fight.

"What in hell were ye doing down there in the hall?" he shouted at her.

"What was *I* doing?" she asked. "I was enjoying a civil conversation with a civilized man before ye interrupted us acting like a madman."

"I won't have your games, Moira. I put up with them when I was nineteen, but I won't now," he said as he backed her up against the door. "I'll no stand by while ye

flirt and bat your eyes and God knows what else with another man!"

"We have an important guest," she said between her
teeth. "I was merely being a gracious hostess—not that
it's any business of yours."

The edges of his vision turned blood-red. "Does being
a gracious hostess involve taking our highborn guest to
bed?"

He had released her arms, which was a mistake. Moira
tried to slap his face, but years of practice with a sword
made him far too quick for her. He caught her wrists
again and pinned them against the door.

"What do ye mean, it's no my business?" he said an
inch from her face. "I thought we had an understanding."

"An understanding?" she said, her eyes narrow slits of
blue fire. "And what understanding would that be?"

"That you're mine."

Duncan kissed her—not the sweet, tender kisses he
had been giving her, but hard on the mouth. She said she
was no fragile flower, and he hoped to God she was right,
because he was in no mood for caution. His need for her
was as violent as the storm that had torn their boat apart.

Ever since he had found her again, he had banked his
passion, made himself be the gentle lover she needed him
to be. But he could hold back no longer. Control was beyond him. His hunger for her was boundless.

He wanted to strip her bare to her soul and make her
his, utterly and completely.

Moira gripped her hands in his hair and held on as
he thrust his tongue into her mouth and devoured her
with his kisses. Her nails dug into his shoulders through
his clothes. When he grasped her buttocks and lifted her

against his throbbing erection, she wrapped her legs around him in a vise. He wanted desperately to take her right now, fast and hard against the door.

But he had spent too many nights in his younger years dreaming of her in that bed.

Without lifting his mouth from hers, he carried her to it. When he broke the kiss to pull back the bed curtains and set her down, she looked at him with velvet eyes that were dark with desire.

"Ye don't seem quite so concerned about propriety now," she said in a throaty voice as her mouth curved up in a slow smile. When she ran the tip of her tongue over her swollen lips, all the blood in his head went straight to his cock.

This was the old Moira. Without realizing it, Duncan had been waiting for her—the wild and free Moira he had first fallen in love with. And yet, she was so much more now. He loved this complex, deeper woman even more than he had loved the carefree girl.

"Just because I want to protect ye," he said between harsh breaths, "does not mean I think you're weak."

Moira fisted her hands in his shirt and pulled him down. They fell across the bed, legs tangled and hands tearing at each other's clothes with a frantic desperation. Duncan ignored the sound of her gown ripping as he pulled the bodice down and filled his hands with her full, rounded breasts. While he rubbed his thumbs over her nipples, he moved down her throat with his mouth, leaving his mark on her with sucking kisses. She moaned and arched her back, egging him on.

His, she was his.

He licked the salt of her skin, breathed in the smell

of her desire. As he sought more bare skin beneath her clothes, he kissed her breasts and pressed his cock against her thigh. There was far too much cloth between them, and he was desperate for her.

"Hurry, Duncan, hurry," Moira pleaded in ragged breaths as she jerked at her skirts, trying to help free them. "I want ye now."

The lass was going to kill him. With a final tug, he had her skirts up around her waist.

"I love ye so much," he said. "And I do know you."

Moira clamped her legs around him and lifted her hips to meet him. As he plunged into her, he squeezed his eyes shut against the rush of pleasure that surged through him. He paused, deep inside her, reveling in the sensation. This was where he was meant to be. She was his. And God knew, he was hers. He had been since the beginning of time.

"Aye, aye," she gasped as he began moving inside her.

She was everything he wanted, and he was claiming her, body and soul. She tossed her head from side to side and held on to him, making frantic little noises as he thrust deeply, again and again.

"Don't stop," she pleaded as he reached the very edge of his control.

They cried each other's name as they came together in an explosion of pleasure that was so intense it blinded him. He rested his forehead on the bed beside her, gasping for air. He was trying not to crush her, but he could hardly hold himself up. Finally, he gave up and collapsed beside her. They lay side by side, breathing hard, their skin damp with perspiration.

Duncan stared up at the fancy drapes that hung around

her bed. That hadn't resolved anything, but he felt a whole hell of a lot better.

"I'm leaving to take Trotternish Castle now," he said. "And ye had best be waiting here for me."

"And if I'm not?" Moira said, raising her eyebrows.

"I will come find you." He cupped her cheek with his hand and held her gaze. "You and I are one, and we will always be."

CHAPTER 33

As Duncan made his way down the hill to meet Alex's boat, he was glad for the dense fog that had rolled in with the night, covering the sea and the shore. No one would see them slip out of the bay. Duncan was twenty paces from where Alex's boat was pulled up on shore before its black outline emerged from the dark gray billowing fog.

As Duncan drew closer, he could make out the figures of the men in the boat—and one man leaning against it. He knew it was Connor even before he was close enough to recognize the long, lean frame.

"Duncan," Alex called out in a soft voice from the boat, and Duncan raised his hand in greeting.

"We must talk," Connor said. "In private."

Duncan sighed inwardly. Connor was furious with him—and rightly so—for carrying Moira out of the hall like that, declaring to the world that he was bedding the chieftain's sister. Though Duncan knew they must have this conversation, he had hoped to delay it until after they had taken Trotternish Castle.

"Ye shouldn't leave the castle without guards," Duncan said when they had walked through the fog far enough to be out of earshot of the others.

Connor chafed under the constraints for his personal protection that came with being chieftain, but he understood what his death would mean for the clan so he usually complied.

But not tonight.

"I have important business with ye." Connor put a hand on Duncan's shoulder, but there was no mistaking the steel in his voice. "We need to discuss my sister."

Though he and Connor had been his best friends since the cradle, Connor would put the interests of the clan before their friendship. Duty to the clan was ingrained in Connor's soul, and it weighed even more heavily on him now that he was chieftain.

"What is it ye wish to know?" Duncan asked, delaying the inevitable.

Connor squeezed his shoulder harder and leaned close. "Ye know damned well what I'm asking."

Connor, Ian, and Alex had always treated Duncan as an equal, but others had not because his father was unknown. Duncan had worked hard—harder than anyone—until he became a warrior of such strength and skill that he commanded respect in his own right.

Still, asking to wed his chieftain's sister was reaching above him.

"I know this is not what ye want for Moira or for the clan," Duncan said. "But I can't live without her."

"That's a bit vague," Connor said, and Duncan could

feel Connor's eyes drilling into him through the darkness. "What, precisely, do ye plan to do about it?"

"I respect ye as my chieftain, and you're closer than a brother to me," Duncan said. "But I cannot let ye wed Moira to another man. If I must, I will fight even you for her."

The prospect of losing Connor's friendship was like a hot blade piercing his heart. If he lost this lifelong bond, Duncan would never feel whole again. But as much as it would pain him, he was choosing Moira.

"I intend to marry her this time," Duncan said and steeled himself to face Connor's fury.

"It would have been a shame to have to kill ye," Connor said, his teeth showing white in the darkness as he broke into a grin. "With the way the two of ye have been carrying on, the whole clan is talking—and that was before ye carried her upstairs in front of God and everyone today."

"Are ye saying I have your approval?" Duncan was stunned. "I thought ye would want Moira to make a marriage alliance for the clan."

"Ach, marrying her outside the clan has its dangers," Connor said. "If Moira sticks a dirk in you like she did her last husband, I won't have to worry about it causing a clan war."

"There is that," Duncan said with a dry laugh.

"You've always underestimated your value to me and to the clan," Connor said, his tone serious. "If you are the one Moira wants to wed, I'm glad of it."

"Well," Duncan said, and cleared his throat. "Moira has not agreed to it, precisely."

"Not precisely?" Connor asked.

"She will." She had to. "I told her we could not marry until we took Trotternish—and ye made me keeper of the castle."

"Moira was ready to wed, and ye put her off and set conditions on it?" Connor threw his head back and laughed, a rare sound these days. "I wondered what the problem was. Ach, you're both stubborn as mules."

"She's always had a fine home to live in," Duncan said, defending himself.

"If we succeed in taking Trotternish Castle, it will need a keeper," Connor said. "You're the only man I would entrust it to."

"We will succeed," Duncan said.

"Did ye ask Moira what she was discussing with James when you *interrupted* them?" Connor asked.

"I don't want to know."

"She was telling him that Ragnall is your son, not Sean's," Connor said. "She asked him to share that news with the MacQuillans so they would not demand the lad's return after we bring him home to Dunscaith."

Duncan's chest felt tight. While he did not regret carrying her off to her bedchamber, he felt like an ass for shouting at her.

"We should go," Alex called to them. When Duncan and Connor returned to the boat, Alex said, "After your display in the hall, Duncan, a few of us laid wagers on when you and Moira would wed."

"You what?" Duncan asked.

"Don't give me that surly look," Alex said. "I seem to recall you were the one taking wagers before I wed."

Duncan had collected a fine bag of coins from it, too.

"Your chieftain wagered a silver coin on your marriage

taking place in three weeks," Connor said, draping his arm around Duncan's shoulder. "A wise man would remember that."

"We'll see you and Ian at the gates of Trotternish Castle in four days," Duncan said to Connor and climbed into the boat.

"We'll take the MacLeods by land and by sea," Connor called out to them, and they raised their fists and echoed back the MacDonald clan motto.

"*Air muir 's air tìr!*" By land and by sea!

* * *

"We're a couple of miles from Trotternish Castle now," Alex alerted Duncan.

They had made good time and arrived in less than two full days.

"Bring us to shore," Duncan said, "and I'll walk the rest of the way."

A misty rain was falling and the afternoon light was fading, which was good, because everything depended upon no one seeing a MacDonald galley full of warriors land. When Connor and Ian arrived with their galleys, they would take the greater caution of staying out to sea until it was full dark.

"Quiet, lads," Alex said as he guided the galley toward a stretch of beach with no cottages in sight.

The soft, regular splash of their oars was the only sound the men made as the boat approached the shore. As one, they lifted their oars, and Duncan felt the soft scrape of the hull on the rocks as they glided in.

"Two nights from now, after the household has gone to bed, I'll signal from the tower window if it is safe to proceed," Duncan told Alex, though they had gone over this a dozen times before.

"I'll be waiting," Alex said. "When I see the signal, I'll send a man to tell Ian and Connor to have their men ready."

The plan was for Duncan to drop a rope from the tower room. After Alex and a handful of his men climbed up, they would make their way to the castle's gate, subdue the guards, and let their main force in through the gate.

"I hope ye haven't grown too weak from your lax training to climb the rope," Duncan chided him.

Alex just laughed.

"If the sea is rough," Duncan said more seriously, "it will be difficult to bring your boat close enough to the cliff to reach the rope."

"Ach, I could do it with my eyes closed," Alex said. In the dark of night, it would be much the same as doing it blind, but no one was a better sailor than Alex.

"By then, the castle folk should be accustomed to seeing me and won't be watching me closely." Or so Duncan hoped.

"I'd wager that a few of the women will still be eyeing ye," Alex said with amusement in his voice. "You're usually blind to the lasses' attention, but ye ought to be mindful of it this time. I advise ye to pick one of them when ye first arrive, and that will discourage the others."

"I'll be wed soon," Duncan said, offended.

"I'm no saying ye need to bed the lass," Alex said. "Just flirt with her—make the others believe she's the one ye want so they don't follow ye about."

"I'll make certain no one follows me," Duncan said and changed the subject. "With any luck, we'll surround the MacLeods while they're still sleeping in the hall, and the fighting will be over quickly."

"We can hope," Alex said, sounding doubtful. "Otherwise, this is bound to be bloody."

"Remember," Duncan said, gripping Alex's arm, "the keeper of the castle is mine."

"And you remember," Alex said, "that MacLeod hostages are more valuable to us than dead MacLeods."

Not this one. Duncan picked up the bag that held his pipes and prepared to drop over the side of the boat into the shallows.

"It will all go as smooth as cream down a cat's throat," Alex said, which they both knew for a lie, and put his hand on Duncan's shoulder. "All the same, you'll be alone in there, my friend, so be careful."

CHAPTER 34

Moira could see her breath as she paused to watch the clouds traveling over the lush green hills wet with rain. Duncan did not believe it, but she would rather live here on the Sleat Peninsula of Skye in a small cottage than live in a castle anywhere else. For her, this was home, and there would never be a place she loved as much.

She turned to gaze across the wide inlet toward the misty peaks of the Cuillins. Beyond them, on the farthest corner of the island, lay the Trotternish Peninsula. Duncan and Alex should be arriving there now. Trotternish was starker, less green than Sleat. The castle, sitting high on its forbidding cliff, reminded her too much of the MacQuillans'.

Moira had wandered the hills for hours with Sàr. Since Duncan's departure two days ago, she had much to think about. She understood that Duncan must serve as the keeper of Trotternish Castle. After prying it out of the thieving hands of the MacLeods, the clan needed its fiercest warrior to be the castle's protector and defender. But would she go with him?

Aye, she knew she would. Perhaps she could live without him, but she did not want to.

She had faith that Duncan would take Trotternish Castle, but she wished he had enough faith in her to wed her without it. At least he did not think of her as fragile anymore. She smiled to herself. The way he had made fierce love to her before he left was rather persuasive on that point.

When it started to rain, she suddenly remembered that Connor was leaving for Trotternish with most of their warriors tonight. The day had gotten away from her. She started back, hoping to reach Dunscaith in time to see Connor and the others off.

As she ran on the muddy path along the windblown ridge of the hill, Moira noticed a boat and two figures on the shore of a small cove below her. All of the Sleat Peninsula was firmly in the hands of the MacDonalds, so these would be her clansmen. Sailing back to Dunscaith would be much faster, and it was growing dark. She decided to take advantage of being the chieftain's sister and ask them to take her back to Dunscaith in their boat.

The rain was coming down harder all the time. She left the path and went slipping and sliding down the hillside through the tall wet grass with Sàr on her heels. When she reached the thick brush near the shore, she had to slow her pace.

Moira was close enough now to call out to the pair, but she stopped herself when she recognized the woman. *What is Rhona doing here?*

"Quiet, boy," Moira whispered when she heard the low rumble of Sàr's growl beside her.

She knelt and put her arm around him to hold him back. As she watched, Rhona embraced the man and gave him a good, long kiss.

"Hmmph. It didn't take Rhona long to find a way to comfort herself over the loss of Duncan," she whispered to Sàr. "At least I won't have to worry about her poisoning my food now."

Moira reconciled herself to walking the rest of the way back to Dunscaith in the pouring rain and missing saying good-bye to Connor. She was not about to interrupt the tryst on the beach. With a sigh, she got to her feet to leave.

Just then, the man with Rhona broke their kiss and turned, showing his profile. Moira froze. For a long moment, she thought she was seeing her father's ghost.

But no, her memory was playing a trick on her in the fading light of the rainy winter afternoon. Moira felt a deep pang of sorrow. The man on the beach was only a man with a large frame and dark gold hair the color her father's had been when Moira was a young girl.

Her father was dead.

As Moira climbed back up the hill, she suspected that what had triggered the memory of her father even more than the man's build and hair color was seeing him in an illicit embrace with a woman. Her father always had women about. Some said that his infidelities broke her mother's heart. Others said her mother put a curse upon her father, which she may have. Despite all his women, Moira was his last child. At least, she did not know of any others.

By the time she reached Dunscaith, Moira was chilled and drenched to the bone. And she had missed saying good-bye to Connor.

* * *

Soon I will be master here.

The words echoed in Duncan's head as he passed through the gate of Trotternish Castle.

As he crossed the castle courtyard, a man coming the other way gave him wide berth, and Duncan realized he was walking as he normally did. Though it went against every instinct, he hunched his shoulders and lowered his head.

Once inside the keep, he scanned the hall from under his hood, instinctively counting men and weapons and finding no more than last time. His gaze came to an abrupt halt at the high table. Ragnall was sitting next to his friend Sarah, just a few seats down from Erik.

Duncan should not have been caught off guard by Ragnall being invited to sit at the high table, though he had not been there last time. After all, the MacLeods believed Ragnall was the MacQuillan chieftain's only son. But Duncan could feel the evil emanating from Erik MacLeod, and he disliked having his son anywhere near him.

Ragnall was leaning his head on his chin and had a scowl on his face. When he saw Duncan, his expression brightened, and he sat up straight. Much as it warmed Duncan's heart that the lad was pleased to see him, it could spell disaster. If Ragnall acted overly friendly toward him or came too close, it was possible someone could notice the resemblance between them.

When Duncan gave his head a slight shake, Ragnall dropped his smile at once and looked away. Ragnall's quick perception of Duncan's signal spoke of lessons learned from living under the threat of Sean's temper. Though it was useful at the moment, it troubled Duncan. He had much to make up for with his son.

"I see you've returned to eat my food, piper," Erik called out, drawing Duncan's attention to the center of the high table. "Let's have a lively tune."

Erik's rudeness was boundless. Duncan forced himself to lower his eyes so Erik would not see murder in them. When one of the serving maids brought Duncan a stool and gave him a saucy wink, he remembered Alex's advice.

"What's your name, lass?" he asked loud enough for those nearby to hear.

"Mòrag," she said, tossing her hair over her shoulder. "But for you, I'll answer to anything."

Luckily, the lass did not require much encouragement. Now, if someone caught him in a part of the castle he should not be, he could say he thought that's where Mòrag had told him to meet her.

Duncan felt Erik's gaze burning holes in him as he began to play. Damn the man's suspicious nature. When Erik threw that apple at him last time, he should have let it hit him in the head. Duncan had seen it from the corner of his eye and caught it instinctively.

He could afford no more mistakes like that.

* * *

Erik was aware that one of the guards on duty at the front gate had come into the hall and stood behind him, but he made him wait. He was vigilant about reminding the men of the importance of his position. While he kept the guard waiting, he watched the piper.

"What brings ye back from the MacCrimmons so soon?" he called out when the piper finished a tune.

"Well," the piper said, "the MacCrimmons are a bit too protective of their daughters for my taste."

Erik laughed. That was too true. Reassured that at least the piper had been where he said he was, Erik leaned back in his chair and waved the guard forward.

"That MacDonald pirate is here," the guard said close to Erik's ear.

Hugh Dubh must finally have news about his nephew's plans.

"Send him in," Erik said.

CHAPTER 35

With Erik's gaze fixed on him, Duncan kept his own on his pipes and continued playing.

All the same, he was aware when someone entered the hall and approached the high table.

"Ragnall," Erik called out. "Come meet your mother's uncle."

Duncan missed a note and struggled to pick up the tune again. From the back, the visitor standing before the high table could be one of Moira and Connor's Clanranald uncles from their mother's side. Duncan did not pray often, but he was praying hard that whichever uncle it was did not recognize him. He played softly, using his music as an invisible shield as he let it float behind the conversations in the hall.

"This is your uncle Hugh Dubh," Erik said.

Hugh. They should have guessed that Hugh would be consorting with the MacLeods again to stir up trouble.

"Come, lad," Erik said, waving to Ragnall.

Icy fingers stole up Duncan's spine as he watched Ragnall go to stand beside Erik with only the width of the table between him and Hugh. His son looked so small and vulnerable, like a wee rabbit caught between two circling hawks.

Duncan's every muscle tensed, ready to fight to protect his son. He envisioned himself stealing a claymore, running across the room to reach Ragnall, tossing him over his shoulder, and then escaping with him out of the hall, across the bailey yard, out the gate, and through the open fields to safety. He would never make it—but for a long moment, he considered it.

Duncan did not realize he had stopped playing until Erik shouted, "Another tune, piper, to welcome my guest!"

Time seemed to slow as Hugh turned and looked straight at Duncan. Hugh's eyes went wide. Duncan was already on his feet when Hugh flung out his arm and pointed at him.

"I know that man," Hugh shouted. "That's Duncan MacDonald!"

Even without his claymore, Duncan took down half a dozen of the MacLeods who came at him. But there were too many of them, and eventually they held him long enough to tie his hands behind him. Through the melee of men grabbing and pushing and women screaming, Duncan caught a glimpse of Ragnall. His son's expression was closed but his eyes seemed to take in everything, and his wee friend, Sarah, was holding his hand.

The next time Duncan looked, the two children were gone.

* * *

Moira and Ilysa discussed the week's menu as they melted tallow for rush candles. Servants usually did this task—and the smell was dreadful—but staying busy helped keep their minds off their worry over the men who had gone to Trotternish. After the kitchen was cleaned up from the midday meal, Ilysa had shooed the servants out so it was just the two of them. Moira had grown fond of Duncan's sister and was glad for the time alone with her.

"We'll run out of fresh meat soon," Ilysa said. "Tait had some lads drop lines out the sea gate, so perhaps we'll have fish for supper."

"Speak of the devil," Moira said, giving Tait a friendly wink as he came into the kitchen.

"Good day to ye both," Tait said. "Have ye seen young Fergus?"

"Not today," Moira said and glanced at Ilysa, who shook her head. "Why?"

"He's gone missing." Tait leaned forward, resting his hands on the worktable, and spoke in a low voice, though no one else was in the kitchen. "No one has seen Fergus since he was on guard duty last night."

"I won't believe Fergus is our spy, if that's what you're suggesting," Ilysa said, pulling her delicate brows together. "He's a simple young man."

"What else am I to think?" Tait asked. "Connor was very clear that no one was to leave the castle until he returned. He was taking no chance of the MacLeods being forewarned."

"I saw Fergus with Rhona yesterday," Ilysa said. "Perhaps she knows."

"What business does Rhona have with a sixteen-year-old guard?" A cold dread settled in Moira's belly. "Let's split up and search the castle for the two of them."

"No need to alarm the household," Ilysa warned.

Half an hour later they met, as agreed, in Connor's chamber.

"Neither of them is in the keep," Moira reported.

"I checked all the storerooms along the wall," Ilysa said.

"I didn't find them, either. But the men guarding the gate with Fergus last night saw him and Rhona fook—" Tait halted midsentence and turned bright red. "Sorry."

"By the saints, Tait, just tell us," Moira said.

"Well, when the other guards saw that Fergus and Rhona were...um, *occupying* themselves against the wall, they took a walk," Tait said.

"The other guards 'took a walk'?" Ilysa asked, arching her brows.

"Ach, it happens," Tait said, squirming under Ilysa's gaze. "Night guard duty is long and tedious, and if a willing lass..."

"Just tell us about Fergus and Rhona," Moira interrupted.

"When the other guards returned, the pair was gone," Tait said. "The men assumed Rhona and Fergus had found a more private place to carry on their business."

"The guards did not report that Fergus had left his post?" Ilysa asked, with her hand on her hip.

"Men cover for each other for something like that, expecting—or at least hoping—to need the favor returned." Tait was shifting his weight from foot to foot, clearly uncomfortable explaining this to sweet-faced Ilysa. "They wouldn't dare if Duncan were here for fear he'd skin them alive when he found out—which he would—but Duncan has been away a good deal lately."

"Regardless, the pair of them are gone," Moira said. "But if they are spies, why sneak out of Dunscaith now? 'Tis too late to warn the MacLeods. Connor left with our war galleys two days ago."

"I can't believe Fergus would be disloyal," Ilysa said. "If he's involved, Rhona must have duped him into helping her."

"Fergus is not the sharpest knife in the kitchen, if ye know what I mean," Tait said, glancing at Moira.

"Rhona was here at Dunscaith when Hugh held the castle," Ilysa said. "I was never certain, but I suspected she was one of the women who was *friendly* with Hugh then. After the four returned from France, however, Rhona attached herself to my brother like a leech."

While Tait blathered on about the danger of a scorned woman—as if he knew—Moira tried to puzzle it out.

"I saw Rhona meet a man some distance from the castle shortly before Connor sailed out," she told them. "I thought she was meeting a lover for a tryst, but I suppose she could have had another purpose as well."

"Who was the man?" Ilysa asked.

"For a moment, I thought it was my father's ghost." Moira started to laugh at herself for her foolishness, but then she clutched Ilysa's arm. "Do you suppose it could have been my uncle? I haven't seen him since I was a bairn, and I don't remember him at all."

"If your father and Hugh had not been fifteen years apart," Tait said, "they would have looked very much alike."

"Then the man I saw with Rhona could have been Hugh," Moira said. "But if she is Hugh's spy, why would she leave now, two days after Connor set sail for Trotternish?"

"I don't know, but I sense trouble," Ilysa said.

"We need to find Rhona and Fergus—and stop them," Moira said.

"I'll go after them," Tait said.

"No, Connor left you in charge of the defense of the castle," Ilysa said. "We don't know that Rhona poses a danger, and with most of our warriors away, Connor would not want you to leave."

"He did take most of the able-bodied men," Tait said.

"I wish I knew for certain which of the warriors he left behind are trustworthy..." Ilysa narrowed her eyes, considering. "We must be very careful who we share this with."

"Aye," Moira agreed. "We need a man we can absolutely trust."

At a knock on the door, the three of them jumped like guilty conspirators. A moment later Niall hobbled in using a thick stick for a cane.

"I've got Duncan's boat fixed as good as new," he said. "Either of you lasses want to go for a wee sail and try her out?"

Niall was perfect.

"Here's our man," Tait said, slapping Niall on the back.

No one was more trustworthy, and Niall was strong and well trained. And yet, Moira's gaze kept shifting between his young, open face and his injured leg. While the other two told him about Rhona and Fergus, she gathered her courage.

"I'm going with Niall," Moira said and stood up.

"You?" Ilysa blinked at her.

"Look at him," Moira said, pointing at Niall's leg. "He can't sail the boat alone."

Even more than that, Niall was far too softhearted when it came to women. He would be no match for Rhona.

Moira would not have the same problem.

* * *

Hugh was drinking copious amounts of Erik's best whiskey.

"I expect payment for alerting ye to the presence of a MacDonald spy in your midst," Hugh said as he helped himself to more whiskey.

Damn it, Erik had known something was not right about that piper. Erik felt a begrudging admiration for Duncan MacDonald's fearlessness in entering his enemy's castle alone and under such a ruse. If Erik were not so furious, he'd have a good laugh over it.

"That was pure luck," Erik said. "Ye had no idea he was here."

"'Tis true that I didn't expect to find the captain of Connor's guard inside your castle pretending to be a piper." Hugh pointed his finger at Erik. "But I did know that he left Dunscaith in the dark of night. That meant the attack would come soon, so I came to warn ye."

Hugh did not know half as much as he pretended. "What I need to know is why your nephew sent the captain of his guard here."

"He's scouting things out in preparation for the attack." Hugh leaned back and stretched out his legs as if he had a right to be here in Erik's castle. "Why else would he be here?"

"Did ye see the MacDonald war galleys set sail?" Erik demanded.

"No, but I was told that the men were packing up the boats." Hugh speared a herring from the platter that had been left on the table and commenced to eat it. "I expect they'll be here anytime now."

Hugh was guessing, but it was possible. Erik would double the guard.

"Connor's cousin Ian was also preparing his boat at Knock Castle." While he spoke, Hugh picked at his teeth with his dirk like a heathen.

"But ye know nothing at all about how they plan to make the attack?" Erik asked.

"No, but ye have the captain of Connor's guard in your dungeon," Hugh said as his gaze followed a dimpled lass with an ample behind. "Get it from him."

"My men have tried for a night and a day already," Erik said. "He hasn't said a word, and I don't believe he will."

It was pointless for Duncan MacDonald to keep his mouth shut now that he had been discovered. Whatever his task was here, he had no chance of completing it, and the attack would surely fail. Erik thought the man's honor was senseless, but he did admire his stubbornness.

"Feed him salted pork with no water," Hugh said around another mouthful of food. "A man dying of thirst will talk—if it doesn't make him go mad first."

"That takes too long," Erik said.

Besides, Duncan MacDonald was likely to know that trick. Though most men could not help eating the salted pork anyway, Erik suspected this MacDonald was tough enough to refuse to eat it no matter how long they starved him.

"I showed ye the spy and brought ye valuable information," Hugh said, interrupting Erik's thoughts. "Give me the lad now."

"The MacDonalds don't have enough warriors to take this castle," Erik said. "But if you're right and the MacDonalds do attack, you can have the lad then. No one will blame me if he is killed or disappears in the chaos of the battle."

Erik had given the MacQuillan lad very little thought, but he pictured him in his mind now. He was a fine-looking lad, tall for his age, and surprisingly quiet for having fiery red hair.

Red hair... No, it couldn't be. There were ginger-haired men and lads all over Scotland and Ireland. Yet the more Erik thought of it, the more it seemed to him that there was a resemblance between the MacDonald spy and the lad. And the lad's mother was Moira MacDonald.

"Ye say our spy has been friends with the MacDonald chieftain since they were lads?" Erik asked. "Was he friendly with the chieftain's sister as well?"

"Duncan's mother was nursemaid to Connor and his sister Moira," Hugh said with a shrug. "They all grew up together at Dunscaith."

So it was possible... The lad was supposed to be MacQuillan's, but, God knew, women were deceitful. Erik would not risk his life for a son, but many men would. This Duncan MacDonald struck him as that sort of man.

"From what I hear, there's more between Duncan and

Moira than childhood memories," Hugh said as he leaned forward to spear another herring with his dirk. "They say Moira is a rare beauty like her mother—and that she is Duncan's only weakness."

Erik smiled to himself. If he was right, he knew how to get the attack plan from the MacDonald spy.

It was almost too simple.

CHAPTER 36

Duncan kicked furiously at the rat crawling toward his foot. Frustration burned through him. God help him, he had failed on a grand scale. While the safety of his clansmen, including his son, his chieftain, and his best friends, depended upon him, Duncan was in the dungeon of Trotternish Castle chained to the goddamned wall like an animal.

"Arrgh!" He jerked the chain again, though it served no purpose but to cause the chain to bite into his bloody wrists.

He tried to guess how long he had been in this godforsaken hole. Judging from the quiet above him, it was night again. That meant Alex would be in his boat, watching for the signal and waiting for the rope that would never be dropped.

Duncan leaned his head back against the wall to keep the blood from running into his eyes. The beatings were getting fiercer, but he'd suffered worse. Though he was chained, the men seemed afraid to get close enough to do him serious harm.

The silence was broken by the echo of boots on the stone steps on the other side of the iron grate. Only one man this time, so he was braver than the others. Duncan got to his feet. He would be prepared if the guard gave him the slightest chance to overpower him.

When the man reached the bottom step, the light from the torch he carried shone on his face—and Duncan saw that it was Erik. Rage roared in his ears.

Erik waited to speak until he unlocked the iron grate door and stepped inside. Unfortunately, Duncan's chains were not long enough for him to reach Erik.

"You can save us both trouble and tell me now what I want to know," Erik said. "Or ye can wait for me to bring the lad down here."

An unfamiliar jolt of fear went through Duncan. *No, Erik could not know about Ragnall.*

"What lad?" Duncan attempted an indifferent tone, though his heart was pounding so hard Erik could probably hear it.

"I'm talking about your son," Erik said. "Ragnall."

Erik paced in front of Duncan, just beyond his reach. A few inches closer, and Duncan would wrap his chain around Erik's throat and strangle the life out of him.

"He's just a bairn," Erik said. "Don't make me hurt him."

"You wouldn't." Duncan forced himself to speak calmly. "Your chieftain undertook a solemn duty to protect him."

"His duty is to the MacQuillans," Erik said. "But Ragnall is not a MacQuillan, is he?"

"What man can truly know if a child is his?" Duncan shrugged. "The MacQuillans believe Ragnall is their chieftain's son, as does Alastair MacLeod, and that's what matters."

"'Tis true that my chieftain feels an obligation to the lad." Erik folded his arms and shook his head. "But there are so many ways a child can have an accident. And if it should look suspicious, I can blame Hugh Dubh. The fool as much as told my chieftain that he wants Ragnall dead."

Duncan believed Erik was capable of harming a child, and he knew for certain that Hugh was. Together, they were like a two-headed viper.

"If ye want to save your son, ye must tell me the things I need to know."

God have mercy on me. To buy time, Duncan said, "I was to report on any weaknesses I saw, that is all."

"Perhaps that was your task the first time ye entered my castle," Erik said, then he ticked his questions off on his fingers. "For what purpose did your chieftain send ye here a second time? How does he plan to attack me? And where does he have his men waiting now?"

Duncan tried desperately to think of lies that Erik would find convincing. And yet, he knew it would make no difference. Erik could not be trusted to keep his word. Even if Duncan was fool enough to tell Erik the truth and sacrifice the others, Erik would not spare Ragnall.

Duncan met the hard stare of his enemy and considered telling him that he was his son. He had envisioned telling Erik after he took this castle from him—and while he held a blade to Erik's throat. Confessing the truth as a plea for sympathy while he was humbled in chains was the last thing Duncan wanted to do.

He doubted that Erik would believe him. And if he did, Duncan had no illusion that Erik would spare him. But the question Duncan had to ask himself was whether there was a chance that the truth could move this cold-hearted man to save his grandson.

"Think on it tonight," Erik said. "I'll come back in the morning with the lad, and then we'll see what ye have to say."

* * *

"One of the small boats the young lads use for fishing is missing from the shore," Tait reported. "I expect that's what Rhona and Fergus took."

"They'll be moving slow in that," Niall said. "Still, they're half a day ahead. And worse, I don't know which way they went."

"I hate sending ye on a goose chase," Ilysa said. "Go see Teàrlag first. She may be able to tell ye where Rhona and Fergus have gone—and why."

"But Connor said no one was to leave," Tait said.

"He didn't mean me and Niall," Moira said, not bothering to hide her impatience. "We're not spies."

"We?" Niall said, cocking an eyebrow. "Duncan and Connor will both have my head if I take ye with me to chase after Rhona and Fergus."

"We're only going to Teàrlag's now," Moira said and headed for the door.

"Take Sàr with ye," Ilysa called after them.

It was growing dark when Moira and Niall reached the cove below Teàrlag's cottage. Moira followed Niall up the steps of the steep cliff to the ancient cottage. Niall managed surprisingly well, using his stick for a cane, but Moira slipped several times. Finally, she reached the top—and nearly plunged to the sea below when a voice came out of the darkness.

"About time ye came!"

Moira squinted into near darkness and saw the old seer standing above her on the top step.

"Hello, Teàrlag. It's me, Moira. Niall's here as well."

"I know who ye are." Teàrlag turned around and walked off toward her cottage, mumbling, "Ungrateful lass."

Moira followed her inside with Niall, hoping she would be welcome. Niall had told her on the sail over that Teàrlag had left her cottage for the first time in many years to give a prediction about Moira and to urge Duncan to leave for Ireland without delay.

"Leave your beast outside. I don't want him frightening my cow," Teàrlag said as she shuffled to her small table and lit the lamp.

There was no room in the tiny cottage for Sàr in any case.

"I'm sorry I haven't come to thank ye." Moira set the basket of food they had brought on the small table and gingerly took the stool across from Teàrlag.

The seer had looked older than the mist for as long as Moira could remember. Except for shrinking a bit more, she had not changed much.

"I knew that blood in my vision wasn't yours." Teàrlag's shoulders rose and fell as she made a sound that could only be called a cackle. "But I knew ye needed help, and it did get that big lad in his boat."

Only Teàrlag would call Duncan "that big lad." Moira was relieved that the old seer appeared to have accepted her apology. Teàrlag was not above threatening to curse someone for what she deemed a lack of courtesy.

"I suppose you've come to ask me about that troublesome lass, Rhona," Teàrlag said as she peered into the food basket—which was probably what had gained Moira forgiveness. "Couldn't Ilysa tell ye?"

Moira turned and raised her eyebrows at Niall, who had joined them at the tiny table.

"Ilysa's been learning the Old Ways from Teàrlag," Niall whispered, his knees bumping hers as he leaned forward. "Some say she's developed The Sight."

Calm, circumspect Ilysa is a seer? Moira could not imagine her weaving back and forth and waving her arms like Teàrlag did when she had a vision. But then, Teàrlag did make the most of her gift.

"The Sight comes and goes with Ilysa," Teàrlag said, shaking her head. "She lacks faith in herself."

Not something Teàrlag suffered.

"Can ye tell us why Rhona and Fergus left the castle?" Niall asked. "Are they a danger to the clan?"

"Rhona is not the danger," Teàrlag said. "But there is a danger to our returning warriors, and Rhona knows what it is."

"We must find her then," Moira said. "Do you know where she and Fergus are?"

Teàrlag rolled her eyes back and made a strange humming noise as she swayed in her seat. After a time, she stopped and blinked several times.

"Well?" Niall asked.

"I can't see their destination," Teàrlag said. "But

they're sailing south along the coast of Sleat toward the point of the peninsula."

"Is there anything else ye can tell us?" Moira asked.

"Rhona has vengeance in her heart," Teàrlag said. "And she is looking for Hugh Dubh."

CHAPTER 37

A sound pricked Duncan's ears. *Footsteps?* They sounded too light, and no torchlight shone on the stairs.

Clink, clink. Duncan heard a key turning in the lock, followed by the slow *creak* of the iron door swinging open. Perhaps the guards had returned for another attempt to beat the plans for the attack out of him, though they should know by now that it was hopeless. A few men could not be broken, and Duncan was one of them. He did not take special pride in it, but he knew it to be true nonetheless. He closed his eyes for a moment, steeling himself to bear the pain to come.

"He's in here!"

Duncan's eyes flew open at the unexpected sound of a little girl's high-pitched voice. It was so black in the dungeon he could not see anything.

"Hush!"

That was Ragnall's voice this time. Duncan thought he must be having a waking dream, as men do when they're beaten and kept in darkness, but then he sensed someone standing next to him.

"Ragnall?" he asked.

"We brought a mallet for the chains," Ragnall said.

"That was my idea," the girl said.

Duncan felt laughter bubbling inside him, like a madman. Surely, God was having a joke with him—or giving the famed warrior a lesson in humility—by sending two bairns to rescue him.

He took the mallet from Ragnall's hand and felt for the chain that shackled his legs to the wall. Then he slammed the mallet against the chain again and again until one of the links broke. He did the same with the chain that held his arms to the wall, and he was free.

"We must be very quiet as we go up," Duncan warned the children. "Ragnall, you'll come with me. Sarah, we'll see ye safely to your bedchamber door first. Where is it?"

Sarah had been permitted to sit at the high table with Ragnall, and she appeared to have free run of the castle and time to play. That meant she was from a highborn family and would sleep in one of the bedchambers, rather than in the hall or the kitchens. She was probably being fostered here like Ragnall.

"I'm not going to bed," Sarah said. "I'm staying with you and Ragnall."

"There will be trouble tonight, and ye must be safe in your bed with your clanswomen," Duncan said. "Now, which bedchamber is it?"

"I'm not telling."

Ach, she was stubborn enough to be a MacDonald lass. "Ragnall, where is it? 'Tis far too dangerous for her to come with us."

"Two floors above the hall," Ragnall said.

Sarah made a sound like a growl, which Duncan ignored. With that settled, he led the pair through the iron-barred door, up a set of steep stone steps, and along a narrow passageway. At the end of it, light shone around the edges of the low wooden door that led into the undercroft. Duncan put his ear to the door. It must be late indeed, for there were no voices or sounds of clanking pots coming from the kitchens.

"Where are ye taking Ragnall?" Sarah asked.

"To his mother," Duncan whispered, using up the last of his patience. "Now hush, Sarah. Not another word—unless ye *want* to see me back in that dungeon."

Duncan opened the door and made sure no one was in sight, then the three of them walked on silent feet past the kitchen and up the stairs that led to upper floors of the keep. Duncan heard the snores and snorts of the sleeping men as they passed the entrance to the hall and continued up the stairs.

Duncan patted Sarah's head and left her outside the door of the bedchamber she likely shared with several clanswomen. He was relieved to have that task done. Now he could go to the tower room. He hoped her family would not punish her too severely when they learned Sarah had helped them—but then, they would never know unless she confessed, which seemed unlikely.

Duncan took Ragnall's hand and hurried back down to the ground floor, all the while praying that the guards had already made their last check on their prisoner for the night. He half expected to hear shouts and see men come running at him from all directions.

Very carefully, he eased open the door that led into the

building adjoining the keep. The MacLeods expected no threat from within, so this inside door was unguarded. He and Ragnall crept up the stairs to the large room where he had found the children playing with wooden swords.

It was empty, as he had expected. He had learned that this was where Alastair MacLeod slept when he came to the castle. If the ghost existed, apparently she was gracious enough to stay in her tower and not disturb the chieftain's sleep.

Before opening the door at the far end of the room, Duncan checked to see that the bit of twig he had stuck in it the day he arrived was undisturbed. Relief surged through him when he found that it was still there. No one had entered the turret room after he was here.

As soon as he closed the door behind them, Duncan dropped to his knees to retrieve the rope, flint, and rush lamp he had hidden under the narrow bed. Then he opened the shutters, and prayed that Alex was still waiting for the signal.

"If the guards chance to see a light that comes and goes," he told Ragnall as he lit the lamp, "they'll believe it's the ghost." Or so he hoped.

He held the lamp to the window, counted to a hundred, then closed the shutter. Then he did it all again three more times.

"Are ye taking me to my mother now?" Ragnall asked.

"The other MacDonald warriors and I must first take this castle from the MacLeods," Duncan said, crouching down to rest his hands on his son's shoulders. "Ye must wait here for me until the fighting is over. You're not afraid of the ghost, are ye?"

Ragnall shook his head. Since most of the castle folk

were afraid to enter the turret room, Ragnall should be safe here.

"As soon as we have secured the castle, I'll come back for ye," Duncan said. "You'll be on the first boat sailing back to Dunscaith."

Duncan tied one end of the rope around the leg of the bed, and then he leaned out the window to drop the rope. The sound of the surf crashing on the rocks fifty yards below filled his ears as he watched the rope disappear into the darkness. The blackness of the sea below was broken only by whitecaps.

Duncan stayed at the window, waiting. He was hours late with the signal. The others could have assumed things had gone awry—which they had for a time—and left.

Come on, Alex.

After what seemed like a long while, Duncan saw the shadow of a boat below him. From the way it was gliding impossibly close to the cliff, that had to be Alex. Duncan shook the rope to make it easier for the men in the boat to see it. A moment later he felt the rope grow taut.

"They're here," Duncan said, turning to nod at Ragnall.

Alex was the first on the rope, his fair hair visible even in the dead of night. It was a long climb, and the wind was blowing hard. When Alex was a few yards away and close enough to hear him, Duncan made the soft sound of a dove to let him know it was safe.

When Alex finally reached the top, Duncan took his hand and pulled him through the small window. Then he jerked the rope to signal for the next man to start up. Duncan could not find a single rope long enough to scale the cliff, so he had tied three together. Because the knots made it weaker, the men were climbing one at a time to be sure the rope would hold their weight.

When Alex saw Ragnall, his eyes widened; then he glanced at Duncan and raised an eyebrow. Duncan ignored the question.

"I'm Alex MacDonald, your mother's cousin," Alex said.

Ragnall examined Alex but said nothing in reply.

"The lad is spare with words and smiles." Alex rubbed the back of his neck. "Reminds me of someone..."

Duncan gave him a look meant to end the conversation. Alex was a good friend, but he never knew when to be quiet.

Alex turned his back on Ragnall and said in a low voice, "Have ye told the lad?"

Duncan shook his head. "That's for his mother to tell him."

"It won't wait. You'd best tell him before someone else remarks upon it." Alex glanced over his shoulder at Ragnall. "They will, ye know."

Duncan did not respond, but he considered Alex's advice as he helped the next man through the window. The tiny room was soon cramped with MacDonald warriors, so he lifted Ragnall to stand on the bed.

When the last man was up the rope, Alex shook it again to signal to the men remaining in the boat to leave. "I hope to hell they don't scrape my galley against the cliff."

"There are half a dozen guards at the gate and another half dozen patrolling the walls," Duncan said, imparting the critical information quickly. "They don't sleep, so we must be cautious."

"All right," Alex said, and the others nodded.

"These MacLeod warriors are well trained," Duncan continued. "We'll wait for Connor and Ian at the gate. If something's happened and they don't come, we can escape that way. No sense dying for nothing."

Duncan, however, would have to return here first for Ragnall.

"I need a moment with the lad," Duncan said to Alex. "Take the men into the room just below."

"Be quick," Alex said as he led the others out.

Duncan put his hands on Ragnall's narrow shoulders.

"Are you my blood relation as well?" Ragnall asked.

Duncan met his son's direct gaze and promised himself he would never lie to him. "Sean was not your father," he said. "I am."

Ragnall blinked several times, then gave him a slow nod.

"I did not know it myself until a short time ago," Duncan said, and he hoped that one day both Ragnall and Moira could forgive him for their years with Sean. "I'm very glad to be your father."

Alex leaned his head in from the next room. "Duncan, we must go!"

What does a man say to his son when he is going into battle? Duncan never had a father to show him.

"I must leave ye now to fight for the good of the clan," Duncan said. "I do it for you, for your mother, and for all the members of our clan."

Ach, what a trite and useless thing to say to a six-year-old lad. Duncan felt wholly inadequate, but he did not know what else to say.

"My mother says that is what a man of honor does," Ragnall said.

"Your mother has taught ye well," Duncan said, and for the first time thought of how hard it must have been for Moira to raise Ragnall under Sean's roof. "I'll return for ye as soon as I can."

"Be careful," Ragnall said.

Duncan ruffled his son's hair. "I'll make quick work of these MacLeods and be back before ye know it."

Ragnall surprised him then by throwing his arms around Duncan's neck. As Duncan held his son, he realized how much he already cared for this child, blood of his blood, begat of a young love. Duncan had put his life in danger for others a thousand times because that was what honor and duty required. But he knew with absolute certainty that there was nothing he would not do to protect this child.

CHAPTER 38

Duncan and Alex crept through the courtyard to the gate as silent as shadows while the four other MacDonald warriors went up on the wall to take out the guards above. There were more guards at the gate than Duncan had counted before, but they were not expecting an attack from within. Before the men knew they were in danger, Alex and Duncan had them bound and gagged.

Duncan shoved back the bar that braced the wooden doors of the gate. As soon as the MacDonald warriors who had gone up on the wall rejoined them, Duncan motioned for two of them to go inside the gatehouse and crank up the portcullis. The weight of the iron grille, which had spikes at the bottom to impale attackers, made it easy to drop quickly, but slow to raise.

While the iron chain creaked and moaned, making an ungodly noise, Duncan stood next to Alex with his back to the gate, his claymore ready, and every sense alert.

With each turn of the crank, he expected to see MacLeods pour out of the keep.

Finally, the portcullis was up. Duncan and the other men kept watch over the courtyard while Alex went out to alert Connor and Ian. If something had gone wrong on their end, Duncan and Alex would learn of it now. Duncan recognized the sound of Alex's dove call. A short time later, he heard two faint dove calls in the distance.

"Is that them?" the MacDonald warrior next to Duncan whispered.

"Aye," Duncan said. "Be ready."

His blood pounded in his veins in anticipation as he heard the muffled footfalls of a hundred MacDonald warriors running up to the gate. The time had finally arrived. This night, the MacDonalds would retake Trotternish Castle from the MacLeods.

Tonight, Duncan would take it from Erik and be made keeper in his place.

Though it was dark, Duncan recognized the familiar shapes of Connor, Ian, and Alex as they came through the gate at the front of the men. Connor clasped Duncan's arm in greeting.

"I don't know if he still is, but Hugh was here," Duncan said to him in a low voice.

"Hugh?" Connor said. "Catching him here would be good luck. 'Tis past time I settled matters with my uncle."

"The MacLeods are bound to hear us soon," Duncan said. "We should go quickly into the keep."

"Lead the way," Connor whispered back. "You deserve the honor."

Duncan raised his claymore high and waved it for the men to see in the darkness, then started running for the keep. As planned, they did not shout their battle cry. Surprise and cunning would win this night.

Duncan burst into the keep and through the doors of the hall. Some of the MacLeod warriors, who were sleeping on the floor and benches, sprang to their feet with their weapons in their hands, while others seemed slow to recognize the invasion for what it was. In moments Duncan's clansmen had encircled the room.

"Put down your weapons and ye won't be harmed!" Duncan shouted.

The clank of swords and shouts of alarm filled the air as some of the MacLeods began to fight. A few recognized that too many of their warriors had been caught off guard for them to prevail and relinquished their weapons. Others charged the doors to escape. Duncan knew that the MacDonalds would not capture them all, but holding too many captives had its own risks and was generally more trouble than it was worth.

After fighting a short time, Duncan could see that victory was close at hand. He clenched the hilt of his claymore in frustrated fury as he scanned the room. *Where is Erik?*

Connor appeared at his side and shouted over the noise. "Have ye seen Hugh?"

"I don't see him or Erik," Duncan said. "Hugh could have left the castle before tonight, but Erik is here somewhere. I'm going to find him."

* * *

The devil take me, this is a disaster.

One glimpse into the hall and Erik could tell that the castle would be lost. Though he knew he must get out quickly, he stood for a long moment staring at Duncan MacDonald. How could he have been fooled into believing this powerful warrior was a piper? Erik's men were falling before the man's sword like oats to a scythe.

Yet the captain of the MacDonald guard was not as tough as he ought to be. Any MacLeod warrior who gave up his sword to him, Duncan spared. He had a weakness for honor that could be used against him.

Erik remembered the lad.

A hostage would increase his chances of escape—and what better hostage could he hope for than the MacDonald chieftain's heir. If he held a blade to the lad's throat, they would let him out the gate. Later, he would decide whether to give the boy to Hugh Dubh or slit his throat himself. He would enjoy telling Duncan MacDonald how he did it the next time they met.

And Erik would make certain that they did meet again.

* * *

Erik must have been asleep when the attack began, but Duncan wondered why he had not come down when he heard the fighting. Well, Duncan would bring the fight to him.

As keeper, Erik should have the bedchamber right above the hall. Duncan pushed men aside as he ran to the arched doorway that led to the stairs. After racing up the circular stone steps, he paused outside the bedchamber on the next floor. Unlike the keeper, the men who guarded his bedchamber door had left their post to join the battle downstairs.

Battle lust pulsed through Duncan as he slowly lifted the latch. At long last, he would have his revenge for the shame Erik MacLeod had brought upon him and his mother. All the years of fighting to prove himself worthy and to raise himself to a position of respect within his clan would come to an end in this room with Erik's death.

Duncan eased the door open. His sword made a soft *whoosh* as he swung it in front of him and stepped inside. No one was waiting on the other side. With his heart pounding, Duncan waited until his eyes adjusted and he could make out the curtained bed.

As much as Erik deserved an ignoble death, Duncan would not kill him in his bed. It was not Duncan's own honor that held him back as much as his pride. Duncan wanted to do battle with his enemy, fight him warrior-to-warrior, and crush him.

When he heard the rustle of bedclothes, he tensed. He held his claymore at the ready, waiting for Erik to emerge through the bed curtains with a blade in his hand.

But nothing happened.

"I'll give ye time to get your sword," Duncan said, "and then I'm going to kill ye."

"I don't have a sword!"

The voice was a woman's. Duncan backed up, turning his head side-to-side, searching the shadows for Erik.

"Don't kill me!"

The lass sounded terrified. Duncan moved the curtain aside with the tip of his sword. She was fair-haired, pretty, and far too young to be here. And she was alone in the bed.

"I've come for Erik," Duncan said. "Where is he?"

"I don't know," she said. "He left when we heard the shouting coming from the hall. Then he came back in a fury and said he was looking for the lad."

Duncan's blood turned to ice. "What lad?"

"The quiet one with the red hair," she said. "Sarah's friend."

* * *

Please, God, don't let Erik find Ragnall before I reach him. Surely, Erik would not think to look in the turret for him.

Duncan flew down the circular stone steps three at a time. He was moving so swiftly that he almost crashed into the small figure before he saw her. Just in time, he lifted her up. He carried her down several steps before he could stop.

"Sarah," he said as he set her on her feet again, "what in God's name are ye doing wandering the castle?"

"I was looking for ye," she said, slipping her small hand into his. "Erik has Ragnall, so ye must come quickly."

No! The devil had his son. "Where, Sarah?"

"I followed Erik into the other building and up to the turret."

"Get back into your bedchamber and stay there!" he shouted and took the rest of the stairs in one leap.

By the time he reached the long room that led to the turret, Duncan's heart was pounding hard enough to explode. He flung the door to the turret open and froze.

The room was empty.

CHAPTER 39

Duncan tore at his hair. Where could Erik have taken Ragnall? MacDonald warriors were guarding the gate so he could not get out that way. Erik could have taken Ragnall over the wall. It was a long drop, but that's how many of the others were escaping.

From the corner of his eye as he left the turret room, he saw the rope they had left hanging out the window. Something bothered him. He started down the three steps to the other room, then halted abruptly and looked back. The rope was taut.

"No!" he shouted and ran to the window.

The wet wind lashed at his face as he leaned out, trying to see down the rope through the darkness. A rush of terror went through him as he imagined Ragnall falling down, down the side of the cliff into the black swells far below.

Then, finally, he spotted what he was looking for— a movement halfway down the cliff. In the darkness, he could barely make out a shape against the black rock. He could not tell if it was one person or two.

Duncan climbed out the window and started down. Moving dangerously fast, he let the rope slide through his hands as he rappelled off the wet, slippery side of the cliff with his feet.

He felt the rope strain under his hands and hoped to God the knots would hold under the weight of the three of them.

"Don't come any closer," Erik shouted when Duncan was fifteen feet above them, "or I'll drop the lad."

"You do that, and your life is over," Duncan shouted back. "Are ye all right, Ragnall?"

"I'm scared!"

Lord help him. Duncan was close enough now to see that Ragnall was on Erik's back and holding on to Erik's neck—which meant he did not have a hand on the rope.

"I'll let ye go, Erik," Duncan shouted. "Just let me have the boy."

Erik continued climbing down the rope. Soon he would be near enough to the water to risk dropping. It was not far to shore for a grown man who was a strong swimmer. But in this rough sea, a boy would never make it. And if Ragnall fell, it was far from certain that Duncan could find him in the water before his son disappeared under the black swells of the sea.

He thought of Moira's suffering if he failed to save their son—and knew he simply could not fail.

"Let him go, Erik," Duncan said over the wind as he closed the distance between them. "He's just a wee lad, an innocent."

"There are no innocents!" Erik shouted.

"I can't grab you and also save the boy," Duncan shouted. "Let me take him, and you can escape."

"How do I know ye will choose his life over taking mine?" Erik shouted back as he continued climbing downward.

"He's my son!" Anguish tore at Duncan's heart.

Duncan was nearly close enough now to grab hold of Ragnall. He stretched his arm out, praying Erik would not pitch the boy into the sea before Duncan's fingers grasped Ragnall's shirt.

Erik released one hand from the rope to swipe at Duncan's arm with his dirk. As Erik's body swung to the side, Ragnall cried out. Duncan's heart stopped as his son was rammed against the sheer rock cliff.

"Hold on, Ragnall!" Duncan shouted.

In one motion Duncan kicked Erik's face with his boot and swept down to catch Ragnall by the back of his shirt. He felt the shirt ripping as he jerked the boy up. Before it gave way, he caught his son's small body between himself and the rope.

"I have ye." Duncan held his son against his chest and gasped for air.

"Arrgh!" Erik started up the rope, swiping his dagger at Duncan's legs.

Why in the hell wasn't Erik going down the rope and escaping with his life while he had the chance? Erik was coming at him like a madman. Duncan kicked him in the head, hard enough to stun him. This time, Erik dropped like a stone. The sound of the splash was lost in the wind and the roar in Duncan's ears.

Duncan feared Ragnall's thin arms might be too tired to hold on to Duncan's neck—and he just did not want to let go of him—so he started climbing up the rope one-handed. It was slow going, hauling the two of them up with one arm, then wrapping his feet in the rope to give him the leverage to push up and grasp the rope higher again.

Duncan's hand slipped on the rope. Ragnall screamed as they dropped a foot before Duncan could brace his feet and stop their downward slide.

"It's all right," he said. "It's all right."

Damn it. His hand was wet with blood. Erik's blade must have sliced his arm. Now every time Duncan moved up, he had to stop and wipe the blood on his shirt so he could grip the rope again.

Duncan was breathing hard when he finally reached the top and heaved himself up to the window. The light from the lamp still burned in the turret room with a welcoming glow. When he looked down to lift Ragnall inside, he saw that the boy's eyes were squeezed shut and his fingers were latched on to Duncan's shirt like barnacles on to a rock.

"You can let go now, son," Duncan said. "We made it."

* * *

Erik fixed his gaze on the castle he had lost while Hugh's boat carried him farther and farther away. As he watched the castle's outline disappear against the dawn light, he thought of all the wasted years. He had devoted himself, utterly and completely, sacrificing all else to his goal of rising from his poor beginnings to the exalted position of keeper of one of his clan's strongholds.

In one night, that damned Duncan MacDonald had ruined everything. Erik had escaped with his life and nothing else. After losing Trotternish Castle, he would never have the respect of his chieftain or clan again.

It did not improve Erik's mood to know that he had the slippery devil standing next to him to thank for his escape. He was tempted to kill Hugh Dubh for that black favor.

"You'll want revenge." Hugh said.

"Revenge," Erik repeated, and the word tasted sweet on his tongue.

"I know how ye can get it," Hugh said.

A new purpose took root in the ashes of his ruin. Erik would pursue it as ruthlessly as he had pursued his ambition to rise in his clan.

He would destroy Duncan MacDonald and everyone he cared about.

CHAPTER 40

Moira was not in the best of moods. She was un-accustomed to sleeping with cows, and Teàrlag's had mooed half the night. Then black rain clouds had blown in as they sailed out from her cottage this morning. After searching the coastline for hours, they had not seen a sign of the missing pair or the boat they had stolen.

Moira was frozen and drenched. At least the rain was washing the smell of cow off her. And she was learning to sail.

"The weather is getting worse," Niall said, watching the sky to the west. "Perhaps we should turn back."

"No."

"Then watch for a fire along the shore," Niall said with a sigh in his voice. "They're in that small boat. They will have gone ashore to wait for the weather to clear."

Two hours later, they were nearing the point of the peninsula, and the storm was blowing full force.

"Teàrlag must have been wrong about them sailing

south," Niall said. "We should head back to Dunscaith."

"Just a bit longer." Moira wiped the rain from her eyes as she searched the shore. "Niall! Look there, is that a fire?"

The column of smoke was barely distinguishable through the rain and gray light of the winter afternoon.

"Aye, it is," Niall said. "Let me talk to Fergus when we land. He and I are near in age, and we trained together."

As Niall brought the boat into shore, Moira could make out two figures huddled together under a plaid by the fire. Relief flooded through her. They had found Fergus and Rhona at last.

"Fergus!" Niall shouted. "It's me, Niall!"

Rhona and Fergus got to their feet and appeared to be arguing. But then, Fergus put his arm around Rhona and waved back at Niall.

As soon as the galley scraped bottom, Moira jumped out into the rough surf. Though Duncan's boat was a small galley, it was a struggle for just the two of them to pull it in because of Niall's injured leg. As Moira tugged it in, she turned her head to glance up at Fergus by the fire, hoping he would lend a hand.

Just when she looked, Fergus crumpled to the sand. Then Rhona took off at a dead run. Moira's mind felt slow as she tried to comprehend what had just happened on the beach. All she knew for certain was that she did not want Rhona to get away.

"Sàr, get her!" she shouted.

The wolfhound leaped into the water with a great splash and then loped like a deer across the beach in the direction Rhona had gone. As soon as they had the boat safely on the shore, Moira scrambled up to Fergus, who was still lying prone next to the fire.

Niall joined her and fell to his knees on the other side of the moaning man. When he saw the blood pouring from Fergus's throat, he pressed his hand against the wound.

"Fergus, what happened?" Niall asked.

"She stabbed me," Fergus said, his eyes wide with incomprehension. "Why would she do that? She said she loved me."

Niall met Moira's eyes, and she could see that he thought Fergus could not be saved. Though Niall was only seventeen, he was an experienced warrior and had seen death often enough to know.

A mix of sorrow and rage swamped Moira. She took Fergus's hand and held it to her cheek. Such a waste of a young man's life!

"Can ye tell us where Rhona was taking ye?" she asked in a soft voice.

"She said she had never sailed past Castle Maol before," Fergus said in a fading voice.

Moira and Niall exchanged another look. Castle Maol was the stronghold of the MacKinnons, who were close allies of the MacLeods.

"Rhona begged me to take her." Fergus's voice was so weak now that Moira had to lean close to hear him. "I knew we weren't supposed to leave Dunscaith, but she said..."

Tears blurred Moira's vision as she watched the light leave Fergus's eyes.

"I never would have believed Rhona was capable of this," Moira said, wiping her nose on her sleeve.

"I wonder what is at Castle Maol," Niall said, "that Rhona believes is worth murder."

A burst of barks and a woman's screams filled the air.

"I intend to find out," Moira said and leaped to her feet.

"Wait for me." Niall grimaced as he struggled to stand. "She's dangerous."

Moira took Niall's arm and helped him up. Together they followed the barks and shrieks over the rough ground toward the thick shrubs that grew near the shore. When they broke through the tangle of brush, Moira saw that Sàr had Rhona backed up against a boulder. The wolfhound was so tall that his snapping jaws were level with Rhona's chest, and he clearly had the woman terrified.

"Sàr, by me!" Moira shouted.

When Moira took hold of the wolfhound's rope collar, he moved back, but a low growl still rumbled in his throat.

"We should let the wolfhound rip ye apart with his teeth after what ye did to Fergus," Niall said.

Rhona looked Niall up and down with a sneer on her face. "Ye don't have it in ye to kill a woman."

"I do," Moira said, barely containing her rage.

Rhona met Moira's gaze, and her sneer faded. "Duncan always underestimated how tough ye are."

"Tell me why ye were headed to Castle Maol," Moira said.

"I was going to visit some acquaintances," Rhona said.

"You're not some Lowland noblewoman who 'visits acquaintances,'" Moira said, taking a step toward her. "I know you've been spying for my uncle Hugh because I saw ye with him."

That revelation appeared to startle Rhona.

"'Tis all your fault," Rhona said. "If ye hadn't left your

husband and taken Duncan away from me, I never would have gone back to Hugh."

"You've never had a shred of loyalty," Moira said, and suddenly she knew what Rhona had done seven years ago. "It was you who told my father about Duncan and me, wasn't it?"

Rhona laughed. "So ye finally figured that out?"

"What information did ye give Hugh?"

"There wasn't much I could tell him except that Duncan had disappeared again," Rhona said with a shrug. "Hugh already knew that Connor was getting the men and galleys ready to set sail. He figured they were going to attack Trotternish Castle and said he was leaving to warn the MacLeods."

"I understand how you could betray me," Moira said. "But how could ye betray your clan—and murder poor Fergus? He thought you loved him."

"Love?" Rhona scoffed. "That's not what men want."

"So what did you want from Hugh?" Moira asked. "He must have promised ye something."

"When Hugh becomes chieftain, he's going to make me mistress of Dunscaith," Rhona said, lifting her chin. "Perhaps I'll let ye be my maid."

"You're a fool if ye believe Hugh would do that," Moira said.

"If Hugh has gone to Trotternish," Niall said, "why were you going to Castle Maol?"

Rhona looked back and forth between Niall and Moira. Clearly, this was the one question she did not want to answer.

"I will do whatever I must to protect this clan." Moira pulled out her dirk. "Duncan taught me how to kill a man with this. If ye have a heart, I imagine it's in the same place."

"Ye can't stop Hugh with just the two of ye," Rhona said, but her eyes were fixed on Moira's dirk.

"Tell us now!" Moira demanded and took a step forward with Sàr.

Rhona held her hands up. "Keep that beast away from me!"

"If ye want to live," Moira said, "you'd best tell me quick what I want to know."

"Hugh said that Connor's forces would be greatly weakened after the battle for Trotternish Castle, whether they won or lost," Rhona said, her gaze shifting between Moira's blade and Sàr's teeth. "He plans to lie in wait for them north of Castle Maol and ambush them as they sail home."

Castle Maol overlooked the narrow strait between Skye and the mainland. The MacDonald boats would have to sail through it to return home from Trotternish.

"And I felt sorry for ye because I thought ye truly cared for Duncan," Moira said. "You'd have him killed, along with all our men."

"Hugh says he only wants Connor," Rhona said. "He promised me he won't harm Duncan."

"And ye believed him?" Moira asked, her voice rising high in disbelief. "You and Hugh deserve each other. You're both liars, traitors, and murderers."

"We should bury Fergus before we leave," Niall said, then tilted his head toward Rhona. "But what do we do with her?"

* * *

"This is a great day for the MacDonalds of Sleat!" Connor shouted as he stood before all the men in the hall, flanked by Duncan, Ian, and Alex. "Thanks to Duncan Ruadh Mòr, the finest captain of the guard any chieftain ever had, we have taken this castle that was stolen from us."

The MacDonald warriors raised their fists, and the floor vibrated with their shouts. "Duncan Ruadh! Duncan Ruadh!"

Duncan raised his claymore to acknowledge their cheers. He felt gratified that they had taken the castle with so little loss of life, but the close call with Ragnall still weighed heavily on him.

"Our former MacLeod guests have kindly left our kitchens well-stocked," Connor called out. "So today we feast on MacLeod hare, pork, and mutton."

"I'm looking forward to finding out if MacLeod whiskey is as good as they say," Alex said, causing a round of laughter.

The day was young, but the men had been up all night with the attack and were starving. While the others enjoyed their celebration fueled by victory, trays laden with roasted meats, and whiskey that was as fine as the MacLeods claimed, Connor signaled to Ian, Alex, and Duncan to follow him out of the hall.

On his way, Duncan stopped to speak to Sarah, who sat at the end of one of the benches eating.

"Why did ye not leave with the others?" he asked as he knelt beside her.

Connor had kept the captured MacLeod warriors as hostages, but he had allowed the servants and all the women and children to gather their belongings and leave the castle. Duncan was annoyed with himself for not noticing that the child had been left behind.

"I want to stay here with Ragnall," she said, swinging her legs. Sarah was so small that her feet did not touch the floor. "How long will he be asleep?"

"Ragnall is tired after... what happened," Duncan said. "You should be with your own clan."

Sarah shrugged, apparently unconcerned about being stranded in a roomful of warriors from her enemy clan. Duncan sighed. It would not be easy returning her to the MacLeods now. She would probably have to remain here until a deal was made for the hostages.

"Tormond." Duncan waved over a young warrior who had half a dozen younger sisters at home. "You'll look after Sarah until we get some of our own women here."

When Tormond looked as if he would complain, Duncan gave him a hard look, and the young man closed his mouth.

Duncan went up the stairs and found Connor, Ian, and Alex in deep discussion in the chamber that had been Erik's a few hours earlier.

"I've decided to remain here and make Trotternish Castle my home," Connor said as Duncan was lowering himself into the empty chair at the small table.

Duncan sat down hard. "Stay here? Why?"

"By making this the chieftain's castle, I'm sending a message to the MacLeods, the Crown, and our own people that I mean to hold this castle—and to take all of Trotternish Peninsula back for our clan," Connor said.

"That will make the MacLeods all the more determined to retake this castle," Ian said.

"Let the MacLeods come," Connor said. "I will not

hide from this fight or let others stand before me. I am chieftain, and I've made my decision."

Duncan saw that it was no use pointing out the risk to Connor's safety. From their faces, he could tell that Ian and Alex had already made the argument and lost.

"Duncan, I need you to take charge of Dunscaith," Connor said.

The image of Dunscaith, sitting on its rock island with the sea and mountains behind it, came into Duncan's head. It was the castle where Scáthach, the mythical warrior queen, had her legendary school for heroes. There was no place on earth Duncan loved more.

"'Tis an honor beyond me," Duncan said.

"No, 'tis an honor you deserve," Connor said.

"I swear to you," Duncan said, thumping his fist against his chest, "no one will take Dunscaith from our clan so long as I am keeper."

"There is one condition," Connor said raising his finger. "Ye must marry my sister in a fortnight, and I'll return to Dunscaith then to make sure ye do."

Relief and joy spread through Duncan. If he could give Moira Dunscaith, she would never leave him.

"If Moira gives ye any trouble about it, you can tell her that I command it," Connor said.

"You tell Moira that, and I'll wager she won't wed ye for another six months, no matter how much she wants to," Alex said, and the others laughed.

"I fear it would work against me," Duncan agreed.

"Let's set sail for home," Ian said, putting his hand on Duncan's shoulder. "The defense of the Sleat Peninsula depends on us—and I miss my wife."

CHAPTER 41

Erik glared at Hugh's men. Their drunkenness and lack of discipline—which began with Hugh himself—disgusted him.

"Don't mix with them," Erik said, returning his attention to the dozen MacLeod warriors still under his command. While most of his men had been at Trotternish Castle at the time of the attack, Erik had kept a smaller group in a former MacDonald settlement on the east coast of Trotternish Peninsula to maintain control there. It had been an easy matter to collect the men on the way to this end of the island.

Despite Hugh's slovenly ways, Erik had to admire the man's cleverness. His plan to ambush the MacDonalds as they sailed through this narrow strait on their route home was brilliant. After taking the MacDonalds by surprise and killing their chieftain, they would sail around the Sleat Peninsula and take Dunscaith Castle.

Hugh was an untrustworthy snake, but then, so was Erik.

After they took Dunscaith, he was going to kill Hugh and take control of the MacDonald stronghold himself. A dozen disciplined MacLeod warriors were worth fifty of Hugh's men, who were clanless pirates. Once Hugh was dead, most of them would slither away.

By taking the legendary fortress of the MacDonald chieftains, Erik would redeem himself with his chieftain and his clan. And he would have his revenge as well. Hugh had told him that Duncan was likely to remain at Trotternish as its keeper, so Duncan would not die in the ambush.

Erik smiled to himself. The revenge he had planned would be far worse than death for Duncan MacDonald. When Erik took Dunscaith Castle, he was going to cut off Moira MacDonald's head and have it dumped at the gate of Trotternish Castle.

* * *

"There's Castle Maol, up ahead." Niall pointed with one hand while he held the rudder with the other.

Moira's heart went to her throat as she looked at the MacKinnon stronghold, which stood on a headland overlooking the strait between the Isle of Skye and the mainland.

"The strait is so narrow that it makes a perfect place to trap our boats," Moira said. "Perhaps we should have brought Rhona. She might have been able to show us where Hugh has set his ambush."

They had left Rhona where they found her and pushed the little boat she stole out to sea.

"Well, I know I slept better when we camped last night not having to worry about her slitting my throat," Niall said, sounding cheerful. "Besides that, she would have tried to cause trouble and alert Hugh once we got here."

"You're right," Moira said. "We're better off with her stranded miles away."

"Our men won't be expecting an attack from MacKinnon lands," Niall said. "We had some trouble with the MacKinnons shortly after the four returned from France, but none since."

"Will the MacKinnons let Hugh attack our boats from their lands?" Moira asked.

"The MacKinnons don't want a clan war with us, but they're not our friends," Niall said. "They'll turn a blind eye to Hugh's boats and afterward pretend they didn't know Hugh was there or why."

Moira's heart raced as their boat approached the MacKinnon castle. She half expected to hear the guards on the walls shout the alarm.

"You've heard of Saucy Mary?" Niall asked.

"Tell me about her." Moira knew the tale, but she was grateful for the distraction.

"They say that Castle Maol was built in the old days by the Norse invaders, and it came to the MacKinnons through the marriage of their chieftain to a Norse princess, known as Saucy Mary. This princess and her MacKinnon husband exacted a toll from all the boats that passed through this strait. Some say they forced the toll by tying a line of boats together from Castle Maol to the mainland, while others say it was an iron chain. Either way, the sailors happily paid. When they gave up their coin, they would look up at the castle, and Saucy Mary would reward them by exposing her ample breasts."

The humorous tale seemed in marked contrast to the

dark and ominous keep standing guard over the strait.

"If the MacKinnons try to stop us," Niall said, "you can distract them by doing what Saucy Mary did."

"Saucy Mary mustn't have minded getting her *ample* attributes wet," Moira said and pulled her cloak over her head against the rain.

"Don't tell Duncan I suggested that," Niall said.

Moira was about to say that it was no one's business but her own what she did—not that she wanted to expose her breasts to strangers—but she stopped herself. Duncan did not try to tell her what to do because he took pleasure in controlling her like Sean did, but because he wanted to protect her. Of course, that did not mean he was not misguided in his concern or that she would do as he wished.

Perhaps Moira could learn something from Saucy Mary. When Duncan found out what she was doing now, baring her breasts might not be a bad trick to distract him.

They were right beside the castle now, sailing mere yards from the walls of the formidable fortress. Moira held her breath. When they glided past without incident, she let it out and sent up a quick prayer of thanks. Then she looked up the coastline for Hugh's boats.

"Where do ye suppose Hugh has set his ambush?" Moira asked. The strait was so narrow here that she could almost throw a stone from the boat and hit either side.

"That's where I would be if I were Hugh." Niall pointed to a tree-covered point that jutted out into the strait some distance ahead. "They could hide their boats on this side of the point where our galleys coming into the strait from the north would not see them and post lookouts on the other side to watch for our boats' sails."

Moira imagined a murderous spray of arrows launched from the trees pelting a passing boat at close range. Aye, the point was the perfect place for an ambush.

"Our problem now is that Hugh knows this little galley of Duncan's," Niall said.

It was an unusual boat, smaller than a war galley, and specially built for speed and maneuverability.

"Hugh's men are probably waiting at the point now," Moira said. "How do we get past them to warn our men before they sail into the ambush?"

"Either we wait until dark to sail by—"

"But it's only morning," Moira objected. "Tonight could be too late."

"Or we go ashore here and circle behind Hugh's men by foot," Niall said. "We can climb that hill that rises behind the point and come out well up the shore, where we can watch for our boats and hail them."

"That's what we'll have to do," Moira said.

Niall steered their boat into a small cove. When he jumped out of the boat, Moira caught the grimace on his face and knew his leg was paining him. After they dragged the boat up under the shrubs to hide it, Niall sat down on a rock.

"Let's have a look at that leg." Moira knelt beside him pushed his knee-length tunic up his thigh before he could object.

"It's fine," Niall said. "I just need to rest it a wee bit before we start up the hill."

"Ach, blood is coming through the bandage." Moira unwound the bandage and sucked in her breath when she saw the wound. "Oh, Niall. You're not walking anywhere on this leg."

The wound had broken open completely, and it looked bad.

"Just bind it up again," Niall said, his eyes intent on hers. "We must warn our men of the ambush."

"I can do it alone." When Niall started to object, she said, "It's a stroll through the woods—I'm not having ye die just to keep me company."

"I'm going with ye," Niall said and started to get up.

Moira put her hands on his shoulders. "I'll be much faster without ye. If ye want to save the others, you'll stay here."

CHAPTER 42

Moira helped Niall make a lean-to using a blanket she found in the boat. The rain had eased to a drizzle, so it should serve well enough to keep him dry.

"I want ye to rest while I'm gone," she said as she cut strips from her shift for a new bandage. "Ye should have told me the wound had reopened."

She looked at his pale face and wondered how long he had been hiding it from her. Ach, men.

"We should sail past Hugh's men tonight instead of you doing this alone," Niall said, but they both knew that if all had gone well at Trotternish, their boats should be passing through the strait today.

"Don't fret. 'Tis a wee walk through the woods, and I'll have Sàr with me." Moira brushed Niall's hair back and kissed his forehead. "You've become a fine man, Niall MacDonald, and I'm proud to call you cousin."

He was a worry to her, but there was no more she could do for him now. When she climbed out from under the shelter of the lean-to, Sàr was waiting for her. He gave her a forlorn look from beneath his shaggy brows. But when she whistled to him, he followed her up the hill.

Moira knew she was walking into danger. As she made her way up the steep hill through the trees, she thought about all the times she had stood on the beach in Ireland, longing to take her son home to her clan on Skye where they would be safe. Then she thought of the peril awaiting the returning warriors. If Hugh succeeded, her clan would be destroyed and none of them would be safe. Not Connor, not her cousins Ian, Alex, and Niall, not Duncan, and not her son.

Moira regretted so much. At long last, she and Duncan could have been together, if she had been able to forgive him for the past. She had been too bruised and too fearful to trust him. But when she remembered how he looked at her while he sang the song about his dark-haired love, she knew in her heart that he did truly love her. If she lived to see him again, she would not waste another day denying their bond.

Moira squeezed the hilt of her blade as she marched up the hill. She intended to live a long life with Duncan and Ragnall. When this was over, she was going to be the damned happiest woman in all of Scotland, and nothing and no one was going to stop her.

The sound of male voices brought her attention abruptly back to the present. She signaled to Sàr to stay close and be quiet. Then she crept a few paces down the hill to peer through an opening in the trees.

O shluagh! Hugh's men were no more than thirty yards below her. They appeared to be enjoying themselves, throwing dice and drinking around campfires, as if they were celebrating a feast day instead of waiting to murder her kin. But then, Hugh's pirates were rough, clanless men who raided the coasts and stole winter stores from poor folk whose children would go hungry. And woe to any women they caught.

Hugh had far more men than Moira expected, which made it all the more important that she not fail to warn her returning clansmen.

Moira climbed higher up the hill to make a wider circle around their camp. When she was above the trees, she scanned the sea to the north. Far out on the horizon, the sky had cleared, and streaks of sunlight shone on the sails of three galleys. They were too far away for Moira to recognize them, and yet she knew they were the MacDonald boats returning from Trotternish.

Down in the trees, the men would not be able to see the galleys yet, but it would not be long before their lookouts spotted them. Moira's heart pounded. She had to get to the shore north of the ambush in time to signal her brother's boats.

She ran as fast as she could across the side of the hill with Sàr on her heels. Her lungs hurt, and her breath came in deep gasps, but she kept running. She flicked her gaze back and forth between Hugh's camp and the arriving boats, trying to judge how soon she dared to drop down to the shore. She had to go down soon enough to warn the MacDonald boats but not so soon that Hugh's men could reach her and haul her away before she gave the warning.

* * *

Erik had not risen from nothing by being slack. While Hugh relied on a couple of lookouts to watch the passage into the

straits—and threw dice and drank with the rest of his men—
Erik remained vigilant to every sound around him.

That was why he was the only one who saw the dark-
haired lass slipping through the trees high above them. A
shiver went up his back when he saw the beast following
on her heels. For a moment he thought the hounds from
hell were coming for him, but it was only one of those giant dogs from Ireland.

The woman was probably a local lass on an errand.
But there was an urgency in her step that made him suspicious. And that dog was all wrong. A warrior who
ignored his instincts did not live long, so he followed her.
He did not owe his men an explanation and gave them
none.

After the lass went above the tree line, she began running. Erik ran on a parallel path below her, keeping in the
trees. After half a mile through rough terrain, in which
she did not slacken her pace, she dropped down through
the trees. He hid behind a boulder so she would not see
him.

A low growl snapped Erik's attention away from her.
As he turned, he picked up a large rock. The dog was ten
feet from him, with his teeth bared. Before it could spring
on him, Erik hurled the rock. It hit the dog between the
eyes and dropped the animal to the ground.

As one of the greatest MacLeod warriors who ever
lived, it was not Erik's fate to be killed by a damned dog,
no matter how large.

He turned back in time to see the lass run by him as
she came down the hill—and he caught his breath. She
was the most beautiful woman he had ever seen. Her eyes
were an unusual violet color, her lips were full and red,

and her hair was black as midnight. It was a testament to the startling beauty of her face that he was able to take his eyes off her voluptuous curves.

She continued past him and did not slow to a walk until she reached the shore. Despite her dirty gown, this was no farmer's daughter. She held herself with the self-assurance of a princess. Erik would wager his life that this lass was close kin to a chieftain. Very close kin—a wife, a sister, or a daughter. And usually, if a woman was one, she was all three.

So what was this gorgeous, highborn lass doing here? When he followed her gaze and saw the three MacDonald war galleys sailing into the strait, he knew at once who she was. The MacDonald chieftain had no wife. This had to be his sister, Moira MacDonald, a lass famed throughout the isles for her beauty.

Erik almost regretted that he was going to slit her throat.

* * *

Moira climbed up on a rock and waved her arms. The galleys were only fifty yards away. The wind filled their sails, and they were moving fast. She glanced over her shoulder. She thought she had come far enough that Hugh's men could not see her, but she could not be sure.

Were the MacDonald men blind? She was beginning to wonder if she would have to show her breasts like Saucy Mary to get their attention, when the first boat finally veered toward her. As it drew close to shore, she saw that the man standing in the bow was not her brother or Ian. It was Duncan!

Joy filled her heart as Duncan sprang over the side of

the galley. While he ran toward her through the surf, she jumped off the rock and, clutching her skirts in her hands, raced across the beach to meet him. When they collided, she leaped into his arms, and he lifted her off her feet in a crushing embrace.

"What in God's name are ye doing here?" Duncan asked as he squeezed the life out of her.

Then he kissed her, and everything felt right again. The beach, the pirates, all her fears and worries faded away, and she felt safe and loved.

"Are you two ever going to stop?"

When they reluctantly broke the kiss, Moira saw that Ian was standing beside them and that the two other boats had come to shore.

"Now then," Ian said, folding his arms, "perhaps Moira can enlighten us regarding how in the hell she came to be here—and why."

"Niall and I came to warn ye that you're sailing into a trap," Moira said. "Hugh has his men hidden just ahead on that point, waiting to ambush ye."

While Moira went on to explain about Niall, it occurred to her that Duncan would not be returning home unless they had lost the battle for Trotternish Castle. Ach, poor Duncan. He would lay all the blame for the loss on himself.

Then she noticed that one of the galleys was missing. Dear God, how many of their men had perished? Moira looked for her brother among the MacDonald warriors who were now crowding the beach. Tears sprang to her eyes when she did not see him.

"Where is Connor?" She could not make herself ask if her brother had been killed. "Is he hurt?"

"Connor is safe and well," Duncan said, squeezing her shoulders. "I'll tell ye all about what happened after we deal with Hugh and his pirates."

"Is there anything else ye can tell us about this ambush?" Ian said to her.

Moira told them quickly exactly where she had seen Hugh's men camped and how many she guessed were there.

"Mother!"

Time stopped when Moira heard her son's voice calling to her. When she turned, she saw Ragnall's bright copper head leaning over the side of the boat Duncan had sailed in on.

A thighearna bheannaichte! Blessed Lord!

"Don't jump, I'll come get ye," Duncan called, and he trotted back to lift Ragnall out of the boat.

Moira's knees felt weak as Duncan brought her son to her. Finally, she had Ragnall in her arms.

"Duncan brought ye safe to me," she said as she held him close. "I missed ye so much!"

"We should go," Ian said after a moment.

"You and you," Duncan said, pointing to two warriors. "Stay and protect them with your lives."

Duncan ruffled Ragnall's hair, then swept Moira into one more kiss.

Moira held her son's hand as she watched Duncan lead the MacDonald warriors up the hill. They reminded her of the wolves, running silent and swift through the trees.

Please God, watch over my love. Watch over them all.

* * *

Erik smiled to himself. The big, red-haired warrior had embraced Moira MacDonald as if she were his own bit of heaven. Finally, Erik's luck had turned.

Ach, revenge would be sweet, indeed.

CHAPTER 43

Duncan ran through the trees, leaping over rocks and fallen logs, with Ian right behind him, until he neared the place where Moira said Hugh's men were camped. After waiting for the other men to catch up, he signaled for them to be cautious, then crept forward. Hugh's pirates were vile, but Duncan did not make the mistake of underestimating their fighting skills.

As soon as he spied the enemy camp, he waved at the men to spread out through the trees. They moved forward in silence, forming a net through which none of their enemy could pass.

Duncan exchanged glances with Ian. When Ian nodded, Duncan raised his claymore high over his head. When he brought it down, the MacDonalds stormed the camp shouting their battle cry, *"Fraoch Eilean!"*

The pirates scrambled for their weapons. Duncan swung his claymore in swift, powerful strokes and cut them down as they came at him in twos and threes.

While he fought, Duncan noticed a group of men who neither looked nor fought like pirates and worked his way toward them. He knocked the sword out of the hands of one of them and pinned him to the ground.

"Who are ye?" Duncan shouted in the man's face. "A MacKinnon or a MacLeod?"

"I'm a MacLeod."

"Who brought ye here?" Duncan demanded.

"Erik, the keeper of Trotternish Castle."

Erik is here. As soon as Duncan heard of Hugh's ambush, he should have known Erik would be part of it. He was not one to accept defeat lightly.

Anxiety balled in his stomach as he scanned the chaotic battle around him and did not see Erik. Although scores of men were in the camp, Duncan would see him if he were here. Erik was a man who stood out and gave orders.

Duncan gripped the front of the MacLeod warrior's shirt. "Where is Erik?"

In the distance, he saw movement on the shore. True to their reputation for avoiding capture, some of the pirates were running for their boats now that the outcome of the battle was clear. And first among them was Hugh Dubh.

Duncan roared in frustration as he watched Hugh pushing off in his galley. When he turned his attention back to the MacLeod warrior whose chest he was sitting on, the man had terror in his eyes.

"I don't know where Erik went," the man said. "He went up the hill through the trees like he was stalking a doe."

Duncan's heart stuttered in his chest.

"Ian!" he shouted as he jumped to his feet. "I'm going back to our boats. Moira and Ragnall are in danger!"

Ian looked up from where he was tying a pirate's hands while resting his knee on the man's back. "Go! I'll come as soon as I can!"

Duncan was already running. He jumped over a pair of men grappling on the ground and shoved a couple of others out of his way as he left the camp.

Duncan's heart seemed to pound in time to his steps as he raced the half mile back to where he had left Moira and Ragnall. Though he had chosen two of his best warriors to guard them, he could not shake the feeling that he had left them exposed and vulnerable. As he ran, he prayed to every saint he could think of to protect them, and then he called on the faeries as well.

* * *

Erik was a patient man. He waited until he was certain the MacDonald warriors would have reached the point and be engaged in battle so that they would not hear any screams or shouts for help.

He fixed his gaze on the dark-haired lass and her son, who sat on a blanket leaning into each other and talking. Duncan MacDonald had made a grave mistake. Such a fine warrior should know that attachments to women and children make a man vulnerable. Erik would see to it that Duncan paid dearly for his weakness.

All the MacDonalds would pay. Erik would use the beautiful, dark-haired lass and her son to get back what belonged to him. And then he'd kill them slowly so that the knowledge of how they died would torture Duncan MacDonald for the rest of his days.

* * *

Moira sighed with happiness and smiled down at her son as she brushed his unruly red locks back from his forehead.

"I can't wait to see Sàr again," Ragnall said and rested his head against her.

"I brought him here with me," she said. "He must have run off chasing a deer, but he'll be back soon."

In all the excitement, she had not noticed that the wolfhound had disappeared. That was odd. Though Sàr frequently went off alone, he had a keen sense of danger. She was surprised he had left her side with the pirates nearby.

"Get behind us!"

The shout of one of their guards startled Moira. She spun around and gasped when she saw a tall, heavily muscled warrior coming toward them with his claymore in his hands. The strange warrior carried himself like a man who was a formidable fighter and knew it. Though his hair was graying, his stomach was flat and the corded muscles of his arms and neck flexed as he swung the claymore from side to side.

But it was not his size that made Moira's mouth go dry so much as his eyes. They were hard and cold—and exactly as she imagined Duncan's looked when he fought an enemy. He held her gaze, as if the two warriors who stood between them were of no concern to him. Moira pulled her son closer.

"That's Erik MacLeod," Ragnall said under his breath. *Duncan's father.*

Erik moved so quickly that Moira did not even see

his blade strike one of their guards, but suddenly the MacDonald warrior crumpled at her feet. When she looked down at his empty eyes and saw the blood seeping between his lips, she finally screamed.

The other guard was engaged in a desperate fight with Erik. Fear and panic gripped Moira, for she could foresee the outcome. Erik fought with a strength and easy agility that she recognized. It was obvious that Duncan's natural skills as a warrior had come from his father.

The clank of swords meeting rang through the air as Erik forced the MacDonald warrior back and back again. For a moment it looked as though the MacDonald warrior had the better of Erik when Erik failed to block his sword. But Erik dropped low, letting his opponent's blade slice through the empty air above him. Then Erik sprang to his feet and sank the blade of his dirk under the man's breastbone.

Erik took his time wiping his blade on the shirt of the brave warrior he had just killed. Then he lifted his gaze to her. Moira's blood froze at the smile of satisfaction in his eyes.

She pushed Ragnall behind her.

CHAPTER 44

Erik laughed to himself when the MacDonald lass pulled her dirk. She looked even prettier up close.

"Where's your protector now?" he taunted her.

"Duncan is fighting the murdering scum you're traveling with," Moira said, her eyes spitting fire. "I suggest ye leave before he comes back."

Erik chuckled again. She was a hot-blooded one.

"The murdering scum serve a purpose," Erik said, resting his hands on his belt. "They'll keep the MacDonalds busy while we disappear in one of their boats."

"We're not going anywhere with ye," Moira said.

The lad had his arms around his mother's waist and peeked out from behind her to shout, "Ye touch us, and my father will kick ye in the head again!"

The little shite. Erik did not appreciate being reminded of that kick. He had blacked out and might have drowned if the freezing water had not jarred him awake. Erik felt better when he thought of how easy it would be to control the mother once he got his hands on the brat.

"Without us, ye have a chance of escaping," Moira said.

"You can climb into the boat or I can toss ye into it," Erik said. "Makes no difference to me."

"If ye think you can take us and get away, then ye don't know Duncan," Moira said. "He's relentless. He'd follow ye to the gates of hell to get us back."

"The man does have a weakness for ye, I'll grant ye that." Erik was counting on it. "Would ye care to make a wager on whether he'll give up Trotternish Castle to see ye alive again?"

"Ye can't ask him to choose between his duty to the clan and to us," Moira said, her eyes going wide with indignation.

The lass was amusing.

"I can do what I damned well want to," Erik said. "We'll find out soon enough which is more important to Duncan—you and the boy, or his ambition."

Erik considered whether to kick the dirk from the lass's hand. Ach, he'd just grab it.

"Ye don't know who Duncan is, do ye?" Moira said, as Erik took a step toward her, and the gleam in her eye stopped him. "He didn't tell ye."

"I know who he is," Erik said and spit on the ground. "He's the MacDonald who stole Trotternish Castle from me."

"He's more than that to you." Moira paused. "He's your son."

Erik was a trained warrior and hid his reaction, but he felt as if he had been punched in the gut.

"You're lying," he said.

"Ye stole his mother from the beach near Dunscaith Castle," Moira said. "Her father was a MacDonald, but her grandfather on her mother's side was a MacCrimmon piper."

How did she know about the MacCrimmon piper's granddaughter? That was years and years ago. Was it possible that what she said was true? No. And even if it was, what difference did it make?

"That lass caused me a good deal of trouble," Erik said between his teeth. "Unfortunately for you, I don't share Duncan's weakness for lovers or kin."

"Duncan is your son!" Moira's violet eyes were intent on his, as if she thought she could make Erik believe that her words changed everything. But she was wrong.

"A man can always have another son," Erik said. "A castle is considerably harder to come by."

* * *

At last, Duncan saw the opening in the trees that led to the cove where he had left Moira and Ragnall. He pulled his claymore from the scabbard on his back.

He burst out of the trees at a full run—then came to a dead halt at the sight that met him on the beach. The two warriors he had left behind lay sprawled on the ground in the awkward positions of the dead. Moira and Ragnall stood alone on the shore with the man who had killed the two guards.

Duncan had found Erik MacLeod.

Moira and Ragnall were backed up against the side of one of the galleys and facing Erik, who stood a few short feet away from them with his back to Duncan. Since Erik had not killed them yet, Duncan assumed Erik meant to take them hostage. Duncan was too far away—he had to be cautious. If Erik saw him, he might well decide to kill them to make a quick escape before Duncan could reach them.

Ducking low, Duncan worked his way through the shrubs and tall grass that grew above the rocky shore until he was as close to the three on the beach as he could get without being seen.

Moira was speaking to Erik. Hopefully, she was trying to keep him calm. Duncan inched forward on his elbows through the tall grass. He wanted to hear what they were saying to better judge when to make his move.

"You disgust me!" Moira said. "You're every bit as worthless as those pirates."

Duncan could not risk waiting. Damn, Erik was too close to Moira and Ragnall. He would have to move very fast, or Erik could grab one of them to use as a shield.

"Duncan will send you straight to hell where you belong!" Moira shouted.

The instant Erik started forward, cocking his arm to strike her, Duncan sprang to his feet. He heard Moira shriek and Ragnall shout as he hurtled through the air. He and Erik crashed to the ground. Before Erik had time to stick his dirk in Duncan's side, he rolled off Erik and onto his feet.

"Get up!" Duncan roared as he stood over his enemy. "We're going to finish this now."

Erik got to his feet slowly and, keeping his eyes fixed on Duncan, picked up his claymore.

"Moira told me you're the son of that troublesome lass I took from the beach that day," Erik said as they began circling each other. "She was a pretty thing, fair and slight as a faery child."

Duncan swung so hard that when their swords met, the force of it vibrated up his arms.

"I enjoyed bedding her for a time," Erik said. "But she grew tiresome."

"My mother was a good woman." Duncan swung his claymore, but Erik met his blade again. "You will pay with your life for the shame and misery ye brought her."

Duncan was constrained by how close they were to Moira and Ragnall. As he and Erik clanked swords, he tried to ease Erik farther and farther away from them so that he could fight without caution.

"Ye knew she was with child when ye sent her to the MacCrimmons, didn't ye?" Duncan said.

"It could have been anyone's," Erik said.

Duncan knew Erik was trying to goad him into making a mistake. But Duncan's anger was like his sword—cold and hard and deadly.

"Your mother was weak," Erik said. "I didn't expect her to give me a son worth claiming."

"The only good deed you ever did was not claiming me."

Duncan knew that now. Having no father had given him a kind of freedom. As a lad, he had looked around him, at the good men and the bad among his clansmen, and made a choice about the kind of man he wanted to be.

"If I'd known ye would take after me, I would have claimed you," Erik said.

"I don't take after you in any way that matters."

Duncan struck again and again, keeping one eye on Moira and Ragnall, who were caught between their swinging swords and the side of the galley.

"You're the warrior ye are because ye have my blood," Erik said, and then grunted with the effort of swinging his sword toward Duncan's thigh.

Duncan blocked the swing and forced Erik back another step. Finally Duncan had enough distance from Moira and Ragnall to fight without worrying about them being harmed in the fray. He whirled and dodged, striking again and again in an uncontained fury.

Then Duncan came straight at Erik. Back and forth, back and forth, he swung his two-handed sword in deadly arcs. Though his opponent met each swing, Duncan was forcing him to step back and back again.

Erik was strong, but he was tiring under the onslaught of Duncan's relentless blade. Duncan sensed the end of their battle drawing near. And for the first time, he wondered if he could kill his father. Aye, he would strike him dead without remorse if he needed to.

Erik deserved no mercy. But if Duncan could simply disarm him, he would.

Erik attempted to strike Duncan across the chest, and they crossed swords, arms straining and faces inches apart. As they leaned into each other, they were so close that Duncan could see the drips of sweat on Erik's brow.

"You're a MacLeod," Erik said, his face and neck muscles straining with the effort of holding his sword against Duncan's. "Claim your heritage and Trotternish Castle for the MacLeods!"

"I will live and die as a MacDonald," Duncan said between his teeth and shoved Erik back with his sword.

"So be it," Erik said.

Duncan swung his sword with all his might toward Erik's side. But Erik was quick for his years and at the last moment ducked under Duncan's moving blade. Duncan knew what Erik was going to do next before Erik did. Mercy was no longer a choice. When Erik sprang back up with his dirk, Duncan's was already in his hand, ready to plunge into Erik's throat.

But just as Duncan was about to strike, he caught a glimpse of movement from the corner of his eye. It was Ragnall, and he was running straight for Erik.

Everything happened so fast that Duncan acted on pure instinct. He lunged for his son and caught him midair as Ragnall launched himself on Erik. After rolling on the ground with him, Duncan sprang to his feet, placing himself between Ragnall and where Erik had been the moment before. He managed to do it all without either of them being caught by Erik's blade.

But his enemy had also moved quickly.

Erik held Moira against him, and his blade was at her throat. Duncan died a thousand deaths as he saw the fear in her eyes.

"Ye hurt her," Duncan said, "and I'll kill ye before ye take your next breath."

"I believe I have the upper hand here, and I'm taking her with me," Erik said as he dragged her toward the boat. "Make one move I don't like, and I'll slice the lass's throat."

"Don't take the coward's way out," Duncan said. "Fight me."

"There was a time when I could have taken ye," Erik said. "But I don't need to fight ye now that I have her."

"Do ye care nothing for your own life?" Duncan asked. "If ye take her, I will track ye down and kill ye. Ye could never have taken me in your prime, and ye surely can't now."

Duncan held himself back, every muscle taut with the need to murder this man who dared threaten the woman he loved. But Erik was using Moira's body as a shield, and his blade was a hairbreadth from her ivory neck.

"Ye set your sights even higher than I did, crawling into bed with your chieftain's only daughter and getting her with child," Erik said. "Shame it didn't lead to the advantageous marriage ye hoped, but it was a grand scheme. Perhaps I'll try it myself. "

"Ye will not harm her," Duncan said, shaking with rage.

Moira struggled against Erik as he began dragging her backward toward the boat. Panic surged through Duncan. He had to stop them. If Erik got her onto the boat, he feared he would never see her alive again.

Duncan dropped his sword to the ground. "Take me instead."

Erik did not loosen his grip on Moira or lower his blade, but he did stop to stare at Duncan.

"I'm the one who took Trotternish Castle from ye," Duncan said as he removed the dirks from his boots and the hidden one strapped to his thigh and tossed them aside. "Take your revenge on me."

"You'd do that for a woman?" Erik asked.

"Aye," Duncan said as he started walking toward Erik. "There is nothing I would not do for her."

CHAPTER 45

Duncan walked slowly and deliberately toward Erik. He would take the man down with his bare hands or die trying.

"Stay back," Erik warned.

Duncan hesitated, judging the risk to Moira. Then he saw Erik's eyes widen. An instant later, he felt a rush of wind beside him as a blur of gray flashed past. It was the wolfhound.

"No!" Duncan shouted, fearing Erik's blade would slide into Moira's throat.

But before the word was out of his mouth, the wolfhound leaped through the air and dropped Erik and Moira. Sàr was snapping and growling over them like a wild beast, while Moira and Erik writhed on the ground.

Moira's screams filled the air as Duncan raced to them. When he reached them, the dog had his teeth in Erik's neck. Duncan lifted Moira to her feet with one hand and grabbed Sàr's rope collar with the other.

While Sàr barked and strained against his collar, Moira flung her arms around Duncan and buried her face in his neck. His knees felt weak as relief coursed through him. She was all right.

"Enough!" he commanded Sàr, who was still pulling at his arm, fighting to get to Erik.

He knelt beside Erik, who lay ominously still on the ground. Judging from the blood pouring from the ragged cuts on his throat, Sàr's teeth had found a vital vessel.

Erik was choking on his own blood. Duncan should be glad of it, but he was not. Erik was struggling to speak so Duncan leaned down to hear him.

"You're a man who looks after his own," Erik said between gurgling breaths. "I want ye to take care of Sarah."

"*Sarah?*" Duncan asked, bewildered by the unexpected request.

"She's your half sister."

"Sarah is your daughter?" Duncan asked. How could such an evil man have begotten a wee angel like Sarah?

"Her family threatened to go to my chieftain when her mother died, so I had to take her in." Erik's voice was growing faint. "I didn't intend to let her become a weakness, but…"

"I will look after her. Always," Duncan said and squeezed his father's hand as the light faded from his eyes.

Duncan was heartened to discover that his father did have a kernel of decency. Though he had shown no regard for his children in life, Erik had used his last breath to assure the welfare of his young daughter.

* * *

Duncan buried his father on the beach and buried his bitterness with him.

He was grateful to Ian for keeping the other men back. Ian understood that Duncan needed to do this alone.

With each shovel of sand, he felt released from the burdens of his childhood. All his life, he had felt something was wrong with him because his father refused to claim him. Once he was past boyhood, Duncan had understood that the fault lay not with him, but with the man who had sired him. Now Duncan finally believed in his heart, as well as his head, that his father's failure was no reflection on his worth.

Duncan was his own man, and he had chosen to be a man of honor.

Erik had been right about one thing. Having to prove himself to everyone, especially to himself, had driven Duncan to become a renowned warrior. But unlike his father, Duncan employed his skills for the protection of others, and he showed mercy to his enemies when he could.

Duncan thought of his own son living under the oppressive influence of Sean MacQuillan, and he paused in his shoveling to rest his hand on Ragnall's shoulder.

"Will ye teach me to fight like you do?" his son asked.

Ragnall had explained that he ran at Erik because he saw him making the same move that had killed one of the men Duncan had left to guard them. Though the lad's interference had nearly caused a disaster, it showed he had the natural instinct and bravery that would serve him well as a warrior.

"Aye," Duncan said, meeting his son's serious gaze. "'Tis a Highland man's duty to protect his clan and his family, and so I will teach ye to be a great warrior."

But Duncan hoped to teach him much more than how to swing a claymore. He wanted to go sailing and hunting with him and to sit by the hearth listening to the *seannachie* tell the old stories of their clan. Perhaps Ragnall would want to learn to play the harp.

Duncan finished covering the grave and put his arm around Moira as she said a brief prayer.

Then he left his father to God.

* * *

After helping Duncan unfurl the sail, Moira settled beside him and lifted Ragnall onto her lap. Duncan put his arm around her, pulling her close, while he held the rudder with his other hand. When Sàr joined them in the stern, he lay across Moira's feet, keeping them warm. The rain had stopped, and it looked as though it would be smooth sailing all the way home to Dunscaith.

Moira sighed and leaned her head back against Duncan's arm to watch the clouds passing overhead. They were quiet for a long time, enjoying the peaceful sail and the comfort of being together after the strain of the last days. When Ragnall fell asleep in her arms, it felt so good.

"I hope Niall recovers quickly," she said in a low voice so as not to wake Ragnall. "He seemed no worse than when I left him."

"Except for being mightily annoyed at missing the fight with the pirates." The corners of Duncan's mouth tilted up as he gave her a sideways glance.

"I'm glad it's just the three of us and Sàr sailing home in this small galley," Moira said.

One of the other men captained the war galley Duncan had sailed from Trotternish, and Ian had taken Niall in his war galley.

"Ragnall's had a rough few days," Duncan said, looking down at his sleeping face. "You must be tired as well, *mo leannain.*"

"I'm tired to the bone, but I'm too happy to sleep," she said, smiling up at him. "I want to stay awake and enjoy it."

"Ye were so brave to come to warn us." Duncan pulled her close and kissed her hair. "Ye saved many lives today."

Moira's heart swelled to bursting at his praise. She had been trying to decide how best to bring up the loss of Trotternish Castle, which she knew must be a grave disappointment to him. His remark gave her the opening she needed.

"I threatened to murder a woman, argued with a man who wanted to murder me, sailed in the freezing rain for countless hours, and even slept with Teàrlag's cow," Moira said. "So I hope ye can see that I'm no damned princess."

Duncan laughed. "What you are, *m' eudail,*" my treasure, "is a warrior princess."

Moira liked the sound of that.

"What I'm trying to say is that ye don't have to give me fine things to keep me," Moira said, looking up into his eyes. "All I need to be happy is you and Ragnall."

"I know that now," Duncan said. "I'm blessed to have the love of the strongest, bravest lass in all the isles."

"I am sorry ye did not succeed in taking Trotternish Castle from the MacLeods." Moira rested her hand on

Duncan's thigh. "I know how important that was to ye. But I'll be content to live in your cottage on the hill."

"We did succeed in taking the castle," Duncan said.

Moira swallowed her disappointment over leaving Sleat. Her home would be wherever Duncan was. It was Duncan, not Dunscaith's walls, that made her feel safe.

"I'm so proud of ye." Moira pulled him down so she could kiss his cheek without disturbing Ragnall. "But why aren't ye at Trotternish Castle now? If my brother did not choose his best warrior to be its keeper, he'll answer to me."

"Connor has decided to make Trotternish Castle his home," Duncan said. "I am to be keeper of Dunscaith."

Dunscaith! Moira was too stunned to react for a long moment—then she threw her head back and laughed. After torturing her for seven years, the faeries were finally smiling on her, making her every secret wish come true.

"Take the rudder, and I'll lay Ragnall down where he can sleep better," Duncan said as he unfolded himself and stood up.

Duncan lifted Ragnall from her arms and carried him to the bow, where he made a bed for him out of blankets. Then he snapped his fingers, and Sàr got up off Moira's feet and went to lie down by their son.

When Duncan returned, he knelt on one knee in front of her and took her hand.

"I know I'm seven years late—and I'll try to make up for it every day—but, Moira MacDonald, *a chuisle mo chroí*," pulse of my heart, "will ye marry me?"

"Of course I'll marry ye," Moira said, smiling at him. "Now that I know how to sail, ye couldn't get away from me if ye tried."

"I love ye with all my heart," Duncan said, cupping her cheek with his hand. "I always have."

"I'm looking forward to all that making up," Moira said and pulled her warrior down into a long kiss. "I believe it was closer to seven and a half years."

When the boat veered sharply to the side, Duncan broke the kiss to grab the rudder, which she had abandoned. Then he kissed her again and again.

"The moment we get home to Dunscaith," Moira said, her voice breathless between kisses, "we'll call everyone in the castle into the hall, say our vows before them, and have a grand feast to celebrate."

"I wish we could," Duncan said. "But that's a wee bit soon."

"What?" Moira leaned back and gave him a hard look. "You'd better have a damned good reason for keeping me waiting again, Duncan Ruadh Mòr MacDonald."

CHAPTER 46

Two Weeks Later

M mmm." Moira snuggled next to Duncan. Of course, he had been right that they should wait to say their vows until Connor arrived. It seemed churlish not to wait for him when he was coming specially for it—and after he had given them Dunscaith.

Besides, Moira was enjoying these last days of clandestine meetings. Though everyone in the castle knew, they pretended not to.

"I'll miss sneaking away to your cottage," Moira said, running her hand over Duncan's chest.

"We can come up here any time we want after we're wed," Duncan said.

"But will it be as much fun when we're married?" she teased him.

Duncan rolled onto his side and took her face between his hands. "Everything will be better when we're married," he said, fixing his serious eyes on her. "I promise."

"How can it be better than this?" she asked, her throat suddenly tight. "I'm so happy now."

"That's all I ever wanted," Duncan said and then kissed her with a tenderness that let her know how precious she was to him.

His body was all hard muscle, and yet his lips were soft and warm on hers. Moira sighed against his mouth and pressed against him. Eventually, their kisses grew heated. No matter how many times they made love, they wanted each other again.

After all the time apart and how much they both had suffered, she cherished these intimate moments together. If this joy between them had come easy, perhaps Moira would not know its worth. But now, she would never take it for granted.

Sometime later, she was collapsed on top of Duncan, her limbs limp and every muscle relaxed. She thought it would take the cottage catching on fire to get her to move—but it only took someone pounding on the shutters.

"Get out of bed, you sinners! I've come a long way for a wedding!"

Moira laughed when she recognized Alex's voice.

"Connor's galley is nearly to the castle." This time the voice calling through the shutters was Ian's. "Sìleas and Ilysa sent us to fetch the bride so they can help ye dress."

"That's the end of this." Moira grinned at Duncan and gave him a quick kiss. "From now on, I'm only making love to my husband."

* * *

Duncan stood before his clan in the castle he had grown up in and loved, but which had never truly been his home until today. He knew every stone of its keep and every hill and mountain that could be seen from its walls.

Connor faced him, holding a new claymore, an expensive and symbolic gift to mark the occasion. The flat of the unsheathed blade, which rested across his palms, gleamed in the light from the lamps and candles that filled the hall.

"As chieftain of the MacDonalds of Sleat, I entrust this castle and my clansmen who rely on its protection to a great warrior," Connor said in a voice that carried through the room. "Let our enemies beware that Duncan Ruadh MacDonald is now keeper of Dunscaith Castle!"

The roar of voices and stomping of feet was so loud that it seemed to shake the walls as Duncan accepted the sword. Fortunately, their clansmen knew Duncan and did not expect a speech.

"I'm grateful for this honor to serve you and our clan," Duncan said to Connor over the continuing clamor. He held the gaze of his friend and chieftain and saw the pride he felt reflected in Connor's eyes.

"Who thought we would see this day, my friend, when I was chieftain and you the keeper of a MacDonald stronghold?" Connor said, his silver-blue eyes gleaming. "And now, to make you my brother."

At Connor's signal, the hall went quiet and then the wondrous music of Uilleam MacCrimmon's pipes filled the room. Duncan had sent word to him as soon as he and Moira had returned to Dunscaith and was pleased Uilleam had received the message in time to come.

Duncan slid the new claymore into the scabbard strapped to his back, then turned and held his hand out to his bride. As always, Moira took his breath away. She was stunning in a dark blue velvet gown that matched her vibrant eyes, set off her dark hair and ivory skin, and clung to her full curves like a lover.

But it was the glow that shone about her, as it had when he first fell in love with her, that made her truly beautiful to him. His darling Moira was fearless and full of laughter once again.

Moira touched the sprig of white heather in her hair, like the one pinned to his plaid, and winked at him. "I hear 'tis not easy to find heather this time of year," she whispered under the music of the pipes, "unless ye know where to look."

White heather, which was a wedding token for good fortune, had been especially hard to find.

Duncan nodded to Alex and Ian when they came to stand on either side of Connor. Ragnall, Sarah, and Alex's daughter Sorcha stood at the front of the crowd, where they could see. Ilysa was with them, along with Ian's wife Sìleas and their babes. Alex's wife, whom Duncan was very fond of, was pregnant and too near her time to travel.

When Uilleam finished his tune, Duncan and Moira turned to face each other.

Their marriage would be blessed by the church, along with all the others that had taken place over the last year, when Father Brian came on his annual visit to the island. Since the marriage contract had already been signed, all that remained was for them to say their vows before witnesses. In the contract, Duncan had given Moira his cottage, which was all he had. Moira had been inordinately pleased, though her *tochar*, dowry, was worth far more.

Duncan and Moira first exchanged rings, circles with

no end that represented eternal love. Then they held up their right hands and joined them, palm-to-palm, entwining their fingers. Moira locked gazes with him as he wound a long, cream-colored strip of linen around their wrists three times.

"I, Duncan MacDonald, take you, Moira Catriona, great-granddaughter of the Lord of the Isles, granddaughter of Hugh...," Duncan began. Moira's name took considerably longer than his to recite because of her illustrious lineage. He saw the amusement in her eyes as he concentrated to say it all correctly. Finally, he reached the essential promise. "...to be a faithful and loyal husband until God shall separate us by death."

Duncan said the traditional final words though he believed that even death could not separate them. Their souls were entwined and bound together like their hands were now.

"I, Moira MacDonald," she said simply, breaking the rules as she liked to do, "take you, Duncan Ruadh MacDonald, to be my husband, before God, our chieftain, and all our clansmen. I promise to be a faithful and loyal wife to you until God shall separate us by death."

A sense of peace settled over Duncan. At long last, Moira was truly his. As he leaned down to kiss his wife, the hall erupted in cheers. The kiss was like stepping into warm summer sunshine from the cold winter that had been his life without her.

Uilleam MacCrimmon took up his pipes again as their clansmen surrounded them, wishing them happiness with the traditional blessings.

"*Guma fada beò sibh.*" Long may you both live. "*Guma slàn dhuibh.*" Health to you both. "*Móran làithean dhut is sìth.*" May you be blessed with long life and peace. "*Le do mhaitheas is le do nì bhith fàs.*" May you grow old with goodness and with riches.

Under Duncan's glare, the men were cautious with the traditional kisses to the bride and limited themselves to circumspect pecks on Moira's cheek.

"You've taken my best man from me," Connor said as he took his turn and kissed his sister.

"I have," Moira said, smiling up at Duncan in a way that made him feel all soft inside.

Connor turned to him, and they gripped forearms in the ancient greeting of warriors and friends.

"I don't know what I'll do without ye," Connor said, his eyes intent on Duncan. "But it warms my heart to see ye happy. No man deserves it more."

Ian and Alex had joined them, rounding out the foursome.

"Well, Connor, 'tis obvious to the rest of us what ye ought to do," Alex said, his green eyes sparkling with amusement. "'Tis time ye found a fine lass to take that dreary look off your face."

"As chieftain, you're slacking in your duty to produce heirs," Ian added.

"If you've forgotten," Alex said, "the activity we're talking about is a good deal more enjoyable with a partner."

Connor's laugh was strained. "The times are still too unsettled for me to know which marriage alliance will be best for the clan."

He went on about the rebellion and court factions fighting, but they had heard Connor's reasons for waiting before, and none of them was listening.

"There's nothing that says that when ye choose a

wife," Ian said, slapping Connor on the back, "ye can't serve the clan *and* please yourself."

"My father and grandfather pleased themselves, and look what that did," Connor said.

The prior chieftains' relations with multiple women had caused the clan endless strife and grief. Connor was determined not to follow the same path.

"I believe I won our wager," Connor went on, changing the subject. "Pay up, lads."

"'Tis hardly fair when ye told Duncan when to wed," Alex said.

"One of the few advantages of being chieftain," Connor said, and held his hand out.

Duncan was pleased to see Connor's humor returning.

"I don't know what made ye bring Sarah with ye, since ye didn't know that she is Duncan's sister," Moira said, and rested her hand on her brother's arm. "But I'm so glad ye did."

"'Tis hard to say nay to that wee lass," Connor said, shaking his head. "Sarah wailed and wept until I gave in."

Duncan expected there would be shouting at times between Moira and Sarah, as they were both strong-willed and Sarah was unaccustomed to a mother's firm hand. But he was equally certain that there would be plenty of love between them as well to smooth their way.

"The wedding feast is ready," Ilysa said, after coming up quietly behind them. "Everyone is waiting for ye to take your seats."

Duncan was starving.

"Ilysa intends to go to Trotternish and set up Connor's household there," Moira whispered to Duncan as they made their way to the high table.

"I won't permit it!" When Moira dug her fingers into his arm, Duncan lowered his voice. "If she's running the chieftain's household without her own family there, everyone will think she's his mistress."

"Finding her a husband will solve the problem," Moira said in a low voice.

"Hmmph. I'll leave that to you," Duncan said. "I must help Connor choose a reliable man to be the new captain of his guard. Tait is loyal and a good fighter, but he's no leader."

Duncan did not like the idea of Connor sitting up there at Trotternish Castle surrounded by MacLeods. And then there was Hugh, who was as intent as ever on murdering him. Alex had brought word that Hugh was already gathering more men in the outer isles with promises of plunder—and there was even a rumor that Rhona was with him.

Tomorrow, the four of them would discuss Hugh and how to force the MacLeods off the lands they had stolen. But today was Duncan's wedding day, and it was a glorious day.

"Let's sit down and enjoy our wedding feast," Moira said, smiling up at him.

It was a grand meal, with a good deal of toasting and laughter.

"I'm lucky to have a husband with a voracious appetite," Moira said and gave him a wink as he speared another slab of roasted pork.

He squeezed her thigh under the table and wished it was time for the bedding part of the wedding. But after the food was cleared away, there was music and dancing.

Before Caitlin MacCrimmon would agree to dance with Niall, she insisted on lifting his tunic to make certain his wound had healed well enough. As the wound was quite high on Niall's thigh, this caused a bit of a stir.

"All three of the MacNeil lasses look disappointed," Moira said in Duncan's ear after the girls' mother scolded them for staring and dragged them away.

Duncan waited impatiently through a few tunes before he caught Uilleam MacCrimmon's eye. Uilleam nodded and then stepped into the center of the hall playing his pipes. When he had everyone's attention, he stopped playing and announced, "The groom has a song to sing to his bride."

Duncan stood where he was and sang unaccompanied.

Black is the color of my true love's hair
Her lips are like some roses fair

He took Moira's hand and helped her to her feet. Then he lifted her in his arms and continued singing as he carried her around the hall. Moira's cheeks turned pink, but she was laughing and enjoying herself.

She has got the sweetest smile and the gentlest hands
And I love the ground whereon she stands

When the people in the hall realized Duncan was carrying her to the bedchamber, they clapped and cheered.

I love my love and well she knows
I love the ground whereon she goes

Duncan kicked the door shut behind him. The bedchamber was hardly recognizable from when it was Connor's. Moira and Ilysa had decorated the entire room with holly and other greenery, and the grand chieftain's furniture and tapestries had been returned to it.

Duncan's bride looked up at him with violet eyes that were full of love. He had waited until he and Moira were alone to sing the final lines of his song to her.

> *Now the day has finally come*
> *When you and I will live as one*

Duncan felt as if he had waited his whole life to become one with Moira. After loving her for so long, she was his at last and forever.

EPILOGUE

Moira heard her husband's voice coming through the window from the courtyard below and paused to listen.

"Have ye paid no mind to what I've been teaching ye?" Duncan said. "You'd let yourself get killed over a wee bit of rain in your eyes?"

That was odd. While Moira could well imagine Duncan using those words as he trained the men, his tone was soft and reasonable.

Moira stuck her head out the window, wondering if the faeries had stolen her warrior-husband. When she saw he was with Ragnall and Sarah, she smiled. The two children were squinting up at Duncan through the rain and holding their wooden swords in front of them. Duncan held a wooden sword as well, which, with his size, made him look a trifle ridiculous.

"Do ye think the MacLeods will wait for a dry day to attack us?" Duncan asked them as he crossed swords with first one and then the other. "Or the MacKinnons? Or the Macleans? Or the—"

"Duncan," Moira called down, "it is raining a bit hard now."

Duncan looked up at her and broke into a smile. "I suppose it is."

"Can I wipe the rain out of my eyes now, Da?" Sarah asked with a sour expression on her face.

Sarah had decided to call them Mother and Father, which seemed right to them. While Duncan was bound to spoil Sarah and their future daughters in other ways, they were both determined that their girls would learn the skills to defend themselves. They lived in dangerous times in a dangerous world. Should the girls ever need to, they would know how to steal a boat and use a dirk.

"Let me help," Duncan said to Sarah and wiped her face with his sleeve.

Moira patted Sàr next to her. Duncan was like the wolfhound—profoundly loyal and gentle with his family and the fiercest of warriors in protecting them.

"Ye both did well today." Duncan scooped up a child in each arm and rubbed noses with them in turn. "What do ye say we meet your mother in the kitchen and find ourselves a treat?"

Moira ran down the stairs with the wolfhound on her heels. A short time later, she and Duncan stood in the kitchen doorway watching the children eat honeyed nuts and chat with the cooks. Every time Ragnall smiled at something one of them said, Moira's heart felt lighter. He would always have a more serious nature than Sarah, but the dark cloud that had hung over him was gone.

"I have a different kind of treat in mind for us." Duncan's warm breath tickled her ear as he leaned down and whispered to her. "What do ye say to sneaking off to your cottage with me, princess?"

"Ye know that if ye sing to me first," she whispered into her ear, "ye can get me to do anything."

Much later, Moira lay in her warrior's arms, thinking of all her blessings.

"Teàrlag told me our new babe will be another boy," she said, resting her hand over the new life inside her, "and the next one will be a girl."

"Then it must be true," Duncan said and cupped her face with his hand. "I have great faith in the old seer, for she's the one who told me that trusting in a woman's love would change my fate."

Moira smiled into his eyes. Her husband had a true heart she could always depend upon. He had promised her everything would be better once they had wed, and he was a man who kept his promises.

HISTORICAL NOTE

I always have "aha!" moments when I do my research for a book. Usually, this happens when I come across a colorful historical character I can use to add an intriguing twist to my plot. With this book, my great finds were a dog and a song.

Once I decided to include a dog in this story, I looked for a breed that existed in Scotland in the early 1500s. I considered making him a Scottish deerhound until I stumbled across its cousin, the Irish wolfhound, which I could have my heroine acquire in Ireland. I did not know much about the breed, so I met with a local woman who owns three. What amazing dogs! The owner told me they are aptly described by the phrase *Gentle when stroked, fierce when provoked*. The wolfhound's quiet devotion, fighting prowess, and huge size made it seem like a canine version of my hero, Duncan. I named him Sàr, which means "warrior" in Gaelic.

Duncan was musical in the previous books, but I had not planned to have him sing until I heard the words to "Black Is the Color of My True Love's Hair," a traditional song from Appalachia that is believed to have originated in Scotland. The man's longing and the description of the woman made this a perfect song for Duncan. Continuing in the folk tradition, I did change a few words.

Meticulous readers may remember that Duncan's whistle was made out of metal in *The Guardian*. I've learned since that was a mistake and consequently changed it to bone in this story.

I apologize to connoisseurs of Scottish "whisky" for using the spelling *whiskey*, which is more familiar to most American readers.

As I portrayed in this book, the Highland clans of the Western Isles had close cultural and kinship ties to northern Ireland. The Irish MacQuillans were on-and-off allies with the MacDonalds of Dunivaig and the Glens, a branch of the MacDonalds that had lands in both Scotland and Ireland. Sean and his brother Colla, however, are pure fiction.

As I have mentioned before, researching clan histories of five hundred years ago presents both challenges and opportunities for the fiction writer. For my story, I assumed that the MacCrimmons were already serving as the hereditary pipers to the MacLeods and that they were just starting their famous school, but I am not certain when either actually occurred.

The MacLeods of Dunvegan and the MacDonalds of Sleat had a long and bloody rivalry. I confess that I moved their fight over the Trotternish Peninsula forward by several years. And so far as I can tell, the MacDonalds did not take the castle on Trotternish before taking the rest of the peninsula.

Finally, I changed the name of this castle from Duntulm to Trotternish Castle to make it easier for the reader to distinguish it from Dunvegan, Dunscaith, and all the other castles that begin with *Dun*. The castle is in ruins, but the site is gorgeous. The day my daughter and I visited, the sun was out, and it seemed as if we could see forever from the ruins on top of the bluff. (I have photos on my website, www.margaretmallory.com.)

The MacLeod chieftain, Alastair Crotach, married late and lived a remarkably long life. I hope readers find this real historical character as fascinating as I do, because you will see more of him in *The Chieftain*.

Look for the conclusion of
this sizzling series featuring
fearless Highlanders!

Please turn this page
for a preview of

THE CHIEFTAIN

PROLOGUE

Fornicator, philanderer, liar," Connor's mother called out as she circled the crackling fire dragging a stick behind her through the sand. "*Mo mhallachd ort!*" My curse on you!

Connor hugged his knees to his chest as he watched her long, unbound hair swirl about her in the night wind like black snakes.

"May your seed dry up, Donald Gallach, chieftain of the MacDonalds of Sleat," she said in a high, quavering voice as she circled the fire a second time, "so that no woman shall bear you another child."

Connor wished his friend Duncan or his cousins were here, instead of asleep in the castle hall with his father's warriors, as he should be. His father said a seven-year-old who slept on a pallet next to his mother's bed would never be a great warrior and had forbidden it. But his father was away, and Connor had been afraid something bad would happen to his mother if he did not stay close to her.

"May your sons already born by other women die

young," his mother said as she raked her stick around the fire again.

She had been weeping and tearing at her hair for days. She was like that sometimes. Other times, she was like sunshine that was so bright it hurt your eyes.

But she had never done this before.

"Three times 'round, and the spell is bound." His mother straightened and raised her stick in the air. "And may ye know it was I, your wife, who cursed you!"

Connor heard running feet coming through the darkness just before a familiar voice called, "No, Catriona!"

Connor's heart lifted when Duncan's mother, Anna, appeared next to his mother. Her soft voice and kind words could sometimes soothe his mother. But if Anna saw him, she would send him back to the castle. While her attention was on his mother, Connor crawled through the beach grass until he was safely out of the firelight.

"Please, ye mustn't do this," Anna said. "An evil spell that's unwarranted can come back on ye."

"Donald Gallach deserves every evil wish," his mother spat out. "With passion and sweet promises of eternal love, he persuaded me to leave a man who adored me. And now, I discover he's been keeping a woman up at Trotternish Castle—and she's borne him a son!"

"Men have done far worse." Anna put her arm around his mother's shoulders. "I beg ye, take back this curse before it's too late."

"It was too late the moment he took another woman to his bed," his mother said and pushed Anna away. "I swear I will make that man regret what he's done to me for the rest of his days."

"I'm certain you're the only one the chieftain loves,"

Anna said, brushing his mother's wild tangles back from her face. "Please, return to the castle and rest."

"If he believes I will accept this and remain here, a dutiful wife, he has forgotten who I am." His mother stared into the fire and smiled in a way that frightened Connor. "How he will rage when I leave him for another man."

"Ye can't mean to do that," Anna said. "What about your children?"

Connor held his breath, trying not to cry, as he waited for her answer.

"Ye know very well that Highland children—especially a chieftain's children—belong to their father," she said.

"But they need their mother," Anna said, gripping her arm again. "And young Connor adores ye."

"You're better at mothering them than I am, and I know you'd never let Donald Gallach touch you," his mother said. "Promise you'll take care of Connor and Moira after I leave."

"I will, but—"

"Don't go!" Connor ran to his mother and buried his face in her skirts. As always, she smelled of rose petals.

"My sweet, serious lad." His mother dropped to her knee and embraced him, then she leaned away from him and asked, "Ye want your mother to be happy, don't ye?"

Connor nodded. If she were happy, she would stay.

"You were begat of fiery passion, when I owned your father's heart," she said, holding his face between her hands. "Every time your father looks at you, he will remember how it was between us then and regret what he's lost."

* * *

One night, Connor slept too soundly, and his mother disappeared.

When he awoke, a storm raged outside, and the castle was in an uproar. His father had returned after weeks away and was bellowing at everyone.

"Ye follow your mother about like a dog." His father lifted Connor off his feet, shook him, and shouted in his face. "Ye must have seen her with someone. Who did she leave with? Tell me!"

His father's fingers dug into his arms, but Connor did not say a word. Even if he had known where his mother was, he would never betray her. And if he was very good, she might come back for him.

His father sent his galleys in every direction, despite the storm. By the next day, an eerie calm had settled over the sea. Connor was outside with Ragnall, his father's son by his first wife, when one of the boats returned. As soon as he saw a warrior carrying his mother from the boat, her limbs and long black hair swaying with his long strides, Connor starting running.

"No, Connor!" Ragnall shouted.

He darted out of his brother's reach and scrambled down to the beach. But Ragnall was ten years older, a grown man, and he caught Connor before he reached her.

Ragnall neither chastised nor tried to soothe him, but simply held Connor against his solid frame, heavily muscled from constant training. Connor strained to see his mother through the warriors who had crowded around her.

"Even in death, she commands the attention of every man," Ragnall said under his breath. "By the saints, your mother was beautiful."

Was? Connor did not understand, but fear knotted his belly.

The men suddenly parted to let the chieftain through. As their father brushed past Connor and Ragnall, his gaze was fixed on the limp body that was draped over the warrior's arms like an offering.

"Their galley capsized in the storm, and all were lost," the warrior said when Connor's father came to a halt before him. "A farmer found her body washed up on shore."

The muscles of his father's jaw clenched and unclenched as his gaze traveled over her.

"Let me see her!" Connor wailed, reaching his arms out to her.

His father pivoted and fixed his fierce golden eyes on him. Ragnall tightened his grip and turned sideways to protect him from their father's wrath, but Connor was too distraught to fear him.

"What's wrong with her?" Connor usually kept silent in his father's presence, but he had to know.

"She was unfaithful, and now she's dead," his father said, anger vibrating off him. "There will be no weeping for her."

Grief sucked the air from Connor's lungs, and it was a long moment before any sound came out. Then he howled, "No!" and clawed at his brother's arms, trying to get down. "Let me see her! Let me see her!"

"Praise God I have one son who is a fit heir to lead this great clan," his father said.

"Connor's only a bairn, Fa—" Ragnall started to say.

The chieftain cut him off with an abrupt wave of his hand. "Keep her son out of my sight."

CHAPTER 1

1516

Y e can't go with Connor," Duncan said.

"Who else will set up his household at Trotternish Castle?" Ilysa continued sorting and packing her clothes while her brother, who was twice her size and all brawny muscle, glowered down at her. "Ach, there will be so much to do."

"I won't allow it," Duncan said, crossing his arms.

Ilysa paused to give her brother a smile because he meant well, though she was not going to let him stop her. "For heaven's sake, Duncan, why shouldn't I go?"

"If you're keeping his household, everyone will believe that you're also warming his bed," Duncan said in a low hiss.

"I've been managing his household here at Dunscaith Castle since he became chieftain, and no one thinks that." It would not occur to any of them, least of all Connor. Ilysa stifled a sigh and returned to her packing.

"That's because I live here as well," Duncan said. "Ye grew up here, this is your home. Following the chieftain to Trotternish Castle is a different matter altogether."

What would she do if she remained here? Now that Duncan had married Connor's sister and been made keeper of Dunscaith Castle, Ilysa had lost her place. Though she had become good friends with Duncan's new bride, there could be only one mistress of a castle.

"If you're troubled about this, why don't ye speak to Connor?" Ilysa asked. "He's been your best friend since the cradle."

"I won't insult my friend and chieftain by suggesting he'd take advantage of my sister!"

"But you'll insult me?" Ilysa asked, arching an eyebrow—though if Connor MacDonald wanted to take advantage of her, she would faint from pure happiness.

"I'm no saying anything would actually happen between the two of ye," Duncan said, raising his hands in exasperation. "But if the men think ye belong to the chieftain, you'll never get another husband."

"I don't recall saying I wanted one." Ilysa held up an old cloak to examine it for moth holes. "Should I take an extra cloak? They say the wind is strong on the north end of the island."

"Ily—" Duncan stopped abruptly.

Years of fighting had made her brother's instincts sharp and his reflexes quick. Before Ilysa could draw a breath to ask what was wrong, Duncan had run out into the castle courtyard and pulled his claymore from the scabbard on his back.

Through the open door, Ilysa heard shouting and raced out after him.

"What is it?" Duncan called up to one of the guards on the wall.

"Three riders are galloping hard for the gate," the man shouted. "One looks injured."

Please, God, don't let it be Connor. He had gone for a last hunt with his cousins before his departure for Trotternish. Usually, Duncan would be with them, but he had stayed behind to be with his bride. And to lecture Ilysa.

Ilysa followed in Duncan's wake as he ran through the warriors who were flooding into the courtyard. Through the open gate, she saw the three horsemen riding hell-bent toward the castle. Her stomach dropped when she recognized Connor as the injured rider, flanked by his two cousins. He was slumped forward, looking as if he was barely holding on. The rest of his guard was several yards behind them.

As the three riders drew up to the narrow bridge that connected the castle to the main island, Duncan ran across it and blocked her view. Ilysa wanted to scream in frustration as she alternately rose on her toes and leaned to the side, trying to see.

"Clear the way!" Duncan shouted as he came back across the bridge.

The world fell away as Ilysa saw Connor enter the castle between his cousins, Ian and Alex, who were half carrying him. His black hair hung over his face, and the front of his tunic was drenched in blood.

"Run and fetch my medicines," Ilysa told a serving woman who was next to her, before she ran after the others into the keep. As she entered the hall, she called out to another woman, "Bring blankets from my brother's bedchamber."

With one sweep of his arm, Duncan sent cups and platters clattering to the floor, clearing the high table just before Ian and Alex lifted Connor onto it and laid him down.

"*O shluagh!*" Ilysa said, calling on the faeries for help, when she saw the arrows sticking out of Connor's chest and thigh. *How many times will our enemies try to kill him?*

When Connor tried to sit up, Duncan held him down with a firm hand.

"I'm no badly hurt," Connor objected, but his face was gray.

"We rode hard for fear that he'd bleed to death before we reached the castle," Alex said as he sliced Connor's tunic open with his dirk to expose the wound.

"The arrows came from rocks above us," Ian said. "We were in the middle of an open field where we were easy targets, so we couldn't stop to take care of his wounds."

"We'll take the arrow out of his chest first, then the one in his leg," Ilysa said after she examined both wounds. She held her breath and prayed as she rested her fingertips on Connor's wrist. "'Tis fortunate that ye have the heart of a lion, Connor MacDonald."

Connor started to laugh, then winced. "Just get the damned things out of me. They hurt like hell."

"Someone bring us whiskey," Duncan shouted. "The rest of ye, out!"

When the whiskey arrived, Duncan cradled Connor's head and poured it down his throat.

Ilysa noticed the blood running down Ian's arm, but his injury could wait. Connor's could not. Still, this was not as serious as that other time, shortly after the four of them had returned from France. She shuddered as she re-called Ian carrying Connor's broken body into the seer's tiny cottage. Connor had been more dead than alive. With God's help, she and Teàrlag had snatched him back from death's door.

"Cutting the arrow out will be a wee bit messy," Alex said as he wiped his long dirk on his tunic. "I'll do that, Ilysa, and ye can do the sewing."

"I think we'll need all of ye to hold him down," Ilysa said, knowing the men would take that better than telling them a delicate hand was needed with the blade. "If Con-nor moves it will make things worse."

While the men poured more whiskey into Connor, she made a poultice.

"Ready?" Duncan asked Connor. When he nodded, Duncan took the tooth-marked strip of leather from Ilysa's basket of medicines and put it between Connor's teeth.

Ilysa exchanged glances with the others, then took a deep breath and willed her hands not to shake. The arrow was deep, and it was barbed, so she had to work carefully. Thankfully, Connor passed out long before she finished.

After she cut out the arrow, Ilysa cleaned the wound thoroughly with whiskey and covered it with the poultice. Then she did the same with the arrow in his thigh. The three men were skilled at dressing battle wounds, so she sat down on the bench next to the table while they wound strips of linen around Connor's chest, looping the cloth under his left arm and over his right shoulder.

Now that it was over, a wave of nausea hit her, and she leaned forward to rest her forehead on the table. She slipped her hand into Connor's. When he was so badly injured the last time, she had washed his naked body with cool cloths to break his fever. Somehow, holding his hand now felt more intimate.

Ach, she was pathetic. She sat up and ran her gaze over his face, which was eased of worry for once. Though his looks were the least of what drew her to him, a lass would have to be dead not to notice how handsome he was. He had scars all over his body, attesting to the battles and attempts on his life, but his face was unmarked. He was perfect, an Adonis with black hair and silvery-blue eyes.

Since Connor returned from France to find his father and brother dead and their clan near ruin, he had devoted himself with single-minded determination to restoring the clan's lands and making their people safe. If he lived long enough, he would be one of the great chieftains, the kind the bards told stories about. Whatever Ilysa could do to help him, she would.

"Connor will be fine," Ian said, squeezing her shoulder. "Ye did well."

"Let me see to that cut on your arm." Ilysa chastised herself for daydreaming while Ian needed tending, and she pushed up his bloody sleeve. "Looks like an arrow grazed ye."

"'Tis nothing," Ian said.

Ilysa rolled her eyes and set to work on it. "Connor's wounds are deep and will bear watching," she said for her brother's benefit. "He'll need a healer to travel with him to Trotternish."

"There must be healers in Trotternish," Duncan said.

"None that we can trust," she said as she tied the bandage around Ian's arm. "A healer wouldn't even have to poison him, though she could. 'Tis easy to let a wound go bad."

* * *

It should have been a clean kill.

Lachlan mulled over what went wrong as he waited at the meeting point for Hugh's galley, which would take him back to Trotternish. He had wasted his first arrow on the wrong man. When the rider entered the clearing, he fit the description Lachlan had been given: a tall warrior near Lachlan's age with a rangy build and hair as black as a crow. Fortunately, the man's horse had jerked to the side and saved his life. Lachlan was relieved he had only winged him. He did not make a practice of killing men who did not deserve it.

As soon as the next man charged his horse into the clearing, Lachlan realized his mistake. He could not have said why, for the two looked much alike, but he had known immediately that the second man was the chieftain. There was something about him that bespoke his position as leader of the clan.

Odd, how the chieftain had ridden directly into Lachlan's range when he saw the arrow strike his companion. Connor MacDonald had not hesitated, not spared a glance behind him to look for someone else to do it.

It was the chieftain's unexpected willingness to put the life of one of his men before his own that had caused Lachlan to falter, just for an instant, and send his next arrow into the chieftain's thigh instead of his heart. Lachlan recovered quickly, and his third arrow struck the chieftain in the chest, though it may have been too high to kill him.

Next time, he would not falter.

* * *

The four men were in deep discussion when Ilysa slipped into the chamber with a tray. She glanced at Connor, who had no business being out of bed a day after he was wounded. Though he hid his pain well, she saw it in the strain around his eyes.

"We haven't found the man who shot those arrows yesterday," Ian said. "His tracks were washed out in the rain."

As Ilysa started around the table refilling their cups, Duncan gave her his icy warrior's stare to let her know that their earlier argument was not finished. Ilysa responded with a serene smile to let him know that it was.

"We all know Hugh is responsible for this attack," Alex said, referring to Connor's half uncle who was set on taking the chieftainship from him. "He's tried to have Connor murdered more than once."

"The MacLeods wouldn't attack us here on the Sleat Peninsula where we are strong," Ian agreed. "This was a single archer, and my guess is he was one of our own."

"We have vipers among us!" Duncan slammed his fist on the table, causing their cups to rattle.

As Ilysa refilled their cups, Ian shot her a quick, dazzling smile, and Alex winked at her. She had always been fond of Connor's cousins, though the pair had been philandering devils before they settled down to become devoted husbands. Ian and Connor had gotten their black hair from their mothers, who were sisters, while Alex had the fair hair of the Vikings who had once terrorized the isles.

"Will ye reconsider your decision to live at Trotternish Castle?" Ian asked Connor. "Up there, ye won't have us to guard your back as we did yesterday."

"Hell," Alex said, "if someone kills ye, we're likely to end up with Hugh as chieftain."

"By making Trotternish Castle my home," Connor said, "I'm sending a message to the MacLeods—and to the Crown—that I am not giving up our claim to the Trotternish Peninsula."

Connor's deep voice reverberated somewhere low in Ilysa's belly, making her hand quiver as she poured whiskey into his cup. For a moment she feared he would notice, but she needn't have worried.

"I want them to know," Connor continued, "that we will fight for the lands the MacLeods stole from us."

"*A' phlàigh oirbh MacLeods!*"—A plague on the MacLeods!—the four chanted in unison and raised their cups.

Ilysa could see that she had arrived just in time with more whiskey.

"If you're intent on this," Duncan said, "I should remain as captain of your guard and go with ye."

"I need ye to protect our people here, just as I need Ian and Alex to hold our other castles," Connor said. "I'm sailing for Trotternish in the morning, so I suggest we discuss how to remove the MacLeods from our lands."

Ach, the man should let his wounds heal before leaving. Ilysa would have to watch him closely on the two-day journey.

Ilysa took her tray to the side table and stood with her back to them, pretending to be busy. Because they suspected Connor's uncle had spies in the castle, Ilysa had always served them herself when Connor's inner circle met in private. The four men were so accustomed to her coming and going that they never noticed when she stayed to listen.

"The MacLeods are a powerful clan," Ian said. "We won't defeat them without a strong ally fighting at our side."

"If ye want us to take Trotternish," Alex said, "ye should make a marriage alliance with another clan."

Ilysa tensed, though she was certain Connor would say it was not yet time, as he always did.

"Several clans have already left the rebellion, and it will end soon," Ian said. "'Tis possible now to judge which clans will have power—and which won't—when it's all over."

"Ye always said that's what ye were waiting for," Alex said. "Of course, we think ye were just stalling."

"You're right," Connor said. "'Tis time for me to take a wife."

Ilysa's vision went dark, and she gripped the edge of the table to keep from falling. Concentrating to keep her feet under her, she sidestepped along the table. When she reached the end of it, she turned around and half fell onto the bench that was beside it against the wall.

From the long silence that followed Connor's announcement, the men were as surprised by it as she was.

"We prodded the bull by taking Trotternish Castle. Alastair MacLeod could strike back at us at any time," Connor said. "The sooner I make a marriage alliance, the better."

Soon? Ilysa took deep breaths trying to calm herself. What was wrong with her? She had known Connor would wed eventually.

"God knows, ye need a woman," Alex said. "How long has it been?"

When the others began making ribald remarks, Ilysa

knew they had forgotten her completely and was grateful for it. Connor's apparent celibacy since becoming chieftain had been the subject of a good deal of speculation and gossip. The men of the castle seemed almost as amazed by the chieftain's failure to take any lass to his bed as the women were disappointed.

The distance to the door suddenly seemed too far. As soon as Ilysa could trust herself to walk, she forced herself to get to her feet. She crossed the floor with her head down and bit her lip hard to keep from weeping.

THE DISH

Where authors give you the inside scoop!

♥ ♥ ♥ ♥ ♥ ♥ ♥ ♥ ♥ ♥ ♥ ♥ ♥ ♥ ♥ ♥

From the desk of Margaret Mallory

Dear Reader,

I've been startled, as well as delighted, by all the positive comments I've received regarding the deep male friendship—the "bro-mance"—among my four heroes in the Return of the Highlanders series. If my portrayal of male camaraderie rings true at all, I must give some credit to my younger brother, who always had a gang of close friends running in and out of our house. (This does *not*, however, excuse him for not calling me more often.)

Looking back, I admire how accepting and utterly at ease these boys were with each other. On the other hand, I am amazed how they could spend so much time together and not talk—or talk only very briefly—about trouble in their families, divorces, or other important things going on in their lives. They were always either eating or having adventures. To this bookish older sister, they seemed drawn to danger like magnets. And I certainly never guessed that the boys who shot rubber bands at me from behind the furniture and made obnoxious kissy noises from the bushes when I went out on dates had anything *useful* to teach me.

Yet I'm sure that what I learned from them about how male friendships work helped me create the bond among my heroes in the Return of the Highlanders. These four

Highland warriors have been close companions since they were wee bairns, have fought side by side in every battle, and have saved each other's lives many times over. Naturally, they are in each others' books.

Ever since Duncan MacDonald's appearances in *The Guardian* and *The Sinner*, readers have been telling me how anxious they are for Duncan's own book because they want to see him find happiness at last. We all love a tortured hero, don't we? And if any man deserves a Happily Ever After, it's Duncan. In truth, I feel guilty for having made him wait.

Duncan, in THE WARRIOR, is a man of few words, who is honorable, steadfast, and devoted to duty. With no father to claim him, he's worked tirelessly to earn the respect of his clan through his unmatched fighting skills. His only defeat was seven years ago, when he fell hard for his chieftain's beautiful, black-haired daughter, a lass far beyond his reach.

He never expected to keep Moira's love past that magical summer before she wed. Yet he accepts that his feelings for her will never change, and he gets on with his duties. When he and his friends return to the Isle of Skye after years spent fighting in France, every stone of his clan's stronghold still reminds him of her.

Moira's brother, who is Duncan's best friend and now chieftain, is aware that Duncan loves her, though they never speak of it. (Thanks to my brother and his friends, I do know it's possible for them to not talk about this for seven years.) When the chieftain hears that Moira may be in danger, he turns to the man he trusts most.

The intervening years have not made Moira trusting nor forgiving, and the sparks fly when this stubborn pair reunites. After the untimely death of her abusive husband, these star-crossed lovers must survive one dangerous adventure after another. They will find it even more daunting to trust each other and face the hard truths about what happened seven years ago.

I hope you enjoy the romance between this Highland warrior and his long-lost love—and that my affection for the troublesome boys who grow up to be the kind of men we adore shines through in the bro-mance.

I love to hear from readers! You can find me on Facebook, Twitter, and my website, www.MargaretMallory.com.

Margaret Mallory

♥ ♥ ♥ ♥ ♥ ♥ ♥ ♥ ♥ ♥ ♥ ♥ ♥ ♥ ♥ ♥

From the desk of Jennifer Delamere

Dear Reader,

Have you ever wished you could step into someone else's life? Leave behind your own past with its problems and become someone entirely different?

I'm pretty sure everyone has felt that way at times. When you think about it, the tale of Cinderella is such a story at its essence.

When I was in college, I saw a film called *The Return of Martin Guerre*, starring the great French actor Gérard Depardieu. It was actually based on true events in medieval France. A man has gone off to war but then stays gone for over a decade, essentially abandoning his wife.

One day, though, he does return. The good news is that, whereas the guy had previously been a heartless jerk, now he is caring and kind. The wife takes him back, and they are happy. The bad news is that eventually it is discovered that the man is not who he claims to be. He is an impostor.

Ever since I saw that movie, I have loved stories with this theme. One thing I've noticed is that so often in these tales, the impostor is actually a better human being than the person he or she is pretending to be. In the case of *Martin Guerre*, Gérard's character *wants* the life and the responsibilities the other man has intentionally left behind. The movie was remade in America as *Sommersby*, starring Richard Gere and Jodie Foster. Richard Gere's character grows and *becomes* a better man over the course of the events in the film. He does more for the family and community than the real Sommersby ever would have done.

Please note that a sad ending is not necessarily required! There are lighthearted versions of this tale as well. Remember *While You Were Sleeping*, a romantic comedy starring Sandra Bullock? Once again, she was a better person than the woman she was pretending to be, and she was certainly too good for her fiancé, the shallow man she thought she was in love with. In the end, her decency and kindness won over everyone in the family. They were all better off because she had come into their lives, even though she had initially been untruthful about who she was. And—what's most important for fans of romance!— true love won out. While Sandra had initially been starry eyed over her supposed fiancé, she came to realize that it was actually his brother who was the right man for her.

The idea for AN HEIRESS AT HEART grew out of my love for these stories about someone stepping into another person's shoes. Lizzie Poole decides to take on another person's identity: that of her half-sister, Ria, whom she had no idea existed until they found each other through an extraordinary chain of events.

Lizzie is succeeding in her role as Ria Thornborough Somerville, a woman who has just been widowed—until she falls in love with Geoffrey Somerville, the dead husband's brother. And aside from the fact that it would have been awkward enough to explain how you had suddenly fallen in love with your brother-in-law, in England at that time it was actually illegal: The laws at that time prevented people from marrying their dead spouse's sibling. So Lizzie is left in a quandary: She must either admit the truth of her identity, or forever deny her love for Geoffrey.

In a cute movie called *Monte Carlo*, a poor girl from Texas (played by Selena Gomez) impersonates a rich and snobbish Englishwoman. During her week in that woman's (high-priced, designer) shoes, she actually ends up helping to make the world just a bit better of a place—more so than the selfish rich girl ever would have done. She finds a purpose in life and—bonus!—true love as well.

Maybe I'm so fascinated by these stories because of the lovely irony that, in the end, each character actually discovers their *true* self. They find more noble aspects of themselves than they ever realized existed. They discover that who they *are* is better than anyone they could *pretend* to be. They learn to rise up to their own best natures rather than to simply be an imitation of someone else.

As the popular saying goes, "Be yourself. Everyone else is taken."

Jennifer Delamere

♥ ♥ ♥ ♥ ♥ ♥ ♥ ♥ ♥ ♥ ♥ ♥ ♥ ♥ ♥

From the desk of Roxanne St. Claire

Dear Reader,

I'm often asked if the fictional island of Mimosa Key, home
to beautiful Barefoot Bay, is based on a real place. Indeed,
it is. Although the barrier island is loosely modeled after
Sanibel or Captiva, the setting was really inspired by a
serene, desolate, undiscovered gem called Bonita Beach
that sits between Naples and Fort Myers on the Gulf of
Mexico.

On this wide, white strip of waterfront property, I spent
some of the most glorious, relaxing, deliciously happy days
of my life. My parents retired to Bonita and lived in a
small house directly on the Gulf. On any long weekend
when I could get away, I headed to that beach to spend
time in paradise with two of my very favorite people.

The days were sunny and sandy, but the best part of the
beach life were the early evening chats on the screened-in
porch with my dad, watching heartbreakingly beautiful
sunsets, sipping cocktails until the blue moon rose to turn
the water to diamonds on black velvet. All the while, I
soaked up my father's rich memories of a life well lived.
And, I'm sorry to say, a life that ended too soon. My last
trip to Bonita was little more than a vigil at his hospital
bed, joined by all my siblings who flew in from around the
country to share the agony of losing the man we called
"the Chief."

My mother left the beach house almost immediately to
live with us in Miami, and more than twenty years passed

before I could bear to make the drive across the state to Bonita. I thought it would hurt too much to see "Daddy's beach."

But just before I started writing the Barefoot Bay series, I had the opportunity to speak to a group of writers in that area of Florida, and I decided a trip to the very setting of my stories would be good research—and quite cathartic.

Imagine my dismay when I arrived at the beach and it was no longer desolate or undiscovered. The rarefied real estate had transformed in two decades, most of the bungalows replaced by mansions. I didn't have the address, but doubted I could find my parents' house anyway; it couldn't have escaped the bulldozers and high-end developers.

So I walked the beach, mourning life's losses, when suddenly I slowed in front of one of the few modest houses left, so small I almost missed it, tucked between two four-story monsters.

The siding had been repainted, the roof reshingled, and the windows replaced after years of exposure to the salt air. But I recognized the screen-covered porch, and I could practically hear the hearty sound of my dad's laughter.

I waited for a punch of pain, the old grief that sometimes twists my heart when I let myself really think about how young I was when I lost such a fantastic father. But, guess what? There was no pain. Only relief that the house where he'd been so happily retired still stood, and gratitude that I'd been blessed to have had him as my dad.

And like he had in life, my father inspired me once again. For one thing, despite the resort story line I had planned for the Barefoot Bay books, I made a promise to keep my fictional beach more pristine and pure than the real one. I also promised myself that at least one of the books that I'd set on "Daddy's beach" would explore the poignant, precious, incomparable love between a father and a daughter.

That book is BAREFOOT IN THE RAIN. The novel is, first and foremost, a reunion romance, telling the story of Jocelyn and Will, two star-crossed teenagers who find their way back to each other after almost fifteen years of separation. But there's another "love" story on the pages of BAREFOOT IN THE RAIN, and that's the one that brought out the tissues a few times while I was writing the book.

The heroine is estranged from her father, and during the course of the story, she has to forge a new relationship with the man she can barely stand to talk to, let alone call "Daddy." Unlike my father, Jocelyn's dad can't share his memories, because Alzheimer's has wiped the slate clean. And in their case, that's both a blessing and a curse. Circumstances give Jocelyn a second chance with her father—something many of us never have once we've shared that last sunset.

I hope readers connect with Jocelyn, a strong heroine who has to conquer a difficult past, and fall in love with the catcher-turned-carpenter hero, Will. I also hope readers appreciate how hard the characters have worked to keep Barefoot Bay natural and unspoiled, unlike the beach that inspired the setting. But most of all, I hope BAREFOOT IN THE RAIN reminds every reader of a special love for her father, no matter where he is.

Roxanne St. Claire